Dart River Valley

Patricia Snelling

A Family Saga set in the Southern Alps, New Zealand. This is an omnibus edition. Each of these volumes is a stand-alone story.

WHEN HOPE WENT SOUTH
JESSIE'S HIGH COUNTRY HEART
MACK THE GOOD SHEPHERD

Disclaimer

These novels are written using British English with New Zealand colloquialisms or Kiwi slang.

Harold Joyce Cover Art
Martin Joyce Graphic Design

Website: **www.patriciasnelling.com**

WHEN HOPE WENT SOUTH

Contents

WHEN HOPE WENT SOUTH

Chapter One

A Little Town Called Bethlehem
Bay of Plenty, New Zealand 1971

Frank Petersen tottered along the path towards the front door of Number 10 Penny Lane. He coughed and spluttered, briefly stopping to get his breath.

His legs threatened to buckle while he blindly fumbled in his pocket for the door key. Grabbing the handrail with one hand, he inserted the metal into the lock with the other. Suddenly the door flew open, as the key failed to find its destination.

Myra, his wife, stood glaring while Frank lurched forward, almost landing on the dining table.

'There you are—paralytic again! Your food is in the oven and probably dried up. I don't know why I even bother cooking for you.'

Hope listened to the commotion. Her father was drunk again, for sure. The loud bang of the front door slamming caught her breath.

More shuffling and a crash. She wondered what he'd stumbled over this time. Tomorrow he would probably forget how he got the bruises.

Hope pulled the blankets over her head, as her stomach formed a knot. She turned a deaf ear to the yelling and ugly words. Inky, her cat, slid under the duvet and rubbed her nose on Hope's cheek. The softness of the black cat offered some comfort, but it didn't stop the angry words bouncing off the walls of the small house. When will this end? She can't stand much more. Her faithful companion's fur soaked up her tears until sleep pulled her into oblivion.

***

Doug was arriving home today. Although ten years older than Hope, he never treated her like a bothersome little sister. He was her friend and protector. Even after serving in Vietnam as a radiographer and returning home changed, broken. That's the word she'd use. He even drank like her dad. Never as much, though.

Sitting by the window made her feel closer to him as she imagined him on his way home for a brief leave from the hospital in Auckland. Was he still on the plane, or had he left the airport already, making the last short trek to their house?

'Hope! Come here and help me with this chicken. You can sew it up with this when you've finished stuffing it.' Her mother handed her a needle and thread with a bowl of herbs with breadcrumbs. 'You'll need an egg to bind it, remember?'

'What time is Doug arriving? I can't wait to see him.' She parted the Venetian blinds and looked down the driveway.

'He'll be here soon— that's if the shuttle from the airport doesn't do a huge round trip. After you've finished stuffing the chicken, you could set the table for dinner.'

'I hear a car. I think it's the shuttle.' Hope rushed to the sink to rinse her hands under the tap. She wiped them on her jeans and dashed to the door. 'Come on Mum. Let's go to the gate and meet him.'

Her mother scooted to the mirror in the hallway. She pushed at her auburn curls that wouldn't behave then hurried to the back door. 'Frank, come inside. Doug's here.'

2

Too late. Doug had turned the corner of the house with Hope hanging onto his sleeve. Taking two steps at a time she rushed up the front stairs, her arm looped through Doug's almost pulling him off balance. Her face brimmed with a smile on a toothpaste advert. Doug stopped as his father grunted something from behind and plodded towards him. He turned to greet him.

'Dad. How are you?' His father put out his hand. Instead of shaking it, as usual, Doug ignored it and put his hand inside his jacket. He extracted a packet of Tasman Light pipe tobacco.

'Gee, thanks, boy. I've just run out of the stuff.' He took a deep whiff. 'Smells good.' As Frank continued to sniff the tobacco loudly, his wife pushed past him to get at Doug. She threw her arms around him then stood back, looking him up and down.

'What have they been feeding you? Wasting away to a shadow again, I see. I'll have to fix that.'

Hope knew, the way Myra had always doted on Doug, that he was the apple of her eye. She dragged Doug by the hand through into the lounge. He stripped off his brown corduroy jacket and slumped into the leather couch. Hope plonked herself down next to him, about to fire questions at him about his leave. Myra entered the lounge and glared disapprovingly at Hope.

'Help me bring in the tea trolley, please. Pop the scones underneath. There's a pot of raspberry jam on the bench.'

Hope trundled back in with the trolley to see her mother had hogged Doug's attention. As usual, Frank shrunk into a seat in the corner of the room while Myra handed everyone a plate.

'Help yourselves. I'm done for the day.' She dumped herself in her special armchair and leaned forward, rubbing the side of her foot. 'Must get these awful shoes off.'

'This is very formal. I rarely get scones on arrival.' Doug had guzzled a whole one. He pulled out his handkerchief and wiped the jam from the corner of his mouth. Hope handed him a paper serviette.

'It was Hope's idea because you haven't been home in ages. She had me making scones early this morning.' Myra gave a half smile.

'How long are you home this time?' Frank finally got a word in.

'Not long—going back in a week. I'm on call after this and we're flat out. Lots of staff off sick.'

***

Doug's leave had flown by, and the week was almost out. Not enough time to spend doing the things Hope had planned to do with him. She'd asked him to take her fishing at the beach. There was also the waterhole she had discovered a few weeks ago near Misty's paddock and she'd hoped he would swim there with her. But today was one of the many days when her mother took up his time.

'Sorry, Hope. I promised Mum I'd mow the lawns today. Maybe we could go tomorrow. Dad doesn't do much to help her these days.'

Her head started pounding. She could feel the stress on her amalgam fillings as she clenched her teeth. That's how she'd fractured one of them recently.

'I know that! Dad doesn't help her around here much at all. I'm always finding her up on the roof painting the corrugated iron or mowing lawns and weeding gardens. That's when she's not in the orchard picking fruit or packing tomatoes. She gets so grumpy when she's tired and takes it out on me. Dad just disappears somewhere between the tomato rows until dusk to stay out of her way.'

4

Doug put his arm around her shoulders, leaning gently on her. 'I know, sweetie. That's why I need to help her when I'm at home.'

Resentment burned a hole in her soul. If it wasn't for her dad's drinking, she could have had a fun holiday with Doug. It had always been the same whether her father was drunk or sober. This was her lot. Will it ever change? Perhaps it's time to escape it all.

***

Thank goodness for the Returned Servicemen's reunion. Hope and Doug had barely had five minutes alone together since he'd arrived home. Now they had a whole evening ahead of them. She raced down the hall from her room and stopped short. She'd planned a night of card games with her big brother, but his furrowed brow and tight lips didn't look like anticipation. They spelt angst.

'There's something I think I need to tell you, something important.' He patted the seat next to him on the couch.

'What do you mean? What's up?'

'I'm telling you this because you'll soon be leaving school and you've already told me you want to go places, find work, and go to university.'

'What are you trying to say, Doug?'

'Something Dad said to me in one of his drunken states one night. You know how verbal he gets when he's been drinking.' His voice croaked as if he was struggling to get the words out. He locked her gaze. 'He told me you're not his daughter and that it's always been a family secret.'

Hope leaped to her feet. Her stomach heaved as she swallowed the remains of her last meal that lingered in her stomach, burning her throat. 'What are you talking about? He was just drunk and probably talking rubbish.'

He reached out to her, taking her hand.

'It's true. He confirmed it one day when he was sober and told me I must never tell you or anyone else. He said he should never have told me.'

She fought back tears. 'I knew there was something wrong. All my life I believed I was adopted or perhaps a foster child. I knew I didn't fit in.' She clenched her fists. 'Why didn't Mum tell me all these years? I wouldn't have had to find out like this.' She wiped her glass-like tears with her sleeve as they scalded her hot cheeks.

'Do you know who my real father is? Please, Doug! I have to know. Please tell me!' She pulled on his arm, glaring at him bug-eyed.

'I can only guess who it is, but I have no evidence. I might be wrong, then I'll be in trouble. Only Mum can tell you.'

'Well, she won't! She hasn't done all these years, and I'm nearly nineteen years old. I'm going to give her one chance and if she refuses to tell me the truth, I'll leave home!'

Tears welled up in her eyes again. She quickly wiped them and as she looked up at Doug, she could see that his eyes were moist too.

He lowered his head, looking at his feet. Then he stood and wrapped her in a hug. His embrace warmed her but did not fill the new broken places in her heart. She took a step away.

Doug lifted her chin. 'You'd better get to bed now. They'll be back from the reunion soon and it's late. We can talk about it tomorrow.'

Hope sloped off to her bedroom and crashed onto her bed. Her entire body ached, calling out for sleep. Yet it didn't come. She had almost pried the truth out of him, but he was loyal to the end.

Hope's sick of all the arguments when Frank comes home drunk every night. And her mother with all her deceit. How could they keep such a secret all these years? She must get away from it all. She'll have to pick her moment to confront her mother, so she won't get Doug into trouble.

Her head almost burst with the pent-up emotion. She struggled to get off to sleep with a throbbing headache, tossing and turning and hoping to be asleep before they arrive home to start the arguments all over again.

***

Finally, school was done. Hope sloped into the living room. Her stomach twisted as she approached her mother.

'Mum—now that school has finished, I'm going to take a gap year. I'll find a job in some stables or do farm work for a year before I go to university.'

Her mother stood in the doorway, frowning at her. 'I don't know why you don't want to go nursing. You don't know what's good for you!'

'No, Mum! I told you I'm not interested. Just because you think it's a noble profession, it doesn't mean that I have to take it up!' She stifled the urge to scream at her. 'You can't keep trying to live your broken dreams through me.' Hope crossed her arms in defiance.

Myra scooped up a pile of clothes from the laundry basket, dumping them next to the ironing board.

'It will always provide you with job security and you'll be able to travel all over the world as a nurse.' She slammed the iron down roughly. Hissing steam spat from it like an enraged creature.

'I've made up my mind already. You know my passion is to work with animals. I want to have a career with horses.'

'You'll never get a proper job doing that. I doubt it. In fact, I've already told you that without qualifications you'll become nothing!'

'That's right. That's why I'm doing a diploma that specialises in equine health.'

'What a load of rubbish. You won't get into a university doing something like that.'

'Sorry to disappoint you, but I've already been accepted for the Diploma in Agriscience Equine in Dunedin. I'm doing it through correspondence. That way, I can do casual work learning to train horses as well.'

'Is that right?' A sneer appeared on Myra's lips. 'You said nothing about it.' She snapped.

Hope rolled her eyes. 'I knew you would try to stop me. I applied for a place when I passed my college exams just to see how far I would get. Look, Mum. You should be happy for me.'

'I didn't see any letters from the university.' Her mother stood stiff, bracing herself with her hands on her hips.

'That's because I had them sent to Jessie's house.' Hope looked down at her floor.

'That was very deceitful, don't you think?'

Hope jerked her head back up and glared at her, anger rekindled.

'No, not deceitful. Cautious. I didn't want you ruining my chances. That would be selfish, don't you think?'

Myra backed off. She pressed her lips together, as she always did when she was working an impossible problem.

'Well, I've never heard such utter rubbish in all my life. You'll never amount to anything doing that—you mark my words.'

'It would be nice for you to encourage me, just for once. You always put me down.' Hope's eyes blurred.

'Well, I just thought it would be wiser for you to stay and go nursing. You could live at home and save money. Here—take these blouses to your room and hang them up.'

She just wants to keep me here as her slave.

Memories of having a copper for boiling water pushed forward in her mind. Hope hated going into the outside laundry in the old, corrugated iron shed where it stood amongst the cobwebs and bugs. She'd felt sorry for Doug, that it was his job to stoke it and carry the scalding hot water into the house for their baths. He'd only been a teenager then but was required to carry the water in the heavy metal buckets three times a week when he arrived home from school. *Well—I won't end up like that. Poor Doug.*

Hope hung up her blouses in her wardrobe and walked back into the dining room. She picked up a rag off the dining table and began and cleaning the heavy Venetian blinds, each blade one by one. This was her mother's favourite job for her.

Drawing her brows together, she narrowed her eyes. Working and working—receiving no reward. Her pockets were still bare.

Hope threw the cloth back on the table. 'I know Frank isn't my real father. And I need to know the truth!'

'What? Where did you get that? Who's been talking to you?'

'Frank, in one of his drunken stupors spilt the beans. Why did I have to find out this way? You've both deceived me.' Hope's tone was brusque. She swallowed around the lump in her throat and blinked back tears, willing herself not to break down. It was no good. She cracked. Tears gushed down her face. She grabbed a tissue from her pocket, blew her nose, and shoved her fringe roughly out of her eyes.

Her mother blew on her glasses that appeared fogged and wiped them with the corner of her blouse. Her lips pursed. She glowered at Hope, then shifted her gaze straight ahead. Frozen tears filled her eyes.

'He's talking rubbish. Anything comes out of him when he's drunk.'

'I believe him. Why would he say that if I were his daughter? You're lying. If you don't tell me the truth, I'm leaving home ... for good.' Hope stood up abruptly, pushing her chair back and stood up. 'Anyway, I've decided to go away for a month or so. Jessie's father has some farm work for me until I get a regular job. I have some thinking to do.'

'When are you going? This is ridiculous.' Her mother barked.

'Jessie's picking me up in the morning. If you don't tell me the truth before I leave, I'll be thinking about moving out when I get back.'

'Moving ... where? You are over-reacting!'

'Overreacting—you're in denial. How can you say such a thing?'

'I don't know what you're talking about.' Myra persisted. 'You are over-reacting to something you don't understand. Oh, well—if that's the way you want to go.'

'I want to save some money before I begin my studies in a year. I'll be looking for a proper job while I'm staying with them.'

Hope stormed off into her room. *Over-reacting, she says. Now I know I have to get out of here.*

Hope lay on her bed thinking how different family life was at Jessie's house. Mental weariness drained today's events out of her. Sleep was an attractive proposition and oblivion came quickly.

Waking feeling unrefreshed the following morning, Hope got a whiff of fresh toast emanating from the kitchen. She bolted her breakfast down, dressed, then hurried outside, looking for Frank. She thought it best to tell him she was off to Jessie's for a month.

Myra hung her head out the kitchen window.

'Hope—I need to talk to you before you go.' She bellowed.

Frank kept his head down as he continued to hoe the trenches he'd prepared for planting the potatoes. It was as if he knew there was trouble brewing, but said little to her.

'Off you go then. Try not to upset your mother and let her know your plans.'

As if he really cared about her plans. Hope cleverly hid her lack of respect for him for not having the spine to bring the truth out into the open. But deep down, she felt sorry for him.

She went back inside to fetch her backpack and dumped it at the front door. 'What is it, Mum? Jessie will be here soon.' She thought her mother was about to confess. Or was it just wishful thinking?

'What are you going to do about Misty while you're away?' Hope's neck tensed. Her mother was still in denial.

'Someone needs to care for her and check her water trough. I can't. I'm busy with the Women's Institute fundraising this month.' Myra's nose twitched, the way it always did when she justified her behaviour.

'Peter said he'll look out for her. You know, Joel's friend in the carpentry workshop whom he used to work with. He loves horses and knows Misty well.'

'But he isn't there all the time. He only works part time like Joel used to.'

'That's okay. Misty has everything she needs. She just has to be checked every few days.'

'I'm glad that's all sorted, then. It's been years since I've had to handle a horse.' Myra scowled at her.

A horn tooted outside on the street. Jessie was there. Hope gave her mother a quick peck on the cheek and met her gaze. 'Please, Mum, do the right thing.' As Hope turned to walk out the door, she saw that Myra's eyes had lost all expression.

***

Jessie's parents, Wyatt and Prue Lee, owned a large cattle farm on the outskirts of Bethlehem and welcomed Hope with open arms. Hope counted on Wyatt giving her work and references. She was sure she could convince him she was a top-notch farm worker. Thank God he was giving her the chance. She arose each morning when the rooster crowed and worked from daylight to dusk to prove to him her worth.

One evening, when Jessie's parents were in bed, Hope opened up. She poured her heart out to her friend about the devastating revelation that Frank was not her biological father and how Doug had blown the whistle on his parent's deception.

'It was pretty selfish of your mother, not telling you who your real father is all these years. Especially after you begged her.' Jessie put an arm across Hope's shoulders.

'She fears a scandal, Doug says. It has been the family secret for years.' Hope began picking at her fingernails.

They talked until late into the night, stuffing themselves with Fanta, popcorn and chocolate.

'Jessie—there's something else ... something that I'm worried about. But I suppose you want to go off to sleep now.' Jessie had returned to Hope's room in her winceyette pyjamas covered in Panda bears.

'No, I'm fine, really I am. Wait—I'll make us some hot chocolate. I'll bring it in here.'

Hope got ready for bed. She pulled out a photo of Misty from her backpack. Her eyes became glazed, like deep blue glass marbles. They filled with tears, and she quickly put the photo back as Jessie walked in with the hot drinks.

'Are you okay, Hope?'

'Oh—I'm fine. Just a touch of hay fever I get at this time of the year.'

'What did you want to tell me?' She placed a mug of steaming hot chocolate milk on the bedside table next to Hope and plonked herself down on the bed next to her.

'It's Doug. There's something wrong with him.'

'What do you mean ... Is he sick?'

'Kind of. He was in the permanent army from the age of seventeen, and you already know he's a Vietnam war veteran. When he left the army, he was psychologically damaged. His personality has completely changed.'

'Poor Doug. Can't he get some help?'

'He's had a lot of counselling, but no one can stop him from getting terrible flash-backs. The few times he has come home for a weekend or on holiday, we've been woken by his nightmares. He yells out in his sleep. My room's next to his and it freaks me out.'

Hope leaned forward, bracing her arms on her thighs and gazed at the floor. She continued. 'One night I saw a flashlight in the hallway and heard him yelling. I got up to find him running around in the dark with a torch and Mum got up to see what the commotion was. He kept on saying, "They're out there ... shush ... they're out there!" He meant that the Viet Cong were outside.'

'Wow! He sounds so messed up. So sad. He needs help. He uses alcohol to numb the pain, and I think he doesn't care about anything anymore.'

'Would you like me to say a prayer for him? That's all we can really do. I can ask God for a healing of memories.'

'Thanks Jessie, I'd love that.'

After Jessie had prayed for her, Hope wandered back to her own bedroom and as she lay in her bed, an unusual sense of peace came over her she'd never experienced before.

***

The monthly Farmer's Market was something Hope had not experienced, though she had always wanted to.

She linked arms with Jessie. 'I can't believe I go back home tomorrow. The time's gone by so fast.'

'Nor can I. It's been such fun having you here the last month. I'll miss you. So will Dad. He said you were worth every word he wrote on your reference.'

'I'll miss you, too.' Hope examined the wares of the farmer's market stalls as they strolled, especially the oversized cheeses. She stopped. 'Wait a minute, Jessie. I think she's a girl I know from Pony Club.' She pointed at someone at a stall opposite.

The girl in Jodhpur pants and elaborate looking riding boots walked towards them. She looked up. 'Hope—what are you doing here? I wondered where you had gone. Where's Misty? I rode past her paddock yesterday and couldn't see her. Are you grazing her somewhere else these days?'

'Sally...what? What do you mean? She must be there. I haven't moved her.'

'I had a look around her paddock. Your horse float isn't there either. I thought you must have taken her to a show or a hunt.'

Hope's heart raced. Misty had to be there. She just had to be. 'I'll go back and look for her and make sure. Thanks for that. I've been staying with my friend Jessie for a month and return home tomorrow. But I'll have to get back and check on Misty now.'

The two friends said their goodbyes, and Jessie led Hope to the market exit. What if Sally was right? She couldn't have escaped by herself. Someone must have let her out. Or taken her. No, it couldn't be. Sally probably just didn't notice that Misty often lies down behind the willow tree. That was it. Her beloved horse had to be where she'd left her a month before.

The rest of the day dragged on as her thoughts continually returned to Misty. She'd been dreading going home, but now she couldn't wait. When they arrived back from the market, Hope explained to Jessie's parents that she needed to return home straight away in case Misty had escaped.

'You know you're welcome here anytime.' Wyatt and Prue waved her off after they both gave her a bear hug.

Jessie drove Hope home and dropped her off at the gate. 'Thank for everything.' Hope embraced Jessie, almost crying. 'I'll let you know the outcome later this evening.'

Jessie pulled out of the drive tooting as she drove up the road. Hope's feet were heavy with reluctance as she dragged them up the front steps and flung open the door.

Her mother stood in the kitchen peeling potatoes.

'I'm back,' Hope muttered as she shot straight past Myra and headed towards her bedroom. She offloaded her backpack and rushed back out of the house.

Misty! She has to put her eyes on her horse. The paddock can't really be empty. She just can't fathom it.

She grabbed her bicycle and sped off to where the horse grazed. Her mother's voice chased her as she yelled, 'Wait, Hope – we need to talk.'

She continued cycling as fast as she could, a fifteen-minute ride to the paddock that felt like an eternity.

Misty was Hope's sweetheart. The noble, white Anglo-Arab mare was her best friend and the type of horse that was highly sought after in equestrian circles. During the hard years at home, when Hope felt invisible, Misty comforted her. The horse always met her at the gate, waiting for a carrot treat and then rub her head up and down Hope's back as a thank you.

She cycled like a lunatic, almost toppling off. Her cheeks burned tomato red as she swiped away the beads of salty perspiration stinging her eyes. With fire in her belly, she jumped off her bike, throwing it aside. Her legs kept pumping, propelling her to the fence.

But this time, Misty didn't approach the gate as Hope sped down the track towards her paddock, calling her name. 'Misty,' she yelled. The paddock was empty.

Clambering over the wire fence, not bothering to open the wooden gate, she caught her leg on barbed wire.

Blood ran down her leg. 'Stupid fence,' she bellowed. 'Misty, please come. Where are you?'

She scanned the field of long grass. Her beloved companion was nowhere to be found. Misty was gone. But she couldn't have disappeared on her own.

Hope dropped to the ground, tears streaming down her cheeks. She wailed. Had the ground swallowed her? If it hadn't, she wished it would.

'Who would do this?'

Normally, she'd run to Joel who once worked part time in the carpentry shop next to the paddock when he wasn't training horses. But eighteen months ago he'd left his job and disappeared from the Bay of Plenty.

Hope hauled herself up and trudged to the tack shed. It was empty too. The well-oiled saddle, bridle, and grooming kit were all missing. Even the horse float had gone. Her knees buckled; a flood of tears wet the ground beneath her feet. It felt as if a rock dropped into the pit of her stomach. She shook from head to toe. How would she get through this?

No answers came to mind as she fell back on the grass. Dark clouds above matched the ones in her mind.

Chapter Two

The tyres on the bike were almost flat, slowing her down as she tore down the street towards her house. Panting, her heart in her mouth, she stomped into the kitchen.

'Where is she? What have you done with Misty? She's not in her paddock!' Her legs shook like jelly, and her heart missed a beat. The strain was too much.

Her mother leaned over the stove, about to put a roast in the oven and paused. She stood aside, wiping her hands on her apron and put a hand on the bench to steady herself. 'I'm sorry, Hope. We thought it best to sell her.'

Hope stood with hands on hips, her face muscles taut. She swiped a wringing wet fringe from her eyes and burst into tears. Slamming a fist on the kitchen bench, she glared at her mother.

'What do you mean? You can't do that—she's mine. You had no right!'

'After you left here for so long, your father and I thought it was the right thing to do. You can't exercise her if you are out gallivanting around. And the horse is just a distraction when you go nursing.'

Why can't her mother just accept that she is not going nursing?

'Just stop it! I'm not gallivanting around. I'll be looking for work. And stop calling Frank my father. I haven't called him my father ever since I found out the truth. You had no right to do this behind my back. I hate you!'

'Don't talk like that. He's been your guardian all these years.'

'What! For the few times that he's been sober. And all this time you still haven't told me the truth. Anyway—what have you done with Misty?'

'She's gone to someone who'll take her to horse shows and hunts, just like you.'

'Where—where has she gone?'

'The South Island. To someone who wants to enter her in events. You don't need to know more than that.'

Hope collapsed back into the hard wooden chair. She leaned her head on crossed arms on the table briefly. She wanted so much for this scene to just be a bad dream. Soon she would awaken, and her life would be back to how it used to be. Abruptly she sat bolt upright with renewed ardour, pushing the chair away.

'Why down south—so far away? You could have sold her locally!'

'It was someone who wanted a white Anglo-Arab like Misty, her breed and her capabilities. They'll take good care of her, I promise.'

Hope thought she would never trust her mother again, let alone believe her promises.

'I'm going to find her. And I already warned you I would move out completely if you continue to withhold the truth about my father from me. I'm an adult and can take care of myself. I'm leaving!'

Hope wilted. She was nauseated with the powerlessness over losing her beloved Misty. She sloped off to her room and stared at the ribbons and trophies she had won with the mare. Crashing on her bed, she howled like a baby, then lay on her back, emotionally exhausted.

How could she be so cruel? I'll never forgive her.

She wanted to go back to see Jessie and tell her what had happened, but it was dark outside. But she was afraid to bike in the dark and had run out of energy. Jessie would be upset, too. They had been riding companions for years. Hope was grateful that Jessie was home from university for the holidays.

She lay on her bed, upsetting herself with pessimistic thoughts about the bad things that might happen to her precious horse. This latest betrayal was for Hope the last straw.

Myra and Frank were stretched out on their worn-out couch watching television, sharing a bar of chocolate. Hope crept into the hall so as not to alert them and picked up the telephone.

'Jessie! I'm glad you picked up the phone.' Her throat seemed to have closed up as she choked on the words. 'It's Misty ... Sally was right, she's gone! Mum sold her!'

There was silence on the other end of the line, except for the sound of Hope sobbing into the phone. 'Please Jessie— can you come and pick me up again? I'm so angry with my mother. I can't stay here any longer.'

Having been given a car for her nineteenth birthday so that she could get to her university, Jessie had previously told Hope to let her know if she ever needed a ride anywhere.

'Sure, no problem. That's pretty mean of your mother. I'll leave now. Stay as long as you want, and I'll talk to Mum and Dad.'

Hope scurried around, grabbing as much clothing as she could pack into a backpack, including all her photos of Misty. She walked into the lounge to inform Myra and Frank that she was leaving for good. They just sat there, speechless for the first time. Hope had grown up. Myra sat with her face in her hands, looking totally bewildered.

***

Hope's home life had always been tumultuous. Frank's drinking had got out of control and there were increasing arguments between him and Myra. Her bedroom was off the dining room. When Frank walked in drunk each night, she was kept awake by her mother yelling at him. This time, she had had enough.

Jessie pulled up outside the house, tooting the horn a few times. As Hope opened the door and ran towards the car, Jessie saw the lounge curtain being drawn aside and Myra standing at the window her eyes shooting daggers at them.

 'Quick, let's get out of here before she comes out to start a drama.' Hope dared not turn her head as Jessie drove off.

'Are you sure your folks don't mind me coming back again? I'll work for your father until I find a job.'

'It's alright, they know that. Dad has plenty for you to do. Anyway … you can ride one of our horses while you're here and we can go on a few treks.'

Jessie's family was completely different to Hope's—kind and respectful towards each and people of faith.

***

Once again, Jessie's parents welcomed Hope back as one of the family. It made her feel secure, but she felt drained. Her neck and shoulders ached from the emotional tension, so she excused herself early that evening as her body longed for sleep.

That night, the house fell silent as the full moon lit up Hope's room like a searchlight. The light-weight curtains were no match for this moon. Hope pulled back the soft white sheets. The unusual pillowcases with Swiss embroidered edging welcomed her head, heavy from the pent-up emotion that plagued her. She lay still, listening to the sound of a cow crying out for its calf. *Hurry Mum*, she wanted to call out.

Hope imagined what life could have been like if she had a family like Jessie's and was going to make sure she made the most of it … at least for now.

The next morning, a rooster stood crowing from the top of a hen house opposite Hope's room, while the Border collie working dog ran around outside yelping.

There was a knock at her door. 'Are you awake, Hope? Mum's cooking breakfast. A special one for you.'

She tumbled out of bed, still half asleep. Her shoulders ached from the stress of the last few days as she opened the door to Jessie who was already dressed.

'That's sweet of her. She shouldn't go to any trouble.'

'Take advantage of it. Believe me, it might not happen again for a while.'

'Oh, okay, I'm quite hungry. I'll just jump in the shower and be there shortly.'

Jessie was waiting in the dining room when Hope walked in with her long, voluminous black hair—still wet from the shower.

'I thought perhaps we could go over some of your plans to find Misty. If there's any way I can help, I will. Come—let's eat first. I'm famished.'

Jessie directed her to a French farmhouse style dining table set with old-fashioned Wedgewood crockery placed neatly around the table on place-mats.

Hope listened intently to the healthy communication going on at the dining table—pleasant conversations between Jessie, her parents and her brother. She enjoyed the way they involved her, which made her feel part of the family.

Breakfast was over quickly, as Wyatt, Jessie's father had a busy schedule on the farm that morning.

'Here, girls—grab a tea-towel each. After that, I think Wyatt wants to show you the jobs he has lined up for you,

Hope.' Prue placed fresh tea-towels on the bench in front of them.

'You don't have to start the jobs today,' Wyatt interjected. 'Start tomorrow. I'll give you lassies the day off so you can help sort Hope out, Jessie.' He winked affectionately at his daughter.

'Great! Come on, Hope. Let's saddle up and take off to the beach. Twinkle, the horse you'll be riding, loves the water.'

***

They arrived at the beach close to Jessie's home and took the horses into the sea on the incoming tide. Twinkle almost reared with exhilaration. Suddenly, he plunged forward. 'Hey! Whoa!' Hope kept her balance and tried to pull his head up, as the feisty gelding seemed to sink in the sand. 'Jessie, help me! I think we're sinking,' she screamed.

Jessie was further up ahead and had taken her own horse through a deeper part of the estuary where it was less muddy. She turned her horse around and hurried back towards Hope. She stopped a few metres away.

'Wait! I have a rope on my saddle, and I'll try to pull you out. Can't come any closer, though.'

Jessie threw Hope the long rope with a large clip attached.

'Attach the clip to the ring on your saddle. It's a strong one.'

Hope followed Jessie's instructions. 'I'm ready.' *What now? She's done this before*, Hope thought.

'Here—give me your reins. Just hang on tight. I'm going to pull you out.'

Hope held her breath. Her body went rigid. 'I hope we don't sink any further.' She shrieked.

'Don't panic. I've done this before.' Jessie leaned forward to speak into her horse's ear. 'Now then, Rusty—you have to pull very hard.'

Rusty pricked up his ears as she nudged his sides with her heels. He swayed back and forth as if to find his footing then lurched forward, grunting as he heaved. Suddenly, Twinkle gave a loud whinny and forged forward, following Rusty out of the hole.

Hope shook. A large shot of adrenaline raced furiously through her body like an electric current. 'I'm feeling wrecked. I need a break!'

They rode up onto a large patch of grass along the foreshore. Hope flung herself off her muddy horse, although she'd almost fallen off him in shock. Her legs trembled. She found a small hand-towel in her saddle-bag and clumsily trudged to the foreshore to soak it in the incoming tide. She began to wipe the mud from Twinkle's coat with the wet towel.

'Poor boy. I'm so sorry Twinkle to get you into this. I'll give you a good warm wash down when we get back.' She wrapped her arms around Twinkle's neck and squeezed it tight.

'Whew! That was close.' Jessie gave her a sheepish look.

'You may have saved our lives, Jessie. How strange that the ground just went from under us. I've never been in quicksand before.'

'I'm sorry, Hope. I am so used to coming this way with riding companions who are familiar with the area. I just didn't think that you wouldn't have known.' Jessie's voice quavered.

Hope turned and looked straight at her, eyebrows raised.

'You mean you knew it was boggy before I went in there?'

'I should have warned you, it's not real quicksand, just boggy in parts. If you know where to go, it won't be a problem. It happened to another friend in the past. I just forgot to let you know. So sorry—please forgive me.'

'It's okay. You're forgiven, I suppose. I'm safe now, but I won't come this way again. Let's eat.' Hope could already see her friend's fair complexion, that usually resembled that of a porcelain doll, had turned a strawberry colour.

She pulled her packed lunch out of her saddle-bag and dumped herself on the grass. She gulped down the cold drink that Jessie's mother had packed for her.

'I'm feeling shattered. I wonder how my Misty would have reacted. Twinkle was very calm despite the danger.'

'He's a lovely boy. Sure-footed. We'll have to give them a good wash when we get back. Look—I have an idea. What about saving some money from your jobs and hire a truck to bring Misty back up here when you find her?'

'No. I won't be able to bring her back. Mum's put our paddock put up for grazing.'

'Really? Don't worry. We can graze her on our farm with my horses. Dad won't mind. I'll ask him.'

'You seem to be quite confident that I'll find her.'

'You will I'm sure.' Jessie's long, slender fingers stroked the back of her hand.

'I'm going to pray that you do. You could hire a car and tour around for a while. There are those free relocation vehicles that have to be dropped off in towns with airports.'

'Yeah, I might look at that.'

'You could visit local Pony Clubs and make enquiries about Misty. Take some photos with you to show the riders.'

'That's a great idea!' Hope's face lit up.

'I wonder if the new owner will keep her name the same.'

'Mum says he would—but I don't know if I can trust her anymore.' Hope frowned.

'I suppose we'd better get back. I don't like the look of the dark clouds up there.' Jessie pointed upwards. They packed their lunchboxes back into their saddlebags and untied the horses.

Hope said nothing during the ride back to the farm. She let Jessie ride ahead while troublesome thoughts were living rent-free in her head. *What will Misty be doing right now? Who is with her?*

Chapter Three

After six weeks of working on the farm, Hope had saved up enough money for the airfare to Christchurch. Wyatt had paid her well, and she'd worked from daylight to dusk. They didn't even charge her for her lodgings.

'Let's check your plans.' Jessie picked up Hope's papers and looked at the itinerary in front of her.

'Where are you staying in Christchurch? You haven't written it on here.'

'I don't want to stop there. I'll just keep driving towards Queenstown and if I get tired, I'll find a holiday park or backpackers for the night.'

Hope noticed Jessie was acting overly concerned as she sat obsessively, looking over her itinerary several times.

'I've booked a relocation station wagon from the airport, which I'll have to drop off at Queenstown Airport in four days' time. After that, I'll take public transport or hire another car from there. I'm needing to find more work so I can afford to buy Misty back.'

'You said your Uncle Joel has a sister in Geraldine. Perhaps you could find her. Didn't you say that his family came from around there somewhere?'

'Yes, perhaps he's living there now.'

'How will you find out?'

'His sister will be in the phone book, I guess. I'll pay her a visit. Surely she must know where he lives. He's the only one who might help me find Misty.'

'Well, looks like you're all set for your big adventure. Promise you'll write the minute you arrive in Queenstown. I'm going to miss you terribly. Dad's going to run you to the bus terminal so you can get the Road Services bus to Auckland International Airport.'

Jessie threw her arms around Hope, teardrops rolling down her pink cheeks. 'I'll say goodbye now as I have to feed the calves tomorrow and need to stay back here. Going to miss you heaps.'

'Pity you can't keep me company at the airport as I'll have a four-hour wait for my flight. I'll miss you too, Jessie. Don't know what I would have done without your help. I would probably be stuck at home depressed. Thanks so much.'

As Jessie stood in the doorway, Hope grabbed her and hugged her tight and walked towards her room.

Jessie looked back, hesitating. 'Don't be upset, please. You can come up for the holidays sometime and stay at my flat. Anyway, you're going to be busy searching for Misty. Just keep the letters coming ... okay? I'm off to bed now. If things don't work out in the South Island, you could always come and stay with me.'

***

During her short flight on the DC-10 plane to Christchurch, Hope had been trying to solve a problem in her mind. Something just didn't sit right about Joel taking off in a hurry for no reason. And according to her mother, he had gone to the South Island, and she wouldn't tell her where. Why was everyone so secretive?

The airline stewardess, with the soft voice, interrupted her thoughts.

'Excuse me, dear, but we'll be landing soon. Please fasten your seatbelt. Can I offer you a lolly?'

'Um ... Oh, it's okay, thanks.'

'It helps to stop your ears from blocking up.' The old woman sitting next to Hope nudged her as she unwrapped her own lolly.

With that, Hope quickly put her hand out for a sweet before the stewardess walked on down the aisle.

'Thank you,' she said to the woman. 'I think we're about to land ... I hate this part.' She squeezed both armrests tight.

'Me too. I just close my eyes and hope for the best.' The woman placed her hand on hers and smiled.

'Do you live here in Christchurch?'

'No, I'm on my way to Queenstown. I've more travelling to do yet.'

'How are you getting there—is someone waiting to take you?'

'No. I've ordered one of those relocation vehicles, which I can have for four days. I have to drop it off at Queenstown airport. They are free except for petrol.'

'Sounds lovely, dear. Look—you can drive by my house first if you like. It's near here, and I can give you something to eat and a cup of tea. I was going to get a taxi, but if I ride with you, I can show you how to get there.'

Hope thought that the old lady was just looking for a ride home from the airport. She told Hope that she had been away for a few days visiting a new grandchild in Auckland.

'I don't mind giving you a ride home, then I would like to get on my way as I want to make good mileage before it gets dark. Thanks for the offer, though.'

At the arrival gate at the airport, Hope saw a large placard, waving in the air with her name on it.

HOPE PETERSEN – SOUTHERN RENTALS

She collected her backpack from the carousel and walked to the exit gate towards the man in a suit holding the placard and waved at him. He waved while hurrying over to help carry her luggage.

'Do you mind waiting a moment? I promised a lift to an old lady who sat next to me on the plane. She lives near here. I'll just help her with her luggage.'

'No worries, madam. As long as she doesn't take too long. I have another job after this. Our office is just down the road, so you'll have to drop me off first and sign the paperwork.'

'Hold on—here she is.'

The woman trundled slowly towards them, pushing a trolley.

'So sorry to keep you both waiting. Elsie's my name.'

The man in the suit helped them both load their luggage into the vehicle. After the paperwork was completed, Hope dropped Elsie home. The woman gave her a bar of chocolate and waved her on her way.

***

The station wagon was a spacious one, big enough for a large family, and Hope found it easy to handle, as she had driven one once before. She'd been warned by the rental company about black ice on the roads and not to take corners too fast, especially if it was windy.

Before she set off on her intrepid journey along one of the most scenic routes in New Zealand, she stopped to study her map. She'd a general idea of where she was headed but wanted to make sure she didn't get onto the wrong highway, as the thought of getting lost in the South Island was daunting for her.

***

The station wagon was comfortable to drive, except that Hope became quickly fatigued from the intense concentration of driving in the wind. The vehicle roared along the highway until it started veering to the left and right as she struggled to keep it on a straight path in the strong southerly wind. She wished she had someone with her to take turns driving. She would have to harden up.

Hope was relieved when she saw a green, overhead road sign that said "Geraldine" and slowed her pace. Pulling into a rest area just out of town, she spotted a dairy. She pulled over and went into the store, and asked the shopkeeper if she could browse through the local phone directory.

'Here she is! Nelly Grey. Primrose Avenue number 11.' She jotted the details down.

'Thanks so much. I just hope she's there, that's all.' She waved to the shopkeeper as she walked out the door.

The man behind the counter called back to her. 'You can use my phone to call her if you like.'

Hope hesitated as if she wanted to walk back into the shop, then changed her mind. 'No, thank you. I'll just drop by and see if she is in.'

She chanced it. If Nelly wasn't home, she'd keep going through to Lake Tekapo and stop at the camping ground there.

She parked the car outside an old, freshly painted villa. It was typical of a home of someone Nelly's age. An ornately adorned wire archway covered with deep pink, climbing roses provided a welcome feature at the front gate. As Hope walked into the entrance of the property, she noticed the pull-up windows were open and to the left of the home, white cotton sheets blowing in the southerly breeze.

'Can I help you, dear?' An elderly woman caught sight of Hope and popped her head out of the window.

Hope's eyes darted back and forth to see where the voice came from. 'Oh, sorry—I wasn't sure if anyone was home. Are you Nelly ... Nelly Grey?'

'Yes—yes, I am. Wait. Come around to the front door will you, dear.'

Hope scurried around the front, holding up a small bunch of flowers she'd purchased from a roadside kiosk and pushed them in front of Nelly's nose.

'I'm Hope ... Hope Petersen'. She handed Nelly the half-wilted flowers.

'They're lovely, thank you. Oh, my goodness. You have grown up. I haven't seen you since you were about ten years old. Come on in, dear.'

Nelly sat Hope down in a cosy floral armchair while she hurried into the kitchen and returned with a cold drink.

'Would you like one of my oat biscuits? I baked them last night. They're nice and crispy with a little ginger. You can take a few with you on your journey. Now tell me where you are headed.'

Hope took a handful of the biscuits, wrapped them in her paper napkin, and slid them inside her bag.

'Actually, I'm here for a reason. I'm trying to locate Uncle Joel. My mother said he's living in the South Island somewhere. He just up and left suddenly a few years ago and I don't understand why. But I need to ask him something important. I thought he may be around here somewhere, near his old hometown.'

'Oh, yes. My elusive brother—he did stay here for a short time after he left your home. Since he moved south, I see him less than when he lived up north with your family.'

'Do you know where he is? I need to find him urgently.'

'Goodness. That sounds serious—somewhere near Queenstown, I think. I can't remember what he said.' Her brows knitted in a frown. 'I can't remember if he said it was Wanaka or Queenstown.'

She let out a deep sigh. 'Sorry, Lass, my memory's almost gone. He said he had purchased a piece of land and now runs horses on it—trains them he said. But to be perfectly honest, that's all I know. In fact, I can't do much travelling nowadays. I had his phone number somewhere, but it's a toll call and I can't afford it.'

She rummaged through a drawer in her kitchen, looking for her address book.

'It should be in this book,' she mumbled, her forehead puckering as she realised the number was incorrect.

'Sorry, dear, I only have his old number. Perhaps he might be in my phone directory. I'll just take a look for you.'

Hope's heart sank. She'd driven all that way for nothing. Joel was her only hope of finding Misty.

Nelly handed her the book and saw that Hope's face had dropped.

'I can't see his name in the main phone directory. Perhaps you'd better see if you can find it. Your eyes will be better than mine.'

It was futile. Hope's attempt at trying to track Joel down through Nelly had failed. Where to now?

'I'm so sorry to have put you to all this trouble, Nelly. I'll go to the public library in Queenstown and look through the phone directories there. But I really have to get on the road before it gets dark.' She jangled her keys and picked up her bag.

'Of course—it's no trouble at all. But I don't like the idea of a young girl like you travelling so far by yourself. You're welcome to stay here the night if you like.'

'I'm nearly nineteen, so not so much of a girl. That's kind of you, but I wouldn't want to put you to any trouble.'

'No, really. I welcome the company, and I see you've turned into a lovely young woman.' Nelly quickly corrected herself. 'Are you going to Queenstown tomorrow?'

'No, I want to see the alpine lakes and stay in Wanaka. Maybe I'll get to see Mount Cook from there and take some photos. I'll then head down to Queenstown.'

'Why not let me make you a nice hot dinner and then you get a good night's sleep before your big trip tomorrow?'

'That's so kind of you. I really appreciate it.'

'It gets lonely in these parts. I'm grateful for the company.'

Nelly lit the fire and started singing. Hope could see that she was happy to have a guest for the night.

The woman brought out a crock pot with a hot lamb casserole and placed it on the dining table.

'Now you sit yourself down here and tuck into this. I have apple crumble and custard to follow.'

When the meal was over, Hope wanted to find out more about Uncle Joel. She scanned the row of black and white photos in frames that skirted the oak hutch dresser and spotted a younger version of Joel.

'Do you mind telling me a little about Uncle Joel and his family life?'

'Of course. I'd love to.' She walked to her cabinet and pulled out a small photo album.

'You know Joel was born here in Geraldine where he spent his youth on my father's farm, hoping one day to take it over from him. While he was on active service during the last World War, Joel's American wife ran off with an English pilot and it took him years to get over a broken heart.'

'Oh—I didn't know. That's terrible, poor man.'

'Then our father died of a heart attack on the farm while Joel was still overseas ... a double whammy. Mum and I had to put the farm up for sale. Dad had bequeathed the farm to Mum, Joel and me equally.'

'It's a pity he couldn't take over the farm. He would have loved that.' Hope picked up a photo of Joel riding a horse.

'When Joel returned from the war, he had to face the fact that his dream of managing the farm had ended. Mother had moved to Bethlehem to be near her relatives and Joel moved in with her.'

'That's when he met my family. You didn't go with them, Nelly?'

'No. I had good friends here and didn't want to move. I worked as a journalist for a firm in Christchurch by correspondence and bought this little cottage with the money from the estate.'

The sad talk about Uncle Joel's past bereavements drained Hope.

'Thanks so much for the delicious food and for talking to me about Uncle Joel. I'm tired now and need to get some sleep.'

As Hope was about to get into bed, the ageing spinster stood at the door to say goodnight.

'I promise I'll note down Joel's phone number if he rings me after you've gone. Keep in touch with me now and then, if you can, and I'll let you know if I hear from him. Get some sleep now and don't worry.'

Chapter Four

'Thanks for the cooked breakfast.' Hope reached out and hugged Nelly as though they were old friends.

'Here's a little something for your journey.' Nelly handed her a basket full of home baking. A delicious aroma wafted out through the tea-towel that covered it. 'You don't need to return the basket. I have two of them.'

Hope was eager to start her journey. She only had four days left before the car was due back. It was a comfortable trip from Geraldine along State Highway 79 until she missed the turnoff at Fairlie junction for State Highway 8 to Lake Tekapo. She had to turn around and drive back to the junction, about fifteen minutes out of her way, which annoyed her. She pulled in at Fairlie for a quick break when she spotted a tearoom where she could ask directions for the turnoff to Lake Tekapo.

After travelling along State Highway 8, she felt weary after not having slept well at Nelly's house worrying about how to find Joel. She knew that tiredness was risky when driving long distances, stopping when she got to Lake Tekapo.

Arriving at the lakefront, she couldn't believe her eyes. The view was breath-taking. An abundance of pink and purple lupins formed a technicolour carpet on the lake shore. It appeared like a stunning tapestry from a distance.

As Hope drove closer to the shore, she saw the renowned Church of the Good Shepherd, the quaint stone church framed by the famous Southern Alps.

She stood on the foreshore taking photos, not forgetting the lovely bronze statue of the collie dog, representative of the honoured sheep dogs of the Mackenzie country. Hunger pangs gnawed at her as she eagerly headed over to the tearooms. She hesitated, as she abhorred crowded cafes. Although this one was full of tourists, she battled her way along the queue to the food cabinet. She headed towards a small corner table and devoured her meat pie, one of her dietary weaknesses.

The starchy pie made Hope sleepy. She climbed into the back of the car, stretching out for a brief power nap. Reluctant to pass through the mountains in the dark, she set her alarm clock to wake her before sundown.

Thirty minutes later, the alarm startled her from a deep sleep and awoke to a penetrating, raw chill.

Quickly climbing into the driver's seat, she started the engine to warm herself, grateful there was heating in the vehicle.

Reaching over to the passenger seat, Hope picked up her clearly marked map.

'Mmm ... where are we? Oh, right here. I'm headed for the Lindis Pass, then on to the backpackers in Wanaka. This route is long and desolate, like most alpine passages. I'd best get through it in daylight,' she mumbled to herself while an onlooker in a nearby car stared as Hope continued her self-talk.

The road along the Lindis Pass was long and windy, and dangerous in places because of the narrow, deceptive bends. The prolific clumps of brown tussock grass and expansive, brown, stark hills became monotonous, and her eyelids were heavy. Although sleepy from boredom, she didn't want to stop and get out of the car as she knew she was vulnerable, a girl in a remote area alone. She opened all the windows and turned the radio up.

The car wound its way up the long windy road towards the summit, arriving at the lookout point. There before her was the awesome sight of the Southern Alps with a thin coating of fresh snow which glistened in the last rays before the sun disappeared behind the hills.

The temptation to get out of the car and take photos of the majestic, mountainous view was too great. She looked at the rugged landscape surrounding her, and all she could see for miles was wide open spaces with brown tussock and bare hills with no vehicles in sight.

She put on her fleecy-lined bomber jacket and got out of the car, placing her car keys on the vehicle's roof while she pulled her new merino beanie over her ears.

The sleet had made the ground slippery. She opened the rear hatch and pulled out a pair of suede boots with rubber soles, and as she fastened them, she glanced up. The view took her breath away.

She stood for a few minutes taking a short video of the snow-capped Southern Alps providing an artist's background to the expanse of brown rolling hills that reached for miles. She realised that once the sun faded, the alpine pass could be treacherous, and she quickly and cautiously walked back to the car.

As she approached the vehicle, she caught sight of a large green parrot-like bird circling her car. It spread its wings, hovered over the vehicle momentarily, and landed on the roof. As she tentatively edged herself closer, she noticed there was something in its beak, a sparkling metal object, and to her horror, the bird had picked up the car keys.

As she walked towards it, she could see that it was a kea, a bird often seen in this location. She also knew that they were drawn to anything shiny.

'Hey! Drop it!' Instead, the bird spread its wings like an eagle, revealing a myriad of rainbow-like colours and took flight. Hope froze, then the horror intensified as she had fleeting thoughts of being stranded miles from anywhere, as dusk was about to descend. For an instant, she wished she knew how to pray like Jessie and if her dear friend was with her, she would do that for her right now. Deep inside, she heard her own spirit cry out silently, 'Help me, God!'

The bird darted sideways, encircling a log in a field over the fence near her parked car. It appeared to be fascinated with its new toy and to Hope's relief it appeared unable to grip the bulky keys in its beak. It just sat on the log jangling them, tossing them to and fro.

Hope clambered over the wire fence with difficulty, as there was no stile in sight. This was her last chance of retrieving her lifeline.

She crept up to the bird slowly. It must have been accustomed to being around tourists, as her advances did not frighten it. The bird continued to toss the keys about.

'Shoo, confounded bird! Let go of my keys—let go!' She charged at it, stumbling, muttering under her breath.

The creature glared at her, squawked defiantly while dropping the keys, and flew high into the sky. She rifled through the rough tussock grass to see where they had dropped and spotted them shining in the sunlight.

'Thank you, God!' She sat sprawled on the log crying and quite shaken up. This escapade had thwarted her endeavour to reach Wanaka before dark.

The landscape through the Lindis Valley was in autumn splendour with trees covered in yellow and orange leaves. A sign that summer was drawing to an end.

The road appeared to go on forever, seeming to lead to nowhere. Again, she regretted taking this trip alone and felt lost and isolated. Then, to her relief, she saw a truck in the distance—a huge petrol tanker. Another vehicle appeared approaching from the opposite direction, and then it was still.

She nibbled at some biscuits Nelly had given her, and as she looked around for a ladies' restroom, she found there was none in sight. She knew she had to wait until she came out the other side of the Lindis Valley at Tarras. When she arrived there didn't waste any time pulling in at Tarra's restroom and then did she not stop again until she arrived in Wanaka.

***

The Wanaka Backpacker's sign was a welcome sight as the car rumbled into the small township.

'Mmm—I could die for some hot chips,' she muttered, looking for a takeaway shop before they closed. She spotted one near the backpackers, ordered a meal, and sat by the lake as she watched the sun go down. She opened the car window to listen to the unusual night sounds of the bird life, revelling in the peace. From where she was sitting, she could see the bright lights of the backpackers. Glancing at her watch, she started the car and hurried off to book in.

After a well-earned sleep, she woke just in time for the light breakfast she had paid for.

'Where are you off to today, Mount Cook?' The woman behind the reception desk came out from behind her computer. 'The weather has changed and there's a chill in the air so make sure you've plenty of warm clothing.'

'No, I'm heading to Queenstown to drop off my relocation vehicle, unfortunately. I'd love to go up onto the mountain, but there's no time. But thanks, anyway.'

'Which route are you taking? The road through Cromwell, or the Crown Ranges, which is a more scenic route.'

'I've been told the Crown Range is much more interesting and the views are better.'

39

'That's right, as long as you don't mind heights, as it's scary in parts where it's steep. Just be careful on that windy road in case of ice.'

'Yes, I've been told about the dangers of icy roads. I used to go up Mount Ruapehu with my friend, Jessie. She could use one of her father's cars and we took a few friends up there. Sometimes she'd let me drive after I got my own driving licence. It was unnerving sometimes, but I got used to going up there in the car with chains.'

Hope wished she could have slept in longer as she was weary after the long trip through the alpine pass and the distressing episode with the kea bird.

There was something important she knew she had to do before leaving Wanaka. Try to locate Uncle Joel.

She walked back up to the woman at the reception desk. 'Excuse me ... I need to get hold of a local phone directory, please. Do you have one I could look at?' The woman with the horn-rimmed glasses looked her up and down. 'Can I help you perhaps, dear? I know many people in this area.'

'Um ... I don't exactly know what area he lives in. I just know that he may live near Wanaka somewhere.'

'That's vague ... who is it you're looking for?'

'His name's Joel Grey. He's my uncle.'

'Ah, let me think ... no, sorry, I don't know anyone around here called Grey. Are you sure he lives around here? I think I just about know everyone and there's been no one around here with that name.'

Her heart sank. 'No,' she mumbled in a low voice. 'It doesn't matter. I'll look in the library directories when I get to Queenstown.' She walked towards the door like a scolded dog with its tail between its legs.

'I think I can help you—Joel Grey, did you say?' The farmer placed the cartons of free-range eggs on the reception desk. 'Chuck's my name.' The farmer shook Hope's hand.

'He was a great mate of mine when he used to live around here. Didn't come into town much. Went further south I think.'

Chuck pointed towards the hills. 'He did some work on my farm up on the ridge. Said he wanted his own piece of land and had some special plan in mind but didn't say what it was.

'Do you know where he lives now?' Hope thought she was on the brink of a breakthrough.

The expectant look on Hope's face appeared obvious to the man. 'Sorry, he didn't say as he didn't know himself at the time except that he wanted to go down the line to look around Lake Wakatipu for some acreage. He told me he wasn't much of a letter writer, so I haven't heard from him since he left.'

'Oh, I see. I'll try to track him down around there when I arrive. Thanks anyway. I have to get on my way now.'

Things were looking up for Hope. Now at least she knew to search around Lake Wakatipu, though she knew the area was expansive. She sat in the car, perusing the map again.

'Um ... let me see. I'll stop somewhere halfway, perhaps in Cromwell where all the yummy stone fruit is for sale.'

It was a clear, crisp autumn day, not a cloud in sight. Leaving Wanaka, she filled the car with petrol and drove along the highway, trying to enjoy the enchanting surroundings without obsessing about Misty's whereabouts and the likelihood of finding her. She tried not to think about what she would do if she couldn't find Joel. But he just has to be somewhere near Lake Wakatipu. If she was Jessie, she'd be praying and asking for God's guidance. Perhaps that's what she needs to do now. She prayed loud and clear, in the same fashion that Jessie used to do when either of them had got themselves into trouble.

'Please, God! I don't know where to look. Uncle Joel seems my only hope of finding Misty. If you could help me find my horse, I promise I'll always believe in you.'

She started a plea bargaining with her maker—desperate—hoping that he was the loving and merciful God that Jessie knew.

Chapter Five

The clear, crisp days were a change from the humid weather that Hope had experienced up north all summer. She wasn't used to snowy conditions with treacherous windy roads with ice. She heeded the advice of several people at the backpackers to drive carefully even in autumn. But to her relief, there was no ice on the road.

As she drove along the highway heading towards Cromwell, she became euphoric from the magnificent sight of Mount Pisa while passing through the scenic area.

Approaching the Clutha River, she spotted a jetty with a parking area nearby. She pulled in and parked where she could sit and look at the sweeping views of the large stretch of land opposite the river. The riverbank boasted trees covered with autumn leaves of, bright orange, red, yellow, crimson and gold.

Her back hurt from sitting behind the wheel so long. She wished she could stop for longer to soak up the changing autumn scenery, but her desire to get to Queenstown to look for Joel was greater.

Near the parking area was a small tearoom where she could get a cream bun and a small mince pie to take on her journey, along with a bottle of cold Fanta.

She walked up to a tour bus driver sitting outside puffing on a cigarette, to get some directions.

'Excuse me—I'm heading down to Queenstown. How far is it from here please?'

'It should take around an hour to get to the centre of town.'

'Good. That's not too far then. Thanks very much.'

'Better be careful going through the Kawarau Gorge. There's pea soup fog up there right now and the road is treacherous. Take it slowly.'

A shiver went through Hope at the thought of driving in the dangerous conditions. It was bad enough driving through the Lewis Pass on her own and now this. She thought she'd made a foolish decision taking this route. Perhaps she should've taken the less scenic, boring route from Dunedin up through the middle of the island. But she'd been looking forward to this trip with some of the most picturesque scenery she'd ever seen.

To her delight, the fog had lifted. It was only at its worst at the beginning of the Gibbston Highway. There was even regular traffic along that road, which made her feel more secure. After she'd driven at a snail's pace for most of the journey, hemmed in by a Kingswood station wagon pulling a caravan, she pulled over on the side of the road to take a few more photos of the autumn splendour that had monopolised the trip.

As she drove towards the end of the highway, she noticed the overhead billboard stating Welcome to Queenstown Lakes District and breathed a sigh of relief that, although it had been spectacular, the long, lonely drive was over.

She had to get the rental car back the next day. Where to now? She didn't even have a place to stay.

Hope put her head out the window and asked a pedestrian where the Youth Hostel was. She found it easier to be told than to keep looking up everything on her roadmap.

'Not far, Miss ... it's down by the lake.'

The man, who appeared to be a local, gave her clear directions to the hostel, which was only a ten-minute drive away.

The large prominent, cedar building was the largest Youth Hostel she had ever seen and appeared super modern. It had a vacancy sign in front and all Hope wanted to do was sleep. The drive through the gorge had taken it out of her.

She parked outside in the visitor parking area and wearily dragged her heavy backpack through the hostel door, tripping on the doorstep.

'Whoops! Do you need a hand there? That's a huge pack you're carrying.' The woman behind the front desk, moved towards her to help.

'No, I'm fine, thanks. I've just been driving a long distance and need a break. Can I book in, please? I have a current Hostel membership.'

'Sure thing. Pat's my name. If you could just fill out this form here, I'll see which room might suit you. You can either share with others in the women's dorm, which will keep the price down, or pay more for a single room.'

'I'll have to sleep in the dorm as my funds are getting low.'

'Well, you're in luck right now. There's just one other girl in there who is from Sweden and nobody else has made a booking.'

Hope looked up from the form, struggling to remember some details. 'That's great. I'm trying to find my membership card. It's in my backpack somewhere, sorry!' She started opening all the backpack's pockets.

'Don't worry, just tell me your full name and address and pay me for the first night. When you find your card, you can give it to me later.'

Pat led her along the corridor to a pleasant room with six double bunks. She put her backpack on the floor next to a bottom bunk near the window, which let a lot of light in.

The blue and white cotton curtains looked fresh and fairly new. In the corner stood two large wooden dressers with lots of drawers, to Hope's delight.

As she unpacked the rest of her belongings and hung her clothes in the wardrobe, the other guest walked in and welcomed her. Hope was surprised to find she spoke good English.

'Nice to meet you,' said Hope, as she rummaged in her backpack for her flannel and towel. She rinsed her flannel in the basin in the corner of the room and started washing her face to freshen up.

'Did you come from far today?' The Swedish girl spoke good English to Hope's amazement.

'Not too far. I drove from Wanaka but the road was windy and there was a thick fog at the beginning of the Kawarau Gorge, so I had to drive slowly in case there was ice on the road. Now I just want to sleep for a bit.'

'I understand. Hey ... my name's Helga. I'm from Stockholm in Sweden. If you like, I can show you the lakeside after your nap. It's beautiful down there and lots to see. Did you come here to go sight-seeing?'

'Hope's my name. The South Island is awesome, but I've come from up north to search for my show horse. My mother sold her to someone down here and I am trying to locate my uncle who might know what happened to her. He may be here in Queenstown, and I think he might know my horse's whereabouts.'

'Really! That sounds serious. Does your mother not know where your horse's new owner lives?'

'Yes, I think so ... but she won't tell me. She doesn't want me riding her anymore. Look—it's quite complicated. I'll tell you later when we go for a walk.' Hope was careful about not divulging too much of her personal business to this stranger, although the woman appeared to be sincere. Perhaps she is someone with whom she can share her burden. She appears old enough to be her aunt or big sister. A problem shared is a problem halved, so the saying goes.

When she awoke, the curtains had been pulled across, blocking the sun, which Hope gathered Helga had kindly done.

Her newfound friend crept quietly into the room. 'You were dead to the world. Must have been exhausted. Do you feel like a walk soon?'

Hope yawned loudly and peered out the window, squinting from the strong sunlight as she opened the curtains. 'Looks nice out there. What a clear blue sky. Yes, a walk along the lakeside would be great. I'll grab my camera.'

As they arrived at the lakeside, the steamship TSS Earnslaw had just pulled into the wharf and started unloading its passengers.

'Wow, look at that! Isn't it gorgeous? I love old boats. I wonder how much a cruise like that costs.'

'Let's see—the ticket office is over there.' Helga pointed to the building with a long queue of people standing waiting to make bookings.

'I don't think I want to stand in a queue like that. Let's look at that billboard over there.'

Hope pulled on Helga's arm, directing her towards the signage while Helga hurried along, trying to keep up with the exuberant young woman who appeared to be full of life. But little did Helga know that underneath the bubbly facade, was a young woman with a broken heart in more ways than one.

'Oh no, look at those prices. I don't think I should spend that kind of money. My funds are getting low.' Hope put her wallet back into her shoulder bag.

'Look ... I have enough money for both of us. Please let me buy you a ticket.' Helga touched her arm and looked her in the eye.

Hope was far too proud to take this stranger's money. She did have funds in the bank and enough cash in her bag, but she knew if she started splurging it on tourist attractions it would run out. She realised quickly she had to get a job.

'That's really kind of you, but I can't accept this right now. I'll come with you another day. What I need to do is look for some casual work.'

'What ... today? You've only just arrived!'

'No, but soon, though. First, I need to return my rental car back to the office tomorrow morning. It has cost me nothing except for petrol, as it was a relocation vehicle. I might have enough money to hire a compact car while I'm job hunting. That's if it doesn't take me too long to get work.'

'Goodness! Queenstown Lakes District is a vast place to get around if you have no car. I hope you find work soon.'

'Me too. I heard there's a lot of casual work on the farms around here. That's what I'm used to. I hope to do an Agricultural Science Diploma specialising in equine health. But I've chosen to take a year off to find my missing pony and get some money together.'

As they wandered along the path around the lakeside, Hope went mad with her camera. She was overawed by the sight of the Remarkables, the mountain range covered with snow, even in autumn. The sun glistened on the peaks, which made them even more spectacular. The TSS Earnslaw steamship had started up and chugged its way across the lake towards Walter Peak Station full of passengers again. Hope wished she could have been on it, but she was a diligent budgeter and knew her funds could only go so far, particularly if she bought a little car.

Nelly had shown Hope an album with photographs of Queenstown the night she stayed with her, and she remembered the photos of Walter Peak Station and Lake Wakatipu.

Perhaps she could find work over there on a sheep station around the lake. She was in a little world of her own imagining finding a job with horses on a sheep or cattle station. Helga startled her suddenly by tugging her arm and brought her swiftly back to reality.

'Sorry, Hope. We're at the end of the walkway. How about we go back and at least let me buy you a hot roll at that kiosk?'

'That's nice, thanks. Would you like to come with me into town to return the car? If I can rent one from there, I'd like to go to the car yards and look for a cheapie to buy. I've been saving up for months for one. When I get a job that pays well, I can swap it for a better one.'

Helga hesitated. 'Sure ... I'll come. Where do we start?'

'I've made a list of some car yards—here, look.' She handed her the piece of paper.

'Why don't we pick up some hot rolls at the kiosk and sit where we can talk.'

The girls purchased their food and milkshakes. By the time they'd eaten, they had all their plans mapped out.

Chapter Six

Hope woke to another clear, fine day. The sunshine was not as warm as it had been. Snow flurries had fallen during the night on the Alps.

After a hasty breakfast, Helga was waiting for her at the front door of the lodge as planned. 'I hope you have plenty of thermals on today. There's been a cold snap, and it'll get colder with that southerly wind blowing.' Helga clucked over Hope who found her over-protectiveness irritating as it reminded her of her mother's behaviour.

I suppose she means well. I should be grateful that she's looking out for me, I suppose.

When she dropped the vehicle off at the car rental office, she explained to the salesman that she was needing a cheap rental vehicle to use, so she had some wheels to go hunting for a vehicle to purchase.

'You say you just want to buy something cheap, and you don't mind how old it is? I think I've just the thing for you here to save you going to the car yards.'

'What do you mean? I thought you just rent cars, not sell them.'

'Ah ... but we have another string to our bow. We've ex-rental vehicles that we sell at a cheap price. Most of them have done over a hundred thousand miles but they last forever.'

'What cars?'

'Come over here, lassie, and I'll show you.'

Hope was surprised when she followed him to the back of the building, to find a long fleet of used cars in tidy condition.

'Take your pick. Any idea what model you're after?'

'I've been told the Toyota Corollas are the most reliable. Do you have any?'

'Funny you should ask. We just added this one to the stock this week. I'd say it would be just what you're looking for. If you take this, you won't have to rent one or go looking to buy one. It could take you days to find one if you don't know your way around.'

Hope turned to Helga. 'What do you think? Do you know anything about them?'

'Yes, I do. My father had one a little bigger than this. He told me they are reliable and the engines last forever. I'd go for this one Hope, honestly, I would.'

They took their time inspecting the mustard coloured car and were both impressed.

'Wow! Beautiful upholstery. Looking at it, you wouldn't think it's an ex-rental. It's been well preserved.'

'Yes, you're sure right about that. We look after our cars, as we know how they can depreciate. Well, what do you want to do, ladies?'

'Is there a warranty on this car?' Helga asked, as though she was experienced in car buying.

'Yep. Three years, or if you pay a bit more—five years.'

Helga looked at Hope. 'I think you should take it.'

'How about a hundred dollars off if we pay cash today?' Helga was used to bargaining in her own country.

The salesman hesitated, looked at the car papers, and studied the girls momentarily.

'I suppose it sounds like a done deal. Come into the office and I'll sort out your insurance if you want that now too.'

***

Hope drove into a tree-studded glade alongside the lake and turned on the car radio.

'Well, my girl. You're now the proud owner of a very nice car. And you won't get lost in this one. I've never seen a mustard coloured Corolla before. You'll have to give it a name.' Helga passed her a bag of potato crisps. 'Do you think we should eat these in your tidy new car, Hope?'

'I don't think it matters as long as we don't wipe our greasy hands on the upholstery. I've some moist wipes I keep in my bag. I know—Sunflower! I'll call it Sunflower!' They both laughed.

'Where do you go from here? It's a good thing we both booked out of the hostel, and you don't need to go back to get your luggage.' Hope was ready for a new adventure.

Helga took Hope's hand. 'Sorry, Hope, but I'm headed for Milford Sound. As I've got some time to kill, I would appreciate a ride to the bus station where I'll book my luggage. Until my bus is due in, I'd like to take a walk around the town.

'Yes, that's fine. I'm going to the Post Office to look up the directory for my uncle's address and can drop you off first.'

'Thanks, Hope. I've really enjoyed hanging out with you, though. It's been an inspiration hearing about your great road trip adventure.'

They found a coffee bar in town and then went their separate ways after swapping addresses. Hope was disappointed she wasn't able to give Helga a stable address, as she didn't know where she would be in the future.

After Helga walked off in the opposite direction, Hope realised how she needed a buddy and just how much she missed her closest friend, Jessie, now that she was alone again.

Hope thought she'd better get in touch with her parents and stopped at the nearest stationer's shop for writing material and postcards. As she entered the Post Office, she remembered she'd redirected her mail to Post Restante and walked to the counter to request it.

'Here you are, Hope. Looks like there's a bit of mail for you.'

To Hope's surprise, there were some letters. One lengthy one from her mother, one from Doug, and two from Jessie.

'Thanks so much. Um ... do you know if there's a camping ground near the lake anywhere? I was hoping to get my tent up.'

The lady looked her up and down. 'Camping, you say. Surely it's too cold for that now. There's snow on the Alps. But if you insist, You'll find a decent Holiday Park about two miles south of here if you follow the lake around. It's opposite the Golf Club. They have cabins too if you change your mind about the tent.'

'I have a mountaineer's tent, an alpine sleeping bag, and all the thermal clothing. My brother used to take me camping in the National Park and we were warm as toast with snow on the summit.'

'Rather you than me. They also have a hot spa pool if you need to thaw out.'

'Not in this weather. I think I'll give that one a miss.'

'Here are the directories you asked for. I hope you find what you want.'

She sat down and waded through the phone books, not knowing where to start. There were four of them and she scanned each one for Joel's name and address, then slumped back in her chair, despairing.

This is hopeless. This is her last chance at finding some clue as to Misty's whereabouts. What is she to do now?

She gathered the heavy directories and slapped them back on the counter.

'Thanks very much. I've finished with them.'

'Found what you were looking for?'

Hope turned to look at the woman whose face appeared kind. 'Well—no. I can't find the person's name anywhere.'

'Maybe I can help. Who is it you're looking for?'

'My Uncle Joel—Joel Grey. Apparently, he purchased a block of land around Lake Wakatipu somewhere and I need to see him about something important. I've driven down from Christchurch where I flew in from Auckland.'

'That was a big trip you made. Grey, you say. Mmm ... sorry dear, I haven't heard of any Greys around here. What does he do?'

'He breaks in horses and trains them. He also does a bit of farm labouring.'

'Have you come all the way down here just to look for him? Couldn't your parents tell you where he is?'

'It's a long story. Sorry to bother you. I'll get on now.' Hope grabbed her bag and sloped out the door despondently. Again, she didn't feel like telling this perfect stranger all her private business.

'Wait! Wait a minute—perhaps I can help you.' The woman appeared hot and flustered, running after Hope. 'I have a spare room in my modest little abode close to here. I often take students from the Bible College nearby, but the room is free at present and they're all on a long break.'

'Oh, that's kind of you, but I really enjoy camping and the great outdoors. It's like being on one big adventure. Thanks, but I'll be fine.'

The woman wrote some details on a piece of paper and handed it to her. 'Here is my name, address and phone number. Grace is my name, Grace Rogers, but you can call me Gracie. Please phone me or drop by if you need anything, anything at all.'

'Thanks, but I'll be okay once I find work. I'll probably stay on here in Queenstown until I track down my uncle.'

'There's plenty of work in hospitality if you like waitressing or hotel work.'

'No thanks. I'm looking for farm work, preferably with horses.'

The woman ducked under the counter then stood up handing her a business card.

'Here is the name of a high country station owner who picks up his mail from here. In fact, I know him well as his daughter went to the Bible College here, and I gave her a room for a while. Jock Weston is his name.'

'Where's his station? I don't know the area that well.'

'It's just out of Kingston at the southern part of the lake. I hear he takes on casual workers and I've sent some of the Bible students to him for work. If you like, I can call him and let him know you might be in touch.'

'Um ... I suppose that will be okay, but I can't promise I'll phone him.'

Hope didn't want anyone to take over her life after she'd escaped her mother's control. She changed her mind quickly.

'Sorry—but I'd rather you didn't phone him. I have his card and if I decide that it's right for me to approach him, I will. I really appreciate your help, though.'

Hope was aware she was disappointing Gracie though she knew she had to keep her boundaries.

'Promise I'll be in touch if I need help. Bye for now. I'll see you next time I collect my mail.'

***

Hope thanked the woman and drove in search of the camping ground. As she drove around the lake, Aspen Holiday Park appeared and to her relief, a vacancy sign.

She trundled into the office and rang the bell then leaned on the counter and glanced at the brochures in front of her.

'Hello there. Sorry, I was out back. Have you been waiting long?' Hope averted her eyes as an over-weight man with his belly cascading over his belt waddled in behind the counter. He wiped his mouth as though he had been eating.

'No, not really. Do you have any vacancies?'

'Depends on how many nights you want to stay.'

'I'm not sure yet. I have to find some casual work so it might take a while. Perhaps a few nights to start with. What's my cheapest option?'

The man looked her up and down as if he was trying to work out if she was a person of means or not then spotted the old car.

'We have basic cabins for twenty dollars a night or tourist flats which are a lot dearer. That's if you aren't thinking of camping, which of course is the cheaper option. One night will be ten dollars. I'll show you the cabins if you like.'

'Um ... no thanks, I'll take a tent site. I hear it won't be snowing for another month, only on the mountain peaks. I have plenty of warm gear.'

The manager led her through the camp to her tent site, shaking his head as if she was mad. She chose a spot near a family who were just settling in opposite her, which made her feel a little more secure.

'Kitchen and shower block are just over there.'

He handed her a small bottle of milk.

'We have basic supplies in our office and apart from that there is a shop just along the road and a minimart in town.'

'Thanks for that. Okay if I park here?' She pointed to an area next to the tent site.

'Of course, as long as it doesn't encroach on the next tent site if anyone arrives.' The man hobbled off, scuffing the dusty ground in his rubber Jandals back to the office.

Hope looked around to check out her neighbours. There was the family opposite her who appeared to have well-behaved, older children. They were about fifteen metres away from her tent, which was next to a paddock full of sheep. To the left and right of her, the tent sites were unoccupied, but further along the row was a young couple who waved and smiled at her. She did not feel so alone.

She hastily dragged her gear out of the boot of her car and erected her igloo-shaped tent. As tiredness set in, she couldn't remember how to erect the tent poles.

'Can I give you a hand? My kids have the same tents, and I'm used to putting them up.'

The middle-aged man from across the way grinned jovially at her and picked up a pole.

'Oh, you don't have to. I'm sure I'll eventually work it out. It's just that it's been a while, that's all.'

Hope turned slightly, staring at the pole in her hands so that the man would not see the warm flush spreading up her neck.

Within minutes, the tent was up and she expressed her heartfelt gratitude.

'Why don't you come and join us for supper. I think we are playing cards tonight.'

'Ah ... thanks very much, but I'm pretty tired. I think I'll shoot along to the fish and chip shop up the road, then turn in. Perhaps another evening.'

She zoomed off in her car and sat by the lake eating fish and chips, wondering where all this was going to end. When she'd finished, she cleaned her hands using the wipes she kept in her car, then pulled out her mail she'd been keen to read.

The first letter she opened was from her mother who admonished her for taking off to the South Island and upsetting her. Then Myra's tone softened when she manipulated Hope into going home to start a "real" career. She went on to say that she needed Hope there, as Frank was ailing, and she couldn't manage all the tomato picking on her own. The local teen who had been working for them had left.

'There you go. That's why you need me to come home—typical!' Hope spewed out her frustration at her mother's guilt-trip.

She read the rest of the letter which left her cold. No mention of her Uncle Joel, Doug, Misty or anything or anyone she held dear. Her mother knew she was grieving over these losses but showed no compassion.

Hope quickly stuffed the letter into the glovebox of the car and started on the next letter. It was from Doug, and she knew this one would give her some degree of comfort

Dear Sis

I have just arrived home and heard from Mum about your incredible intrepid journey down south. Please let us know if you are safe. You can send a telegram. Mum is a nervous wreck, though I know she caused you grief by selling Misty behind your back. She said you took off down south to find her. Have you tracked her down yet? Where are you, Sis?

I have moved back to Bethlehem and decided to stay at home for a while to help Mum out with the tomato picking. She said she had insisted you come home to help out too now that Dad is ailing, but you don't need to do that. I know you want to have a gap year before you start university. Jessie told me about that when she was in town on her break. She sends her love and has already written to you.

I think it will be good to work and save money before you start your studies. I am enclosing a cheque for you, a belated birthday present which is some of the superannuation I received from the army. Sorry I was not around for your birthday. I hope this will make up for it. I want you to use it to tide you over until you get a job. And promise me that you will get straight on the first flight home if your luck runs out!

I forgot to tell you. I have been seeing a counsellor at the local Anglican Church near my flat in Auckland who has

helped me deal with my flash-backs. I think I'm getting well, Hope. He is a Pastor and has been giving me spiritual help too.

Thinking of you

Lots of love
Doug.

Chapter Seven

It was starting to get dark, and the sun had disappeared over the Remarkables while Hope sat in the car reading the mail. She cried after reading Doug's letter.

She decided to read Jessie's news when she gets back to her tent where she can read with her lantern. She started to get cold and hurried back to the camping ground.

As she pulled in, she noticed the tall pine trees about the camp were swaying in the wind. The weather had changed, but she'd been reassured by the camp owner that there was no sign of rain, according to the weather forecast.

She gathered her torch and lantern and made her bed ready for the night. She wasn't keen on sleeping on the ground, but her tent was watertight, and her airbed was comfortable. She'd inflated it before she'd set off for her takeaway meal.

She snuggled into her duck down sleeping bag zipping it up to her neck. A welcome rural odour emanated from the cow paddocks through the fence.

There was a full moon that illuminated the tent, as she lay still fascinated by the night sounds of owls and other birds settling in for the night. Then she started to think about the journey she'd made, such a long distance for a young woman alone. And for what? Nothing had worked out for her. No sign of Uncle Joel anywhere. He must be here somewhere. What will she do if she can't find work? Or what if her money runs out? Then she remembered the cheque for five hundred dollars she had in the envelope from Doug.

If her money runs out, she's not going home. She'll go and stay with Jessie in Palmerston North and find work there.

She lay there trying to talk to God out loud.

'Please, God, I'm not very good at this as you already know. I've got myself into quite a pickle by landing down here with Uncle Joel nowhere to be found. No job and no place to go. I said that if you help me find Misty, I'll always follow you. I promise I will, but first I need to track down Uncle Joel. Please help me!'

Suddenly a strong gust of wind shook the tent and startled her. The wind seemed to increase in force until she began to worry that her tent would blow away. She remembered that it was anchored to the ground sheet and her weight would stop it from going anywhere.

Then in the bright light of the moon, she saw large shadows towering over her, things that appeared like giants. She shuddered. The muscles between her ribs tensed so she could hardly breathe.

The strange figures began to sway back and forth until she realised they were the silhouettes of the tall pine trees along the fence-line. She lay there imagining they were huge angels sent to watch over her while she slept.

She recalled a story Jessie had told her about the archangel Michael and imagined him to be one of the figures standing over her tent protecting her. She drifted off to sleep.

***

The early morning sun woke her and streamed through the mesh window in her tent flap. She needed to go to the camp bathroom and reluctantly crawled out of a warm sleeping bag as the cold air bit her face when she unzipped the tent. She pulled on her fur-lined boots, donned a thick jumper over the track pants she slept in and stumbled over to the shower block, combing her fingers through her matted hair.

As she walked back to her tent, she saw the woman from the caravan opposite. She was standing outside in the crisp morning air in her pink pyjamas. She smiled and waved at Hope then disappeared back inside the caravan.

After visiting the camp bathroom, Hope scratched around in a hamper for the muesli and fruit she packed for breakfast. She mixed up a little milk powder with the water from her drink bottle. She tipped some coffee into a mug and wandered into the kitchen to get boiling water for a welcome hot drink.

'Are you heading off today?' a voice from behind.

It was the husband of the woman with pink pyjamas. He dumped a pile of dishes in the sink and started washing up.

'I'm not sure yet. It depends. I have to find work but I don't know where to start.'

'That's a real pity. Now I feel guilty going off skiing today. I hope you find something. Did you know there's an employment office in town? They have job vacancy listings in their window and might be able to help you.'

'That's really helpful, thank you. I'll try there first. I'm dying for a hot shower. Hope they are good ones.'

'They're really good, lots of pressure. Unlike some of the camps we've stayed at.' He trundled off to his caravan with the bucket of clean dishes.

Hope ate her breakfast in her tent then walked over to the utility block for a shower. She went back to her tent to look for her work resumes and references then drove her car into town to find the employment office.

She was astounded by the sight of the Remarkables at sunrise. Majestic, snow-capped peaks that appeared like pink and orange gelato ice-cream glistening under the dawn sunrays. In spite of the strong winds during the night, the morning sky was clear and not a cloud in sight.

As she entered the building, there was a long queue right up to the door. The young men stood staring at Hope, as she was the only young woman in the queue. After a long wait, her name was called.

'Hope Petersen— come with me please.'

As she followed an officious looking woman down the passageway, Hope's spirit fell, and she did not feel in a secure position. She'd heard there was very little work in Queenstown for women except in retail which she abhorred but plenty of work for men on the farms.

Who's going to take on a girl Hope's age with all these great strapping young men waiting in line for farm work? She sneered at the queue and continued to torment herself, then sat down in front of the recruiter's desk.

'Good to meet you, Hope. I've had a look at the application form you've filled out and there's not much in the way of work experience listed. We can only offer you a position in retail or hospitality, which is the work we have available for women.'

'Oh! But I'm not interested in that kind of work.' The hairs on the back of her neck bristled.

'Well, I'm sorry. The only work left is for farmhands or ranchers, and there are plenty of young men available for that. It would be far too strenuous for a girl like you.'

'That's untrue. Didn't you read what I wrote on my resume about my farm experience? I can handle horses really well and have general farmhand experience.'

'I'm sorry, but we're unable to offer you anything at this time. Perhaps come back in a month and see what's available then.'

'It's okay, I have some other options.'

The recruiter could see from the look on her client's face that there was no point in continuing the conversation. Hope roughly grabbed her documents and stormed out of the building. As soon as she was back in her car, she sobbed with exasperation.

What's she going to do now? No job, no leads on Misty or Uncle Joel, and only enough money to provide food and accommodation for a few weeks. She'll have to keep the money that Doug gave her in case she finds Misty and needs to buy her back from her owner.

She pulled out the business card that Gracie at the Post Office had given her and decided to phone the high country station manager. This may be her only chance.

She sped back to the camp, this time not taking as much care on the road as usual and almost knocked over a pedestrian.

As she entered the camp, she parked near the office and wandered inside to ask if she could use the phone.

'That'll be twenty cents. You can put it in that jar, thanks.' The camp owner went through to the back of the office to give her some privacy.

She managed to get hold of Jock, the station manager and came off the phone beaming. 'Thank you!' she called out to the camp owner. 'I've finished now.'

Things were starting to look up for her, as the farmer said he was short of staff and would be interested in giving her a trial. She couldn't believe her luck that he'd invited her to come for an interview that afternoon.

The road leading to the sheep station was bumpy and dusty. As she drove to the crest of the hill overlooking Corriedale Hills Station, she was amazed at what she saw. There must have been thousands of acres spread out for miles covered with sheep that appeared like tufts of cotton wool in the distance. The spectacle was something she'd never seen in her life before.

The road seemed to go for miles and eventually she arrived on time at the station. She approached the homestead down a long driveway lined with gold popular trees giving it a stately appearance. It was as though she was entering the Taj Mahal.

As she approached the colonial homestead, it reminded her of home with its billows of smoke escaping the chimney and the strong smell of macrocarpa wood burning. She also caught sight of a tall burly man and a well-built woman walking back from the barn to the house waving at her, showing her where to park. There were two cars, an old land rover, and a truck parked in front of the house.

'You'll be alright over here, next to the Land Rover. Meet my wife Gilly— and you are Hope, isn't that right? I couldn't quite pick up your name over the phone.'

'Yes, that's right—Hope Petersen. Pleased to meet you.'

'Jock and Gilly Weston—Come and take a seat.'

She shook hands with them both and followed them inside.

'I've just made a pot of tea if you would like to join us.' Gilly went into the kitchen and brought back a tray and placed it on the table.

'Do you mind if we sit at the dining table? There's more room there for us to sit around. Just easier I suppose.' Jock pulled a seat out for Hope then quickly stoked up the Kent fire while she sat down and instantly relaxed.

'Can I pass you a lemon muffin? Just fresh this morning.' Gilly passed the plate around.

'Thank you ... how do you find time to do all this with such a large sheep station?' Hope assumed Gilly worked on the farm.

'We have a few station hands. There's also Hamish, our son who assists Jock, and our daughter Charity who helps out when she's back home between Mercy Ship missions.' Gilly went to the lounge and looked out the window.

'She should be home soon. She's on leave and just popped into town to go shopping.'

'What's the Mercy Mission?' Hope remembered that Gracie at the Post Office told her that Jock's daughter stayed with her when she went to Bible College.

'It's a hospital ship that provides free health care to people in desperate circumstances.' Gilly poured another cup of tea for Hope then one for herself.

'Jock just drinks coffee. I told him it will be the death of him one day, but he never listens.'

'What does Charity do on the boat?' Hope asked.

'She's a volunteer school teacher and comes home every four months. At least she's back home for six weeks between voyages.'

Jock looked agitated, as though he wanted to get to the reason for Hope being there. He darted a glance at Gilly.

'Well, Missy, what experience have you had with farm work? Any references?' Jock sat there scrutinising her while she pulled out her documents.

She showed him the inflated job reference she'd received from Jessie's father and her letter of acceptance from the university to study Agricultural Science. She pulled out all her pony club certificates and photos to show that she was a proficient horse rider.

'Excellent. That's what we need. Someone who knows how to manage a stock horse. In this high country, you can't work without being able to ride. I've just the one for you. I'll take you over to see her a bit later. How about I give you a week's trial and if you're as good as you say you are I'll keep you as a casual worker? That's until our two station hands are back from the shearing competitions up north. How does that sound?'

'That sounds great, thanks. You mean ... as a volunteer for the week?' Hope's fine jaw set as if stressed. 'Except I need to find a proper paid job though.'

'Oh, for goodness' sake, no! It's illegal for me to not pay you. I don't practice slave labour. Of course, I'll be paying you the going rate for a novice station hand, regardless of whether I keep you on after the trial or not. That's minus food and accommodation which leaves you a bit you can put aside for yourself.'

'Can I work overtime?'

'If you still have the energy. The work is hard, and you'll be tired at the end of the day. Tomorrow we're docking the lambs' tails and that'll take it out of you. I'll get Charity to give you a quick rundown on it tonight.'

'You mean ... I'm hired! Have I got the job?' Jock melted when he saw her eyes almost popping out with delight.

'You don't think I can let you go after all those convincing testimonials you gave me. As long as you can handle the pace, you should go well. You'd better get back to the camp and pick up your things. You might just be back in time for dinner.'

***

Charity placed her shopping bags onto her bed. She wandered down the hallway and to meet the guest in the bedroom next door. As she approached Hope's room, she found her busy emptying out her backpack and placing her carefully folded articles of clothing in the drawers of the dresser provided.

'Hi, there! Welcome to Corriedale Hills Station. Mum said you'd just arrived. Charity's my name. Dad asked me to show you around the station before dinner. How does that sound?'

Hope was excited and couldn't wait to get onto the high country property which evoked a flood of nostalgia about working on Jessie's farm.

'Yes, sure. I'd love to. I'll just change into my jeans and jumper. I'll be there in a minute.'

'You'd better wear a warm jacket as it's pretty cold up here in the hills. The southerly wind bites.'

Charity went outside to wait for Hope and sat on a hay bale until she arrived.

They spent an hour walking around while Charity gave Hope the "grand tour". She showed her one of the mares she could ride and to Hope's astonishment, the horse was a white mare just like Misty, and although not an Anglo-Arab, she was beautiful in Hope's eyes. Hope was ecstatic.

'Why don't we go and sit in the barn and chat before dinner. I'd like to hear all about this great adventure that you've been on and why you've come all the way down here from the Bay of Plenty. You don't look much younger than I am. Dad said you're almost nineteen.'

'Yes, I am. What about you—how old are you?'

'Twenty-two.'

Hope thought, judging by the girl's maturity that she was older. She told her all about her search for Misty and how she could not find her Uncle Joel and that he might be the only one who would have an idea of Misty's whereabouts. *Could Jock and his family help*?

Chapter Eight

After the first week of working the sheep on horse-back, Hope was exhausted but invigorated. She and Charity finished moving a paddock of sheep then they tied up their horses and stretched out in the sun and rested.

The wind was biting just as Charity had warned.

'I'm glad you told me to wear plenty of warm clothing. I'm wearing three layers of merino undergarments.'

She passed the thermos flask of coffee back to Charity. They both pulled out their packed lunch that Gilly had provided and talked at length about their lives.

When Hope told Charity the truth about her grudge against her mother including her extreme sadness at losing Misty, her confidant could see that she was holding back tears and handed her a clean handkerchief.

'Thanks, I feel silly now ... but I'm desperate and don't know what to do. Look—this is Misty.' Hope passed her a small photo she'd removed from her jacket pocket.

'It may sound strange, but I think I have seen that mare somewhere at a show.' Charity took a closer look then handed it back.

'We don't see many white Anglo-Arabs around here at the local shows. But I was at one we had here recently when I returned from the Mercy Africa on leave. I entered the dressage event and noticed a distinctive white Arab mare that was getting ready to enter the show jumping event across from me. We rarely see an animal like that in these parts.'

'Who was riding her, do you remember?'

'A girl I think, younger than you. I can't quite recall, sorry.'

'That must be Misty, it has to be! How can I find out? There must be a way.' Hope's voice shook. She cleared her throat.

'I suppose we could contact the show and ask for a copy of the program of events. The names of the competitors will be on it ... wait on—I think I still have one in my bedroom. Come on, we best be getting back. Dad needs us for the drenching this afternoon. I'll take a look after dinner.'

***

'Charity! Can you give me a hand to dish up the meal? And Hope, dear, would you mind setting the table?' Gilly took the lamb roast out of the oven and started carving it up while Hope took the cutlery into the dining room and started laying the table. Jock walked in.

'We need to have a chat later, Hope. I want to talk about your trial period and give you some feedback.' He had a bottle of Stout in his hand, flipped the lid off, and sat down at the dining table.

Hope realised she would have to make up her mind. If she stayed on at Corriedale Hills, she would have no time at all to search for Uncle Joel or Misty. And what if the horse that Charity saw really was Misty? She was perplexed and knew she needed to work although her wages and the money from Doug would keep her going until she found another job. Perhaps Jock would keep her position open for a week while she went back to Queenstown to make enquiries about Joel.

'Come on— let's eat while it's hot.' Gilly had just poked her head around the kitchen door.

70

When they'd all finished the meal and gone to sit in the lounge, Jock invited Hope to join him in his office to discuss her trial period that had just ended. Hope sat holding the sides of the chair, feet crossed, and waiting for Jock to break the bad news.

'Well, Hope, we're all flabbergasted. To be honest, none of us believed that you'd be able to keep up with us all. Our station hand and Charity and I were amazed at your riding ability on the steep hills as well as your stamina. And you were like a torpedo when you were helping with docking and drenching the sheep. You could keep up with all of us.'

She pressed her hands to her cheeks as the usual pink colour suddenly returned to them.

'I can offer you a permanent position here if you'll take it.'

Although it was good news, Hope felt put on the spot. She knew she needed the money, and this was a top job with a perfect family including accommodation, food and horse. But she had to open her mouth now and beg Jock to employ her after a week's break. She needed time to follow-up the lead on Misty.

She spewed it out and told him the whole story, including the lead she had from Charity. When she'd finished talking, Jock excused himself to go back into the lounge to discuss the situation with his wife and daughter.

'Hamish is back next week and so are our two part-time station hands who've been on holiday.'

Gilly untied her apron strings and wiped her hands. 'I think you should take Hope on after a week's time when she has finished her investigations. She is distraught over losing her horse.'

'Yes, I know. I've got a feeling I may have met that bloke Joel she's talking about. I could make some inquiries about him and make a phone call to Federated Farmers.' He walked back into the office and found Hope waiting with her head in her cupped hands.

'Hope, cheer up! We'd be more than happy to have you back here again in a week and I'll give you full-time work. But it will initially be on a casual basis. That's in case you need more time off to sort this out further down the track.'

'I'm so grateful, thanks so much. If I find Misty, I'll have to have work to be able to afford to buy her back if the owner will agree. It might be at a high price.'

'I think I've met your uncle, Joel Grey, in fact, I think I was introduced to him at a Federated Farmers meeting earlier this year. He had a ranch somewhere outside of Queenstown, but I can't remember where. Does he break horses in, do you know?'

'Yes, that's him. He broke in my horse, Misty. He's also a trainer. His sister in Geraldine said he bought some land down this way, but no one seems to have heard of him and she doesn't know where he lives.'

'I can find out from the Federated Farmers. They have a list of names and addresses of members.'

'Oh, please will you? That'll be amazing if you can find him for me.'

'I'll do my best. Where will you stay if you leave here? You're welcome to stay on here while you're doing your search. Except we're a bit far away from everything, I suppose.'

'That's really kind of you, Jock. But it's best I stay in a backpacker or Youth Hostel in Queenstown as it may be more practical.'

'Well, I'll look forward to having you back here in a week. Pity you won't be able to meet Hamish before you go, but he will be here when you get back.'

'I might go and pack now. I have to make a list of places to go to make my inquiries.'

'I'll make a few phone calls tonight to try and help you. Don't give up hope of finding Misty. You'll get her back, don't worry.'

While Hope was busy filling her backpack, she couldn't stop herself from looking at her mini photo book of Misty and suddenly had a meltdown. She crumbled in a heap on her bed and sobbed. In desperation, she prayed 'Please, God, I'm at my wit's end. Please help me find her, I can't stand it anymore.'

There was a gentle knock at the door. Hope saw Charity standing in the doorway and she quickly wiped her eyes.

'Sorry ... Hope, are you alright? I knocked twice but you couldn't have heard me. Will you let me pray with you?'

Hope remembered Charity had been at Bible College. Jock gave thanks for the food at the table each night and Hope guessed they were all believers.

'Um ... if you like, thank you.'

That night, she slept peacefully for the first time since she'd arrived in Queenstown.

She awakened to the sound of Jock scolding one of the dogs for bringing a rabbit inside the house. She showered and dressed then joined the family at the dining table early.

'I've some news for you, young lady.' Jock took a piece of paper out of his shirt pocket. 'Good news, at that.' He handed the note to Hope. Her heart jumped as she held her breath and then her head spun.

'Oh, my goodness! You did it, you found Uncle Joel!' She looked at the note again. 'But there's no address or phone number. It just says Dart River Ranch, Glenorchy.' The smile on her face vanished as the corners of her mouth turned down.

'The Federated Farmers would not give out personal details for privacy reasons but just the name of his ranch is all you need. We can find that in the yellow pages directory.' Jock had already picked up the directory from the telephone table. He quickly flicked through the pages. 'Here we are ... here's the phone number and the address of the ranch. What do you want to do? I'll write it down for you and you can phone him.' The smile returned to her face again.

In Jock's office, Hope's stomach churned as she picked up the phone. 'Can I speak to Joel Grey please?' A young male voice answered.

'Sorry, he's not here. He's out of town and won't be back until tomorrow. Can I take a message?'

'No— no, thanks. What time do you expect him to be back tomorrow?'

'He should be back by midday unless he stops off somewhere else on the way.'

'I'll come tomorrow afternoon then.' Her heart raced with excited expectation.

'Well, what did he say?' Jock looked intensely at her.

'I spoke to a ranch hand who's looking after the stock while Uncle Joel's out of town. He said he's due back tomorrow, so I'll go out there and find accommodation nearby.'

'Mmm ... Paradise. That's a remote farming valley about twenty kilometres north of Glenorchy village. It's right on the edge of Mt Aspiring National Park.'

'Sounds isolated to me. I suppose there's no accommodation out there.'

'I believe there's a large hostel at Lake Kinloch, about twenty minutes' drive from Paradise. It's supposed to be clean and popular with tourists.'

Charity came into the dining room to clear away the breakfast dishes.

'What am I hearing? It sounds like you've found him ... your uncle, I mean.'

'Yes, isn't it great? Your father's been a great help. I'm so grateful all of you for your support.'

'Well, you'd better get off and get out to that hostel and get settled. I think you might need this.' Gilly handed her a chilly bin full of provisions with ice packs to keep it cool.

'Wow, you're so generous. I don't expect you to do this and you don't have to. I can manage, honest, I can.'

Jock quickly interjected. 'Just take it, lassie. It's the least we can do to help. And you play it safe. Drive carefully and give me a phone call before you come back so that I know what you decide to do.'

Hope drove off down the long driveway then onto the windy highway again, this time really believing that God had heard her prayers.

***

Hope found the drive to Lake Kinloch just as spectacular as the voyage through the Lewis Pass had been. She was overwhelmed by the breath-taking views and couldn't stop gaping at the abundance of forest and greenery all the way to the lake.

This is heaven. No wonder Uncle Joel wanted to live down here. Why did he just up and leave like that? I'll have to ask him what happened—that's if he'll tell me.

As she drove around the lake to Kinloch, she reminisced about the good old times spent with her uncle while she was growing up and pondered on her childhood memories of Joel breaking in Misty and going on the hunts with him.

The drive to the hostel took over an hour. She clutched the steering wheel tight as she drove carefully on the slippery roads. When she arrived at the hostel, to her delight it was not full. 'Great! An empty dorm.' She dumped her backpack on the bare mattress.

In the lounge, the warm glow from the old-fashioned stone fireplace caught her eye. She unpacked her provisions in the small kitchen and placed them in the

75

allotted bag with her name on it then prepared a basic meal of rice risotto with bacon and fresh vegetables.

She went out onto the veranda after her meal, eating a banana for dessert. She was mesmerised by the colours of the electric blue lake and technicolour sunset.

A freshening breeze sent a chill through her. She headed back to the dorm and rested for a while on her unmade bunk, lying on top of her sleeping bag. Though she usually read a novel to relax, she was too tired to read the book she had packed.

An hour later, having woken from a short nap, she went back onto the veranda to look at the changing moods of the lake, dressed in her fleecy bomber jacket and lined trousers. When eventually darkness fell on the lake, she looked up at the sky and saw that it was the clearest she had ever seen, full of sparkling diamonds and shooting stars. It was so still except for the odd sound of an owl or migrating ducks overhead. 'Thank you, God, thank you for bringing me to this heavenly place,' she said quietly, then went indoors to the communal lounge to join a few of the tourists who sat around the fireplace.

Chapter Nine

It was a brisk southern morning, and Hope was glad she packed extra thermals. No more sleeping in the tent for her now. She'd left her wristwatch in the bathroom. When she went back to look for it, she was surprised to find no one had stolen it. She'd been so forgetful lately— it must be all the stress about finding Misty and Uncle Joel. 'Oh my goodness, it's eleven thirty already,' she uttered.

She returned the extra blanket that one of the night staff had given her during the night when she had been woken by the cold. She'd not yet adjusted to the sudden drop in temperature. She handed the receptionist at the desk the rolled up army blanket.

'Thanks, it was a great help. Hope you don't mind but I need a few directions. I can't follow this map. Do you know how to get to Paradise, near Glenorchy please?' Hope handed her the map.

'Sure, I do. Let me take a look.' The receptionist put her glasses back on.

'Do you know where in Paradise you are headed?'

'A ranch on Glenorchy-Paradise Road. It's called Dart River Ranch. Do you know it?'

The girl laughed. 'We know everything and everyone around here. I went on a riding course there last year.'

'Oh, really? Do they have a lot of horses?'

'Yes, heaps. They run a lot of different activities. You can take your own horse there for some training or they'll provide one. They also run treks along the Dart River occasionally which I have done.'

'Sounds amazing. I can't wait to take a look.'

'There are a few hunky ranch hands who work there too.' The girl flashed her a smile and Hope didn't stop to think what the twinkle in her eyes meant.

That must have been one of the ranch hands I spoke to over the phone.

Hope loved the scenic drive to Glenorchy. When she arrived in the village she was surprised there were signs of civilisation. Apart from a pub and a small general store, there was also a school. She stopped to buy some food and sat in the car to eat it. She looked up and saw the sign for Glenorchy-Paradise Road. *At last, I might get a good lead to find Misty.*

She drove along Paradise-Glenorchy Road past Rees Station looking for the gate she was told about when suddenly she saw the sign, *DART RIVER RANCH* with a prominent image of a black stallion. Tall pine trees loomed high, their branches almost shrouding the sign.

As Hope neared the old, colonial farmhouse that presented itself at the end of the long driveway, she held her breath in anticipation.

A young man appeared to be walking back from the stables near the house. He turned and waved then approached her vehicle as she pulled over and leaned out the window.

'You must be Hope—Cole's my name, Cole Digby. You can park here. Come on inside. Joel's been delayed but suggested I show you around the ranch if you're interested. He shouldn't be much longer. Would you like to come in for a coffee first?'

She couldn't help ogling the debonair young man. As she stepped out of the car, he towered above her in his high boots and brown leather Bullhide hat with leather whip stitching around the top. She tried not to stare.

'Oh, thanks, I will. I'm a bit of a coffee addict.'

'Joel has one of those coffee filter machines and fresh coffee beans. Anyway, how do you know him?'

'He's my uncle.' She didn't want to get into the issue that he was probably just an uncle-like figure and not related. Just a close family friend.

'That's strange he never mentioned you. But, then again, he doesn't tell everyone his business. He's quite a private person.' Cole pulled out two well-worn bachelor mugs from the cupboard and opened a packet of biscuits.

'Gingernuts. Hope you like them.'

'My favourite, but usually when I can dunk them and I won't do that in company.' She gave him a sheepish grin.

'Do you live here?' She discreetly looked around at the sleek furnishings that were unlike the usual rugged interior of a high country farmer's abode.

'No, over there.' He nodded towards the large green paddock through the window. Hope spotted a small wooden bungalow she could see in the distance.

'Joel lives here alone. See that cottage over there.' He pointed at the home that Hope had already picked out.

'That's for Joel's ranch hands and I'm the only one he has on the property at present. I'm in my final year at Otago University studying Agricultural Science.'

'Wow! That's unbelievable. I've been accepted for the Agricultural Science Diploma Equine there, as well. It's just a one-year course full-time or part-time by distance learning.'

'I majored in Equine Health as well. That's why I'm here with your uncle. He's been training me in horse breaking techniques and supports me with a horse breeding program I've started.' He poured the coffee into the mugs and passed her the biscuits. 'Anyway ... When do you start your Diploma?'

'I'm having a gap year and wanting to save some money doing farm labouring, particularly working with horses. Next March I hope.'

They finished their coffee.

'Come outside and look around the ranch.' Cole led her out to the back paddocks.

'We've bred some amazing horses with two of our stallions. They are real stunners, a white Arab stallion, and a black Kaimanawa beauty we brought down in the first muster two years ago. The mares and foals are kept in the stables during the cold months until the foals get stronger. I can show you them later.'

'What do you mean in the first muster? Where do you get the horses from?'

'Oh, of course, you don't know. They're the wild horses from the hills around Paradise.'

'I've never heard of wild horses around here. Are there many?'

'I don't think so. We discovered two small herds which you see in those two paddocks over there and we have broken in several of them. The stallions took a lot of work to get to the stage of handling them.'

'Do you do any show jumping or dressage with any of them?'

'Hold on—we'll go and bring the horses down to the front paddock for a feed. They won't hurt us. They're just frisky with all the spring grass.'

'I mean, do you show the horses?' Hope persisted.

'Yeah, we've just been in the local agricultural show recently and our best riders entered the events on our own horses. Wait on—if you could just stand aside while I open the gate to let them through.' He unlatched the long wooden gate.

'Perhaps you'd better stand behind the fence. We shift them into a different paddock each night to give the grass a rest, but some of them can wind each other up and start a kicking match trying to push through the gate.'

Hope stood back and observed how he gathered the horses together with skill and coaxed them through the gate. She leaned against the fence watching each horse trot past one by one then caught a fleeting glimpse of a white Anglo-Arab mare rushing by, which was partly shadowed by another larger horse on her side.

She looked again and froze with shock. She placed her hand on her stomach as the churning started, triggered by her distress.

'Misty! Misty!' she cried out loudly.

Cole looked across at her as he moved towards the gate to close it. 'Are you alright? Why are you calling that name?'

Hope couldn't hear him. She started running towards the horses, tripping over piles of horse dung and stumbling on the uneven ground as she raced towards her mare.

'Slow down, Hope! You don't want to frighten them.' Cole was bewildered at her behaviour. He didn't understand why she was calling out that name, as it appeared she just went over to pat the horses. Then the distraught look on her face was obvious.

She quietly walked up to the herd. A few of them threw their heads in the air and trotted away from her while one white mare pricked its ears and turned towards her, slowly walking in her direction.

'Misty—it is you; I just knew it!' She wrapped her arms around the horse's neck and sobbed. Misty gently rubbed her head up and down Hope's back as if to comfort her.

Betrayed again! Why did her Uncle Joel do this without letting her know? He has a lot of explaining to do. She needed to stop and slow her breathing down. She clutched her chest then leaned against Misty's shoulder with her face buried in the horse's mane and started to relax.

Cole walked over to join her with a puzzled look on his face. Seeing her face wet with tears, he pulled out a clean handkerchief and awkwardly offered it to her.

'Here, it's a clean one. Sorry—I don't understand what's going on.'

She tried to compose herself, struggling to swallow then spoke with a husky voice, 'She's mine, that's my horse. Uncle Joel is the one who bought Misty. He's my friend, so why would he do that?'

She looked Misty over and could see she was in perfect health and appeared content.

'What's he doing with her? I mean, what's he using her for—to breed?'

'No, we have experienced riders who live in Queenstown who don't own their own horses, and we allow them to use our show horses like Misty for jumping events and dressage. But most of them are at university and can only come here during their semester breaks, so Joel and I have to exercise the horses as best we can.'

'Oh, poor Misty. She must have been missing me.' She nestled her head into the horse's mane as the mare responded by nudging her and letting out a soft whinny.

'I'm going to confront Uncle Joel when he arrives and find out the truth. Why did he come all the way back to Bethlehem to bring Misty down here behind my back?' Her mood changed from one of deep sadness to anger.

As Cole shuffled back to the house with Hope, he kept his hands in his pockets and head hanging low. He didn't say a word, as though he was scared to upset her any further.

'Take a seat in the lounge and I'll see what the pot of stew is doing.'

Hope sat enjoying the aroma emanating from the kitchen that reminded her of her mother's cooking. Then she remembered why she was here.

A white Ute arrived out the front of the house. Joel came through the front door and threw off his boots.

'Are you there, Cole? Sorry, I'm so late. There was a car accident causing a traffic jam. I gather that bright yellow banana out there is Hope's car.'

Cole walked back out to the hallway to meet him and chuckled at his comment. 'Oh, yeah ... that's Sunflower.' He struggled to keep his composure.

'Sorry I was delayed, Mate. That mare I went to see seems to be ready for breaking in. The owners are trucking her down from Ashburton next week.'

Joel whispered something to him as he walked into the lounge where Hope was sitting. Cole followed after him. 'What a surprise to see you here!' Joel wiped beads of perspiration from his brow and gave a nervous cough.

'If you don't mind, I'd rather talk to you in private. I've just seen Misty in the paddock out back and I want to know what she's doing here.' Her demeanour was prickly.

Cole took the cue. 'Look, guys ... you two appear to have a lot of catching up to do. I'll disappear back to my digs now and see you tomorrow. Are you staying overnight, Hope?'

'I ... um—I don't know.'

'Yes, she is. You will stay, won't you? Please, Hope. I need some time to explain why Misty is here and why I left your home so abruptly when I did.'

'Well, I suppose I could. I'll have to phone my employer at Corriedale Hills Station and tell Jock I've been delayed.'

'Use the phone in my office. It's not a toll call from here.' Cole tied up his bootlaces and poked his head through the office door where Hope was about to pick up the phone. 'I'll see you in the morning then, Hope. Perhaps Joel will let me take you on a bit of a trek around here on horse-back and show you the Dart River. They need exercise, anyway.'

'I'm not sure yet. Do you mind if I let you know in the morning as I may not feel like doing anything.' The look on her face said it all for Cole and he waved and walked off.

After her phone call to Jock at Corriedale Hills Station, she wandered back into the lounge to find Joel kneeling down stoking the fire. He turned around to glance at her as she entered the room and stood up.

'How did you get on?'

'Oh, he was quite amicable and said I can let him know when I'm ready to start work.'

'Hope—why not hear me out while I tell you why I left under a cloud? But be prepared for some unexpected news. After we've talked, I'd like to give you a good hot meal. Cole has prepared a beef stew in the slow cooker that'll warm you up.'

Hope suspected he was trying to soften the blow as he handed her a mug of hot chocolate. They sat down in the lounge in front of the fire and Joel's old black cat spread itself out on the hearth mat. It rolled onto its back pulling up its front paws, trying to look cute.

Joel sniffed nervously and gave a cough to clear his throat. 'When you had the big quarrel with your mother and went to stay with Jessie on the farm for a month, I received a phone call from her. She was upset that you refused to stay at home and start a nursing career at the local hospital. She said that your horse-riding was a huge distraction from your studies if you were going nursing.'

He stooped down to stoke the fire and drank the rest of his hot drink then continued, 'She seemed obsessed about you going nursing and sounded as though she was determined to talk you into it.'

Hope bristled. 'She was more interested that I live the life that she missed out on and fulfil her fantasy of becoming a nurse!' she snapped.

The deep-seated resentment towards her mother rose again. *How could she be so selfish and scheming?*

'I think she was bitter about me gaining my independence when I went to work for Jessie's father on the farm.'

'The thing is Hope—she kind of coerced me into going up and transporting Misty in your horse float down here so I could take care of her. I didn't buy her. Your mother begged me to take her and made me promise not to change her name.' He sat in the chair wringing his hands and hesitated as if a bomb was about to explode.

'You mean you drove all the way from here to the Bay of Plenty just to take care of Misty. Mum's so mean— but what you did to save Misty from going to a stranger is unbelievable. Thank you!'

'I knew that if I didn't do it, your mother would carry out her threat to sell her, and who knows whom she might have ended up with. I planned to wait until you left home for good and then tell you the truth as I'm doing now. I knew I couldn't get in touch with you. Your mother wouldn't let me.'

Hope leapt up from her armchair and threw herself at Joel, wrapping her arms around his neck and kissing him on the cheek. She was overjoyed instead of being angry with him.

The phone rang in the office. 'Ah, no, not right now. They'll phone back if it's important.' He sauntered back into the lounge, rubbed his hands together and gave another one of his coughs.

'There is something else I need to clear up with you. I'm afraid I've another shattering confession to make.' He stammered as moisture appeared on his temples and started dripping down his face. He wiped it with a handkerchief from his pocket.

Hope jumped out of her seat and walked off to the bathroom. She wondered what on earth he was about to tell her. Perhaps he had cancer, or he was about to move. Or maybe there was something wrong with Misty. The phone rang again. She washed her hands and walked hastily back into the lounge. Joel wasn't there and she could hear that he was on the telephone. The office door was closed and there was only the sound of a muffled voice through the wall. It was a lengthy phone conversation and then he walked back to join Hope. 'So sorry I was so long, but it was your mother phoning. I thought if I didn't answer the phone it would keep on ringing and thank God I picked it up.'

'What? What do you mean? How does she know your phone number?' Hope felt that this was all becoming a can of worms.

'It's a long story, and I was going to tell you. It'll have to wait now. Unfortunately, your mother rang to tell me some bad news as I told her you were here. Your father has just died suddenly in his sleep.' He walked over to her armchair and placed his hand on her shoulder. 'I'm so sorry, Hope.'

She froze and sat in the chair looking like a stunned mullet. She wanted to tell Joel that she knew that Frank was not her father.

'How? Why—what's happened to him? I'd better phone her back.'

'No—she said not to. He's had a sudden massive heart attack, and she's had a lot to deal with right now. Doug's with her and the Vicar is on his way around. But she wants you to go back for the funeral and I said that I'll fly back to Auckland with you. We can get a connecting flight to Tauranga from there.'

Hope couldn't believe her ears. Just when she'd become reunited with Misty and started making a new life for herself away from the unhappiness of home, misfortune struck. *Now I have to go back again.* Her heart sank.

'Poor Frank. I didn't even know he was ill.' She hoped he didn't suffer as she remembered what a kind man he had been in spite of being a drunkard.

'The doctor told your mother he wouldn't have suffered. He had not been obviously ill. It just happens to some people, apparently. His funeral is in two days. Your mother said we can both stay at your house. Why are you calling him Frank? You used to call him Dad.'

'Oh ... no reason. I suppose it sounds modern.'

Joel appeared awkward all of a sudden as though he wanted to tell her something.

'But I won't stay on after the funeral. I have to take care of Misty now and make up for lost time with her.'

'I've been thinking about that too. What do you think about staying on here and working with me? I need help with the horses and I can train you to do the work I do. When you're at university, you can always come here for your holidays and you'll be on wages.'

Hope's mouth dropped open. Suddenly her grim countenance changed to one of elation.

'Really! That would be fantastic. I'll be doing distance study but will have to go there for labs and workshops. But what will happen to Misty while I'm at university?'

'I can take good care of her just as I've already been doing. Cole has done some of his papers by distance study. You could ask him all about it.'

It was like a dream come true for Hope. She was much more focused on this amazing proposition from Joel than she was on the death of her stepfather. Perhaps when she tells Joel what Doug had told her about Frank not being her biological father, he might help her find her real Dad. But she'll have to find the right moment to tell him all about it and now is not the right time.

She sank deep into the armchair with the cat on her lap, with the heat of the fire lighting up her face as well as her heart.

Chapter Ten

Doug stayed on after the funeral and helped his mother to prepare the market garden for sale with the help of one of their casual workers. Joel and Hope stayed for five days then returned to Paradise. As Hope had never experienced any close relationship or bonding with Frank, she did not grieve his loss. During his stay, Joel had detected there was still unnerving tension between Myra and her daughter who constantly bickered with each other.

Hope was relieved that Doug had decided to stay on and share the family home with his mother while he worked at the hospital, which took the pressure of Hope in that she didn't feel guilty about staying away.

'You know you're going to have to forgive your mother someday and the sooner the better,' said Joel, elbowing Hope as he drove to Paradise from Queenstown airport after they flew in.

'Why is that? I don't feel ready to forgive her. She doesn't deserve it and she has always kept secrets from me. Anyway, what were you and Mum having heavy discussions about? I saw you both in deep conversation after the funeral at the cemetery. And later at home too. Mum appeared really agitated.'

'We just had some unfinished business we had to take care of, that's all. Tying up loose ends when I left in a hurry. How about we discuss this as soon as we get back to the ranch?'

For the rest of the trip home, there was silence. Both of them struggling to assimilate the truth that was about to rear its irksome head.

***

Joel unloaded their luggage from the boot of his car. Hope dumped her bags on her bedroom floor and walked back to the kitchen where Joel had just put the kettle on.

'Well, you still haven't told me why you up and left all of a sudden. I remember you were going to tell me the night I arrived when we sat in front of the fire and Mum had rung to say that Frank had died.'

'I suppose I needed to wait for the right moment. I didn't know what state you'd be in after hearing of Frank's death.' Joel's voice sounded full of intrigue.

'I'm over Frank's passing already ... do you know that he's not my father?'

Those words hit Joel with a thud as though he'd been assaulted. He struggled to give a reply, as he was unprepared. He needed time to work out what to say and now she put him on the spot. He grabbed some coffee cups and walked into the lounge with Hope in tow.

'I ... I did know that. How did you find out?' He flopped into his well-worn armchair while Hope sat opposite.

'Doug told me ages ago. He said that when Frank was drunk one night when Mum and I had gone out, he spewed out this confession that he was not my father. He refused to tell Doug whom my real Dad was and made him swear that he would not tell anyone. I think Doug knows who my father is, but he said that even if his suspicions were right, he would never tell me. Will you help me find him, Uncle Joel, please? I don't know where to start.' Her voice quivered.

90

Joel went to the kitchen and poured coffee. He brought it back in on a tray. She noticed a sudden pallor in his face that was not there earlier.

'You're having coffee?' He handed her a cup.

'Thanks.' She took the cup and tried to steady her hand as she placed it on the table next to her.

'It's a long story, Hope—I'm your real father.' He cringed as he said the words then sighed as though he was relieved at having let go of the emotional burden.

'What! First Misty, then this. No wonder my mother didn't want me to find you. Is she a party to all this deceit?' Hope didn't know whether to be happy or to start crying. After all these years, this was a dream come true for her. But it left her confused.

'I don't understand. My legal name is Petersen, not Grey.'

'Yes, I know. Frank agreed to put his name on your birth certificate to avoid a scandal.'

'But Mum was married to Frank, not to you!'

'I'll tell you all about it but you'll need to be patient and hear the whole story. Your mother has given her permission to tell you everything.'

He loosened his shirt collar by undoing his top button that revealed a red, moist neck. 'Do you want a biscuit with your coffee? I have chocolate macaroons in the fridge.'

'Sure.' Her lips tightened, and as she sat staring in front of her.

'Won't be a minute.' He walked slowly to the fridge as if he was deliberately deferring the dreaded moment of truth.

He handed her the packet and sat back in his armchair, this time leaning forward on the edge of the seat with his arms on his knees wringing his hands and peering up at Hope who just sat glaring at him.

'Your mother and I met when we were young, about your age, and fell in love. My parents were not wealthy. They were an ordinary working-class family. My father was a stock auctioneer in Geraldine where he owned a small farmlet. He had a heart condition and retired early then died soon after. My mother and I moved to Bethlehem as Mum wanted to be near her family there. Your Aunt Nelly wanted to stay in Geraldine where she had a good job and friends.'

'Where did you meet my mum?'

'I attended the local pony club and so did your mother. Once a month our farming community in Bethlehem held a dance, a great shindig in the local hall. Your mother and I loved dancing and would always pair up on those evenings and then we gradually started courting. I cycled miles to visit her at her home, in spite of her parent's disapproval. We decided that we would marry one day, but that was way in the future.'

'Why didn't you marry her?'

'I desperately wanted to, but her father was an influential man and convinced her she would end up as a no-hoper without any status or social standing.'

'Where does Frank come into it then?'

He wiped his brow with his handkerchief and continued.

'Well—so much for Myra's high social standing and status. She'd been coerced by her family into marrying Frank Petersen, a marriage of convenience ... a loveless organised marriage.'

Hope grimaced and compassion showed in her eyes.

'Well ... the money didn't come Frank's way and he and your mother struggled for years after the war. When he returned from active service in 1944, Frank began drinking heavily but prior to the war he hardly touched a drop.'

'Oh, that's really sad! I never knew,' croaked Hope, as Joel continued.

'Before Frank went off to war in 1942, Doug was born. He's your half-brother. Your mother suffered the misery of being left with their baby boy whilst trying to manage a market garden alone, with the occasional help of her parents. After the war, she became embittered by another hard blow when Frank confessed to her that he'd become involved in a homosexual relationship in the army and no longer sought intimacy with her. They slept in separate rooms for the whole of your life, I believe.'

'Wow, that's right! Now I understand. I thought they didn't sleep in the same room because of Frank's drinking, but now it makes sense.' The sickness in Hope's stomach returned which she experienced when upset. But quickly she felt a kind of relief at knowing the truth.

Joel continued, gingerly.

'He was a lot older than your mother and didn't keep good health which limited his ability to work. His parents virtually abandoned him because of alcohol abuse and threatened that if he didn't stop, they would disinherit him, which they eventually did.'

'So where do I come into it?'

'When my mother died in 1950, she and Frank invited me to have meals at their home. Myra had become a broken woman from the neglect and strain of living with her alcoholic husband and his secret. We both ended up seeking solace in each other and one night, when Frank had passed out in an alcoholic stupor, Myra came to my home and cried on my shoulders. You can probably guess the rest. I was grieving over the loss of my mother and Myra had caved in under the strain of her life with Frank.'

Joel's face changed colour and Hope wasn't sure where to look.

'How did Frank take that? Did Mum tell him?'

'Yes, she did. He knew he hadn't been a proper husband to her and agreed to support her by raising you as his own daughter. It would have caused such a scandal in the fifties if anyone discovered the truth. All three of us had to keep a pact that no one else would ever know. Frank also had his own skeletons in the closet and that remained a secret too.'

'I can't believe that I've found the truth after so many years. I had my suspicions and gut feeling that something was terribly wrong all my life,' she spouted.

'Look, Hope. I'm sorry to have to tell you all this. It's not pleasant news.' He reached for another biscuit and topped up their coffees.

'Your mother made me promise I wouldn't tell anyone, but I can see the impact that all this has had on your life.'

Once again, Hope was fighting back tears of anger. 'Now I know why I never felt loved or accepted by Frank or his relatives. They aren't even my kin, and I guess they all found out at some stage.'

Joel walked over to her and put his arm around her shoulders, while she allowed him to offer her comfort. Then he tried to talk then stammered, his face appearing flushed.

'I'm so sorry, really I am. Please forgive me, Hope. I've never stopped loving you and it was torture for me to be separated from you.'

'Then why did you? Why did you leave without saying goodbye or leave me a note or something? I thought you didn't care about us anymore.'

'I couldn't take it any longer. I wanted your mother to divorce Frank for years, but she just felt guilty, always driven by shame, even though she had grounds for the marriage to be annulled. She thought he would not have been able to look after himself if she left, although his drinking was affecting her health. I just couldn't wait for her any longer and gave up hope of ever being married to her. I decided to let her go.'

By this time, Hope couldn't contain herself. She was not only feeling devastated by her own grief but also for Joel, her mother and Frank. Joel and her mother had let her down by leading her to believe a lie all these years.

'Look, Hope. At some point, you'll have to forgive your mother, just as God has forgiven you. If you keep holding onto all that resentment, it'll make you sick.'

Hope was taken aback. Until now, she'd not heard any God talk coming from Joel. In fact, she could never remember him attending any kind of church.

'What do you mean? Why are you bringing God into all of this?'

'I've been converted. I have close friends who live locally and who kind of rescued me when I met them at the Horse Breeders Association. They saw the bad state I was in when I purchased this ranch and invited me to their home for meals and then to their local Baptist church.'

Hope didn't know what to say as she was both in disbelief and ecstatic. She wanted to cry out—Dad, you have found faith too, just like Jessie and her family. But instead, she changed the subject.

'Look ... I don't hate Mum. I just feel angry that she betrayed me all these years. I'm not ready to forgive her, not yet.'

'I'll have to work on that now, won't I?' Joel was trying to help Hope loosen up as he could see the strain on her face with the significant disclosures he had made.

'Dad—can I call you that?'

'Of course, my love, you must call me Dad, as I am your father. Look ... we could both get a blood test that can prove it. How about it?'

'Sure. It's not that I don't believe you, but it would make it more real if I could see it in writing. This means that Nelly is my Auntie. You need to talk to her Dad. Tell her the truth too.'

'She already knows, my love. She also kept silent all these years. She'll be relieved to know it's all out in the open now. I'll phone her and we could visit her together sometime.'

'It's pity she hasn't got any children. I would have cousins.'

'But we all have each other. God is gracious.'

'Let's wind it up with a little prayer, shall we? Will you let me pray for us all, Hope? Is that okay?'

She nodded her head in agreement and as she closed her eyes, Joel took her hand in his.

An enormous weight lifted from her shoulders. It was like old times with Jessie when she used to pray for her and hold her hand. For the first time in years, she felt secure and loved.

Chapter Eleven

Eighteen months later at Dart River Ranch

Joel had become involved in the wild horse advisory groups and the horse welfare organisations in the south after he arrived in Paradise.

He took it upon himself to rescue the wild horses from poachers and blood-thirsty pleasure seekers who try to shoot them. The herd included many of the Kaimanawa horses that the renowned ex-army officer, Captain Carl Richardson from Australia had purchased from the army. He'd transported them to his expansive ranch in the Dart Valley, several years prior to Joel's arrival.

There the Captain suffered a devastating blow. As his men were unloading the horses, they failed to secure the pen adequately and his two prized young Arab stallions pushed the fence over. They escaped with the Kaimanawa horses which stampeded and took off into the hills around Diamond Lake. Tourists have seen them appear on occasions, grazing peacefully by the lakeside. The herd has doubled in size.

Due to the loss of the stock and other unfortunate financial setbacks, the Captain had been declared bankrupt and his ranch had become a mortgagee sale. No one in the valley heard from him again. Hunters have tried shooting at the horses each year during the hunting season as they often frighten off the deer. Joel had been given the name "horse whisperer" by the locals and his team of musterers who assisted him each year.

***

Hope became adept at handling Misty on the steep slopes around Dart Valley and was deemed capable enough by her father to be able to take part in the next big muster.

Her university studies by correspondence took up most of her time. This year she'd spent two semesters living in student quarters attending the university full-time and graduated with a Diploma in Equine Health. Even though she'd been to visit her mother in Bethlehem a few times, she only went to keep the peace.

She couldn't wait to get back to her home which was now Dart River Ranch and looked forward to riding Misty.

***

At last, no more study. Hope was ecstatic as her old Toyota chugged its way down the long drive towards Dart River Ranch. Joel stood on the front porch as always, waving as she approached the homestead which was the thing that she looked forward to most. Seeing her father standing there greeting her with his broad smile. It was November and there was still snow in the foothills which meant Joel had the wood fire burning. She could tell, as there was a strong smell of tea tree lingering in the air.

Cole had finished his university degree and had been working full-time for Joel helping him with the breeding program and training young horses.

He peered through his cottage curtains every few minutes, craning his neck to see if the Toyota was parked in Joel's driveway. At last, he heard the familiar sound of Hope's vehicle arriving and pulling to a halt. He quickly ducked behind the curtains, as he did not want Hope to see

98

that he was more than eager to see her. It'd been six months since he saw her last and he wondered how much she'd changed.

Joel walked down the steps, gave Hope a hug, and took her bags as she followed him inside. Then Cole noticed Joel walking back outside again and waved out to him, hoping to catch his attention, which wasn't really necessary. Joel had told him early that morning that he would let him know when Hope arrives so that he could drop over to partake in a welcome-home meal.

Cole ran back into the bathroom and had a last-minute check of his grooming. He was clean-shaven, but today his hair played up. He had thick brown hair that he tied with a band into a small ponytail. It made him look far from effeminate as it outlined his fine contoured jaw and square face. He picked up his brown leather Stetson and raced out the door but as he neared the house, he pulled back and sauntered slowly up the steps onto the porch.

'Are you there Joel? Can I come in?' Cole walked in without knocking.

'Only if you're good looking.' Joel winked at Hope and colour rushed to her cheeks.

'We're in here.' Joel called from the lounge where he'd just lit the fire.

'Oh—Howdy, Hope!' Cole spoke as though he'd no knowledge of her arrival, but his pretence was unconvincing to Hope.

'Hi, Cole. It's been such a while since I've seen you and you look different.'

'Yep, I suppose I do. My hair's grown long and I expect my face is more leathered.' He combed his fringe back quickly with his fingers.

Hope did not let on that the leathered look appealed to her. So did his warm brown eyes. She had not been interested in males at university. She'd thrown herself into her studies and it left no time for socialising. And even then, she'd no previous hankering to get into a relationship. She enjoyed being a free spirit and her horse was the only love of her life. But this time, something unusual awakened in her when Cole walked through the door. They'd only ever had a platonic relationship, and that's how Hope had intended it to stay.

'Right, you two. Why don't you have a good catch-up while I check the roast in the oven?'

'I'll give you a hand.' Hope stood up and followed Joel into the kitchen.

'No, honestly, I don't need any help. I'd rather Cole brought you up to date with what's happening at the ranch and our plans for the big muster.'

Hope and Cole sat awkwardly as though they'd just met and chatted away about the ranch, then Cole changed the subject.

'Your father told me your twenty-first birthday is coming up soon.'

'Yeah, I forgot about that. It's in January, but we have to get through Christmas first. Dad said he wanted to organise a party for me, but I don't know many people around here apart from our staff and a few friends from church who live locally.'

'I can't believe it's been almost two years since you first arrived at Paradise. It'll probably be good for you to get to know some of the locals socially. I think you should give your father the opportunity to do something for you.'

Hope sat there wondering how much Cole knew of her past, but unbeknown to her, Joel had already told Cole he was Hope's father.

'I hope you're ready for the big muster. There are some fine looking breeds up in the hills. A few new ones we haven't come across before.' Cole's hat was still on his head and he hadn't noticed until Joel nodded at him, trying to indicate he needed to remove it. He placed the Stetson next to him on the couch.

'I can't wait. I've been so looking forward to this. What will you do with them all? You won't be able to keep them all on the ranch, surely.' Hope looked at him, eyes wide.

'I don't think there are many left. Perhaps just one or two herds, about twenty horses, I suppose. We'll break them in and sell them, or other trainers will buy them and break them in themselves. We'll use some of them for breeding. Joel has received orders from further up the island from trainers who want new stock.'

Joel poked his head around the door. 'Come on you two. Let's tuck in. Hope, would you mind setting the table? Cole, why don't you pour us some of that Speights ginger beer? It's a good brew that one.'

For the first time since Hope left Jessie's home, she felt like she had a family. Cole had become like a brother to her and her father doted on her as she did him. But this time, she noticed there was a change in her father.

'I think it would be a good idea if we give thanks to the Lord for our food and all our blessings. If you don't mind, both of you, I'll give thanks before we eat.'

***

Hope's life was about to take an unexpected turn.

A cold southerly wind pierced the rugged mountain foothills where the small team of musterers headed. Although it was still autumn in April, the alpine climate cooled everything down rapidly. Hope felt the chill penetrate her lungs in spite of the thick merino garments she wore under her oilskin jacket.

'Now, Hope. You'd better ride with me and remember the instructions I gave you about not getting in their way. If the herd stampedes, you move quickly and follow me.'

101

Joel pulled his horse up alongside Misty and waited while Cole acted as a scout, moving up behind the ridge to see how far away the herd was. He moved quietly and slowly with the dogs creeping silently beside him.

Hope shook with an adrenaline rush. This was her first big muster, a full herd. *I hope I don't muck it up.* 'Shhh, Misty, go quietly now,' she whispered as Misty shook her head a few times then stood still as a post.

'Just stay with me Hope and don't do anything unless I ask you. Things can turn to custard pretty quickly.'

As Hope searched his face, she could see regret that he had brought her with them. It unnerved her slightly. But she had persisted until he gave in.

She felt the strong freshening wind bite her cheeks as she snapped the domes to fasten her jacket collar. The waiting on the ridge for Cole to return felt like forever. Suddenly, like a tornado rushing at them, the horses came towards them, stampeding through the trees.

'Quickly! Follow me!' Joel rushed off towards a group of trees.

Hope could see the wild horses galloping towards them through the forest clearing with Cole trying to restrain his horse along the fence-line.

'What's happened? What's going on?' Hope caught up to Joel looking over her shoulder at Cole further back on the ridge, whose horse was almost out of control. The herd rushed past him.

'Something spooked them. This doesn't usually happen. Hey! Quiet!' Joel growled at one of the dogs that started whining.

'They'll get away on us now. They are far too charged up to muster like this. I'll find out from Cole what happened when he gets down from the ridge.'

Without warning, a tall, black stallion turned around and veered towards them baring its teeth and flashing the whites of its eyes at them.

'Quickly, get in there behind the trees while I deal with this!' He pulled out a stock-whip to protect himself.

Hope dug her heels into Misty, adrenaline racing through her veins. She charged down the ridge behind a thicket of young pines and as she reeled around, Misty lost her footing and went down onto her knees trying to stay upright then struggled back up. Hope flew off and lay sprawled on the grass. Misty had tried not to squash her but had caught her head with a hoof. The culprit stallion let out a mighty grunt and disappeared in a cloud of dust.

Joel was horrified. He dismounted in panic, dropping his reins while his trustworthy steed stood and waited. He slid down the tussock grass to find his precious daughter bleeding and unconscious. Misty stood nearby, back on her feet and limping a little.

'Hope, Hope! Wake up, please!' He felt her throat for a pulse and checked her breathing. She appeared lifeless but breathing. Her pulse raced. Then he saw blood on his hands. When he inspected her head, there was a deep gash at the back of her scalp that bled profusely. By this time Cole had arrived on his horse overlooking the ridge looking down at them.

'What's happened? What's wrong with Hope? Can I help?' He yelled, oblivious to the incident.

'Go to the nearest homestead and call the doctor. Tell him she'll need to be airlifted to the hospital and to come quickly. She's unconscious. Bring a blanket back too. She's in shock and it's freezing up here.'

'So sorry, Joel. My horse got spooked just as I approached the herd from behind. A young Buck appeared from behind a bush. My horse reared, and I hit my head on an overhead branch and yelled. It must have skittled them.'

'What the … the deer aren't usually this far down. It's okay, Cole. I understand … but please go as fast as you can. You'll have to let the workers in the stockyards know. They're still waiting for us below to bring the herd down. Tell them they can go home until further notice.' Cole moved away, carefully winding his way back down the valley.

Joel took off his thick, oilskin vest he wore over his fleecy Swanndri and draped it over Hope's chest. Misty just stood nearby with head hung low as though she knew Hope was hurt. Joel thought she was going to die. She appeared inanimate as he stared at her deathly translucent cheeks. He kept touching her neck to check her pulse. He wiped his tears away with the cuff of his Swanndri and cupped his face in his hands.

'God, why? I've only just got her back again. Don't let me lose her now!' He collapsed onto the cold ground, pounding the earth with his clenched fist.

'I beg you. Please save her! I know I shouldn't have let her talk me into bringing her here. It was my guilt I suppose for having let her down all these years. Now I've made it worse. Please let her be alright.'

Chapter Twelve

Cole brought back the blanket and another jacket for Joel. 'The local doctor can't come as he's attending a birth. He's organised the rescue helicopter and said to turn her onto her side and keep her warm.'

'Thanks—I've already rolled her over. Here ... give me the blanket.' He wrapped the blanket around her and used a corner of it to place under her head on top of the blood-stained grass.

Another thirty minutes of waiting seemed like hours. It was torturous for Joel who kept checking her breathing and pulse obsessively. Suddenly he heard the deafening drone of the helicopter's rotors above and almost cried with relief.

Two doctors and a nurse had to land further down the valley where it was flat. They strenuously clambered up the incline to where the patient lay, dragging the stretcher and medical gear with them. Hurriedly the doctors assessed her vital signs.

'We have to move quickly! She's in shock and her blood pressure is very low.' One of the doctors quickly introduced himself as an Intensive Care Registrar. 'Dave's my name and this is John, another Registrar. Quickly—John, get that intravenous line in. We need to get her blood pressure back up. She's a bad gash in the scalp here and will need stapling when we get to the hospital. I'll apply a pressure dressing for now. We need to get her out of here before she deteriorates.' Dave appeared agitated and kept taking her pulse.

They laid her on the stretcher and asked Joel if he wanted to accompany them in the chopper.

'You might like to come along in case she regains consciousness on the way. You can stay at the hospital until you decide what to do.'

'Yes—yes, of course. I ... sure, I'll come.' He turned to Cole who appeared like a dog that had been scolded, even though he wasn't to blame.

'Cole, I'm sorry, mate. You're going to have to walk Misty and my horse-back to the ranch and get the vet to check Misty. Are any of the boys still down below?'

'Yep. Two of them are still waiting down there in case you need them.'

'They can take our horses back. Tell them I'll sort their hours out later. You can go back to keep an eye on the ranch. But don't forget to phone the vet.'

'I already radioed them. They know what's happened. They're waiting for instructions.' Cole replied before gathered up the other two horses.

'Come on—you need to get into the chopper.' The doctor directed Joel safely onto the aircraft after Hope had been fastened into the receiver for the stretcher. The nurse covered her with more blankets and fiddled with the intravenous tubing.

Joel started blowing on his hands and rubbing them together as if he was feeling the cold.

'Please strap yourself in sir. Here is a blanket for you as well.' The middle-aged nurse in black trousers and a thick jacket with fluorescent stripes put her hand into a deep pocket and pulled out a small bar of chocolate.

'You might need this to help you with shock. It must be difficult for you.' She handed him a small bottle of electrolyte drink then turned her attention back to Hope.

'Thanks, the wind was biting up on the ridge. Please tell me ... what are her chances? How bad is her head injury?'

'It's not really for me to say. The doctors will talk to you when we arrive at emergency care. They'll take her straight to the intensive care unit.'

'I mean ... all the bleeding. Will she be brain damaged?' He took a few gulps of the beverage, suddenly realising how dehydrated he was.

'We can't assess her properly until we stabilise her. We'll know more then. But the gash on the head did not pierce the skull. It's just a deep scalp wound. She'll need a skull x-ray.'

Joel relaxed his jaw as he listened intently. He focused on the nurse with a fixed gaze as she took Hope's blood pressure and shone a small pupil torch into her eyes.

'Still nothing?' Joel went to undo his seat belt as if to approach Hope.

'Ah ... please stay buckled ... It may just be a temporary situation. She could become conscious at any time. You'll find out more once we're at the hospital.'

Joel slumped back into the seat, as though finally accepting his powerlessness over the situation. He softly prayed again. 'Help her ... please Lord. She's not had a happy life, and I want to do things right this time. Please give me the chance.'

The nurse looked back at him, and he looked away, averting her gaze. *I hope she didn't hear me ... I thought I was just praying quietly.*

'Are you okay over there? We should be landing in about ten minutes.' She gave him a sympathetic smile. Even her eyes smiled.

***

Joel was instructed to wait in the room outside the Intensive Care where Hope lay attached to numerous pipes and tubes, though not artificially ventilated.

'Can I bring you a cup of tea or coffee, sir?' A hospital assistant stood in the doorway with a trolley.

'Tea with milk would be nice, thank you.'

'I've been told to offer you a hot dinner. We usually do when relatives arrive for the first time.'

'That would be great. I haven't eaten all day. Just a small one if you don't mind.'

He suddenly saw Hope's doctor leaving the Intensive Care about to walk down the corridor.

'Excuse me—Dave. Sorry, but I need to know what's happening with my daughter.'

'Oh, yes ... I was going to come and talk to you. I'm just going to look at her skull x-rays and I'll be right back.'

Joe thanked him. He slid down into his armchair and wondered what he was going to do if this went on for days. He'll have to phone Cole and ask him to keep the ranch going with back up. What about Myra? She'll have to be informed.

He looked around to see if there was a phone. The hospital assistant came towards him again pushing the trolley.

'I've come to get your dishes. I hope the hospital food was palatable.' She roughly dumped the dishes on top of the over-stacked pile.

'Thanks, the chicken was good. I was wondering if I can make a couple of long-distance calls to let Hope's other family members know what has happened.'

'Of course. Close family can make long-distance calls as long as you keep them short. Just go to the front desk at Reception and ask them to put the call through to the private room. I'll show you where that is.' She gestured to him to follow her down the corridor and muttered something to the receptionist.

'Of course. Mr Grey—just write the number down and I'll put the call through to the private family room.'

'I have two calls to make if that's okay.'

'No problem. There's a limit of six minutes per call. When you finish the first call, hang up, and then dial zero. I'll answer and put your next call through.'

Joel thanked her and walked off, shaking his head. How antiquated the system was. It would be easier to just phone with a coin box.

Myra answered the first time. 'Joel, is that you? How is Hope? I haven't heard from her for a while.'

'That's why I'm ringing, Myra. There ... there's been an accident.' He stammered. 'She's taken a tumble off Misty when the horse went down.' Joel was fighting off the guilt and held his breath, waiting for Myra's reaction.

Her response was predictable. Joel's voice shook, and he struggled to swallow as though he was choking. He longed to be there to comfort her as she said that Doug was out for the day. Now she was receiving the impact of this news alone and he waited for her to compose herself.

His voice softened even more. 'I'll pay for your flight to Dunedin. I can book you into a motel near the hospital but I'm not sure where I'll stay yet. The hospital told me I could spend a few nights on the ward.'

'I have my old friend Elma who lives close by. I'll give her a call.' She burst into tears again.

'Listen—I have an idea. I need to stay here too, so I'll get Cole and one of my ranch hands to bring my Ute up here. I can pick you up from the airport and take you to your friend. Then I can book a room for myself at the motel next to the hospital and come and get you each day.'

Myra calmed down. Now she wasn't alone in all this, and Joel needed her support too. While he was winding up the conversation, Hope's doctor poked his head through the door.

'Sorry to interrupt,' he said quietly. 'I have some results for you.'

Joel waved his hand at him to let him know he had finished his phone call.

'Myra, I've got to go ... the doctor's here. I'll call you back later tonight once they've given me a report. I have to call Cole now too.'

***

The two IC doctors in their blue medical scrubs were hardly distinguishable from the rest of the staff. But they were the doctors who had brought Hope to the hospital. Joel felt relaxed with them as they sat around the table, showing him the x-ray reports.

'Well, we have some good news. Hope does not have a skull fracture. She definitely has had a hard knock and is still unconscious but there have been eye movements. This means she is drifting in and out of consciousness. It's a waiting game, I'm afraid.' Dave appeared to set his jaw, frowning as though he was concerned.

'What does that mean? Will she come out of the coma?'

'There's a good chance she will. Her vital signs are returning and the fact that she's been breathing on her own all this time means she has only sustained a mild traumatic brain injury which we call TBI.'

'Can I go and see her? Will she be able to hear me?'

'You can sit with her but not say anything to disturb her. Just reassure her that you are there and let her hear your voice. Tell her that her horse is safe. She may become disturbed about that if her memory starts to return.'

David accompanied him into Hope's room. Her face was not so pale, and she was breathing normally. When David left the room, Joel pulled the chair close to her bed taking

110

hold of her hand. It was much warmer now. Unlike the hand he had held back on the ridge in Dart Valley which was like that of a corpse—ice cold and motionless.

He kissed her cheek and spoke softly in her ear.

'It's Dad, Hope. I'm here—you're going to be okay. You've had a bad fall but you're in hospital in good hands. I love you my precious and I'll wait here until you wake up.'

He was sure he felt her hand move in his. Perhaps he was just imagining it. He was overcome with fatigue and lay his head on her bed next to her.

He must have drifted off to sleep and awakened with a start. His mouth was dry, and he asked a nurse for a glass of water.

'There's a water fountain along the corridor. I'll get you one. I'll be in to take your daughter's recordings soon.'

The nurse with the kind face gave him a paper cup of water and he thanked her and resumed his night watch at Hope's side.

Later on, when he checked his watch he saw that he must have been asleep for an hour. He took Hopes hand again and chatted away to her as he watched her eyelids flicker. Now and then they would stay open and as he tried to make eye contact with her, he was aware she was in another world.

He started to tell her how well Misty had been doing.

'You wouldn't believe it, Hope. One of our new stallions in the paddock next to Misty has been trying to get friendly with her. Of course, I kept them apart, but he's pretty keen. She missed you while you were at university so you had better wake up so I can take you home to her.'

He made sure he didn't tell her that Misty was limping and had hurt her shoulder when she fell. Nothing serious but will take some months to heal.

Joel could hear the nurse doing her rounds, dragging a small trolley along the corridor with her recording equipment.

Just before she arrived at Hope's door, Joel nearly jumped through the roof with excitement. Hope squeezed his hand. *Am I imagining it?* 'Hope, darling ... it's Dad—I'm here! Please open your eyes.' He felt her squeeze his hand again. 'Oh, my love, you're going to be okay.' Tears stung his eyes.

'Did I hear you say she's waking up?' The nurse stood at the door and Joel wasn't sure how much of his conversation with Hope she'd heard. He quietly resented her interrupting his special moment with Hope as she slowly gained consciousness.

'She's been squeezing my hand. I'm sure it was in response to my voice.'

'That's wonderful. I'll let her doctor know. I've some medication to put into her drip infusion. It'll calm her down as she wakes from her coma, and it'll keep her from becoming agitated.'

'How long do you think it'll be before she completely wakes up?'

'I can't tell you that. None of us can. But she's showing positive signs of having sustained a mild brain injury. I'll continue to monitor her half hourly during the night.'

Joel looked at his watch and calculated that Hope had been unconscious for twelve hours since her fall at ten that morning. His eyes burned as he fought the fatigue but pushed on, determined to be at her side when she gained consciousness.

At midnight, as he started to drift off to sleep with his head on her bed, Hope tugged on his hand and opened her eyes then muttered something incoherently. She startled him. A jolt shot through him sending a shiver down his spine. He reached for the bedside medical call button and her nurse came running.

'She's waking up ... she said something and opened her eyes.' Joel stood over Hope and tried to get her attention, but her eyes stayed fixed on something to the left of him, then to the right. She wasn't able to make eye contact with him. She just lay there staring into space.

'What's happening ... why is she doing that?' He tried hard not to panic.

'It's normal when someone is gaining consciousness. Don't worry. Just give her time.'

Her doctor arrived quickly and began to assess her. Minutes later he turned to Joel with a jubilant look on his face. 'Well, Joel, I think she's going to pull through. She's a fortunate young lady, that's all I can say. Just keep talking to her calmly and reassure her as you've been doing. I'll be back in an hour.'

Both the nurse and doctor left the room. Joel broke down crying with relief. He tried hard to suppress the heavy sobs then blew his nose and sat down in the chair next to Hope's bed thanking God. His maker had come through for him again.

As he prayed, he heard Hope utter the word Dad, then she said Misty's name. At that sound, Joel knew she would soon be home.

Chapter Thirteen

Joel collected Myra from the airport, and they stayed near the hospital for the next three weeks visiting Hope each day. They had a lot of catching up to do and this was a good time to do it. Especially with so much time to fill in outside visiting times. Cole had faithfully dropped off Joel's Ute and gone back to the ranch with his colleague.

He pulled up outside Elma's gate. Myra climbed into the passenger seat. Before Joel drove off, she touched his hand. 'Elma says you can sleep in her sunporch to save you money. As long as you chip in for food and power. She's on a pension and is not well off.'

'Are you sure? That's kind of her.'

'Well, staying in the motel for nearly a month will cost you a fortune.'

'You're right about that. I've been there a week already and they know how to charge. It was the only motel next to the hospital. I'll get my belongings this evening and come over. Let's get back up to the Neurology ward. Her doctor wants to talk to us today.'

Hope had been out of her coma for over a week, but she was muddled and suffered from amnesia. Her doctor directed Joel and Myra into his consulting room.

'There have been some promising signs of recovery taking place but the road to healing can be wrought with twists and turns.' He pushed both hands into the deep pockets of his white consulting coat and sat back on his chair.

'Hope has been having bad flash-backs, yelling out as if she's arguing with someone.'

'What kind of things has she been saying?' Myra pulled nervously at her fingers and glanced at Joel.

'She keeps calling the name Misty. "You can't take Misty from me", and starts crying. Then she acts as though she's lost and looking for her father. She often cries, "No, Mum, you can't stop me!" Do you have any idea what it could all mean?'

Joel's eyes filled with tears and Myra's face showed a tormented expression.

'She appears troubled. Did she experience a traumatic emotional event prior to her fall?' he asked.

Myra tugged on Joel's arm. 'Please, can you tell him … I mean about Misty and you and I?'

Joel gave his nervous cough and sniffed loudly. He spoke with a husky voice and told David the long story. Before he finished talking, Myra had crossed her legs and folded her arms tight, appearing defensive.

'Look, Mrs Petersen. I understand how difficult it has been for you, but while you're visiting Hope, it's advisable not to enter into any dialogue with her until she is in complete recovery. This issue over her horse going missing like that has caused some deep-seated resentment. Her conflict with you is now manifesting itself again. We don't want her to regress at this point in her recovery.'

Myra stammered. 'Are you trying to say I shouldn't visit her? I came all this way to see her.'

'Oh, no, of course not. I just meant that we need to stop her from getting agitated in any way while her brain is on the mend. Just sit quietly with her and let her say something if she wants. She has to stay calm at all times until she is stabilised.'

Myra slumped further into her chair looking even more despondent. Joel leaned over and stroked her arm.

'We can handle this, don't worry, Myra. We'll work this out together.'

Doctor Dave, as Joel called him, left, and they both went to sit at Hope's bedside. She lay quite still then became vocal jabbering away incoherently. Occasionally she recognised Joel or Myra and spoke a few lucid words to them. Myra just sat smiling at her and holding her hand then. Joel placed his arm around Myra's shoulders and held her tight. It was a healing journey not only for Hope but also for Myra and Joel.

***

A month after her accident, Hope was discharged from hospital and could travel back home. She was getting along much better with her mother than ever before and Myra did not want to part with her daughter. She was reluctant to return to her own home and had not yet booked her flight. The day of Hope's discharge, Joel took Myra for lunch at a little café across from the hospital, to say farewell.

He reached across the table and took her hand. 'Look, Myra—Hope has been very happy at the ranch and has been working on forgiving you. We've been attending a little church there and my life has changed too.'

Myra gazed at him and her mouth dropped open.

He continued. 'Why don't you come back with her? You can sit next to her in the Ute. It's very comfortable at the back. Why don't you stay for a week and see how you like it? There's nothing for you in Bethlehem now that Frank's gone and Doug is independent and working at the hospital.'

'What do you mean? Come to live in Paradise?'

'Yes. We could all have a fresh start. You know I've always wanted to marry you, but I couldn't sit back and watch your life disintegrate with a drunken dependant any longer. I

116

saw your soul being eaten up inside and your life disappearing before my eyes.'

'I ... I don't know, Joel. I'll have to sell the house and what about poor Doug? Where will he live?'

'Why sell the house? I have a large home on the ranch with plenty of room. Doug can stay in the house and get someone in to share it with him if he needs company.'

'I don't think he'll miss my company. He's never home and I think he has a sweetheart at work or somewhere he is not telling me about.'

'Myra—why don't you marry me? Please, will you marry me? We've been friends for a long time, and I thought I would never see you again. God works in mysterious ways, and he has used this dreadful accident of Hope's to bring us back together, his way.'

'I suppose you're right. It sounds a sensible thing to do.' She fumbled nervously with her table napkin.

'But do you love me, Myra? Are you still in love with me just as you used to be? I don't want you to do it just because it's sensible!'

Myra could see he needed the reassurance of her love for him and leaned over, kissing him on the lips in public, regardless of the customers watching at the table opposite.

'Yes—yes, of course, I'll marry you. I can't believe this is happening to me. It's a dream come true for me too.' Her eyes began to mist over. The crevasses in her forehead disappeared.

He took her hand, stroking it as they sat and discussed how and when they would break the news to Hope.

'We'll have to wait until she's well out of the woods. We don't want to set her back now she's in a good recovery. I'll just tell her you're coming to stay with us to help take care of her.'

'Don't worry about a ring, Joel. That will make it obvious. There's something I need to say to you. Please listen to what I have to say.'

Joel could see from the way she was twisting her hands and pulling at her fingers that she was struggling to discuss a sensitive subject.

'I'm so sorry my behaviour sent you away. I know you couldn't bear to see Frank wrecking my life. But I had a reputation to keep, and we were running a business. For Hope's sake, I couldn't embarrass her by bringing it all out into the open. What would have become of Frank? He was hardly in a state to care for himself, and I had an obligation as a wife to stick by him.'

'And he had an obligation to take care of you and his family, which he did not. It's a two-way thing, Myra. A woman in that situation can't be a doormat. You have needs for safety and security too.' He stroked her fingers gently.

'And love. I need love too. Just like everyone else. That's why I've been so bitter and bad-tempered with everyone. Poor Hope. I took a great deal of my anger and resentment out on her. Look what damage has been done.'

'Well, I didn't have to leave like that. It's my fault too. We are both to blame for her troubled disposition. If you come back to the ranch for a week or so, we can slowly make her understand how much we love each other. You could go back home and explain things to Doug once Hope is more settled then return here to start a new life. We could get married soon rather than later. Of course, we'll have to do the decent thing. You'll have to sleep in the spare room as Hope has the guest room. It'll only be for a short time.'

When Joel finished speaking, Myra leaned over the table with her head in her hands and started massaging her temples.

'I hope I haven't put you on the spot, my dear. You don't have to make any hasty decisions. If you need more time to think about what I said, that's your prerogative.'

With that, she sat back up and looked at him, anxiously twisting her wedding ring.

'No, I don't need more time to think about it. I've done nothing but think about all this since I came down here. I'll come for a week or so then go home to get the rest of my things. Doug can stay in the house until he decides what he's going to do.'

'That's what I want to hear.'

Myra's forehead puckered again. 'Hold on—how are you going to support Hope and me with just a paddock of horses? Do you have a viable income down there?'

'Oh, of course—I haven't told you about the ranch yet have I? I'm genuinely well-off now. After I left Bethlehem and sold my house, I put some of the money into shares which I don't normally do. I spent a year working as a casual farm labourer and my shares skyrocketed. Within a year I was blessed with enough to buy my own ranch. The stud farm has been a lucrative business for me and shows great promise. That and my horse breaking. It's my passion now. We were going to run some more riding courses this year but we'll have to see how Hope gets on now.'

'You know I'm rather out of practice dealing with horses Joel, but I'm more open-minded about it now and would love to support you and Hope with this endeavour. I remember our Pony Club days when we first met.'

'I think that we could make a fine team.' His cheeks dimpled as he grinned.

Instead of her usual lacklustre smile, Joel witnessed Myra beaming radiantly for the first time in years.

He stood up abruptly, took her hand, and walked her jubilantly up to the hospital ward to collect Hope.

This was no longer just a pipedream, for now, he had the whole package, after waiting more than twenty years.

Chapter Fourteen

Hope was dressed and waiting for her parents, desperate to go home. The staff said they were sad to see her go seeing she'd been an inpatient for so long. Her eyes brightened when she saw Joel and Myra enter her room.

'Mum! I thought you were going back to Bethlehem. When is your flight?'

'Ah … it's … I cancelled it. Your father asked me to accompany you on the long drive home. He needs me to take care of you until you are back on your feet.'

Hope felt baffled. She was still having a few problems remembering certain things, but no longer had amnesia. She sat speechless for a few minutes, sensing a change in the air. Something was happening between her parents. Especially her mother.

'I didn't expect this. I suppose it's okay. Will I have to move out of my room now? We only have the spare room and that's full of junk.'

Joel flinched momentarily as if Hope's remark might offend her mother. 'That's all under control, honey. Your mum is not worried about that. Let's get out of here.'

As they shuffled in a single file past the Reception, the Charge Nurse called out, 'Hold on please, Mr Grey. I have Hope's discharge letter.'

The nurse looked over her shoulder and spoke to one of the receptionists. 'Where is Doctor Armstrong? He needs to sign the discharge letter.'

A voice called from inside the office. 'He's down the ward seeing another patient. I'll get him.'

The doctor trotted hastily towards Hope and her parents, eager to say goodbye and to give a quick summary of his report.

'Hope is incredibly fortunate to have no residual damage after experiencing coma for more than fourteen hours. I tell you, it's nothing short of a miracle.'

Joel looked Hope in the eye. 'It is a miracle, that's for sure. We're really blessed.'

'She may continue to have some post-concussion symptoms such as headaches, fatigue, flash-backs, and memory loss for a month or two, but I'm sure these will eventually subside. Try to avoid stressful situations, Hope and get plenty of rest.' Dave glared at Myra unnecessarily, as the issue between her and Hope had now been resolved.

'What about getting back on Misty? When can I ride again?' Hope interjected.

'Good gracious, Hope. It's a wonder you still want to get back in the saddle. You can get back on Misty in a month, I think. Best to give your brain a good rest first. Make sure you keep wearing your helmet when you're riding.' He looked her straight in the eye.

'I always wear my helmet. I was wearing it when Misty fell,' she spouted. 'Oh, wait on. I think I was wearing my Stetson during the muster. I wanted to be like the others. I mean ... I'm a cowgirl now.'

'No compromise, Hope.' Dave eyeballed her.

'Don't you worry, Doc. She won't be getting back on any horse without a helmet now.' Joel glared at her too.

Myra tucked the discharge letter securely into her handbag as they waved to the hospital staff.

Although Hope was strapped into her seatbelt in the backseat next to her mother, she managed to stretch out her torso and lay her head in her mother's lap. She slept like a baby for most of the long trip back to Paradise. Myra was in heaven—the bridge between her and her beloved daughter that had been broken was now mended.

'Here we are. Alexandra. We've done two-and-a-half hours driving, so time to stretch your legs and stop for food.'

Hope had already just woken up. She looked around, feeling a little disorientated.

'Toilet block over there. Why don't you both pop over while I order our meal?'

'Fish and chips—great. I didn't have that once in the hospital.' Hope came to life all of a sudden.

'It's not exactly health food but I suppose now and then won't matter.' Myra took her arm as they crossed the road to the amenities.

They ate their meal on a picnic table in the sun while it was still daylight. 'Dad ... what's happened to Misty? Tell me the truth. You said she only had a few bruises, but she must have really hurt herself when she went down too.'

'Honestly, Hope. She's another miracle. Apart from a bruised shoulder and ribs, she injured her left fetlock. Cole took care of it by cold hosing the leg and keeping her in the stable away from the other horses. But she can walk on it now. The vet said she can be ridden in a month.'

Hope breathed out loudly, a big sigh of relief.

Joel continued. 'She'll be in recovery along with you. I'll ask Cole to walk her around the arena each day as the vet wants her to have gentle exercises.'

For the next two-and-a-half hours of a five-hour journey, they stayed quiet, contemplative, as though grieving and repining over vain regrets. Or was it perhaps joyful expectations?

***

There was no stopping Cole Digby. He wouldn't take no for an answer and practically begged Joel to let him see Hope who was resting on a couch in the lounge.

'Seriously, Cole. Five minutes only and then you can come back tomorrow when she has settled in a bit more.' Joel was even more protective over his daughter than usual.

'Hold on—you haven't met Hope's mother, Myra.' Cole shook her hand and flashed Joel a look of surprise. 'It's okay, Cole, I'll explain everything tomorrow. Myra's going to be staying on for a week to care for Hope.'

Cole walked in with a bunch of wildflowers he'd picked in the field by his cottage. Hope tidied her dressing gown and pushed her hair into place. She took the flowers from him, sniffed them, and placed them on the coffee table. 'They're nice. Thanks, Cole.'

'Looks like I won't be doing anymore mustering.' Hope gave a half smile. 'I didn't know it could go so horribly wrong.'

'It was a freak accident. I've been mustering for years and nothing like this has ever happened.'

'Don't beat yourself up ... please don't. They tell me your horse spooked and reared then you hit your head on a branch. That could have been Dad or me.'

'That's true. The wild deer don't usually come over this side of the mountain.' Cole lowered his eyes as Hope studied his face.

'Honestly, I don't blame you for any of this. Please believe me!' She tossed her ponytail and passed him a chocolate from the box Myra had given her.

'Come and see me tomorrow. I'm going to get bored sitting around here, not able to ride for a month. Oh, by the way ... thanks so much for taking care of Misty.'

Myra popped her head through the door.

'We'll see you tomorrow Cole, perhaps. You can come for lunch if you like.' She walked him to the door, eager to give Hope a rest.

'Thanks. I'm getting a bit sick of my own tucker. I appreciate the offer.'

As Cole wandered off across the paddock, whistling and swinging his Stetson, Myra and Joel let Hope rest while they chatted away about what an impressive young man Cole appeared to be and how happy they were that the two had become such good friends.

Lunch took place in the same way that Hope had experienced when she stayed with Jessie on her folk's farm. Joel started with praying for the food and a prayer of thanks for all God's grace in the way he provides for his family.

***

A few months after Hope's arrival home from the hospital following her accident, Hope's parents married. It was a quiet affair because of the nature of their difficult past and they did not want the shame and pain regurgitated by inquisitive tongues. Their pastor came to their ranch and married them on their patio alongside Doug and Hope. Cole and the pastor's wife were witnesses. To Hope, her parents were a perfect match and now she had the family she always wanted. Doug bonded well with Joel, as they'd always been good friends. When they were younger, he often took Doug fishing. Hope and Doug also used to accompany him camping in the Kaimai Ranges.

Now it was goodbye to broken hearts, broken dreams, and broken promises for Hope.

***

Hope had been seeing the Neurologist for regular check-ups and the visits were coming to an end.

'Hope Grey, please go to Room Nine!' The voice of the receptionist echoed through the clinic as Joel and Myra followed their daughter down the long corridor to the specialist's room.

'Mr and Mrs Grey isn't it?' The young Neurologist sat them down across from Hope.

'It has been four months since your accident, Hope. This will be your last visit. I think I said I would discharge you this time if there hasn't been any change in your condition since your last follow-up.'

'I'm fine. I haven't had a headache for months and my memory is great. I'm back riding, but not show jumping. Just a bit of dressage.'

He nodded at Joel and Myra. 'How do you think she's doing? Is everything back to normal at home?'

Hope sat biting her lip stifling the urge to say that her parents recently got married and that put a smile on her face. Instead, Joel answered, 'Her moods have been quite stable, and as you can hear, her speech is back to normal.'

'And she's been helping Joel around the farm and is a blessing to have at home. We're very fortunate to have her with us.' Myra reached out for Hope's hand and squeezed it.

'I think I can say with assurance that Hope has made a full recovery. I believe you were both right when you told me at the last visit that your church was praying for a healing miracle. I think that's what's happened.'

In spite of Joel trying hard to suppress tears of joy and gratitude, a few droplets ran down the dark stubble on his cheeks. Myra looked up and spotted his reaction and tears filled her eyes too. She cleared her throat.

'Thank you so much for the good report. So ... I guess she won't have to come back for another follow-up?'

Instead of answering Myra directly, the specialist turned to Hope and smiled.

'No—I'm discharging Hope from my clinic today. Unless of course, there's a problem, you have no need to come back again, Hope.'

***

Joel took advantage of the driving time on their way back to Paradise to chat with Hope about Cole and she had nowhere to go to avoid the conversation.

'Your mother and I were wondering how things are going between you and Cole? It's just that you spend an awful lot of time together on the ranch and he seems very keen on you. Has it become serious? Has Cole let you know his intentions with you?'

Hope sat bolt upright all of a sudden in the back seat, watching her father's piercing eyes in the rear-view mirror and could see he was serious.

'I hope you don't think we're playing around. What are you worried about, Dad? We're just good friends. I'm not ready for a relationship and I've so much I want to do with my life.'

'Really—are you planning on leaving us and going to some far off land? I hope not.' He gave her a broad smile.

'No, not at all. I want to learn to train and break horses like you and become a partner in your business.'

'Which part is that? The breeding or the horse breaking and training? The breeding program involves most of the hard work.'

'All of it. I was starting to get right into it just before my accident.'

'The reason I'm asking you this is that I think that Cole is completely besotted with you— in fact, I'm sure he's been smitten since that day you arrived at the ranch looking for me.'

'Oh, really? I didn't realise he viewed me in that way. Poor Cole. It's not that I don't like him ... I just haven't thought of him as a boyfriend as he's been more like a brother to me. I have to admit I really missed him when I was in hospital and was happy to see him the day I came home.'

'I'm guessing he's picking up your indifference towards him. But don't worry—if you two are meant to be together, it will happen in time, as long as you don't close yourself off from him. Listen to your heart.'

Hope could see her father still watching her body language through his rear vision mirror. He continued.

'I think that you and Cole are very compatible. You have so much in common and you are both skilled riders with similar qualifications. I think we should pray about this, while I'm driving.'

'That's a great idea, Joel. You lead please.' Myra elbowed him. He prayed out loud.

Hope closed her eyes and was instantly reminded of Jessie and her prayers. As her father prayed, her mind drifted off to the times when she desperately grieved not having praying parents and that her parents were not together.

This is a miracle, just one after the other. God has been so faithful and has always come through for me.

***

Max the horse vet patted his hat into place, re-tied his bootlace, and loaded the Ford Falcon Ute with his bags.

'Misty won't need me back here for a while, Hope. You'll be riding her in the next agricultural show I guess. I'll be there with my twins, and I'll look out for you. And I agree— I think she'll make a fine broodmare but just wait until she is completely back to her usual self.'

He turned and shook Joel's hand. 'Just give me a call if you think that mare in the back paddock needs some help. Keep her in the stable overnight.'

Max drove off, swerving to miss a deep puddle on his way up the driveway. Joel looped his arm in Hope's and led her back inside the house.

'Mmm, that smells good.' Hope hovered over the fresh scones that Myra placed to cool on the cake rack and picked at one.

'No, not yet. They need to cool down. Oh— go on. Just one. They're a new recipe, dates with lemon, plenty of lemon. What do you think?'

Hope bit off a large chunk. 'Wow! They're awesome. First time I've had a scone with lemon. Nice work, Mum.'

'Hope—I need to talk to you before we have lunch. Something we need to get sorted.' Joel placed his Stetson on the arm of his chair.

'Sure, Dad. What's up?'

Joel walked into the living room and slumped into his armchair across from Hope. He crossed his legs and clasped his hands as if he was in a business meeting.

'Dad ... don't look so serious. You aren't at a Federated Farmers committee meeting.'

'Sorry, love. I suppose it is a sort of business meeting. I wasn't joking when you first came to live with me that I saw you as a business partner. I think you're old enough. But that's not what I want to discuss with you.'

'Okay, Dad. Get to the point.' She wrinkled her nose as her eyes smiled.

'I know you're keen to have a foal from Misty as she is the right age at seven years old. But you need to understand she'll be pregnant for nearly a year and it would be wise not to wean her foal for at least seven months. It's kinder not to work her during that time.'

Hope squirmed in her seat. 'Oh, I hadn't really thought about all that. I forgot she would be feeding.'

'Just think about it and you need to decide which stallion you want to sire her with. The white Arab stallion is really a grey that turned white, as he got older, like Misty. And Misty is half Arab, so you'll get a stronger Arab breed with that one. It may be interesting to use the white Kaimanawa stallion from the herd we mustered two years ago. He has strong Arab features, is a fast animal, and has already produced great show jumpers and dressage horses with local mares. Our clients say the yearlings are calm and easy to control and ideal for children too.'

Hope stood up and looked out the window where several Kaimanawa stallions grazed. A tall, coal black, noble beast, prominent against the alpine backdrop of snow-capped mountains, stood near a finer built male, a white beauty which caught her eye.

This Anglo-Arab's tail protruded like a flag in the air. His thick mane stood on end in the wind as he raced far ahead of the others horses galloping back and forth. His almost translucent white coat glistened in the last of the late afternoon sun rays. To Hope, he appeared not unlike Misty, apart from the freckles on her mare's face. He raced down the hill towards the fence next to the homestead as Hope's eyes stayed fixated on him. He stood still all of a sudden, staring directly at the lounge window as though trying to convey to Hope a message. Could it be a clue as to what her decision should be?

'I think I know the one that will suit Misty. I'll pray about it, Dad, and let you know. I need to think about all the implications of that decision as you described.'

'Come on, you two. Soups getting cold.'

'Sorry, Mum, coming!'

Chapter Fifteen

'Sorry to hear that, Cole. How long do you think you'll be gone?' Joel stood at the door and looked over his shoulder to see where Hope was.

'I'm not sure, but I'll sort something out with my family and let you know.'

Hope, who was busy at the kitchen bench, had overheard the conversation between Joel and Cole. She wandered out to the front porch where Cole was busy removing his boots. 'What's this, are you going somewhere, Cole?'

'Cole's going to have a bit of breakfast with us before he sets off back to Nelson.' Joel nodded at Cole. 'You tell her, please.'

'To Nelson! Why—what's happened?' Hope froze as if she suspected he was leaving for good.

'It's my brother, Larry. He's had an accident picking apples. The ladder went from under him and he has a badly broken leg. He works with Dad in the orchard in Nelson.'

'Yeah, that's right, I remember you saying you come from Nelson. Is there no one else to help him?'

'Apparently not. There's a shortage of orchard workers where I come from. Dad's lucky to have Larry, especially at his age. He has a Science Degree but doesn't know what to do with it yet.'

'Why don't we talk about it at breakfast? Food's getting cold.' Myra untied her apron and placed the scrambled eggs and bacon in the centre of the table.

'So ... how long will you be away? I suppose until he can walk again?' Hope couldn't let it go. She handed Cole the toast and butter.

'I suppose so. He'll have to stay in plaster for at least six weeks, then who knows how his leg will be after that. I'll get back as soon as possible.'

'Six weeks!' Hope burst forth.

'At least Joel has some casual ranch hands who can fill in while I'm gone.'

'So you won't be here for Christmas again. That's a pity.' Hope wilted. She propped the side of her face on her hand, elbow on the table.

While Cole was explaining the situation, she had mixed feelings about him going away. They aren't even in any kind of relationship. Why was she being so silly?

After breakfast, Joel waved Cole off at the front gate, picked up the mail from the letterbox and went indoors to phone his casual ranch hands. He needed to have cover for the next few months and rang around to arrange extra help.

Hope finished feeding the pregnant mares and mucking out their stables. She wondered how she was going to get on without Cole around to offload her cares on to or to get feedback about her random thoughts and ideas that often invaded her head. She'd always thought of him as a substitute for her brother, Doug.

Joel came off the phone and spotted Hope outside moping around with a disgruntled expression on her face.

'The way she's reacting to Cole's absence—perhaps there's more to this so-called brotherly love than meets the eye,' he uttered to Myra who was standing on the porch. They wandered back inside. Joel went to the wall cabinet and picked up a portrait of Hope hugging Misty.

'Leave her be. She's at that age when she doesn't know what she wants. But I've noticed she's grown out of the horsey girl tomboy stage.'

Myra drew alongside him to look closer at the photo. 'Yeah, I guess you're right.' She said softly.

'She's always been crazy about horses and boys never entered her head. In fact, she once told me she found them boring.' Joel's gaze lingered on the image as if he was reminiscing on days past when he taught Hope how to ride.

'But she's still discovering who she is and it may take a while before she has any kind of love interest. Anyway—we don't need any more dramas at present, do we?' Myra elbowed him then lovingly put her arm around his waist as they shared a special moment.

***

'Well, Misty— Dad is putting you out with your mates, tomorrow. You're now all healed and ready to run with the other horses. What do you think about having a tiny foal to look after ... your own foal? You think about it and let me know. I want to do what's right by you.' Misty nudged her chest, as though she understood then munched away on the carrot she took from Hope's upturned palm.

She spent the rest of the day exercising some of the young horses with her father. It was a tiring day, and she still hadn't regained all her usual stamina.

'I'm packing up now, Dad and going to have a hot bath.'

'Good idea—I told you about not pushing yourself. Just let your body dictate how much you do. I can manage okay with the boys I've got lined up.'

As Hope walked through the living room, she noticed the newspaper sitting on the coffee table.

She called out to her mother who'd just come inside from feeding the hens.

'Is that this week's local paper? I wonder if Dad has seen this article.' The image of the horse on the front page had jumped out at her.

'Yes, it is. Your father brought it back from the mailbox after he waved Cole off. He hasn't read it yet.'

Hope eagerly sat down to read the article on the front page of the local newspaper.

'Hey, Mum! Come and look at this. It's just what Dad's been waiting for. He's put a lot of work into it.'

'What's that, dear?' Myra looked around for her glasses. 'Wait, here they are—Let me see.'

Hope held the paper up for Myra as she peered over her shoulder. 'At last! God has found a way to stop your father from continuing with mustering those dangerous wild horses.' Myra breathed a sigh of relief as she stood with hands on hips in her apron.

'I'm going out to show him the article.'

Hope rushed out the door to look for Joel, beaming from ear to ear. He was by the stables hosing down the black gelding he'd been exercising.

'Dad—have you read the front page of the paper? There's an article about the Wild Horse Welfare Trust and the Bill has been passed.'

'Let's see!' He lifted his eyebrows, quickly scanning the article. 'We've finally succeeded. All the hard work our Queenstown branch did by campaigning and lobbying has paid off.' Joel turned around and embraced Hope tightly.

'So if we aren't going to bring the horses out of the hills to protect them, how will they stay safe from those monsters who want to make dog food out of them or kill them for sport?' Hope's forehead puckered as she waited for Joel's reaction to her comment.

'They'll be fined heavily or even locked up if they're caught. No one can venture into Dart Valley up onto the hills with a huge horse truck without going unnoticed. The offenders will find that the locals in the area won't let them get away with it either.'

'That's good, Dad. I hate to think the horses will be a sitting target.'

'Anyway, madam—after what happened to you, I'm not in any hurry to muster wild horses again. It's an act of God that he has taken it out of my hands.'

'Where are you going to get new stock from to keep our business going?'

'From our broodmares. It'll just take longer, that's all. I have two stallions hard at work out there.' He grinned then stopped short, aware he may have embarrassed his naïve daughter.

'Look, Hope—I've had some more ideas. You could offer riding lessons to novices. The closest riding school to Queenstown is more than three hours away.' He walked back into the tack shed with Hope in tow.

'When Cole comes back, he can continue to help with the breeding programme. Your mother is taking care of the foals, and you could manage the riding classes as a small side business.' He went along the row of bridles, checking each one for wear and tear. 'What do you think—are you interested?'

'I don't know ... I wanted to get Misty back into the shows and some hunts.'

'Ah, no. Can't you remember what the Neurologist said about that? He said no jumping.'

'No, I honestly can't remember. My memory still lets me down and I have some gaps.'

'Tell you what. You go and get that hot bath you were talking about, and I'll get cleaned up and come inside. I want to talk to your mother and after dinner, we can all discuss our plans for the business and try to put them into some kind of order. Oh, and don't use this blue bridle, it needs re-stitching. I'll send it away next week.' He hung the bridle up on a hook opposite.

'Sure, Dad, I'll have a good soak and then help Mum get the meal.'

Hope loved hot baths. She lay back in the blue cast-iron claw bath she'd filled with bubbles. Myra knocked twice on the door to make sure she wasn't falling asleep, which was a risk while she still had post-concussion syndrome.

She propped her feet up on the end of the bath and stretched her long legs out, fantasising about running a riding school and becoming a partner in her father's business. Poor Misty. She loves the shows, and she's too young to give up jumping. But if she goes into foal, she won't be able to do any show jumping or hunting for eighteen months at least. She lay there imagining what a foal from Misty would look like and what a wonderful mother she would be.

'Hope, can you peel the potatoes for me as you promised?' Her mother's voice at the door startled her back to reality. 'Sure, Mum. Getting out now, I'll be there in a minute.' Hearing Myra's voice was different now. Gone was the bitter, harsh admonishing bellow she grew up with when Myra was married to Frank Peterson. Hope had a whole new life now.

'Fresh mint sauce from your herb garden Mum.' Hope chopped up the mint and tossed it into the jug of vinegar Myra had prepared.

'Absolutely. Roast lamb's not the same without it.'

Joel walked in. He rested his palms on the bench next to Hope. 'I was thinking ... once Christmas is over we could plan your twenty-first birthday party. You could invite some of your Pony Club friends and Jessie could come. I can pay for her air tickets to repay her for letting you stay with her all that time.' Hope was aware he was trying to encourage her to socialise more. He had often expressed his concern that the accident had isolated her socially.

Myra quickly jumped in. 'That's a great idea, don't you think, Hope?'

'Sure, sounds okay. I suppose I could make some little cards with photos of me riding Misty and send them out to people I'd like to have at my party.'

'You'd better send one to Cole to make sure he'll return to the ranch by then. I need him here and that might prompt him to get back.' Joel glanced at Hope then quickly diverted his gaze. Her embarrassment was obvious as her neck flushed.

***

Summer was a welcome season for Hope in Paradise. The snow in the foothills had melted but remained on the peaks and the foals and pregnant mares could now be kept outside in the fields instead of inside the stables.

Hope loved to ride Misty up onto the plains and look at the spectacular view of the surrounding mountains. It was like heaven to her, a privileged life for which she gave thanks to God.

As she pulled Misty to a halt to soak up the sun as it began to rise high above the valley, the mare lowered her head to the ground and reached for the new grass. Hope basked in the morning sunbeams that warmed her almost bare shoulders. She suddenly caught a glimpse of Joel waving at her from down below by the front gate. He was gesticulating as if he wanted her to return to the homestead.

As she trotted up to the gate, Joel leaned his bronzed muscular arms over the high wooden gate and looked at her with a cheesy grin on his face. 'I've some good news for you. The lab test results for Misty are back.'

Hope didn't have to ask what the result was. She could read it in Joel's face.

'She's pregnant ... she is—isn't she?'

Joel nodded and patted Misty's nose, allowing her to lick the salty perspiration on his arm.

'Hallelujah! That's fantastic.' Hope wrapped her arms around Misty's neck.

'The vet said she's about five months pregnant. I suspected she was, although all the fresh grass she was eating just made her appear fat.'

'That's what I thought it was. It's hard to tell by looking at her.'

'Anyway—the vet says she's in excellent health. She'll need a scan now, so I'll have to arrange it soon.'

'Wow—things are going to be different around here for you and me now, Misty.' Hope looked the horse directly in the face, as though she understood.

'When Misty's foal arrives, I'll give you the responsibility of it and when it is old enough to be broken in, I'm going to get you to do that. I'll have you well trained up by then.'

'Really? Great! Do you hear that, Misty? You and I and your baby will be a team.' She nuzzled her head into Misty's mane.

'Later on, you'll be able to ride that young horse in the shows. We'll just let Misty have one foal so you can go back to riding her in the shows. No jumping, mind.'

As Joel wandered back towards the barn where he was organising hard feed for a few of the horses, Hope walked Misty slowly back to the paddock that she shared with a few other mares and geldings. Life was about to change for both horse and rider and Hope had come to understand that when one door closes another door always opens. In her case, it had always been for the good of herself and others.

Christmas was a solemn affair at Dart River Ranch. There was just Joel, Myra and Hope sharing a meal. Doug was on call at the hospital during the whole of Christmas but promised to be down for Hope's twenty-first.

On Boxing Day they sat out on the patio finishing off the last of the Christmas mince pies, watching the black and white stallions. They were entertained by them as they chased each other around the paddock bucking and rearing, playfully challenging each other.

There was no word from Cole, except that Joel received a short phone call from him to say he was going to be delayed. His brother's leg would now need surgery.

'What did he say, Dad? Did he say whether he'd be back in time for my party?'

'He didn't mention that. He said he couldn't make any plans until after his brother's operation and wished us all a happy Christmas.'

Joel looked at the despondent look on Hope's face and tried to humour her. 'Have you thought about the proposition I gave you? I think it's right up your alley.'

'Yes, I have and I suppose it'll give me something else to do if I can't be jumping and hunting with Misty. It's something I can offer to the community.'

'That's the spirit. Community service is a great thing. Once you start doing it you'll feel a deep sense of satisfaction and reap the rewards.'

'Okay, Dad. But I'm also interested in some income from it as I need to earn a living too.'

'It'll be your own business venture, and we can advertise it in the local paper. The rest of the time you can spend with Misty exercising her and when she has her foal, you'll be busy with that.'

Joel went out to the kitchen to put the kettle on again. 'Tea anyone? All this talking has made me thirsty.'

'Thanks, love,' said Myra. 'You can make me one too. Can you grab the biscuits in the tin up on the fridge?'

That night, Hope's head was full of the intrusion of busy thoughts—recollections of the day's events and deep conversations. The soak in the hot bath did not calm her mind as she tried hard to get off to sleep. She was thinking how much she had to be thankful for— such loving redeemed parents and a wonderful life the Lord has given her. Especially healing her after that horrific accident. Then why am I feeling so disturbed? She asks herself.

She tossed and turned most of that night until she heard the rooster crowing. The bright morning sunrays dazzled her as they forced their way through the gaps in her Venetian blinds. She decided to sleep in and try to put the intrusive thoughts out of her mind. It was as if there was still something missing from her life, and she couldn't quite put her finger on it. She knew that God should suffice to fill the God-shaped hole in her soul. So why is this happening? She prayed that God would give her the directed she needed.

After that, she yielded, and a peaceful sleep quickly consumed her.

***

Hope's riding courses in Glenorchy district were popular. Most riders who made bookings were mainly university students who came home to Queenstown in the holidays or local children.

Hope was an astute businesswoman and Joel called her a "real natural".

Myra had always been adept at running the market garden business that she and Frank had owned in Bethlehem until Frank's death. Now she was able to help both Joel and Hope, with book-keeping and running the office.

Hope wondered what Cole would be doing. His ongoing delayed return to Dart River Ranch concerned her. He'd phoned Joel a few times to explain that his brother needed a longer recovery period since his leg had been operated on twice. He'd begged Joel to keep his job open and promised he'd be back. Joel was reluctant to lose him, as he was the best ranch hand and horseman that he'd had working for him. Or is there another reason why Joel wants to hold on to him?

After a busy day running a beginner's class for juniors which was often a challenge for her, Hope stood hanging up some bridles and halters that some of the children had lazily tossed onto a hay bale instead of placing them on the rack where they'd been instructed to hang them.

'Here you are. I've been looking all over for you. This place is so big we almost need walkie-talkies, don't you think?'

'Oh—hi Dad. You gave me a fright creeping up on me like that.'

'Sorry, I didn't mean to. I think you'd better come over to the stables. It's Misty … I think she's about to foal. I've already rung the vet.'

Hope abruptly dropped the bridle she'd held in her hand and raced towards the stables. This was the one day she'd been waiting for all year. A special day for her and Misty.

As she entered the stall, her horse gave a soft whinny. Hope quietly approached her and gently stroked her nose. 'It's okay, girl. I'm here now and I'll take care of you. Everything's going to be alright.' Misty rubbed her head on her shoulder and whinnied again.

The vet arrived and declared her fit and well. He suspected it would be a straightforward birth. He spent many hours with Misty while Myra and Hope ran back and forth with cups of coffee and food to keep his energy up.

By early evening, Hope felt exhausted and went for a walk outside under the stars. It was a clear night in early autumn. So quiet one could almost hear a pin drop. As she looked up into the dark abyss at the sparkling diamonds in the sky, she prayed.

'Please God ... grant Misty and her foal a safe and healthy delivery and guide the hands of the vet so he can do everything necessary for a good outcome.'

As she turned to wander back to the stall, Joel poked his head around the corner of the shed.

'You'd better come or you'll miss out on a very special moment.'

Hope took off back to the stall and as she walked in, she saw Misty lying on the ground with two legs protruding from under her tale then witnessed the miracle of her pushing out a black, lanky legged, bedraggled filly which brought tears to Hope's eyes.

'She's black ... I thought ...Dad?'

Joel leaned over and talked quietly in her ear. 'Remember what I told you about foals from greys or whites?'

'Oh yes ... they turn white when they get older. Sorry—my bad memory. They're born black or chestnut you said.' Hope continued to stroke Misty's head while the vet continued to help the animal.

While the vet was dealing with the afterbirth, Hope stayed kneeling next to Misty and kissed her on the forehead. 'You did it, girl. You're going to be a great mother. I just know it.'

Joel was quietly standing behind her. 'What are you going to call her?'

'Um ... I haven't even thought about a name. Let me think.' She looked the filly up and down, curling her fringe around her finger.

'I know—just the right name for her. I'm going to call her Marvella. That means a miracle.'

Hope spent hours that evening with Misty and the filly, reluctant to leave them and go inside. She heard footsteps across the courtyard. It was Joel.

'Are you still in there, Hope? Your mother's been calling you to come in for your dinner. Come on—don't worry about them. The vet said they're both in perfect health and they'll be waiting for you in the morning.'

'I'm going to take myself off for a long hot bath. I'm exhausted after all the excitement of Misty's new foal.'

Joel walked back to the house with her. He put his arm around her and pulled her close. 'You mean your little Marvella. Your little miracle. Hmm ... Marvella ... Marvella. I suppose I'll get used to calling her that someday.' He cajoled.

Chapter Sixteen

Within the two weeks before her twenty-first birthday party, Hope received replies to most of the invitations she'd sent out. But not a word from Cole.

'That's strange, Mum. I thought he would have been one of the first to reply,' she huffed.

Her mother put down the bucket of hard feed cubes she'd been feeding the weaning foals in the stables.

'He'll be hard at work helping his father pick all those apples and apricots he told us about. If he can't come, I'm sure he'll let you know. Am I guessing right that you're a bit smitten with Cole? I thought you'd said he was more like a brother to you.'

'No, Mum, I'm not smitten as you put it. I just need to know if he's coming so we can plan our catering. I expect everyone to at least respond to my invitation.'

Her mother smiled and quickly backed off.

***

The next day Hope got Misty ready to exercise her in the arena. She buckled up the girth and started checking her stirrups when Joel walked up behind her.

'You're up early this morning ... where are you headed now?'

'I thought I should give Misty a bit of exercise.'

'I've something for you to do but you'll have to leave her foal in the stall. Misty can have gentle exercise at this stage, so if you wouldn't mind helping our ranch hand, Mack. He's about to shift the geldings into the back paddock to make room for the mares. They need a good grass feed and the geldings have had a fair go. They could do with slimming down somewhat.'

'Sure, that's okay. Where's his mate, Sam who always works with him?'

'He's off sick, I'm afraid and you might need to help us out until he gets back to work. Your advanced riding courses don't start for another month. Have you got many takers for the classes?'

'Yes, heaps. Thirty people have replied to the adverts already, but I'll have to take small groups of about eight at a time.'

'That's great! That's something to look forward to, your own business.'

Hope blossomed when her father encouraged her like that. He'd never lost his kind nature which she loved most about him.

She mounted Misty who stood perfectly still while she adjusted the stirrup straps and then headed over to the stockyards.

Mack was bent over cleaning dried mud out of his chestnut's hooves. As he looked up at Hope, his horse flicked its tail in his eyes. 'Ouch!' He rubbed his reddened eye with the back of his hand.

'You okay?' Hope asked.

'Yep ... will be in a second. I should watch that as it's not the first time.'

'Dad said I'm to help you shift the geldings. I can come back if you're not ready.'

'No—wait. I've finished now. Let's go.'

They utilised the time to catch up as Hope hadn't seen Mack since he had returned from a shearing contract in Canterbury.

They walked the horses slowly in the heat of the summer's day until Hope beckoned him to stand under the shade of a tall gumtree while she took out her water flask.

'Want a mouthful?' She handed him the flask. He raised his hand. 'No, thanks. I've got a bottle in my saddle-bag. By the way—I haven't seen Cole for a while. Any idea where he is?'

'Oh, he's gone back home to his folks. His brother broke a leg working in the orchard and now Cole has to fill in to help his father.' Hope tried not to show any emotion.

'Is that right? That's a pity. Except, I don't think that pretty, neighbourly girl minds him being back there. He'll be entertained for a while. Who knows, she might talk him into staying this time.'

Hope felt a large rock drop to her stomach.

'Sorry, I don't know what you're talking about. What girl?'

'His neighbour, Sophie who he always goes on about. They were school friends apparently, and she never leaves him alone when he goes back home. It was quite amusing to hear him talk about her.'

Hope didn't find it amusing. She felt irritated by this conversation.

Well—he's a dark horse. Why did he never mention any of this to me? Maybe that's why I haven't had a reply to my invitation yet.

'How old is this girl, Sophie?' Hope said in a disgruntled tone, feeling her neck burn.

'I'm not sure. Cole showed me a photo of her once. Quite a looker she is. Wait—I remember. He went to her twenty-first birthday a couple of years ago. She must be about the same age as Cole. Why the sudden interest in her?' He pulled his horse up as it tugged hard against the bit to grab another mouthful of the rich green grass.

Hope felt a compulsion to interrogate Mack more. But instead, she overcame the temptation and moved Misty on.

'Come on! We'd better get going or Dad'll be out looking for us. By the way … would you like to come to my twenty-first birthday next week? It's on Saturday.' She quickly tried to disguise her disappointment in Cole by inviting Mack, in whom she had no interest at all, to attend her party.

'Sure, sounds like fun. I hope I've got time to shop for a present for you. There's nothing around here so I'll have to get into Queenstown on the weekend sometime.'

'Don't worry, Mack, just bring yourself. Come on, let's get those horses in.' Hope knew it was a knee-jerk reaction she had from hearing Mack's sharing of information about Cole and his neighbourly friend. Is there another side to Cole that she doesn't know about? There has to be a way of finding out. She brooded over this for the rest of the ride.

***

'It's good your party will be over and done with by the time the new riding course starts. We don't want you getting fatigued again like you were after your head injury.' Myra handed Hope the decorations for the grand looking cake she had just finished icing.

'I suppose you're right. It's all been a bit much lately with the new business and trying to get the ranch ready for so many guests. All my Pony Club friends are turning up and Jessie will be arriving tomorrow. She said she'll give me a hand with the coloured fairy lights.'

'Let your father do the fairy lights. We don't want you climbing ladders and risking another fall and Jessie is too short to reach the top of the trees. Just let him do it.' Myra's jaw jutted forward with determination.

Hope's light-hearted mood changed as her mother became overly protective and she tried hard not to snap at her.

'Really, Mum! I'm an adult and I need to live a normal life.'

Hope almost gave in as she saw her mother shrink back as if she accepted her powerlessness.

The nights leading up to her party, sleep did not come easy. Not because of the excitement of her forthcoming twenty-first birthday. But more so because of the intrusive thoughts about her friend, Cole and his friend, Sophie.

Why hadn't he mentioned her name? Hope thought she and Cole had been getting on well and now this.

On nights like these, she jumped out of bed and made herself hot milk with a dollop of honey. That seemed to do the trick.

***

The day before the party, Hope went to the tack shed to check that all the riding gear was in place. She'd planned to take some of her friends riding along the Dart River on her birthday. She took the opportunity this time to rub down the saddles with a leather dressing.

'Where's your elbow grease? You'll have to work a bit harder than that to get a shine up!' Joel stood in the doorway of the shed with a smirk on his face.

'We've had a phone call from Cole. He says he'll be at your party tomorrow but can only stay the weekend. He has to get back to the orchard again as his brother has gone back into plaster after his surgery.'

'Well—it's good he can come but not so good for the ranch that he can't stay, is it, Dad?'

'He said we should rent his cottage out temporarily until he gets back. Mack was looking for another place to live so I'll tell him he can rent the cottage until Cole returns.' Joel lifted the well-oiled saddle back up onto its shelf. He saw the perplexed look on Hope's face.

***

Hope awoke to the sound of the rooster earlier than usual. It annoyed her as she normally slept right through the racket it made at six each morning. She wanted to feel refreshed for her party.

'Jolly rooster! You would have to perch right outside my bedroom. Today of all days.' She opened her window and silently scowled at the rooster, resisting the urge to scream at him.

'Is that you, Hope? You're up early—I thought you said you were going to sleep in this morning to get plenty of rest before the party.'

Myra stood in the doorway holding eggs in the palm of her hand. 'Eggs with your bacon? I want you to have a good breakfast.'

'It was that old rooster. He was so loud this morning. Anyway—bacon and eggs sound great. I'll be there in a minute.' Poor Mother. She just can't come to grips that Hope's a young woman.

Myra kept her talking at the meal table for a reason. Unbeknown to Hope, Joel had been busy in the barn putting up the coloured lights and Mack had arrived with a pile of wooden seats on the back of his Ute.

'Hi, Mack! Thanks mate. Just set them all around the edge of the barn. I can't remember how many she said were coming now, but there are plenty of hay bales for people to sit on. Some guests will stay in the house if they don't want to dance.'

When they'd finished eating, Myra tried to distract Hope from the activities out in the barn.

'Why don't you go and get dressed and then you can help prepare the last of the food. If you don't mind putting all the

149

cutlery and plates out on the trestle tables on the patio. I'll give you a long tablecloth to cover it first.'

'Okay, will do. Jessie's arriving on the two o'clock flight so I'll have to go to the airport at around one o'clock. She might give us a hand with the food when she arrives.'

When Hope was dressed, she wandered out to the patio and set the table up with a white starched cloth. She carefully placed miniature red roses into delicate glasses. She placed a pile of plates in one corner of the table and the cutlery next to it and wandered over to the fence at the back of the garden. Misty stood there hanging her head over the fence. She threw her head back and whinnied softly.

'Oh, you sweetie. You know it's my birthday, don't you? Wait, a minute.'

She quickly went back inside the house to the kitchen. 'Can I have a carrot? Misty has come to wish me a happy birthday. Honest, Mum. She put her head over the fence just now and whinnied at me.'

Hope took the carrot and almost skipped back outside like a child. Misty guzzled the carrot. She licked her hand and gently nudged her chest.

'Thanks, Misty. You're the first one today to wish me a happy birthday apart from Mum and Dad.' Aware that her behaviour was very childlike around her animals, she didn't care. It was always a time when she felt like a free spirit, loved and accepted.

***

Jessie couldn't stop talking during the whole trip back from the airport to the ranch. She had noticed that Hope had changed considerably, especially since her accident. She had always been exuberant, full of gusto. Now she was quieter, contemplative, and reserved.

'Well, come on—out with it. Whom are you dating down here? What happened to that spunky rancher who helped you when you had your accident? Remember you wrote to me about him.'

Hope took the deceptive bends in the road cautiously. She had found it hard to focus since her accident. It was the first time she had driven on the windy road to Paradise since long before her injury. She waited until she was on a straight stretch of the road and resumed the conversation.

'He's just a working colleague and friend and he hasn't been here for the last few months. His brother's had an accident, and he's had to help run his father's orchard.'

'Oh, dear. So he won't be at your party today? That's a pity. I was so looking forward to checking him out for you.'

Hope squirmed and wanted to tell her to be quiet but restrained herself and quickly changed the subject.

'What about you? Any love liaisons on the horizon?'

Jessie bit her lip and hesitated. 'Good heavens, no. I don't have time to waste on boys at university. I'm in the middle of my Masters now.' She tried to keep a straight face then burst out laughing.

'To tell you the truth, there is somebody. I've had a few dates, but we are taking it really slowly.'

They arrived back in time to see Joel and Mack finishing up in the barn.

'You've plenty of time to tell me all about your Romeo while we help Mum to finish off the rest of the food preparation. By the way, I forgot to tell you I've changed my name to Grey, my father's name. It's all legal now.'

'I remember in your last letter you were going to sort that out. It's finally come together. God knows you've waited long enough.'

Hope parked the car to the side of the barn as Joel walked over to welcome Jessie.

'It's been a long time, Jessie. You've certainly shot up tall like your father. I have a surprise for Hope. Hop out the front and come and take a look.' Hope grinned at Jessie. 'Wonder what he's up to.'

Joel picked up Jessie's backpack and put it near the front steps of the house then directed them back to the old barn. He opened the large iron door and switched on the fancy lights.

'What do you think, Hope? Your very own barn dance all ready to go.' He turned on the stereo and played a CD with her favourite tunes while Mack broke into a full tooth-baring smile.

'That's amazing! Oh, thanks so much, Dad. You're a darling.' She quickly dried her tears of joy with her sleeve.

'I think it's about time we had a good old shindig around here. As long as all the local cowboys don't wear you out dancing. Life has become far too serious.'

Joel winked at her and she could see he was doing his best to cheer her up after her long, restricted recovery from her head injury. He placed an arm around her neck and gently pulled her back in the direction of the house. 'Your mother is waving at the window—I think she wants a hand with something. Here, Jessie. I'll take your luggage into the guest room.'

'Okay—thank you.' Jessie caught him up.

Mack quickly spoke up, 'We'll see you at the barn dance then, girls,' and walked away chuckling to himself.

At four o'clock, the first few guests had arrived. Joel was outside busy directing them to the car spaces. Some had even walked a good distance and Sam the casual ranch hand had made a few trips in his Ute to collect some of the local young people.

Meanwhile, Hope and Jessie were inside the house fussing over their last-minute face make-up and dress inspections.

'Come on, Hope. Your guests have arrived, and you need to be out there to receive them.' Her mother untied her apron strings revealing a trendy black and white polka dot flared dress that contrasted strikingly against her thick auburn hair. She was also in celebration mode.

Hope and Jessie came away from the dresser mirror and bustled awkwardly in their high-heeled shoes to the front door.

Who was the first to arrive but Cole. Hope felt like shrinking, struggling with not knowing whether to feel annoyed or relieved to see him. As she walked onto the front porch, he stopped short, as if mesmerised by seeing this tomboy tough girl in a dress and stockings.

'Well—well! You're a sight for sore eyes.' He winked at her and gave her an alluring smile.

Jessie stayed close behind Hope who sensed her friend was trying to avoid taking away her kudos.

Hope's guests admired her eye-catching elegant attire. Her dress, a light blue floral print flare, with sweetheart neck and pink cap sleeve caught everyone's attention. Her white lace court shoes each boasted a silk flower on the toe.

Hope's neck felt uncomfortably warm, and she wanted to hide it while Cole continued to stare at her face.

'Cole! How did you get here? I can't see your car.'

'It's over there by the barn. I've changed it. Dad bought himself a new one and gave me his Chevy pickup.' He pointed towards the truck.

'No one told me. I like the colour. We certainly wouldn't miss seeing you on the road.'

'Yeah. Looks a bit like a fire engine but it's in good nick so I'm happy.'

'It's good you could make it. Come on out to the patio. There's mum's super punch bowl with a fruit cocktail and there are tables under the trees out of the sun.'

Hope ushered the new arrivals including Cole out to the patio. She placed her gifts on a table her mother had set aside in the lounge. Cole followed her, trying to get her attention.

'I was hoping we could catch up later when you're not busy.' He had hold of her arm, whispering discreetly.

'Mmm … I suppose so. I'll be busy with the guests handing around the food and drinks. Perhaps I might have time later after dinner before the barn dance.' She cut him short and walked off, leaving him to mingle with the rest of the small group under the oak tree.

Feeling irked, she toyed with the idea of quizzing him about his neighbourly admirer later in the evening. But then again, she could appear fickle, or worse, a jealous fool if she said something. And they're not even dating. Up till now, they'd just been close friends. He has the right to live his own life.

She recalled the song "Fools Rush in" by Ricky Nelson.

Deep down, Hope knew she wasn't ready for any kind of serious relationship and the few young men she had become close to were far too intense, too serious for her. She just wanted to build a long friendship with a young man and see where it leads. Why is it that they just can't the affairs of the heart the way she does?

When she finished reprimanding herself for almost weakening, she joined Joel outside. He was still busy finding more parking places for the guests who were arriving one after the other.

'It's okay, birthday girl. You wait up on the porch and greet them at the door.' He waved her back.

Finally, the house and patio were full of babbling guests of varying ages, some of them adult couples, her parent's friends.

The best present Hope was given, was the sight of Doug walking through the door. She hadn't seen him in a very long time and almost felt estranged from him.

He kissed her on the cheek, his thick, wiry beard tickling her face. It was the first time she'd seen him with a beard.

'Ooh—now my face is itchy. That must be uncomfortable in this heat. I don't know how you can stand it.'

'This is a symbol of sophistication—I'll have you know. A distinguished gentleman I've been known as.' He loved playing mind games with Hope.

'You mean extinguished.' She elbowed him then led him down the hall to show him where he'd be sleeping.

'Jessie's in the guest room, sorry, so you'll have to be in the spare room amongst all Mum's knitting and crocheting baskets. The bed's all made up. How did you get here?'

'Mum organised one of your ranch hands to fetch me from the airport ... Mack, I think his name is. Very kind of him. Nice fella he is. Told me he is saving hard to buy his own land and start a sheep station. I'm thirsty, where are the beers?'

'Sorry, Doug. It's an alcohol-free party but we've got a large range of alcohol-free cider and wines, even non-alcoholic champagne from an apple orchid in Cromwell, the fruit-bowl of New Zealand.'

'That'll be an experience. I hope I can loosen up enough on that to get you up for a dance, Sis.'

'Mum tells me love is in the air in Bethlehem. Is it true? Who's the lucky woman?' She pulled on his sleeve.

'Mum doesn't waste any time, does she? Just a woman from work I take out now and then. Nothing serious as yet. You just keep the focus on your own love life. I want to hear all about it later.' He wrapped an arm around her waist and walked her back to the lounge. He stretched out in an armchair after he pushed the cat off first.

'Doug—I just want to tell you again how grateful I am that you sent me that money to get down here. In fact, I was able to buy my car, Sunflower, with that.' She bent over the chair and kissed him on the forehead.

'Stop fussing girl and bring me some of that great punch Mum made.'

She brought him a large glass of punch. 'Have some food before it disappears. There are some big hungry farmers around here.'

Meanwhile, Joel turned on the coloured lights that he'd artistically draped around the barn. Earlier in the day, he'd made sure Mack, and another ranch hand had shifted the horses to the far paddocks and Hope had also moved Misty.

He checked the microphone and spoke into it.

'Will Hope Grey please bring her guests to the old barn where the music is playing,' then fired up the music.

Hope walked into the kitchen from the patio with a pile of dirty dishes. She heard the announcement again and went back outside to let the guests know the dancing was about to start.

Doug first got his mother up for a waltz, then Hope who was relieved she'd learned to dance at university. While she was enjoying being twirled around by Doug who was a seasoned dancer, Mack had been trying to get her attention, obviously hoping for a dance.

'Isn't that Joel's ranch hand, Mack sitting over there? Perhaps he wants a dance too.'

'Well. He can ask me when we've finished.' Hope was having such a good time with her brother that she egged him on for the next dance, a foxtrot. By the time the music finished playing, the barn had filled with the rest of the guests, and Doug wandered off to talk to Joel.

Hope edged her way along the ornately decorated table with cold drinks, picking up each bottle of alcohol-free wine to read the label. She settled on a pink sparkling wine and as she lifted the glass to her lips, Cole touched her on the shoulder.

'Sorry—what did you say? I can't hear over the music,' Hope sounded terse, waiting for an apology from him for not trying to find her. Let's face it. He'd agreed to have a chat before the dancing started. He could have at least tried to find her. Typical.

'Let's go outside and sit on one of the benches out there under the solar lights.'

He touched her bare arm and peered at her. Hope followed him outside, wiping her forehead as if to wipe away the tension the conflict had triggered.

Chapter Seventeen

Cole was seated under the pink-blossomed cherry tree. Hope walked up to him and plopped herself on the seat beside him reluctantly. She left a calculated gap between them.

He cleared his throat a few times and waited until he had her attention. 'Hope—I don't know how to put this, especially on your birthday. But I feel that since I've been working on my Dad's orchard there's been more than a geographical distance between us.'

Hope tried to swallow a lump in her throat. 'What do you mean?'

'Please don't go all coy on me. You know what I mean. Something's happened between us ... I feel you've been giving me the cold shoulder since I arrived.'

'Really? I don't think you've been too concerned about our friendship while you've been away. You appear to have had other things on your mind.' She was struggling to say her piece in an agreeably and it was noticeable to Cole. *Don't mention Sophie's name ... he'll think you're an idiot.*

'Look—there's something I need you to know. Please hear me out.' He cleared his throat again and took a mouthful from the bottle of cider he'd propped up on the old wooden bench.

'You and I have been good mates and work together on the ranch really well. You said to me once that I am a replacement for Doug and you treat me like a brother.' He hesitated and drank the rest of the cider rapidly as though it was going to give him relief.

'When you had your accident, I remember reaching the ridge on my horse and hearing Joel yelling out to me. As I drew near, I thought you were dead seeing you lying down the bottom deathly still, white as a ghost. Then your father sent me off to get medical assistance and a blanket.'

'I suppose it was quite frightening for you and Dad. Thank you for going to get help. I don't think I ever really said that before.' She kept crossing and uncrossing her feet.

'That's not the point of me telling you this.' He placed his hand on her arm. She flinched then sat rigid, feeling light-headed. She was hyperventilating and knew to slow her breathing down when that occurred.

'Something happened to me that day. I mean—it dawned on me that I couldn't bear the thought of you not waking up and never seeing you again. There hasn't been a day since I've been on my father's orchard that I haven't stopped thinking of you.'

Hope sat bolt upright, her eyes widened as she turned to him with raised eyebrows. She wanted to trust what she was hearing but needed to check out his story and couldn't restrain herself any longer. He heart pounded in her throat. She couldn't hold off another minute.

'I heard from one of the workers that you have someone else back home, in fact, a neighbour you've been seeing.' She felt her blood rush up her neck to her face and was sure her blood pressure had gone up. As soon as she'd spewed out the words, her glare stayed transfixed on Cole's face, determined to see how he reacted.

He laughed heartily. 'Oh, you mean Sophie my next-door neighbour. Her family and mine have been friends ever since we were babies. She's like a sister and I find her quite annoying, actually. I think she fantasises that our friendship is much more than it is. But honestly, Hope, she's just a neighbour, that's all. I have no interest in her or any other girls for that matter. Just you. I only have eyes for you.'

Hope felt so embarrassed she felt like running a mile.

Now she's done it. He really will give her a wide berth now after her insecure remark.

There was a certain awkwardness between them after Cole's brave act of pouring out his heart to Hope, which she didn't make light of. She just had no idea how to handle his confession.

'Hey, you two! Are you going to stay out there and miss the rest of the party?' Joel had noticed they'd been gone for some time.

'Hope—your mother wants some help with handing around some sausage rolls and you still need to cut your cake before the guests leave.'

'And I'd like the last dance if you wouldn't mind.' Cole ran his hand down the back of Hope's soft black hair and winked. She headed back to the house while he waited in the barn for her. Joel sat down next to Cole to catch up.

'I think Hope's pretty much tickled pink that you were able to make it to her twenty-first. She kept on asking if you'd rung. You'd better make sure you get her up for that last dance, mate.' Joel stood back up and walked off with a cheeky grin on his face.

***

That night, when everyone else was in bed, Jessie and Hope lay awake half the night chatting and catching up on all the news.

Jessie got up and sat on Hope's bed. 'So what happened when you two disappeared from the party? You were outside a long time so it must have been pretty serious. I ended up being cornered by your ranch hand, Mack for the rest of the evening ... though I didn't mind that at all.' Jessie giggled like a little girl.

'Oh—I needed to check a few things out with Cole. I kind of suspected he might have been involved with a girl back home in Nelson, but I was wrong. He seems to be besotted with me.'

'Wow! And what about you? Do you feel the same way?'

'I haven't fallen madly in love if that's what you mean. It's complicated. I really like Cole as a kind of brother or close friend, but I've never had a serious relationship with a man before. I ... um...don't know what it is to be in love.'

'Have you prayed about it? Perhaps you could ask your Dad to pray for you. He's a man of faith now, isn't he?'

'I guess I could ask him. Mum also has God in her life now. Dad led her to the Lord after my accident.'

'That's so amazing! I've been praying for you and your family for so long now. I must tell my folks. And it's a miracle that your mum and dad are together and you are one family now.'

'Yes—thanks to you, Jessie. I really appreciate all your prayers over the years. God's come through for me and my life has changed. It took a huge amount of forgiveness for each one of us. I didn't think I would ever forgive my mother, but God's changed my heart. He's transformed us all.'

'So, what are you going to do about Cole if he's head over heels about you and you feel differently about him?'

'No, I don't feel differently, I really like him a lot. I think about him often too. Is that love? I just never imagined us having a love relationship and to be honest, the reason is— I'm scared of trusting anyone. I mean ... look what happened with my parents who were so hurt and damaged for years after one bad decision. It makes me afraid to make any life-changing choice.'

'I doubt your parents even considered the consequences of their actions at the time. But this is a different situation for you. Anyway—where's God in all this? You told me that you've put your life in God's hands and trust him for the outcome. That was when you first arrived in Queenstown. So maybe you need to start trusting again.'

Hope didn't like being lectured by her friend and quickly changed the subject.

'What do you want to do tomorrow, Jessie? Cole's only here for two days and asked if I'd go for a ride with him along the river.'

'That's okay. I'm here for a week and your Mum said I can spend some time feeding the foals if I want. I'd love that. You and I have plenty of time to catch up. You go and enjoy your ride with Cole.'

***

The morning after the party, Myra and Joel had been hard at work clearing up much of the mess although the guests had been respectful and well-behaved. Cole joined them all for breakfast as they made their plans for the day.

'Hope—why don't you and Cole go for a long ride along Dart River and into the valley? Misty needs a good run and so does your horse, Pedro,' he said to Cole. 'We've been exercising him for you but only on the ranch.'

'And Jessie is going to help me with the foals in the stables, isn't that right Jessie?' Myra passed her another crumpet. 'I hope you don't mind?'

'Not at all. I can't wait to feed the weaning foals.' Jessie's face beamed.

'Are you okay with that arrangement, Cole?' Hope noticed he didn't say much at the table.

'Sure, sounds good to me. The sun is on our side too.' He sat looking like a cat that had found the cream.

They took off along the sandy banks of the glacial fed Dart River on horses that were trying to take the bit in their mouths. The fresh alpine air invigorated them as they trotted through the shallow waters. Then Hope encouraged Cole to do some river crossings and embrace the cool glacial waters.

'Don't go too far ahead, Hope. Stay near me. If you fall into the river I'll have to save you again.' He gave her a half smile.

Hope felt flattered with his gallantry but took umbrage at being held back when she was on Misty. But she held her tongue for fear of scaring him off.

'Look at that spectacular view of Mount Aspiring.' As she looked up, a falcon swooped down into the tussock in front of her and startled Misty. The horse baulked sideways. Hope gripped her saddle hard to keep herself erect.

'See what I mean!' Cole pushed his horse alongside her. 'Remember what that neurologist told you, that you won't survive another head injury.' He wiped beads of sweat from his forehead.

Hope couldn't hold back any longer.

'Cole! You really have to stop this. I'm a skilled rider and Misty is a good horse. She only fell up there on the ridge because it was steep, and her foot went into a rabbit hole. Please—let's just continue this ride and let me enjoy it.'

As they walked the horses the rest of the way along the braided, dry stone river beds, a myriad of colour appeared. There was an abundance of pink and purple lupins which were a welcoming sight after passing the harsh mountainous landscape covered with nothing but tussock grass. They gave the horses a long rein as they made their way along the long windy riverbank.

'Hey—wait! Look over there.' Cole pointed to a pair of waterfowls that were frightened by the horses.

'They are Blue Ducks or waterfowls, and their bills have turned pink because we startled them. I learned all about them when I did my Agriscience Degree.'

Hope pulled Misty to a halt, captured by the surrounding eye-catching panorama. 'Isn't this river water an unusual emerald blue? I've never seen that in the North Island.'

'That's because of the glacial rock and silt that has come down from the mountains called glacial flour.'

'You're a fountain of knowledge, Cole Digby.'

With that, he instantly sat taller in the saddle and placed his hand on his thigh, as if imitating Wyatt Earp with his buckskin Stetson and high leather boots.

Hope looked past him, mesmerised by the view of Mount Aspiring against the clear blue sky.

'Come on, let's do the river crossing now as the horses are chaffing at the bit. You go first and I'll follow behind.' Hope pointed towards the river.

Cole gathered his reins, gave his horse a gentle nudge with his heel. With trepidation, he headed into the water with Hope in pursuit into the river shallows. Both horses frolicked by lifting a front leg in the air then splashing it down hard on the water. After a short time of walking the horses slowly across the river, they stopped on the other side to rest.

Hope looked back over her shoulder then turned Misty around. 'Let's go up into the Red Beech forest up there. There's a lovely bridle path that'll take us back near the ranch.'

They arrived back at the homestead before dusk, climbed off their horses, and rubbed their steaming backs down with wet towels. They continued their catch-up chat while removing the horses' bridles and letting them out into their grazing paddock.

'What a pity you won't be here when I start my new riding course. You could have given me a hand.'

'Yes, I know what you mean.' He flashed her a warm smile. 'It's a jolly nuisance my having to stay on at the orchard. It's been far too long now.'

'Dad will need you in the breeding program soon. Did I tell you Misty's foal was sired by that gorgeous white Arab stallion? You're missing out on seeing her grow.'

'Don't you worry—I'll be leaving the orchard as soon as Larry is back on his feet.'

They walked indoors just in time for a piping hot lamb stew that Myra had just placed on the table.

'Why don't you all sit in the lounge with a cold glass of ginger beer while the stew cools a bit.'

Hope pulled out a few bottles of the ginger beer she and her mother had recently bottled.

'How did you go today, Jessie? Did you enjoy feeding the foals?' Hope glanced at Jessie.

'It was awesome and they're so cute, especially that strawberry-roan. But that didn't take your Mum and me long. She told me I could go for a ride around the ranch, but in the end, Mack took me on a guided tour. He showed me all the horses and gave me a little history about each one, how your father the horse whisperer had broken each one of them in.'

'Really? And all that time I was beating myself up for leaving you back at the ranch.'

'You shouldn't have ... actually—Mack is a really decent kind of guy, I quite like him.'

'Say no more, Jessie before I read between the lines.' Hope playfully tugged on Jessie's blond ponytail.

'I guess you might like to come and stay again during the next semester, eh?'

'Well, I'm not going to say no, in fact, Mack asked if I was going to come for another holiday.'

'Good old Mack. You're right, he's a gem, and I can't understand why he's still single. He's quite shy, I guess. But he's not my type.'

'Ah— but I think we already know what your type is.' She gave Hope a mischievous smile and excused herself to go and get washed up as dinner was served.

Chapter Eighteen

Hope fell flat when Cole went back to Nelson. She felt mixed up, not sure whether she was in love with him or just missing his companionship. How would she know if she was in love? She'd never been in a serious relationship before.

'What do you want to do today, Jessie? Dad suggested we go for a ride out to Diamond Lake. It's beautiful and remote and we may see the wild horses.'

'That would be amazing. Isn't that where you had your accident? It might upset you going back there.'

'No way. I love going to the lake and it doesn't worry me at all to see the wild horses. It was just a freak accident and could have happened anywhere.'

Jessie was always so considerate and attentive which is what Hope liked so much about her friend.

'I'll ask Mum if she'll put together a packed lunch for us. Bring your camera just in case the horses are down by the lake.'

As Joel came inside the house, he overheard Hope telling her mother where they were going. 'Be careful at the lake. Promise you won't go up onto the ridge. We don't want any more rescue helicopters carting either of you off now do we?'

'Of course, we won't, Dad. I'm hoping Jessie will get to see a wild horse down by the lake.'

'Well—make sure you get back before dark.'

'Please don't fuss, Dad. I'm twenty-one and independent. Honest, we'll be okay.'

Joel knew he needed to back off and like Myra, he too had trouble letting Hope grow up since her accident.

The school holidays were over and there were few people at the lake. The girls rode around the side of the lake where they had a good view of the bush and beech trees where the horses usually roamed. They dismounted and led the horses to the edge of the lake to drink then secured their reins to a large log which lay on the stony shore.

'Here—Jessie. Help me spread out this blanket on that grassy patch over there.' She dragged the blanket onto the grass and Jessie stretched out on it while Hope unpacked the picnic box from her saddle-bag. 'I'm famished. Let's tuck in.'

They ate their food and lay on the grass waiting for the sun to appear. It had hidden behind low clouds and they wanted to bask in its warmth.

'Tell me about your boyfriend you've been seeing at university.' Hope rolled onto her front prodding Jessie in the ribs.

'Oh—him. I don't know if he's really my boyfriend. We've just been going out together for a few months. It's kind of platonic I guess.'

'Jessie—quick! Get your camera. Look up there.'

Hope pointed in the direction of a small clump of beech trees. That's where a well-trodden pathway led through the bush and the wild horses were often seen. Just then, in full view, a majestic golden palomino stallion made its way down to the water's edge followed by what appeared to be a palomino mare with its foal. The mare was a little nervous, unlike the bold stallion which was undeterred by a few cars and tourists near the lakeside. Jessie took one photo after another.

'What a pity you and your Dad aren't able to bring down the herd. Do you think he'll have another go at it?'

'No, he can't do that, it's illegal now. Soon after my accident, a Bill was passed for the protection of feral horses and it's against the law to take them out of their natural environment.'

'I didn't know that. When I look at them over there, I can see how vulnerable they are. What about poachers and hunters?'

'Hunters aren't allowed in this area where the horses are breeding. They have designated areas now, as there are other animals that are protected too.'

They sat still, soaking up the awesome spectacle of the beautiful beasts, as Jessie thanked God for the privilege of seeing this little family—a stallion, mare and foal—a witness to her creator's wonderful handiwork.

The sun began to sink gracefully behind the Humboldt Mountains as the horses quietly disappeared into the beech forest.

'Come on, Jessie, we'd better get going back home as it'll be dark soon. You'll have to come here again during your next semester break.'

'I'll look forward to that. I'm going to miss this amazing place. No wonder they call it Paradise. It'll be sad to have to say goodbye to it all tomorrow.'

***

'Are you awake, Hope?' There was a gentle tap on her door as she lay in bed rubbing her eyes, disturbed by the bright sunlight streaming through the crack in her blinds.

'Mum—what's wrong?'

'Nothing's wrong, dear. It's your old employer Jock wanting to talk to you. Maybe he wants you to go back and work for him. Quick, he's waiting on the phone in the lounge.'

Hope scrambled out to the lounge in her pyjamas, half asleep. When she finished her conversation with Jock and hung up the phone, she looked for her mother who was out the front feeding the hens.

'Mum—He asked if we are doing anything tomorrow and would we like to go to Corriedale Hills Station for lunch. He wants to meet you and Dad, as his son Hamish is needing some training in breaking horses. He wants to discuss it with Dad as he heard that he's the expert around here.'

'Really? That sounds interesting. Go and ask your father if he's able to go up there tomorrow. He's in the barn sorting out feed for the horses.'

As she wandered over towards the barn, she remembered her long conversations with Charity, Jock's daughter and the kindness she and the family had shown her when she'd worked for them. The only family member who was an unknown quantity was Hamish their son whom she had not yet met.

'Can we go up there tomorrow, Dad ... please? I would love to see them again as I've only spoken to Charity once over the phone since I left. I think it would be great for you and me to help Hamish learn to break horses.'

'Oh, you do, do you? Who said you'll be involved?' He rubbed the stubble on his chin, hiding the smile on his lips with his hand.

'What ... why? You know I can break in a horse almost as well as you can now!'

'Hah! I thought I might get a reaction. I think you and I could well be a good team.' He couldn't hide the twinkle in his eyes nor could she hide the way her face lit up with elation when her father made her feel special.

***

'It's not far from here, Dad. Just over that ridge and we'll be there.'

Hope pointed in the direction of Corriedale Hills Station. She opened the car's window and appeared almost mesmerised as she gazed at the breath-taking views across the valley of rich fertile pastures covered with sheep that extended for miles. She took in a deep breath. 'Isn't it awesome? I just love looking at the view from here. See the lake down there.'

'The view's certainly beautiful.' Myra craned her neck then also rolled down her window.

'There it is! That's the station down there. Just go down that long driveway with the poplar trees.'

They arrived on time and Gilly opened the door with Jock in tow. They welcomed Hope with open arms, a degree of warmth far removed from one's usual employers.

'Lovely to meet you both finally'. They shook hands with Joel and Myra.

'Hope was such a blessing to us when she worked here— she must certainly be a light in your lives.' Gilly showed them to a seat in the lounge. She offered her guests fresh scones with home-made raspberry jam and asparagus rolls. A teapot with willow pattern stood on a trolley next to them with a jug of orange juice. 'Let me pour you tea.'

'Just milk for both of us thanks. What about you, Hope?' Joel nodded at Hope.

'Orange juice thanks. I'm feeling dehydrated.'

'Jock, where's Hamish? He said he'd be here to meet our guests.' Gilly looked out the window then shook her head. 'He's not the best timekeeper but I'm sure he'll be along soon.'

They all became engrossed in deep conversations, learning all about Hope's accident and their experiences with the Kaimanawa horses. Jock and Myra even disclosed the fact that they had been childhood sweethearts and had recently married. That didn't go down that well. Hope noticed that Jock and Gilly appeared awkward, glancing at each other sideways. But Hope knew them well and did not believe they would judge them.

There was a rattle at the back door, and the thud of leather boots being dropped on the floor. An unfamiliar face appeared in the doorway of the lounge.

'Sorry, Mum. I didn't realise what time it was.'

Hamish introduced himself to Joel and Myra and lifted his Stetson to Hope then placed it on a side table. Hope sat there open-mouthed, gaping at the tall, broad-shouldered young man with thick black hair that contrasted his dark blue eyes. She looked away, as he glanced back at her, obviously aware of her reaction.

He yanked up his new-looking blue denim jeans, tucking his black tee-shirt inside the waist and sat on the end of the couch next to his father.

Joel spoke first. 'Your father tells me you're ready to start breaking horses. Hope here is pretty good at this too. I'd like to involve her in your training if you're happy to start soon.'

Joel hadn't noticed the body language between Hamish and Hope. She felt her throat go dry and her voice sounded raspy as Hamish turned to address her.

'Oh, so you're also a horse whisperer?' Hamish threw her a glance that made her feel as though his intense blue eyes were piercing her soul.

She took a sip of juice. 'Ah, no. Dad's the horse whisperer and I'm just his accomplice.'

'Aw, Hope. Don't be so modest. I'd say that you probably don't need me around when you're breaking any horse in. You're a horse magnet. They go to you like bees to honey,' said Joel, flashing his daughter the warmest smile.

Hamish continued to fix his eyes on Hope while Joel paid tribute to his daughter.

'Come on—perhaps we can show you the horse if you'd like to check her out first.' Jock stood up and showed them out the back.

'Would you like me to show you my garden, Myra? I heard you're an avid gardener at the ranch.' Gilly smiled warmly at Myra and led her onto the deck and down a path that displayed a huge vegetable patch and an English country garden in full colour.

Hope followed the men out to the paddocks where the horses grazed. As they wandered towards the gate, Joel and Jock chatted away while Hamish kept looking back over his shoulder, while Hope lagged behind. He waited for her to catch up.

In a stockyard nearby, stood a remarkable looking Cremello mare pawing at the dusty ground as if bored or frustrated. As Hope approached the gate to look closer at her, the mare stopped scratching the ground with her hoof and glanced up at Hope. Hope was captivated by the animal's mysterious pale blue eyes and imagined how amazing this mare would be for breeding.

Her father interrupted her thoughts. 'What do you think? Gorgeous, isn't she? Three years old and never been ridden. Hamish is hoping, with your help, that he'll be able to saddle her.'

'Is that right, Hamish? I think that's possible and Hope's keen to help you with the basics.' Joel gave Hope a nod.

She felt her throat tighten with a strange kind of discomfort at Joel drawing Hamish's attention to her.

'I'll bet she takes to you like a duck to water.' Hamish flashed her a warm smile.

'No, it's you she needs to take to and bond with. I can just show you how to do it. What's her name?'

'I call her Champagne ... when can you start training her, Hope?'

She looked at her father, waiting for him to reply.

'Oh, Hope won't be able to help you train her until I have handled her first. You'll need me for the initial training of your horse to see how she's going to handle. Hope and I'll work together to start with. She can take over once I see how the horse behaves.'

Joel walked into the pen to see the horse's reaction. He walked around her a few times then left the pen again.

'She's quite calm for an unbroken youngster. Do you spend much time with her?' He looked over at Hamish.

'Yes, I do regularly. I bring her in here with a halter to give her hard feed. I just wasn't sure how to get her to take the bit. I tried to get the bridle on her but she spooked every time.'

'That's not the way to do it. I can see you need some instruction, my boy.' Joel winked at Jock and Hope could see that Hamish didn't take kindly to being called a boy in front of her.

'You've done really well Hamish by getting a halter on her and she's already bonded with you, I can see,' said Hope, coming to his rescue.

Hamish walked inside the pen to give Champagne some pellets from his pocket.

'Good girl.' He rubbed her neck as the horse licked his other hand.

'Well, folks, let's get back to the house and talk brass tacks. We'll have to discuss your schedule and put a plan together, I guess'. Jock removed his hat, scratched his head, and walked back to the house with Joel.

Hamish chose to stay back behind them and take the opportunity to talk with Hope.

'Would you like to come with me to take her back to her grazing paddock?' He stood still, studying Hope's face.

'Sure—I'd love to.'

'Dad! We'll be at the house shortly.' Hamish called out to his father.

When they were finally all together back in the lounge, Joel sat next to Hamish with a diary on his lap.

'How about if I come here for an hour each morning with Hope for a week? After that, Hope can come alone for the following week. I have a quiet time at the ranch coming up the next few months. There are no mares about to birth until later in the year. Hope's still busy with her own mare, Misty's new foal. She starts her new riding course in two weeks. Another little side business she has.'

'How will you manage your ranch if you are both up here so much?' Jock looked across at Joel.

'I'm expecting my best ranch hand, Cole to return soon. He's an asset to the ranch and can help me catch up with the work. I've got behind a bit since he's been away.' Joel had his head in his diary as he spoke.

Hope's cheeks burned at the mention of Cole returning. She looked at Gilly. 'Would I be able to have a glass of water, please? I must be dehydrated.'

'Of course Hope. It's warm out there today.' Gilly brought out a jug of water from the kitchen. Hope's face was still flushed.

'Well, that's settled then. We'll expect you both Monday at ten if all goes well.' Jock shook Joel's hand and patted Hope on the shoulder. Hamish gave Joel his hand then stood awkwardly facing Hope.

'Look forward to seeing ... um ... to having you come on board with us, Hope,' he uttered.

Gilly hugged Myra and Hope. 'It's a pity you didn't meet Charity this time both of you. Next time she's home I must get you all back for another visit.'

On her way out, Myra stood in the hallway glancing at a photo of Charity hanging on the wall. 'I think it's our turn. You must all come to us next time.'

As Joel drove the car down the tree-studded driveway onto the rough country road, Hope went quiet, in deep thought. It was as though she was struggling with some kind of inner conflict.

'Well, Hope, what do you think? Are you still keen on these arrangements with Hamish?' Joel furtively winked at his wife.

'I'll pay your wages, of course. This is all part of our business and as my business partner, you get half of our horse breaking contracts. Jock has offered me a handsome price to break in Champagne for Hamish who wants to use her for showing.'

'Now that you put it that way, I'm super keen!' She couldn't hide the fact that the monetary offer was not the key magnet for her being eager to spend the next few weeks visiting Corriedale Hills Station. Or was it something else that was the magnet?

***

As Hope started on her meal, her mother looked at her husband and gave him a nod.

'Hope—we had a phone call this evening you may like to know about.' Her father tried to cover his wry smile with his hand.

'Ah—was it Jessie? I was wondering when I would hear from her. Is she going to phone back?'

'No, well ... actually, it wasn't Jessie at all.'

'Who then ... Doug, I suppose? I haven't written to him in a while.'

Myra kept her gaze on Hope's face as her father spoke.

'Oh, Joel. Don't keep her hanging like that. Go on and tell her.' Myra frowned at him.

'It was Cole. I'd spoken to him on the phone last week to see if he was any closer to coming back to work and he said he would phone back once he knows.'

'Really.' Hope went into her coy mode.

'Well—is he?' Her eyes suddenly sprang open like whirlpools and her heart missed a beat.

'Yes, my dear. He's arriving at the end of the month and just in time. I was about to employ another qualified horseman to help me. To tell you the truth, it's been a long haul running the breeding program alone.'

'At last—the ranch will get back to normal. And when he's not with you, Dad, he might help me with my program too. Some of the riders in the next lot of classes want to learn how to break in a horse. I should be finished up on Corriedale Hills Station by then.'

'That's good to hear. Cole's had a good teacher—in me of course and has become an expert in horse breaking techniques. They couldn't get a better trainer apart from me ... and you.' Joel squeezed her neck affectionately.

'It's good news, Dad. I'm looking forward to seeing him back here again.'

Hope filled the bath to the brim with hot water and bubble bath. The foam almost overflowed onto the floor. She undressed then opened the bathroom window wide so that she could see the cobalt-blue carpet of bright stars. The full silver moon illuminated the sky above the house.

She climbed into the cast-iron claw bath carefully lowering herself down and sighed at the soothing effect of the silky smooth warm water that saturated her body. She stretched out long like a cat and lay her head back on the sill of the bath. As she stared at the dazzling constellation above, her eyes stayed transfixed on the moon as if her God was there, watching over her.

'What does my future hold, Lord? I'd love to have a glimpse of it,' she uttered. Then a song kept resounding in her mind and she started to sing, 'Que será, será. Whatever will be, will be. My future's not ours to see, que será, será.'

Chapter Nineteen

Hope helped her mother prepare breakfast with an eagerness in her spirit. Today is a special day. For the first time, she'll be coaching her new client, Hamish Weston to break in his horse. Joel will be at her side, but she'll be doing the teaching herself.

'You'd better get a move on, Hope. Finish your toast and I'll meet you out at the Ute. We said we would be there by ten.'

'Okay, Dad. I'll be out in a few minutes.'

She rushed her coffee and the remains of her toast with Myra's popular strawberry jam. She kissed her mother and rushed out the door licking her fingers.

Joel drove cautiously around the deceptive bends in the icy road that was lethal during the spring thaw.

'Have I told you lately how proud I am that you're now taking on private clients? You've become quite a businesswoman. You'll be able to take over this ranch one day when I'm an old man.'

'Aw, thanks, Dad. I hope this contract at Corriedale Hills Station will only take two weeks as you said. My new group of riding students starts after that. I'll have to be back by then.'

'You'll just have to make sure you do a great job of training Hamish so that you won't have to go back up there.' He winked at her playfully.

Hope wasn't sure how to answer that and kept quiet.

The Westons' were pleased to see them, especially Hamish who scurried out to greet them in the driveway.

'We're all ready. Champagne's in the stockyard waiting for you.' He stood beaming at Hope while her father chuckled quietly.

***

By the end of the week, Joel had taken Hamish through the basic handling techniques for an unbroken horse. Mainly he just initiated the main rudiments then Hope reinforced them.

'The first week of your lessons has gone quickly, Hamish. You've worked hard at it!' Joel shook Hamish's hand.

'Thanks to you both. I appreciate you coming and giving up precious time from the ranch.'

Joel turned back to Hope. 'I must say we're a good team, Hope, and I.'

'Thanks' Dad. I guess we'll see the results by the end of the two weeks.'

'Champagne has a quiet temperament for an unbroken mare. She's taken to the bit and bridle easily.' Joel patted the horse's nose gently.

Hamish turned to Joel. 'I reckon you showing me how to bond with her in the pen first off, made all the difference, Joel. I think that's why they call you a horse whisperer.'

Joel laughed. 'You two talk about your arrangements for next week. I'm going into the house to discuss some business with Jock before we leave. Alright, Hope?'

'Sure, Dad. See you out by the car shortly.'

Hope's face gleamed when her father disappeared around the corner.

'I remember your father saying that his services wouldn't be required during the second week when we

179

start saddling Champagne. Are you coming on your own then?'

'I guess so unless he changes his mind. That's if he thinks Champagne is ready to be saddled.'

'I'll look forward to that ... I mean to Champagne being saddled. Everything's gone better than I expected. And you are pretty good at handling a horse, I might add.' Hamish nodded at her, his unusually white teeth glinting under a broad smile.

'You've also worked Champagne well. I reckon you're a fast learner.'

'Thanks. I'll see you back here on Monday.'

Hamish walked tall, broad shoulders pulled back and head high as they walked back to the house. Hope liked the idea of a confident strong male walking alongside her. Particularly one as handsome as Hamish.

'Wait, Hope. I've something for you. I'll just run to the barn and get it.'

He rushed off while Hope saw Joel walking out to the Ute. She walked back towards the house as Hamish approached her with something in his hands.

'I want you to have this.' He handed her an exquisite hand-quilted saddle blanket with vibrant colours. 'My grandmother made it for me when I was given my first horse. I want you to have it.'

Hopes face turned the colour of the red geranium by the front door. She was lost for words. 'I don't know what to say ... it's gorgeous. But don't you think you should hold on to this. It's very special.'

'I've had it for ages and it's time for a change. It's a gift for being so patient with me. I know you've gone the extra mile to teach me.'

'It's a wonderful gift. I need a new one. Thank you!' She wanted to kiss him on the cheek but didn't want to give him the wrong idea. Soon Cole will be back at Dart River Ranch.

She's kept her heart for him all this time, even though he doesn't know it.

'I've got to go, Dad's waiting. See you next week then.' She waved at Hamish as he saw them off in their Ute.

As Joel drove out onto the main road, he couldn't hold back. 'He seems to be quite a decent sort of guy. I think he's a bit smitten with you, Hope. Or am I wrong?'

Hope chose to remain silent, trying to deal with the discomfort of her father raising a sensitive subject.

'What do you think, Dad? Have I done all right this week? Are you happy about me taking Hamish through the saddling and mounting techniques next time?'

'Happy? I'm over the moon with your progress. I probably didn't need to be there the whole week. You don't need me around anymore with your skills.'

'Great! I think I can manage on my own now. Look at this saddle blanket that Hamish gave me.'

Joel's eyes darted to the blanket and back on the road. 'I think it took a lot for him to give that away. I would guard my heart if I were you. Oh, by the way, Cole is due back anytime.' As he said this, he kept looking at her body language, but again she said nothing. She's heard that so many times before that he's coming back. What if he doesn't? She clammed up for the rest of the trip home.

***

As Hope drove up to Corriedale Hills Station the following Monday, her stomach churned with both excited expectation and anxiety.

How does she know that Hamish is to be trusted? She hardly knows him. Her thoughts cautioned her. *Please, God, give me the discernment I need. I'm attracted to Hamish, and he appears besotted with me, but I'm fond of my dear friend Cole as well. I need some kind of sign whether to get involved on a romantic level with Hamish.*

181

As she drove towards the house, Hamish was waiting to greet her with a disarming smile. She couldn't help but flash him a broad smile in return. She was impressed with his appearance. He was dressed in what appeared to be new tan suede pants and a blue and white check shirt. He tipped his Stetson towards her and walked with her to Champagne's pen.

'This is your big day, Hamish. I think Champagne is ready to be saddled but we need to do it in stages.' Hamish picked up his saddle and placed it across his shoulders.

'Today we just use a saddle blanket, so you won't be needing her saddle.'

'Oh, I see. I'll just put this back over the wooden perch then.'

Hope walked on while he placed the saddle back on the perch. She wandered up to the pen where Champagne stood impatiently to be let out and called her. At first, the mare just stood at a distance glaring at her, ears pricked and alert. She started pawing the dusty ground.

Hope took a carrot from her jacket pocket. 'Here you are. Come and see me.' Champagne gave a soft whinny and trotted towards her, stopping directly in front of her. She stretched her neck over the top rail of the fence and took the carrot from Hope.

Hope felt a hand on her shoulder and cringed slightly. Hamish took a step back. 'I can see she's taken a liking to you. I hope she'll be just as amicable when I jump on her back.'

'There won't be any jumping on her back, at least not for the time being. It's going to be a gradual, gentle process. You go in the pen with her, and I'll stand still while I give you instructions.'

'Ooh—that's what I like, a woman in control.'

Hope tried to hide her awkwardness.

'Sorry—just teasing. I didn't mean to embarrass you,' He chuckled.

'Let's get started.' Hamish started exercising the horse with the long reins. After a short time, the mare had made good contact, bonding with him.

'Now place your saddle blanket on her back quietly as you go and once she is accepting it, lean in on her shoulder for a few minutes until she trusts you.'

Within no time, Hamish was able to slide over her back, straddling himself crossways, draping his head over one side and his legs down the other. Within the next hour, he was able to sit on her back without her bucking.

'Shall we stop for lunch now? Don't you want a break,' he asked Hope.

'No! Sorry, we can't stop right now. You have to keep going while she has accepted you on her back. We can introduce the saddle now. I'll get it for you from the perch. Just stay with her and keep the contact but stay off her.'

By the end of the afternoon, Champagne had accepted the saddle and stopped bucking.

'That's it for today. Tomorrow you can try to saddle her straight away and maybe by the end of the day you may be riding her, saddle and all.'

Hope was exhausted. She'd half expected Champagne to buck Hamish off which would not happen if Joel was doing the teaching. But she'd been surprised that the techniques that Joel had drummed into her were getting results and she was now becoming a successful horse whisperer too.

'Hope, I've been meaning to ask you something.' Hamish leaned on the bonnet of her car with his elbow, looking her in the eye.

'The annual hootenanny hoe-down barn dance shindig at the Kingston Hall is on this Saturday night. I haven't anyone to bring and was hoping that you might accompany me as a kind of celebration of Champagne passing her test-ride.' His eyes didn't leave her face.

'Oh, I see. Umm ... I don't know what to say.'

'Just say yes ... please, Hope. I'd love you to come. I'll talk to my folks. I'm sure you can sleep in Charity's room for the night as she's still away. Then you won't have to drive all the way home in the dark by yourself.'

Hope buckled under Hamish's unwavering persuasion. 'I suppose so. I'll check that my father hasn't any jobs lined up for me. We are partners in the ranch and I'm also running riding classes next week. I'll let you know before Friday.'

As Hope drove home after a long day, she felt pangs of guilt, disloyalty at the thought that she might be betraying Cole, even though they weren't in any kind of official relationship. He's not even made his intentions known to her yet. She'd not been to a dance since her twenty-first birthday and was eager to let her hair down.

That evening in front of the fire, Hope she sat stroking the old cat, trying to decide whether to disclose to her parents that change that was in the wind.

'You seem to be miles away, Hope. Come on, what's up?' Joel looked from Hope to Myra and back again, observing the intense expression on their daughter's face, her eyes like blue marbles, staring into the fire.

'Oh, sorry! Just a bit weary from today's efforts.'

'Well, you can give yourself a hug. You've almost caught up to me with your horse whispering. Soon I won't be needed around here.' His eyes smiled.

'But there's something else—want to tell us anything?'

'Oh, Dad. You're so persistent.'

'Leave her alone, Joel. She's worn-out.' Myra pulled on his arm.

'What is it, Hope? Did something else happen up at the station?' Joel persevered.

'Not exactly happen—it's Hamish. He desperately wants me to go to a dance this Saturday.'

'Dance … which one is this?' Myra sat on the edge of her seat suddenly coming to life.

'I think it's called the annual hootenanny hoe-down barn dance shindig held in Kingston Hall.'

'That's a mouthful,' Joel burst into a loud guffaw.

'I know. Hilarious isn't it?' Hope giggled.

'He said he doesn't have anyone else to ask, which I find hard to believe from a guy as good looking as he is.'

'I suppose it can't do you any harm. You don't need our permission. You're an adult now and most young women your age have left home. You would have done so too if you'd not been tied up with the business or had an accident.'

Joel tossed the cat off his lap and put another log on the fire. He slipped into his slippers and flopped back into his well-worn armchair.

'He seems to be a decent guy. Why not go and have some fun for a change? Life has been a bit too serious lately.' Myra handed them both a mug of hot cocoa.

'I wish I was your age again going to a hootenanny hoe-down barn dance shindig.' Joel held his stomach, letting out a roar of laughter again and Myra couldn't contain herself either.

***

By the end of the week, the day before the barn dance, Hamish was already up in the saddle, trotting Champagne around the riding ménage. Hope had spent all day going over some basic dressage techniques.

'I think I'm just about done here. You have all the skills you need now, Hamish. You just have to practise them.'

'Sure, thanks to your expert teaching. I must say I couldn't have had a better teacher to take me through the drill.'

'Yes, you could ... my father. He's the best horse whisperer for miles around here.'

'Oh, that's true, but you come a close second, I'm sure. Hold on—I nearly forgot. Mum said to ask you to stay for dinner. Are you all set to come and stay over tomorrow night after the dance?'

'Yes, I think so. I don't know if I have anything to wear yet. I haven't had time to look.'

'I'm pretty certain that you'll look beautiful, no matter what you wear.'

Hope noticed a glint of delight in his eyes as he spoke.

'Come on, let's go eat. Mum has dinner ready.'

As they walked to the house, Hamish draped his arms around Hope's neck. He's taking liberties. Why is he acting so familiar when he's really just a business client?

The mealtime with the Westons was awkward for Hope this time. She was sure Hamish's parents thought there was a budding romance in the air. No one had thought of asking her whether she had a boyfriend or a person of interest in her life, not once. Not even Hamish.

'Have some more of that lemon pie, Hope. Your mother said you are partial to it. You can take some home with you if you like.' Gilly handed her the dish and Hamish stayed fixated on her.

'Oh, no thanks. It's really delicious but I won't fit into my dress tomorrow night.' Instantly she wished she hadn't drawn attention to the dance.

'Dear me. We can't let that happen and have you not turning up. Hamish hasn't stopped talking about taking you to the dance, all week.'

Hamish's face turned florid as he flashed his mother a disapproving glare. Hope pitied him being embarrassed in front of his new date.

Hamish stood up. 'Let's go for a walk outside, I love this spring weather.' Hope followed him out the back.

'Your Mum sure has a beautiful garden.' Hope bent over to sniff one of a multitude of deep red roses.

Hamish stooped forward. He picked one of the large blooms. 'Here, this matches your complexion. Just to say thank you for all your patience and tolerance while teaching me.'

'Remember I said you've already given me that gorgeous saddle blanket. And your father has paid Dad for the job. I'll be keeping my cut from that too.'

'Well, just to say thank you again to a special lady.' He threw her another one of his charming smiles.

'Look—Hamish ... oh, don't worry.' Hope wanted to tell Hamish she was already spoken for and lost her nerve.

What if I put Hamish off then find out Cole has cooled off me?

'Thank you. I've got to get going back now. I have an early start tomorrow. I'll just say goodbye to your parents.'

'Sorry I can't drop around and pick you up tomorrow night. You're staying with us the night so at least you don't have to drive back home afterwards. I'll meet you at the hall around seven. Look forward to dancing with you.' The Cheshire cat grin did not leave his face.

Hope put her foot down hard and zoomed down the driveway. Why was she beginning to feel cornered? He's only wanting to dance with her because there's no one else.

Thirty minutes into the journey home, the rose lay on the edge of the seat, beginning to droop in the heat of the car. 'Is this a sign, God? Please let me know', she uttered.

Chapter Twenty

As her car veered around the corner and down the long driveway to her home, she braked suddenly. Hesitating before parking her car in its usual spot, she saw a familiar sight that she'd not seen in a while. It was Coles red pickup parked next to the cottage which had recently become vacant.

He's home! Why didn't anyone warn her? She wouldn't have agreed to accompany Hamish to the stupid dance.

'Hope—just in time for dinner. Why don't you go and freshen up? We have a visitor arriving for the evening. I think you may want to change.' Her mother stood in the doorway pointing in the direction of Cole's cottage.

'I've already eaten at the Weston's. I know he's back, Mum. Why didn't you tell me he was coming? This is embarrassing.' Her face spelt annoyance.

'We didn't know either. He drove down from Nelson today to surprise us ... or you, I guess.'

'But I have this barn dance to go to tomorrow.'

'That's okay. Just tell him you are staying with the Westons and will be back on Sunday. You don't have to elaborate.'

'Thanks Mum. I wouldn't have known what to say—I mean ... I'm not lying.'

Joel and Myra held the floor during the meal, to Hope's relief. Myra had already explained to Cole that Hope had eaten because his visit was to have been a surprise for her. Cole told them all about the orchard and how hard he'd worked for his father and brother.

'I don't like orchard work. It's not for me. I missed the ranch so much you've no idea. Especially ... the horses,' he spewed out.

Joel flashed Myra a grin and did not dare glance back at Hope. Myra stifled a titter.

'Let's go for a stroll, Hope. I need to walk off your mother's unbeatable cooking. I'd like to see Misty's foal.'

'I suppose I could let you both of the dishes, just this once.' Myra teased.

'Thanks Mrs G.' Cole strutted out to where Misty and foal grazed, his head held high as he strode across the field in his smart western attire. His skin appeared even more bronzed than his previous return home. Hope couldn't help making furtive spot checks of him.

They went back inside for coffee then Hope said goodbye to him on the doorstep.

'Any plans this weekend? I thought perhaps that we could go into Queenstown for the evening. I'd like to take you to dinner. We've a lot of catching up to do.'

This is just what she's been dreading—being put on the spot!

'I ... ah... I'm going to be staying with the Westons this weekend sorry, I've already committed myself.'

'Are you? That's the people you've been helping to break in their mare.'

'How did you know?'

'Your father told me when I rang to say I'd be arriving today. Are you still working with the horse then?'

'No, that contract has just ended today. I think they just wanted to pamper me to say thank you. The Westons really like me, and they were so good to me when I worked for them and lived in.'

She hoped he would not ask any more questions. She just wouldn't have been able to lie.

'Perhaps we can go for a ride when I get back on Sunday afternoon. I'm going to miss church anyway this weekend.'

'Sure, I'll catch you up on Sunday then.' He gave her a warm smile and went back to his cottage.

Hope went inside and slumped in an armchair. Joel was busy stacking wood beside the fireplace.

'What happened out there? I thought you two were having a good time catching up. Why the sad face?'

'I'm in a pickle, Dad. Now that Cole's back, I don't want to go to the dance with Hamish. I'd like to pull out of it but Hamish is looking forward to taking me, I know he is. I don't want to hurt him.'

'Perhaps you should be really honest with Hamish and tell him you have a boyfriend who has just arrived home.'

'What, Dad? What do you mean my boyfriend? Cole's just a friend, although a dear friend.'

'My dear Hope. I think you need to get real and realise that Cole is besotted with you. Can't you see that? Each time he phoned from Nelson he interrogated me about you.'

'Why didn't you tell me? I didn't know.'

'I thought there was no point with him being so far away and not knowing when he'd return.'

'If only it was Cole who'd asked me to the dance. I don't want to go now.'

Joel walked over and took her hand. 'Listen to me. Honesty is the best policy. I think you should phone Hamish and explain the whole situation to him and apologise. Say you didn't know Cole would be giving you a surprise visit, and that you thought he'd given you up after being up north for so long. Say that you'd misjudged the situation with Cole, and you need to put it right with both of them.'

Hope took her father's advice on board and picked up the phone to ring Hamish.

'Hi, Hamish. There's something I need to talk to you about.' With a knot in her stomach that felt like a heavy stone, she told it exactly as Joel had suggested.

'I can't say I'm not disappointed, Hope. But I'm really pleased you've been honest with me. I know I've been a bit to blame, being so pushy. To be truthful, I've had a few offers to accompany local girls to the dance. Why don't you invite your friend, Cole? You can sit at my table with my dance partner and me if you like. Joel has talked about Cole quite a lot, I think I'd like to meet this fine horseman.'

'Thanks, Hamish for being so understanding. I really am sorry for mucking you around. Perhaps we'll still see you there then.'

Hope breathed a huge sigh of relief and slumped back into her chair by the fireplace.

'All worked out then, has it? I told you so. I think Cole's had his heart set on you for a very long time. And I think you feel the same way but haven't admitted it to yourself.'

'I know, Dad. You're right. I'll tell him this weekend. I can't wait to invite him to the dance tomorrow.' She felt a huge weight fall off her, telling herself the truth in her own mind. Now she just has to find the courage to tell Cole how she really feels.

***

The hootenanny hoe-down barn dance lived up to its name as a shindig—loud, boisterous and packed full of people kicking up their heels to the music of "I hear that train a coming" and such like. Hamish sat with an attractive redhead in the corner of the hall with Hope and Cole. There was a light-hearted atmosphere around the table and Hamish acted as if he wasn't bothered at all by his earlier disappointment. Hope observed his behaviour with interest as he became louder and more egotistical with every drop of drink. He sat there boasting about how he

191

could break in a wild horse and that he was a horse whisperer and never mentioned Hope's name.

'I'm sick of watching him. Let's go outside for some fresh air.' Hope took Cole by the hand and led him outside. They found a seat on a bench in front of the hall.

'I'm so glad you could come here with me. I don't know what would have happened if I'd been here with Hamish on my own. His true colours have come out tonight.'

She caught a strong whiff of cigarette smoke that had drifted her way. She looked up and saw Hamish leaning on the girl's shoulders, blowing smoke over her head. He was inebriated, making a fool of himself swearing and acting common. This was so different to what Hope knew of him.

'Wow—how wrong I've been. One certainly can't judge a book by its cover.' She leaned her head against Cole's shoulder as he placed his arm around her and pulled her close. 'What do you mean?' He frowned and gave her a mystified glance.

'Oh, no matter. I'm just surprised to see Hamish drinking and smoking ... I had no idea.'

'Don't you worry about him. Let's just enjoy this lovely evening we have together.' He leaned his lips into hers and she responded warmly and yielded.

'Tell you what. Let's take off and drive around the lake to Queenstown for a bite to eat away from all this noise, just the two of us.'

It was a clear night, and in the abyss, over the lake, the stars seemed to sparkle brighter than ever. As they headed into Queenstown, a full moon appeared, silver and translucent revealing the ripples that the gentle breeze made on the water.

'Look, there's a Bistro still open and I can hear music, our kind of music.'

As they entered the Bistro, a strong whiff of a delicious aroma emanated from the kitchen.

'Is the food still on?' Cole asked the waiter.

'The kitchen is almost closing so put your order in now.'

They sat at a table eating a light meal while music from George Gershwin aided their digestion.

'A far cry from the boisterous hoe-down, don't you think?' Hope seemed to be on cloud nine as her eyes took on a dreamy appearance.

The music changed to lyrics from Nat King Cole.

Cole jumped up and paid for the meal at the counter suddenly.

'What's happening, why the rush?' Hope's eyes widened.

'Come with me. Come on.'

He took her by the hand and led her across the street to where the car was parked. Instead of opening the passenger door to let her in, he kept on leading her down to the water's edge of the lake where there was flat freshly mown grass.

As the breeze caught the melody of "Unforgettable" Cole started to slow dance with her, leaning his head into her neck.

Hope peaked out from under his head. She could see the bright moon rays dancing on the water and suddenly everything in the world appeared wonderfully surreal. He kissed her more passionately this time, his full lips sinking deep into her soft mouth, and her heart melted. They danced like this for a short time, although it seemed like hours until the music stopped.

Without any warning, Cole went down on his knees. Hope couldn't see what he was doing in the dark. Then she caught the glint of something shining in his hand in the moonlight. He slipped the diamond ring on her finger gently.

'Please, Hope, please marry me. I've been waiting for this day ever since I went to Nelson, and this is the perfect moment to ask you. I've loved you for a very long time and it's great that we're such close friends. But I need more from our relationship.'

'I can't believe it. You just took the words out of my mouth. I never stopped thinking about you the whole time you were away, and I almost gave up hope that you would return.'

They held each other tight and kissed as though they could never get enough of each other. The music started up again. This time it was Elvis Presley's "And I Love You So".

Hope was mesmerised, intoxicated by the music and Cole's voice. She whispered into his ear, 'Yes, of course I will. Why has it taken you so long?'

He pulled her closer. With this next deeply passionate kiss they became lost in a time warp. They continued to slow dance in the moonlight until the last song played.

After the music ended, the barman stood outside the door of the building and waved. Cole leaned over and spoke softly in Hope's ear. 'I had to bribe him to play our special music and turn up the volume so we could hear it over here.'

They walked to the car hand in hand while the wind in the willows whispered the promise of change, of good times to come.

****THE END****

JESSIE'S HIGH COUNTRY HEART

Contents
Chapters 1 – 29

JESSIE'S HIGH COUNTRY HEART

Chapter One

New Zealand 1978

It was six o'clock in the evening when Jessie Lee yawned and arched her spine, stretching out the stiffness in her low back muscles. It had been a long day. She'd been leaning over the surgery's treatment bench attending small animals from early in the morning. Lately, she'd started to weary of her role as a vet at the suburban veterinary clinic in the Waikato. She'd had enough of dealing with small pets, though she loved them.

An ache stirred within whenever she thought of her friend, Hope Rigby who had gone to live in the Southern Alps in the remote rural village of Glenorchy. Jessie thought of her old school friend often. Hope had not only fallen in love with her father's top ranch hand, but the North Island girl also had a love affair with the high country.

The pure mountain air and alpine lifestyle appealed to Jessie too. Especially when riding along Dart River on horseback. But she'd been too busy to get away for holidays in Glenorchy since Hope had married Cole Rigby, even though they'd both invited her to stay at their home on Hope's family ranch.

But now Jessie needed a break. Change was in the air—and a complete change, at that. It was time to take a well-earned holiday, and where could there be a better place but Hope's stamping ground in the far south. How she missed the horse rides with her friend along Dart River and picnics with her at Diamond Lake. But nothing had ever been the same since Hope married Cole and that was why Jessie had not been back to Glenorchy. She didn't want to encroach on the newlyweds' privacy.

But Hope had missed Jessie too and wrote her a letter to invite her to come and stay...

Dear Jessie

Mum and Dad have asked if you'd like to come and stay in their ranch house in two weeks as they are going to go on a bit of a road trip in their motor home. Cole and our ranch hand and I will be keeping the farm going. My folks don't like to leave the house empty so that would be great—you'll have it all to yourself. You won't be intruding, honestly. They'll be away for a month. Please think about it and let me know as soon as you can.

Looking forward to hearing from you

Love Hope

⚜⚜⚜

Jessie looked forward to seeing her young brother. Tom had decided not to go to university in Massey. Instead, he had stayed to partner up with his father on their sheep farm in Bethlehem. They'd stopped running cattle and had decided that sheep would be easier, but it was proving not so, especially with the recent drought. She'd worried about the strain her parents were under running the farm. Tom was pretty clued up, as he'd almost completed an agricultural degree by distance study while working with his father. Now Jessie didn't have to feel guilty about not returning home to help them out. Tom had also been riding her beloved horse, Rusty, as she'd been fretting about leaving the animal behind when she first left home to pursue her veterinary studies.

What kept calling her back to Glenorchy? It couldn't have been the rural life as she'd spent all her life on a farm. Was it just her friendship with her old school friend, Hope? She'd made plenty of friends in the Waikato—in fact, she hungered for relief from the hectic social life of the veterinary fraternity in the Waikato province.

***

Jessie's work day had ended. She left the locking up of the clinic after a long, hot day to the receptionist and wandered out to the backyard. She sat down on the bench under the cherry tree and looked at the view of Mount Pirongia which she had always enjoyed when she had first started working there. Last winter there had been snow on the mountain range but it was nothing compared to the Alps. Now the landscape had become too familiar and was no longer a novelty. They were mere hills compared to the spectacular Southern Alps in Glenorchy.

That was it! She realised the magnet which drew her to the high country, the ache on her heartstrings. That's why she wanted to resign from her job each day.

It was the mountains that called her. The feelings were strong. They evoked wistful memories of her climbing days as a college student. She'd spent many weekends driving to Tongariro National Park with her father and brother learning the art of mountaineering and continued the activity during her university years. Each time she went to stay at Dart River Ranch with Hope Rigby and her family, the call of the mountains stirred inside her again. The yearning returned.

Now she faced a dilemma—whether to accept the offer from the veterinary practice to come aboard as a business partner or leave the Waikato for the mountains. What will it be?

She prayed, Please God, lead me, and guide me in this decision. Please give me the knowledge of your will for me, and the power to carry that out.

Chapter Two

The small church in Glenorchy started to empty out. As Hope Rigby and her husband, Cole walked towards their old red Chevy pickup Max their local vet approached them.

'How's that young filly of Misty's I delivered? I see you've started showing her this season.'

'Hi, Max. Yeah, she's following in her mother's footsteps. So wonderful to ride and a great dressage horse.'

'Actually, I wanted to let the two of you know I'm retiring next month. My wife wants to do some touring with our new motorhome and I'm getting a bit worn-out. We don't get enough time off to spend with our grandchildren in Christchurch. I don't suppose you know of any young vets looking for work who might want to locate to this area. It's just that it's pretty hard to get anyone out here.'

Cole shot a glance at his wife. 'Hope has a vet friend who has been thinking about moving this way. We could find out for you.'

'What skills has he got? Is he a farm or a city vet?' Max leaned on the bonnet of the Chevy.

Hope looked sideways at Cole and cleared her throat.

'Ah, well actually my friend is a woman, a very capable vet. She grew up on a farm and has worked with large animals working alongside her father.'

Max set his jaw and looked back at Hope. He tightened his thick lips.

'Oh, I don't know about a woman—particularly since she hasn't handled large stock on her own before.'

Hope braced herself against the passenger door jutting her head forward. 'Jessie has plenty of experience. I used to spend holidays on her parents' farm. During the calving and lambing season, I watched while she assisted her father with some complicated births, some of which were twins.'

'Oh, that sounds promising,' said Max, jotting this down on his notebook.

Their local vet told her that she'd handled them expertly. She often shared her experiences with me.'

'Is that so? Well, if you and Cole can recommend her, she must be alright. Tell you what—you ask her to send her resume to me and I'll look at it and arrange an interview with her. How's that?' He pushed the notebook back into his jacket pocket.

Hope rushed towards him, appearing to want to throw her arms around him but pulled back and just shook his hand.

'Honestly, Max, you won't be disappointed. She's an amazing person and has plenty of experience handling horses too. I'll phone her tonight.'

***

Dear Hope

Please thank your folks for asking me to house sit. I've been able to take the leave owing to me and extended it to a month. I just can't wait to go riding with you along the Durl River and out to Diamond Lake.

Your phone call about your vet, Max Greaves retiring came at exactly the right time as my boss has been pressuring me into deciding about becoming a partner in their practice.

I have my papers and resume ready to show Max. Now that I have been thinking about it and the possibility of becoming your local vet down there, I would be so disappointed if he chose not to offer me the position. So I hope you bolstered my image plenty. Haha, just joking. I can't wait to get to Glenorchy. Thanks for offering to pick me up from the airport.

See you soon
Love Jessie

***

A week later, Jessie's boss, Peter Cranston approached her again.

'I'm sorry Jessie, but I can't wait for your decision any longer. The board wants to make a choice by the end of this month, and we gave you the first option as we don't want to lose you.'

He spoke as though he had a plum in his mouth, giving him an ostentatious air, but he was a kind and humble man and Jessie had found him to be a great person to work with. He had mentored her ever since she had joined the practice, and she knew he would be unhappy to see her resign.

'I'm taking the leave that's owing to me and return at the conclusion of the month with a decision. If I decide before then, I promise I'll phone you to let you know. I'm off to stay on a high country ranch in Glenorchy. My friend's parents have asked if I'd house sit for them.'

'Goodness, you do get around. I know you're young and free and have the whole world at your doorstep. I'll wait for your decision with bated breath.' He gave a half-laugh, but Jessie could see moisture in his eyes as if he knew she was going to fresh pastures.

***

Jessie's flight had been delayed, so Hope sat at a coffee kiosk sipping a second cup of espresso. At last, her friend veered around the corner of the aisle pushing a trolley loaded with an oversized suitcase.

'Jessie! I'm over here.' Hope waved at her again. 'Is that all your luggage? It's so great to see you.' They hugged. 'You're looking good. The car's parked outside in the drop-off zone.'

Jessie laughed as she approached the car, recalling when she had seen Hope's bright yellow car for the first time.

'Oh, you still have Sunflower.'

'Yep, and she's going like a bomb. The mechanic says she could keep going for my lifetime, but I'm not so sure about that.'

Hope couldn't stop talking the whole trip back to Glenorchy, but Jessie struggled to keep her eyes open after a hectic week at the short-staffed clinic. She opened her passenger window and took some deep breaths. She knew she'd have to stay awake to help keep Hope alert driving around the narrow bends on the country roads.

Jessie pulled a letter from her handbag. 'I forgot to tell you; I received this before I left. A letter from your vet, Max. He wants me to meet with him next week.'

***

After a two-hour drive, they arrived at the ranch. Jessie couldn't believe she had the whole house to herself. Hope's parents' knew her well, since the girls had been at school together in Bethlehem and they trusted her to take good care of their home. Hope and Cole lived in the farm cottage in the field over the fence—an old cottage they had both renovated with assistance from Joel, Hope's father.

Jessie was placing the last of her garments in the empty drawers when there was a knock at the door.

204

'Sorry, I know you need a bit of time to freshen up, but we're putting on the barbeque. Mum left us some lamb steaks to finish up if you'd like to pop over in an hour.' Hope handed her a small bunch of wildflowers.

'Sure, I'd love to. See you there at seven. I might just lie down until then.'

Hope wandered out the back door and Jessie popped the flowers into a vase then crashed onto her bed. She focused on her breathing, inhaling the stillness, apart from the odd lamb calling for its mother. She gained a sense of security from the farm sounds which triggered memories of growing up in the country.

Later that evening, after the barbeque and a stomach full of alcohol-free cider that Myra, Hope's mother had left for them, Jessie had to excuse herself to retire early. The flight, the lively conversations on the way back from the airport and the heavy meal had made her eyelids heavy. Sleep took her by surprise.

She awoke the next morning to busy farm noises, but her sleep had been deep and uninterrupted. Casey, the border collie, rushed into the house to greet her when she opened the front door. Myra had left plenty of food in the pantry for her and although Hope and Cole had said she was welcome to eat with them anytime, it was her choice to remain independent.

Later that morning she accompanied Hope to the stables to check out her mare's filly, Marvella. She was born charcoal black, and during the last three years, her colour had turned grey, almost white, which Jessie knew was usual for the foals of grey mares. Marvella, a beautiful Arab had a soft nature like her mother. She hadn't seen her since she was a foal and the filly was still black then.

'She sure has grown—a real beauty like Misty,' said Jessie as she leaned over the stable door.

'You can ride Misty when we go along the Dart and I'll take Marvella. Misty knows the river bed really well but I'm still training this young filly. She baulks sometimes.'

'Sure, sounds good. I'll help you go and get them.'

'No need to—they're all bridled and waiting in the stables. Cole saddled them up for us. He has gone to help a local rancher present a stallion to one of his mares.'

The two friends trotted their horses along the side of the riverbank, now and then stopping to take in the awesome views of Mt Earnslaw and the wild birds. Overhead a large Kea flapped its wings displaying red, green and gold feathers.

This is what she'd looked forward to when she took her holidays at Dart River Ranch with Hope.

But her mind kept drifting. What if Max decided not to choose her to replace him? Jobs for vets in that district were scarce. Max had been the local vet for thirty years and they didn't welcome female ones. Jessie was in for much opposition, but she was already prepared for that. It did not thwart her, at least not yet.

'Come on—let's go for a ride through that shallow part of the river. The horses love it.' Hope gently urged Marvella on. The horses frolicked in the water. For Jessie, it was like old times.

Cole was waiting at the gate when they arrived back at the ranch. He looked at his watch and stammered somewhat as he spoke. 'I was getting a bit worried, Hope. I thought you were only going for the morning. Leave the horses—I'll hose them down for you.'

The girls jumped off their backs and handed the reins to Cole.

'You're looking a bit peaky, love. Perhaps you need to have a lie down before dinner. I'm going to stoke up the barbeque later.'

'Don't worry so much, Cole. I'm fine, really I am.'

Jessie glanced at Hope and could see the pallor in her porcelain-like cheeks. Perhaps she is sickening for something, she thought.

As evening fell, and they had finished their meal, Hope wandered back to the ranch house with Jessie while Cole offered to stay at the cottage and clean up the mess from the barbeque.

'He's quite the gentleman, isn't he? A real catch—and you both still appear to enjoy married life. Come on in for a quick cuppa before you turn in if you like.'

'I'd rather have some of that Milo drink Mum has in her pantry. It's nice with hot milk.'

The girls sat at the dining table sipping their hot drinks that Jessie had prepared.

'To be honest, I've noticed you're looking a bit pale these days—not like the last time I was down here. You're not getting any headaches or post-concussion from your old head injury are you?' Jessie squinted her eyes, focusing on Hope's face.

'No—you mean my fall from Misty when I first came to live here. Heavens no, I'm completely over that. Look ... I wasn't going to say anything as it's a bit soon, but I'm going to have a baby, that's all.'

Jessie almost dropped her cup, spilling a little in her lap.

'Ow, clumsy me. Well, that is certainly a big surprise.'

'Wait on ... I'll get you a wet cloth. Did you burn yourself?'

'It's okay, just a few drips. How far are you?'

'Only a few months. I'm getting that horrible morning sickness.'

Hope handed Jessie a cloth. 'We weren't going to say anything until the first scan but that won't be until next month. The midwife is sure everything is tickety boo.'

'That's wonderful news, but you shouldn't have been trotting, when we were riding along the river.'

'The midwife says it shouldn't be a problem.'

'I think you should just walk Marvella next time, or better still, ride Misty. She's a bit quieter.'

'Yes, Mum,' she laughed.

Cole came to the ranch house and walked Hope back home to their cottage later that evening.

Jessie lay in bed that night thinking how times were changing and wondering what kind of adventures awaited her. She imagined herself as the local vet building up her business around the Rees and the Dart valleys. She remembered Cole had said he was going to get Max to assist with one of the mares about to foal. In spite of having a head full of all kinds of plans for her possible new career, she fell asleep.

***

Jessie had finished helping Hope feed the horses in the stables and hung around playing with some foals.

'I've really missed this, you've no idea. Especially the smell of the mountain air and the views from up there.' She pointed towards Paradise where they'd been riding early that morning. 'I can't believe I've been here a week already. Max is coming to see me this afternoon, by the way. I forgot to tell you he rang me last night.'

Jessie lifted the bag of horse feed pellets and placed them on the shelf before walking back to the house. 'I'd better go back inside and check that all my documents are in order.'

'That's okay. I'm dying to hear all about it. We'll be in the ranch house during your interview and you can take him out under the umbrella on that garden table if you like. We'll make some coffee inside and bring it out. Just so you don't feel vulnerable here alone with him.'

'Ah, thanks, I would really appreciate it.'

Chapter Three

The meeting with Max wasn't really a proper job interview. Jessie had guessed he'd already made up his mind on Cole and Joel's recommendations and she had excellent credentials. This woman was too good to pass by, even in Glenorchy.

Max handed Jessie back her document folder and stood up ready to leave.

'I don't suppose you could get back to me with an answer by the end of the month. It's just that the position I'm in is a bit awkward now that they are offering me a partnership in the business. I have to notify the Practice Manager in two weeks.'

'Look here, young lady. Do you think I'm going to let you escape? You've no idea how difficult it has been to get hold of a young vet with your experience and qualifications. We've been really scraping the bottom of the barrel.'

Jessie's heart pumped loudly against her eardrums. Was she hearing correctly? Her stomach churned with anticipation.

'Sorry, what did you say? I didn't quite grasp what you meant.' She tugged at the hair behind her right ear, a common habit when she was nervous.

'What I mean is—when can you start?'

Her mouth dropped wide open. The thick portfolio Max had handed back to her left her hand and dropped to the floor.

'Are you offering me the position, really?' Embarrassed, she rushed to the floor and scooped up the documents before Max bent to help her.

'I recognise a skilled professional when I see one. Sorry, but I have to confess I actually know one of those clinicians you work with who has recommended you. I do need to run this past the Board of Directors for the Veterinary Cooperative in Queenstown. They'll want to check your credentials, so I can let you know for sure by the end of the week.'

'Oh, so you have contacted my clinic already?'

'Don't worry, they guessed you were looking further afield or you wouldn't have been delaying and holding off from giving your boss an answer.'

The end of the week couldn't come quick enough for Jessie. She was restless each day and Hope did her best to keep her occupied.

Awakening one morning to a knock on her bedroom door, she stumbled to open it, half asleep. Hope stood there all smiles and rearing to go.

'If you're interested, I was hoping I could take you out to Diamond Lake on the horses later today,' Hope said. 'I've got some stuff to tell you that might put a smile on your face.'

Jessie was up but not quite awake. She stood at the door in her nightwear, scratching her head and yawning.

'Sounds interesting. What time do you plan to go?'

'Cole and Mack are having to shift some sheep to another paddock by horseback. I need to move some horses so you could help me do that if you like. I've packed a picnic lunch to take to the lake after that.'

'Mack ... isn't that Mack whom I met at your twenty-first? We had a few dances together. He kept asking when I was coming down to stay with you again. He was up north shearing the last few times I came here.'

'Yep, he had substantial sheep shearing contracts around the country and used to go away a lot. But he doesn't do that much shearing anymore, except the animals on his own farm.'

'His farm? Oh, that's right. Last time I spoke to him he was looking for land.'

'Well, he managed to buy a hundred acres, a small holding for around here and is trying to convert an old barn into a farmhouse on his own.'

Jessie's face turned pink. She pulled nervously at her fringe. 'That's a lot of work—good for him. I'll just jump into the shower and meet you at your place in half an hour.'

Jessie didn't mean to cut her friend off short but the conversation was beginning to make her feel uncomfortable for some reason.

She couldn't believe what she was seeing when they had arrived at Diamond Lake. Were her eyes deceiving her? On the other side of the lake was a scene she'd not witnessed for several years. The wild horses were back, at least the ones that were left behind.

'Look, they are the remains of the Kaimanawa herd that escaped from that rancher, aren't they?'

'Yeah, they are the ones Dad had to leave behind during the muster when I had my accident. That ex-army officer Captain Richardson trucked them down here when he tried to start a horse ranch. They're the horses that broke free when his ranch hands didn't shut the stock pen fast enough. They're the last of the herd unless there are some foals we don't know about.'

'I remember you wrote and told me that they're now preserved by the Protection of Feral Horses Bill. It's good to see them roaming about here.'

It was peaceful by the lake. Usually, there were tourists scattered around the shore, but this time the girls were the only ones apart from a family having a picnic on the other side.

'Wow, this reminds me of the times we had when I used to come down from university. We would lie on the grass and talk for hours. I've missed this so much. I love the view of Mount Alfred from here. Doesn't it look amazing?' Jessie took out her camera for a quick snapshot.

They sat on the ground finishing their sandwiches and cold drinks while the horses munched on the fresh grass while tethered to a log.

'I can't wait to get down here. I hope I can do this community justice though—I mean it might be difficult to follow in Max's footsteps after all these years,' said Jessie.

'Don't worry about that. You have to be your own person and you're going to bring unique skills and qualities to the role.'

'Yes, I know. It's just that I read somewhere that some of these rural close-knit communities in this part of the country often show prejudice against female vets.'

'Look, Jessie. My father and Cole are totally in support of a woman vet and will completely back you up. Please believe me. You will do just fine.'

'Thanks, Hope. Hey—you were going to tell me something, remember?' She sat back on her elbows, readying herself for some juicy gossip.

'It's Mack ... ever since he bought his farm, he's been asking if I've heard from you and if you are coming down to Glenorchy again.' Hope started to gather up their picnic plates and utensils and wrapped them in a tea towel while

Jessie sat all ears with her mouth wide open waiting to hear the rest of the surprising news.

'And the other day he was saying how lonely it is on the farm.'

Jessie didn't know what to say. What was Hope getting at?

'It's pretty lonely I guess living in a large barn on his own. He has been slowly renovating it, trying to do it himself mostly, and sometimes with help from men at church.' Hope kept watching Jessie's face, looking for her reaction.

'Come on, let's get going. I have to get back and phone my new intake of riding students who are arriving next week.'

Jessie was quiet during the ride back and the girls let the horses have long reins as they made their way back to the ranch just before dusk.

***

Friday came soon enough, and Jessie just moped around the stables feeding the foals and mucking out. She started thinking about what direction her life would take if they rejected her application. The breakfast cereal she had wolfed down had risen to the top of her throat and that sick feeling had returned. She'd forgotten to bring her antacid tablets to the ranch.

'Jessie! Are you there? Can you hear me? There's a phone call for you ... it's Max.' Cole poked his head through the stable doorway.

She swallowed the lump in her gullet, placed the pellet bucket back on the shelf, and rushed out the door.

'Thanks, Cole,' she yelled after him. 'Tell him I'm coming.'

Cole went back into the ranch house with Jessie in tow.

'Hope you don't mind me taking the call. They are often for me about my equine breeding program.' He handed her the phone. The voice on the other end did not sound like

213

Max. He was a lot more serious than the jovial fellow who interviewed her—this time his voice sounded flat.

'I'm sorry, Jessie but we've met with a few obstacles regarding your job application,' he stammered.

Her heart sank and her throat tightened.

'The thing is ... the panel of people who screened your credentials needed to vote for or against your application and it was fifty-fifty. They were all men and half of them did not agree to have a female as the local rural vet for this area. In fact, we seldom see female vets in these parts. I'm sorry, Jessie as I think you are tops.'

'Oh, so what does this mean? I haven't been successful then?' She squeezed back the tears that were threatening to sting her eyes and wiped them away with her hand.

'I don't mean that at all. The Board have accepted your application, thanks to Joel and Cole. They sent strong supportive letters as part of your references. The farmers in this area highly respect these men and the directors could not refuse you on this basis. Of course, the Board had my endorsement as well. It's just that you may get a bit of a hard time from those who had rejected your application, but you just have to stand your ground. Joel and Cole will back you up.'

Jessie's voice quavered. 'What do I do next then?'

'I'll be around tomorrow with your contract. All the directors get one as well. I'll be staying on and working with you for a while before I hand the practice over to you. I'll see you in the morning.'

Jessie couldn't stop thanking him. But most of all she gave thanks to God for standing in the gap for her.

***

That evening, after she'd phoned Peter Cranston to let him know her decision to leave and take up the role of Glenorchy's remote vet, Hope and Cole made a celebration dinner for her. Cole was eager to get her involved in his breeding program with the horses and couldn't stop talking about it. He would require Jessie to certify the mares suitable for reproduction. At last, she was at home in the high country—her dream was about to come true.

Chapter Four

A month had gone by since Jessie's holiday on Dart River Ranch. She'd been flat out winding up her business with the clinic in the Waikato and organising a place to live in Glenorchy. Fortunately one of Hope's church parishioners had come to the rescue. A farmer and his wife had a cottage to rent not far from Dart River Ranch. Jessie had few belongings in the small studio she'd rented near the clinic, so moving was simple.

'Not long now ...we'll be sorry to see you go, I have to say.' Peter Cranston's voice was breaking up. 'I don't blame you though, at your age. You remind me of when I was a young vet. Life was one great adventure, and no one was going to hold me back. You give it your best and I'll be watching the space to see where you end up.'

Jessie avoided his gaze. Peter Cranston had been good to her—a great mentor. She was indebted to him.

'I'll be back up this way to see you all. I have friends in the area, remember?'

The last few weeks flew by and before she knew it, she was back on the Air New Zealand DC-10 flight to Queenstown. She had her belongings sent down by the truck before she arrived.

***

After arriving in Glenorchy, Jessie stayed at Dart River Ranch with Hope who collected her from the airport. The two girls sat up late discussing their plans for the next day.

'I'm going to take you to your new home tomorrow. Lance and Mary, your new landlords will be there to meet you at ten. I'll help you unpack as your packages all arrived here yesterday.'

'Oh, you don't have to go to all that trouble. I have all week and you're busy running your riding classes.'

'No, I haven't any groups for a while. They start again in a few weeks.' Hope sat flipping through the pages of her diary.

'I'm not expected to accompany Max on his rounds until next Monday.' Jessie pulled out the hair tie from her ponytail and refastened it.

'That's good because I have a mare about to foal and I thought you could assist her,' said Cole.

'Don't pressurise her. She may not be ready for that yet.'

'Yes, I am. I can't wait. Even though I've helped Dad with calving for years and did some hands-on during my training, I've never done it unassisted before.'

That night, Jessie tossed and turned, struggling to get to sleep after all the excitement. She couldn't wait to be in her new home and going off visiting farms each day. Hope's father had loaned her an old Ute that was still drivable, although it made all sorts of grunts and gurgles. She had planned to buy a vehicle once she had started work.

The next morning, feeling energised in spite of getting off to sleep late, Jessie was eager to get to her cottage. Joel's boisterous border collie almost knocked her over as he greeted her.

She wandered outside looking for Hope and Cole. They'd already started feeding the animals and checking on the broodmares in the stables. She inhaled deeply, filling her lungs with the clean mountain air. The early morning sun warmed her soul.

'Hi, Jessie. I wasn't sure if you wanted to sleep in so I didn't wake you. We're going in for breakfast now. My folks have already left to visit my Aunt in Geraldine.'

Jessie was ravenous after all the travelling and intensity of the previous day. There was plenty of food on the table so she didn't go hungry.

'How about you get all your stuff unpacked at the cottage and come back here when we think that mare is about to foal. Unless she has it overnight. When she's close, we'll let you know,' said Hope.

'Sure, sounds good to me. I'm only ten minutes away.'

'By the way … Do you remember the young black stallion that was sired by one of the horses in Dad's first muster? He's a three-year-old, stunning Arab. Mack purchased him from my father and has named him, Zoro. He wants to show him as well as use him for as a workhorse on the farm. For a young stallion, he possesses a mellow nature.'

'Oh, really. I'd like to see him sometime... the horse, I mean.'

Cole looked sideways at Hope and chuckled.

'Sure thing, Jessie. I'm sure I can arrange that sometime,' said Cole with a grin.

The girls cleared the table while Cole went back outside.

'Come on. Let's get your things over to the cottage. We can pack both vehicles up. I'll take our Chevy and you can follow me as I know the way.'

Soon after they arrived at the cottage, Jessie's landlords turned up. They presented Jessie with a bunch of multi-coloured hydrangea flowers by Mary who took a large vase out of the laundry cupboard.

'Here—I remembered the last tenants left it and don't want it back. Flowers will help to give the cottage a homely feeling,' said Mary.

Instantly Jessie took a liking to her new landlady.

'And you are our new vet? That will make a change having an attractive young girl instead of a worn-out old codger like Max,' said Lance.

'Hey, cut it out!' Mary elbowed him hard and they both laughed. At least Jessie knew that some people were on her side.

They showed her around the cottage and how everything worked. 'Don't hesitate to ring us if you need anything.'

Hope poked her head in the bathroom. 'Oh, good, a shower.'

'The water pressure is a bit weak but I'm getting someone in to move the hot water cylinder which will fix that. One of us could visit you each week to collect the rent. Hope says you'll be worshipping at our church in Glenorchy. Is that right?' Lance walked back outside, inspecting the water tank on his way out. Jessie followed.

'Yes, I will actually.'

'Well, why don't you just hand me a cheque at church at the end of each week instead. That'll keep you on the straight and narrow now, won't it?'

Jessie begrudged being obligated to attend church so they could collect the rent. She was reluctant to have them come to the cottage every week as though they were checking up on her. Being a modern, independent woman this didn't go down well.

'I'd rather set up an automatic payment at my bank. That way you can guarantee to get your money on time.'

Mary and Lance looked at each other, shrugged. 'I suppose that's your decision,' said Lance, and then driving off.

Hope helped Jessie to unpack.

'Let's get started. With the two of us doing it, we'll have it finished in no time,' said Hope tearing the duct tape off the first box.

***

Her first night in the cottage took Jessie some getting used to. There was a good bed with a firm mattress that Hope's parents had given her. The cotton curtains appealed to her. They were very similar to the ones in her bedroom at her home in Bethlehem— light blue with pink flowers to match the wallpaper.

Jessie's overfatigue caused her to toss and turn. Luckily she was accustomed to all the farm sounds, having grown up being surrounded by noisy cattle and sheep.

Her windows had wire security screens that she locked, but most of all she was never alone. Her relationship with God was stronger than ever and his presence was with her wherever she went. She started to pray to settle her mind—

Surround me with your hedge of protection, God. Bless this house and cleanse it of anything that is not of you. Amen. Finally, her sleep was deep and undisturbed.

***

Jessie woke with sunlight exploding through the crack in her curtains and the phone ringing. She wasn't properly awake as she rolled out of bed to run for the phone and almost fell.

'Morning, Hope. Sorry, I'm not awake yet. I didn't get off to sleep for ages and must have slept in. What's the time?'

'Don't worry ... it's still early ... eight o'clock. Sorry to bother you, but the mare went into labour in the early hours of this morning and she's still going. Do you want to assist?'

'Really? That's wonderful, of course, I do. I'll be there right away.'

220

'Make sure you have a good breakfast as you'll need it. Max has already checked her when her waters broke, and he was happy for you to be there. Dad knows what to do too if you get into trouble.'

Jessie dressed and rushed her breakfast down. She had a good appetite which was usually the case in the mountains.

Driving the Ute was a new experience on the rough, windy road to Dart River Ranch. There was too much play in the steering, and she had trouble keeping it steady. The next thing on her agenda will be a new vehicle, that's for sure.

As she drove up to the ranch house, Joel waved out to her by the stables, followed by Hope. She quickly parked her vehicle and rushed up to them.

'Am I too late? Is everything alright?'

'No, you're just in time. It's your turn now.'

Jessie poked her head over the stable door and let herself in. Hope had gone back to the mare and was sitting on the ground rubbing the horse's neck.

'You need to come to this end, Jessie,' Joel said, winking at her. He loved teasing Hope's friends.

The beautiful mare with the shiny black coat kept standing up and lying down on the deep layer of hay.

Before long, the white foetal membrane slowly expelled itself. Joel verbally coaxed Jessie into gently pulling on the two black spindly legs that protruded. Suddenly her heart was in her mouth.

'Remember to breathe, Jessie,' said Joel.

A skinny, soft body began to protrude from the mare and as Jessie broke open the membrane, the rest of the foal presented itself. Jessie slipped it out, laying it on the hay next to its mother.

'You've done it! There you are—that wasn't too bad, was it?' Joel patted Jessie on the shoulder. 'You did it all by yourself!'

Jessie was so overcome by it all that she threw her arms around Hope.

'Congratulations!' Hope blurted.

'I'll go inside and give Max a call and tell him you don't need any orientation from him. You're a champion,' Joel said to Jessie, who followed him into the house as they left the mare to bond with her foal. Cole had just arrived from visiting a client and couldn't believe his ears when they said that Jessie had delivered the foal. He'd wanted to be back in time. 'Well, what is it—or is it genderless?' He grabbed a bottle of ginger beer from the fridge. 'Anyone else wants a drink?' He handed the bottles around.

'We have another colt. A black one to replace the foal that has gone to Mack,' said Joel.

'When do you start working with Max, Jessie?' Hope popped the top of her bottle.

'Tomorrow—ah no, sorry, I mean on Monday. He's taking me on farm visits straight away. We don't have a clinic out here. With remote rural vets, it's all home consultations and after-hours they have to take smaller animals into Queenstown. I'll still go to the farms for the large animals, as it's part of my job as a remote vet. I'm not too keen on driving after dark but that's just one of the drawbacks of being a rural vet on call.'

'Wow, good on you. I'm sure you're going to do well out here.'

'Max says we're off to a farm to help with calving and later in the week lambing.'

'Well, that's no problem for you after today's session. You're an expert now.' Hope gave her a warm smile and Jessie lapped up the encouragement.

After she washed up, she headed out to her vehicle.

'I'd best be getting back home. I've still got unpacking to do and I'm pretty tired out. Need to be fresh for Monday. I'll be moving the rest of my stuff in tomorrow.'

'You won't stay for dinner then?' Hope asked.

'That's kind of you, but I'm bushed. I'll call you tomorrow and let you know how I'm going.'

Hope and Cole waved her off as the Ute gave a cough and chugged its way down the driveway. Jessie arrived home and threw off her leather boots. Heading straight for her bed, she collapsed on it, forgetting to remove her Stetson, almost crushing it. After tossing it onto the armchair next to the bed, she relaxed and closed her eyes. Tired more than hungry, she soon fell asleep. When she stirred, it was dark, and the cold night air woke her. She hurried outside to secure the Ute and then locked herself in the house. She now had some energy to get herself a meal. If only she didn't have to cook for herself tonight. There was a Chinese food outlet at the end of her street in the Waikato where she could pick up a nutritious meal when she didn't want to cook. Now she would just have to adjust. The nearest grocer, the General Store was a few miles away in Glenorchy and had a limited supply of groceries, so she reckoned on having to stock up once a fortnight in Queenstown.

'Ah!' She remembered she'd taken out a Shepherd's Pie from the freezer—one of the meals that Hope had given her to tide her over until she got on her feet. There were other meals donated to her by her church parishioners that she had frozen too.

Once the meal had been heated up in the oven, she took the enamel dish out and could barely wait to scoop the contents onto a plate. She was so hungry—she smothered it in tomato sauce and sat at the table bolting the food down as if she'd been on a starvation diet.

In the fridge, she saw some of Myra's home-made yoghurt and gulped it down. She was thinking she should start putting her things away into the cupboards and drawers, but she'd had enough for the day.

Hope had told her that there was no television reception in the area, only closer to Queenstown which was a disappointment as she had brought a small TV with her. Perhaps she should have rented something closer to all the amenities. But then she couldn't have it both ways—everything at her finger-tips such as peace and tranquillity. That's what she wanted, and she had right there.

Chapter Five

Monday couldn't come fast enough for Jessie. Max was at her gate right on the dot of nine as she expected. She jumped in beside him in his green, 1973 model, four-wheel-drive Land Rover that stank of dog. She held a piece of toast in her hand, licking the sticky jam from her fingers after she crunched into it.

'We've got a bit of a drive this morning up into those hills way up there. I hope you don't get carsick—it's a rough trip, in fact, most of the roads around here are pretty bad. We have to do plenty of driving in this job so you'd better have a decent vehicle.'

'No, I'll be fine. Back home in Bethlehem, the roads are mostly loose metal, so I'm used to it. As soon as I can, I'm going to buy myself a Land Rover like yours that I can sleep in when I get late-night call-outs.'

'Mmm, I'll have a think about that. There may be one going for sale locally. Now ... my first stop is old Ted Gregory's cattle station. We have to drive through Dart Valley near Mount Alfred. Lovely views on the way. You'll get a chance to assist him with calving.'

'Great, that's what I've been looking forward to.'

'Good, you are wearing the right gear. Did you bring a change of clothes? It can get pretty messy.'

'Oh, I know that. I've helped my Dad do it from an early age. I have them in the rucksack you threw in the back.'

Jessie wasn't normally carsick, but the way Max swerved around the corners in his Land Rover caused the scrambled egg which she'd eaten earlier rise to her throat and back again.

'What do you think of the countryside around here? It's unique, isn't it?' Max sat tall in his seat, gloating.

'That's why I wanted to be down here. It sure is amazing scenery and the mountain air is so clean.'

The vehicle wound its way up to a cattle station that had spectacular views of Mount Alfred.

'Here we are—time to do some work. Roll up your sleeves my girl.'

Jessie was rearing to go. She grabbed her rucksack and followed Max along a broken path that led to the homestead. Ted must have heard the truck, as he was waiting out on the porch in tan corduroy trousers and Swanndri.

'Gidday, mate,' he said to Max. 'You'll be needing something warm up here.' He glanced at Jessie. 'So you're our new vet. Hope you can cope with the work. You need a bit of muscle for this slog, doesn't she Max?'

'I've got a jacket in this bag, and I'm used to cattle. My father runs beef and sheep.'

'Good. At least you're not just a townie.' Ted smirked.

Jessie found his attitude condescending and not welcoming.

'The cows are out the back. I have my motorbike and you can both fit on that old quad bike.'

'Don't worry Missy, I can drive one of these okay,' said Max, humouring her.

The two of them followed Ted to a paddock not far from the house. He had moved the pregnant cows closer to the homestead, so he didn't have far to go to check on them.

Max carried a large leather bag, and Tom had a rope and a few things in a sack.

'She's been going for a few hours, and I think this one is breech.' Ted patted the cow on the neck.

'Oh, she has horns! And all that wool. I haven't seen a breed like this before. My Dad just had Friesians.'

'These are Highlanders. You have to watch those horns.' Max took the calving rope off Ted and pulled on a pair of long rubber gloves. 'Here, Jessie. You'll need these. Remember—stay behind her unless you want to become skewered.'

Max began to examine the cow. 'Sure is breech, but one foot is already protruding.' He took Jessie's hand and guided her arm in to grab hold of the legs. They needed to use the calving rope and there was a lot of tugging and waiting until finally, the calf dropped to the ground. It wasn't breathing at first. Max picked it up and dangled it over the gate to clear its airway. Instantly it perked up. Jessie was impressed.

'I've never seen Dad do that before. He used to throw cold water over their heads to stimulate them.'

'Well, I have to teach you something as you're going to be following in my footsteps. I can't muck that up, can I?'

They took off back to the house. Ted thanked them both and invited them in for some refreshments. He offered some cold beer.

'You know me, Ted—I don't drink and drive, and Jessie here doesn't drink alcohol. Perhaps you have some cold water?'

'I've something better than that. Some of my wife's home-made lemonade with mint. She's gone into town to get the groceries.'

Jessie's arms were still shaking after all the pulling and straining. She wondered how she would have coped with that situation on her own. They both gulped the beverages down in a hurry.

'We'd better get off. Call us if you have any others in trouble, Ted. We'll find our own way out.'

Jessie's knees were still knocking together as she followed Max back down the path to the Land Rover.

She went quiet on the trip back to Glenorchy, wondering whether she really had jumped in at the deep end. There were few women vets doing this kind of work. Did she have what it takes to survive? She prayed silently for courage. It didn't really take so much strength as technique, those difficult births. Other women do it, so can she?

'You're very quiet all of a sudden. You couldn't stop talking on the way up here, girl. Are you okay?'

'Oh, I'm fine. I guess I was nervous on the way to Ted's or apprehensive more like it. I just didn't know what to expect.'

'You did well up there. You've got nothing to worry about. You knew what you were doing. You'll get into the swing of it and the farmer's do most of it, anyway.'

Jessie trusted Max and was secure in the knowledge that he wouldn't have said that if he had not meant it.

'Lambing isn't so difficult. The animals give birth on their own. It's just when they have difficult labour that we intervene. Down in the Rees Valley, there's a ewe with twins and she needs help right now. The farmer radioed me back at Ted's house—oh yes I must show you how to use my car radiophone before I leave.'

When they entered the valley, Jessie kept scanning the hills to see if she could see any of the wild horses that still remained there. As they turned a bend in the road, a chestnut Kaimanawa horse and foal stood under the trees.

'That's one of the horses from the beech forest—you know the ones that had escaped from that mad Captain.'

'You mean from that rogue, Richardson. He's back in the province, I heard. Apparently, he's trying to start up a horse ranch again near Closeburn. I've heard he has some dubious characters working for him.'

'As long as he keeps down there away from us, I don't mind.'

'We'll have to wait and see if they're trouble or not.'

The welcome Jessie received from the farmer with the ewe giving birth to twins was much warmer than the cool reception from Ted. Joe and his wife offered them afternoon tea which was a treat as they'd eaten their sandwiches earlier without a hot drink. The couple sat asking Jessie a myriad of questions before leading her and Max out to the yard where the ewe was in labour.

'She has just started straining, but the sack hasn't appeared yet.' Farmer Joe let Max take over from this point. The seasoned vet took a look at her. 'She's nearly ready. I can feel the sack just sitting there.'

Within minutes the ewe gave a sigh and one foot started to show, and then the second one. After thirty minutes the head and rest of the body made an appearance. Joe presented the lamb to its mother for her to lick it clean while Max prodded Jessie to assist the next delivery.

'Wait on, we've got another one coming, rear legs first. It's a breech birth. Oh well, good practice for you Jessie. Come and kneel here.'

The ewe was already lying down. Max guided Jessie's hands, and it required some pulling but nothing like the efforts needed with the Highland cow.

Within another half hour, the ewe was busy licking both lambs.

Joe showed Max and Jessie to the laundry where they could wash up. They declined his wife's invitation to go back inside the house afterwards.

As Max drove back out onto the main road, he kept looking at Jessie. 'Are you okay? You look a bit pale.'

'I'm okay, honest. I'm just adjusting to a different bed, and I've been doing a lot of unpacking in the last few days.'

'You haven't really had much time to adjust with such a big move and starting work so quickly. Don't worry I won't work you too hard.'

Jessie gave him a half-smile.

'I'm really impressed with your skills. I think you could have handled it all today without my help. Just remember the farmers have experience too, so you're not alone.'

Jessie was wondering if she'd bitten off more than she could chew but she found Max's kind words reassuring.

'I suppose it'll take me a while to get into the swing of things.'

Max dropped her at her gate.

'Coming in for a brew? I'm dying for a cup of tea.'

'No thanks, Jessie. I've got a few urgent calls to make back at the house and I promised Clara I'd put up a shelf for her today.'

'Okay. What have you lined up for tomorrow?'

'I've got a bit of surgery to do near Queenstown in Closeburn. A colleague, Robbie Byrnes from the Vet's Cooperative shares his clinic with me for minor surgical procedures.'

'Oh, great! I love surgery.'

'I want you to come and see what he does, as he'll be a great resource for you. He runs the clinic in Closeburn twice a week. You'll be able to run your own clinic once a week as I have been doing. I'll see you here at eight. I need to get there on time. He has some sterilisations to do and you can assist us.'

When Max drove off, Jessie had butterflies in her stomach that she usually experienced when she didn't know if she was afraid or just excited. Now things were happening. Today she assisted the birth of a Highlander calf and twin Merino lambs. Tomorrow she'll be doing surgery.

Did this mean that she was going to cope with this formidable role of the remote vet after all? She hoped it was the forerunner of ongoing success.

***

At the end of the month, Max completed assisting Jessie with her orientation and departed. This was the last she would see of him for a while as he and Clara were about to embark on a trip around the North Island for a few months. Max reassured her she could call him at any time on her radiophone. Robbie Byrnes, the vet she visited near Closeburn would also be at her disposal.

Max had been generous enough to offer her his vehicle while they were away. He said he and his wife would drop it off in the morning before they leave for their trip.

'We'll slip the keys through your cat door.' Before he drove off, he said he was leaving her to it, that she was highly capable, and he had complete confidence in her. He and his wife live in Glenorchy so he would be able to rescue her if she got out of her depth after he returned from his holiday.

'Wait—I forgot something. I'm going to leave you my Motorola Carphone with battery recharger and batteries. I'll give you a quick lesson first. Unless you already know how to use one?'

'Oh, no I don't. I'd been thinking about purchasing one when I go into Queenstown next.'

'Well, you won't have to for a while. Hold on to it and give it back once you've got one of your own. Now let me show you how to use it.' He went into great detail about the channels and ranges of the Carphone. As he started the engine of the Land Rover, he leaned out the window. 'And remember I said to keep the batteries topped up.' He tooted a few times then disappeared out the gate and around the corner out of sight.

231

Now she was on her own. She was it. The only remote vet for miles. It gave her a foreboding feeling that she kept fighting. At times like this, she prayed for protection, courage, and strength.

***

A month later she had completely settled into her new role and most of the clients so far had been warm and welcoming except for the few grumpy farmers who ruffled her feathers. She was sure she would be able to rise above their prejudice.

Today was her first day off in a long stretch. She had planned to go for a ride on her bicycle in the countryside. She could have gone for a horse ride as Hope had told her she could take Misty out riding any time she liked. But she would rather have her own horse to ride. She intended to buy one, but she told herself the new vehicle must come first.

She pulled her bike out from between all the empty cartons she had thrown into the garage and checked the tyres. Where had she put the bike pump? It was one thing after another that she couldn't find. She'd been so fatigued the first day she was unpacking that she'd just randomly put things away without any kind of system.

She found the pump in her bedside table drawer for some reason. Now, where was her water bottle she took with her on her bike? The one that fits into the bottle holder. She found it crammed into the bottom of her rucksack in her wardrobe.

She was finally ready to go and started to push her bike out the garage door when she heard the phone ring inside the house. She guessed it was Hope and just got to the phone in time, puffing. She was able to say breathlessly, 'Hi Hope. You caught me just in time. I was on my way out on a bike ride.'

'Mack and Cole have organised a hike through the beech forest on Mount Alfred. There are awesome views from up there. I know what an avid climber you are, and when I told Mack that, he insisted you join us.'

'Oh, did he now? I haven't climbed since my school days when Dad used to take my brother and me up Mount Ruapehu. I haven't even got any climbing gear down here.'

'We have all the gear. It can be a bit cold in May but we'll be okay if we have the right clothing. I'll give you some crampons, as you'll need to carry them in your daypack as there is a bit of ice around.'

Jessie guessed she could give it a try as she had missed the mountains when she was in the Waikato, but lately, there had been no time for recreation.

'Drop by at nine on Saturday. You can come with us. Mack says he will meet us at the car park. Why don't you come over for dinner tomorrow night, Jessie? I haven't seen anything of you for a while. Let's celebrate your new role.'

Jessie accepted Hope's invitation the next evening. Once she had eaten a full roast chicken dinner with all the trimmings, she almost fell asleep in the armchair where she sat by the fire in the lounge. The mature low-alcohol apple cider that Cole had uncorked to have with their meal didn't help. It still packed a punch, even without much alcohol and just a small glass with her food was enough to put her to sleep.

'Are you sure you can drive home, Jessie? You can stay in the guest room. I can give you some nightwear.'

'No thanks, I need to do some paperwork before I go to bed. The cool night air will soon wake me up. I'll see you at your house at around nine on Saturday.'

'Wait! I'll just go and get the crampons.' Hope hurried away and brought back the crampons and a thick Anorak.

'Here—you're going to need the jacket as well.'

***

Jessie wound down her window as she pulled out onto the road and took a deep breath of the pure country air. She could smell the newly cut hay in the fields opposite and caught a whiff of fresh silage that gave her a nostalgic feeling reminding her of home.

The full moon lit up the road like a city highway and illuminated the terrified opossums that stood still on the road, dazzled by the headlights of her vehicle. Jessie was aware of them and drove with extra caution at night. She hated seeing animals that had been killed on the road by passing vehicles, even though this was sometimes unavoidable.

She had to force herself to stay awake to do her book work. Now that she was working freelance, she had to complete a report of all her visits at the end of each month for the Vet Cooperative. It was going to be a lot of work for her keeping on top of tax returns and such like. But it would all be worth it in the end. Who knows? Maybe one day she could afford to pay an assistant to deal with that.

Early the next morning her first visit was to a small Hereford Stud near the Rees River. The farmer, Buck, was a widower, one of the grumpy men that Max talked about who didn't like female vets. Some of his cattle needed, health checks, as there had been an outbreak of Leptospirosis in the Canterbury area and due to the recent flooding of his farm, he was worried a few of his herd had contracted it. He had phoned the Vet Cooperative to request a visit but didn't know the vet would be Jessie.

She knocked on the door loudly but still, there was no answer. She then tried the large cast-iron knocker. No one came to the door.

'Who are you? What are you wanting?'

Jessie nearly jumped out of her leather boots as she turned around to see a cantankerous figure standing over her in his threadbare denim dungarees.

'Oh ... hi. I'm Jessie your new vet.'

'What did you say? Where's Max? He usually comes up here.'

Jessie shook inside. This man was one of the difficult farmers Max had warned her about.

'Sorry, didn't you know? Max has retired and is now away on holiday. He has handed his clients over to me. I am a senior vet.'

'Oh, is that right? Well, I don't agree with all these changes, and I don't know if you can handle the cattle.'

'That's not a problem—I grew up on beef and sheep farm. Let me have a look at them.'

'Well, I'm not happy about all this, but I suppose I've got no jolly choice! Follow me then.'

Jessie picked up her leather bag and traipsed along behind him to a large barn where he kept half a dozen heifers inside away from the others. She pulled some rubber gloves out of her bag and other equipment then started examining each animal while Buck held them still. When she'd finished examining them and writing her report, Buck invited her into the house for a cup of tea and offered her a seat in the dining room.

'If you were a bloke, I'd offer you a cold beer.'

'Actually, I don't drink alcohol—I don't like it. I prefer tea, thanks.'

'Hmm. I'll put the kettle on.'

Jessie's awkwardness caused her continual chatter. 'I don't think your cattle have Leptospirosis. It appears to be some kind of cold virus. It would be best to keep them away from the others, especially the one with a cough. Perhaps let them bed in your nice warm barn.'

Buck nodded and handed her a plain arrowroot biscuit. She didn't care much for them but accepted.

'Here is my invoice. You can pay by cheque now or post it to me.'

Buck was taken aback by her self-confident assertiveness. 'Right you are. Just wait—I'll go get my book.'

Jessie's eyes darted over to the photos on his fireplace shelf. It looked like his wife and family.

'Have you been on your own long up here?' Jessie dared ask, handing him the invoice.

'Fifty years we lived up here until my wife had a stroke and passed away five years ago. Not much chop on your own. The kids all live overseas.'

Jessie realised why the widowed man would feel bitter. His coldness towards her was not personal at all—just born out of constant loneliness.

***

Some days later Jessie received a late-night call from Hope. She had rung to tell her someone had stolen the young black stallion that Mack had purchased from Joel. That put the damper on her living alone now that she was aware there were criminals in the area.

A few days later she read in the newspaper that the police had no other reporting of stolen horses. The culprits seemed only to have been interested in Mack's new stallion. But why?

The next day Jessie had the day free and popped in to visit Hope who'd done some baking and invited Jessie to stay for afternoon tea.

Jessie stood on the front doorstep struggling to pull her long boots off. 'I'm sure my feet swell up in the heat. I'll have to sit down to get them off.'

'Come in and have a scone. I made some jam with those strawberries I froze last summer.'

'Delicious. I wish I could make scones like yours. Mine come out like rocks.'

'There's a trick to making them. I'll show you on your next day off if you like.'

'So ... what's happened? You know—to poor Mack's stallion.'

'Apparently, they cut the fence to take Zoro out from the back of his farm where there is a small lane they must have used. Mack was distraught since he had seen blood on the grass by the barbed wire fence. The police believe the horse has been targeted and they must have known it was on the property.'

'How would they know? I suppose one of their friends tipped them off. I wonder why they want him that much, to go to such lengths.'

'At least he still has our branding. He has the mark we freeze branded him with. It has DRR for Dart River Ranch on his rump just by his tail. We photograph all our horses' brandings, so we have a record of it,' said Hope.

'Keep me informed. I'll make enquiries with all my clients and keep an eye out on their properties too.'

***

Saturday couldn't come quick enough for Jessie. She'd been up early, full of anticipation for the climb up Mount Alfred. She packed her truck and headed off to meet up with Hope and Cole who were outside in the driveway packing their Ute already.

'Just in time for a brew before we head off. Sling your backpack into the back of the Ute.' Cole walked over to help her.

Jessie glanced over at Hope and for the first time could detect she was actually pregnant although her slight build seemed to make it not so noticeable. 'Are you sure you should be hiking in your condition? It's not exactly a walk in the park, is it? I hope you have checked with your midwife.' Jessie put her hand on Hope's shoulder to make sure she had her attention.

'Don't worry, I'm fine. Yes, I've checked with my midwife. I'm four months now, and it's okay as I did a few strenuous hikes before I got pregnant. I'm quite fit.'

'Okay, you win. Please be careful.'

They drank their tea while Cole checked the petrol and oil in the Ute.

'Come on, ladies, time to go or Mack will be standing in the car park on his own.' Cole threw the last bag into the Ute.

As they wound their way up through Dart River Valley along the Glenorchy-Routeburn Road, Jessie caught sight of patches of snow on the branches of trees and as they climbed higher up the valley, ice appeared on the road.

'Darn! I heard there had been a bit of snow falling last night but not this low. I hope we won't need chains on the tyres.' Cole leaned out his window to inspect the road.

'Oh ... how are we going to get to the summit if there's snow?'

'You'll be okay. We are carrying all the right gear. It's not a huge mountain, in fact, it's one of the smaller ones.' Cole looked at Jessie in the back seat. She just sat still. Was she quietly regretting she had agreed to come?

'If I can do it in my state, you can Jessie. We can take our time. The sign up there says it takes six to eight hours, but that's there and back. There's no rush, we have all day.'

Mack was sitting on a log eating an apple. His face was much bronzer since Jessie saw him last and he had gained solid muscle. Perhaps he had just grown up. She almost tripped when she stepped out of her vehicle.

'Can I help with anything?' he asked her as she went to the back of the Land Rover to fetch her bag.

'No, I've got it covered thanks.'

'It's been a while since I saw you last. At their wedding, wasn't it?' Mack pointed at Hope and Cole.

'Yeah, I guess so. Golly, it's been that long.'

'I thought you would have been down sooner as you used to like it here so much.' Mack was persistent.

'I would have been down, but the clinic was always so busy and short-staffed. I just couldn't get away.'

'Well, she's here now, Mack so let's make the most of it,' replied Hope, who appeared irritated by his seeming annoyance that Jessie hadn't been around.

'Shall we get going then? I don't know what to expect up there seeing that it snowed up here last night. We'll just have to be careful. Hope—you take a break whenever you want and we'll stop.' Cole was the gentleman, Jessie thought as she imagined what it would be like to have such a kind, caring man in her life. But for now, she'd have to take care of herself. She was even wondering if she could keep up with Hope, even though she was pregnant.

Chapter Six

They walked slowly, stumbling over the large roots and vines that covered the forest pathway, zigzagging their way up towards the summit. The fresh snow became thicker, and icicles appeared on the branches of the beech trees.

Two hours later on the last lap to the top, as they rounded the corner past huge overhanging rocks, a carpet of snow covered the track. A thick mist hung over the whole area giving it a mystical appearance then it quickly disappeared, revealing a bright blue sky that illuminated the white snow.

'Let's stop for lunch. I've packed a thermos of hot chocolate if anyone would like to have some.' Hope pulled it out and placed it on a lightweight rug she had packed to sit on.

They sat eating and talking. Mainly it was Mack asking Jessie all about her work in the clinic in Waikato and her new role in Glenorchy. His eyes stayed fixated on her.

'We need to prepare ourselves if we are going any further as the mountain can be prone to freak blizzards. There was one up here last night. There's usually not so much snow around this early in the year. We'll need to get our crampons on now as I can see ice on the rocks and it's pretty steep going up there. I'm carrying some ropes just in case,' said Cole.

'I've packed some climbing ropes too,' Mack added.

Jessie stopped eating and started fumbling around in her backpack. Her face dropped and furrows appeared in her brow.

'What's wrong Jessie? Is everything okay?'

'Ah, no. I think I've forgotten something and you're not going to be very happy.'

Mack stared at her, squinting through the glare from the snow.

'I've left my crampons behind—the ones you lent me, Hope.'

'Oh no! You won't be able to go up to the summit now. I'll have to stay back with you and let the men go up without us,' said Hope.

'No, she can't continue the climb now. We'll have to turn around and walk back down,' said Cole, gruffly.

'You won't have to do that. I'm wearing special tramping boots for icy terrain. They grip really well. I'll be perfectly fine, don't worry.'

Hope looked over at Mack who was the most experienced climber amongst them. 'What do you think, Mack? Should she continue with all that ice up there?'

'No. I think it would be foolish, but Jessie will have to make up her own mind. Tell you what—I'll accompany Jessie on the steep incline towards the summit and it would be a good idea if Hope sticks close to Cole. What do you all think?'

Cole looked at the two girls and nodded. 'He's right, girls. We need to go in twos from now on and tread very carefully.'

The hike up the last stretch of the mountain was arduous. Hope needed to have several breaks to catch her breath and Jessie began to think it was a bad idea all around for Hope to be taking such a risk. But she was just as experienced a climber as Jessie was and Cole was overprotective. But it was herself she should have been more concerned about, and she was to find it out quickly.

The terrain had changed suddenly from thick, crisp snow to ice and now and then Jessie's boots slipped but she managed to keep her balance. 'Here, take my arm if you think you are slipping,' Mack said, as he stopped momentarily.

'Oh, that won't be necessary—I'm fine. You don't need to fuss.'

Within minutes after saying that, her body began sliding away from Mack's side uncontrollably. Her boots suddenly acted like skis and shot sideways propelling her towards the side of the narrow mountainside where she thought she was going to plummet over the edge. Before she realised what had happened, she jettisoned onto her side causing a stabbing pain in her shoulder. Her body continued to jettison itself then bang—instantly it reached its destination with a hard thud as her back slammed against an ice wall—she had fallen in a deep crevice. The echo of Hope screaming in the distance penetrated her ears.

Her ribs hurt. She had the wind knocked out of her. Worst of all, she peered downwards and all she could see was a blue abyss. As she stayed dead still, she could hear Mack calling from up above.

'Don't move Jessie, just don't move. I'm coming down to get you,' he yelled. Jessie detected a quaver in his voice. All she could muster was a faint, 'Okay Mack.'

He tied the rope around his waist and threw it down to her yelling, 'Grab hold of this loop if you can and place it over your head until I get down to you.'

Cole made Hope stay back and sit on a nearby rock that he had scraped the snow off. He carefully walked over to see if he could help.

'I'm going to set up a belay for you to bring her up on after I have abseiled down to her and set up her harness. What do you think?'

Cole inspected the ice. 'Ah, that's pretty solid. Best test it with your weight first, of course.'

Mack poked around until he found what he thought was solid enough ice for the screws and secured the ropes to the anchors.

Jessie waited patiently for him to abseil down to her. A dark cloud of guilt and regret began to descend on her. What has she done? Why was she so stubborn and put all her friends at risk? Mack will think she is so stupid. Her thoughts tormented her while she waited on a narrow ledge. She prayed quietly—Please God, keep us all safe, and give the men the strength to get us both back up to safety. Thank you.

Waiting the few minutes for Mack seemed like hours. Then he appeared at her side. She could hardly feel her hands in her sodden woollen gloves. She hadn't thought to bring leather gloves with her. Mack helped her remove them and gave her his spare leather pair.

'I'm sorry, Mack. I had no idea what was initially a fine sunny day would turn out like this. We should have listened to the weather report.'

'The report was for fine weather today. It's just that we thought the freak snowstorm last night was in the higher mountains, not here. Let's get on. I'm going to attach some ropes to you and Cole will belay you back up. You will have to dig your boots in as hard as you can to try to give you some lift. I'll be right beside you with and another rope will attach us.'

Cole managed to get Jessie safely back up top with Mack guiding her all the way up. She collapsed with relief, prostrate on the snow. When she had freed herself from the ropes, the weight of guilt bombarded her again. She stood up then trudged over and sat on the rock next to Hope and Mack followed suit.

'I'm sorry I've caused all this trouble. I didn't realise how dangerous it would be without crampons. I was so determined to see the views from up here I lost perspective and put you all at risk.'

'And I should have insisted that you turn back when you asked me what I thought,' said Mack. 'Let's get going back to where the path is safe. I think we'd better get Hope back down out of this cold.' He looked at her. 'Your poor baby must be cold in your little oven.' With that, Cole came to Hope's rescue and helped her back on the path.

Mack's comments warmed Jessie's soul as he revealed his caring and compassionate nature. She was beginning to have strong feelings for him.

'Thanks, Mack. I appreciate your concern,' said Hope, smiling and patting him on his back.

Mack and Jessie started the descent with Hope and Cole in close pursuit as they cautiously made their way back down the mountain.

When they reached the bush and beech trees, they stopped for a rest and some food.

'I've brought another thermos of hot chocolate. It's in your pack, Cole.' Hope nodded at Cole who had removed his pack.

'Oh, so that's why it was so heavy. Let's get into it then.'

'I've got cups in my pack and some choky biscuits,' she said as she took off her own pack and placed it next to a large rock.

As they enjoyed their hot drinks, Jessie sat on an old log looking quite dejected. Mack must have noticed as he came along and sat next to her, putting his arm across her shoulders.

'Look, girl. Don't dwell on what happened up there. We were all at fault. We should have just turned around and come back down. Don't keep beating up on yourself.'

'Thanks, Mack.'

Hope approached and handed them both the packet of chocolate biscuits.

'I've got a bar of dark chocolate so we can have a decadent chocolate indulgence.' Jessie stood up and grabbed a packet from her backpack. She handed around a large bar of dark, almond nut chocolate.

For the rest of the descent down the mountain, Jessie's legs were like jelly from the rush of adrenaline that had been racing through her body. She noticed that Mack was still walking close by her protectively all the way to the carpark below.

When she arrived at the vehicle, Hope was leaning on the bonnet having a discussion with Cole and looked up as Jessie stood behind her.

'Oh, there you are. Are you okay after all the traumas? Mack said you have sore ribs.'

'Oh, they're alright. Just bruised probably.'

Mack joined them. 'I think she was pretty brave back there. I noticed you were super calm.' He nodded at Jessie. 'There's still the mountain climber in you,' he said with a gleam in his eyes.

Hope stood up and stretched her back then rubbed her abdomen. 'We'd better be getting back. I have a heap of papers to sort out before my riding class starts on Monday. It's the school holidays and I have a group of college children arriving,' said Hope.

'Jessie, why don't you ride with me? I can drop you home.'

'That's nice of you, Mack but I can't—my car is at Hope's house. I came with them.'

Mack's face dropped.

'Oh, okay. Perhaps another time.'

'Yes, that would be great. You could pop over and visit sometime.' Instantly Jessie regretted being so forward and impulsive.

'I'd like that. I'll take you up on it.'

Later that night, just as she was about to drift off to sleep, Jessie had been going over the day's events in her mind. She had relieved herself of the guilt but now she wanted to find some way to make it up to Mack. He was the one who had really risked his own safety by rescuing her. How was she going to make it up to him?

She started to plan in her mind how she could help Mack get Zoro back. Perhaps she could fabricate some kind of reason to visit the farms in the area and offer to give their horses a free health examination to check them for the Equine Influenza. The authorities have already quarantined the cases they found. The outbreak started to spread in the Queenstown area. This was the perfect justification for Jessie to visit farms where there are horses as they are now all at risk of getting the disease.

Chapter Seven

Perhaps there was going to be a breakthrough in her quest to find Zoro. Jessie checked all of Max's patients' records to find out which farms carried horses. A week later the replies started trickling in and she had a positive response, no refusals. They were not able to refuse on legal grounds and if they did, Jessie could obtain a Court order to enter their property if she suspected an animal had an infectious disease, especially if there was an outbreak in the area. She spent another week making appointments over the phone. She had more than a dozen farms to visit locally taking tissue and blood samples and identifying diseases in sick animals.

This placed an extra burden on Jessie. In the meantime, Mack had called to ask if he could drop by as he was heading over her way. Jessie's head was spinning, engulfed by the hefty workload with all the extra visits to make. She turned him down and said she would catch up with him, once she had reduced her workload. She didn't tell him her plan to try to find Zoro—not yet. She wanted to wait until she had some positive results to give him.

After two weeks of checking out every horse on fifteen farms in the area, she came to a stalemate. The day she finished the last visit, she went home early and crashed on her bed, every muscle in her body aching, listening to the pounding of her heart hard against her eardrums. She was thinking her blood pressure must have risen to hear her heart that loudly. Within minutes, her eyes drooped, and she drifted into a deep sleep. Two hours later she awakened to the cold and a fly buzzing around her head. She'd forgotten to take the meat out of the freezer for her evening meal and succumbed to eating leftover lamb curry from the previous day.

After wolfing down her food and washing it down with some of Hope's home-made ginger beer, she stretched out on a lounge chair and perused her list of farms she visited. Not one of them had a horse that slightly resembled Zoro, though she saw plenty of black horses. That was it. She wasn't going to be able to prove to Mack that she wasn't an idiot after all.

***

Jessie received a visit from Cole. He told her that Butch had read in the local news that Captain Richardson had purchased a small farm near Queenstown near Lake Wakatipu and had started a horse ranch there. He had some ranch hands that had been acting suspiciously in the area and local farmers were keeping an eye on them. Cole went on to say that he'd been complaining to folk about the Kaimanawa herd he'd lost in the hills around the Rees Valley several years ago and that some local rancher had captured them and taken possession of them. He was carrying a huge grudge, according to Butch and said he would find them and get his horses back. But that would be illegal. Of course, Jessie asked Cole to let Joel know as soon as possible in case there was any trouble from the ranch hands or Richardson himself as she clearly remembered Max telling her that he thought the ranch hands were thugs.

All this set Jessie thinking and later that day she picked up the phone and called Cole back to suggest Butch do some snooping around Richardson's ranch. She believed it was a possibility they could have taken Zoro if they knew he was from his original herd. Jessie suggested that Butch make some excuse to get onto his farm.

***

Butch drove up to the large wooden gate. He could see that Richardson was home as his truck was sitting in the driveway. He walked up to the door, knocked, and peered through a side window to see if there was any movement. No one came to the door. The sound of dogs barking in the field at the back of the farm was evidence that he must have been working them away from the ranch house. Butch wandered over to the stables, hesitated then walked on. In the distance on the far side of the ranch, he caught a glimpse of a tall figure and heard him snarling gruffly at one of the dogs which were busy rounding up a flock of sheep.

Butch walked along through the entrance to the stables and carefully peered into each stall. He had seen four horses but not one of them was black. Zoro wasn't amongst this lot.

He cautiously wandered around the fence line that bordered the ranch house and the paddocks. He scanned each paddock meticulously. In one field there was just a small herd of Jersey heifers. In the next, a couple of bulls and then in the one next to that, to his surprise, more horses. Yes! There was a black one.

As he walked closer to the fence, there he stood, noble-looking—his head held high in the air in such a way it gave him a majestic look, with his tail flying high too. To Butch's amazement, the stallion and two other horses approached him at the fence. Then the other two horses started fighting, rearing, and the black one appeared annoyed, kicking out at them. In a split second, Butch saw it—the letters DRR just below his tail. The other horses galloped off. The young black horse stayed at the fence. When Butch

249

put his hand out, the stallion licked his fingers. 'Well, you're a tame one, aren't you? This isn't your home and we are going to get you out of here.' Butch could see that the horse had a wound, a deep cut that hadn't healed properly and obviously festering.

'Hey! What are you doing here? Clear out!'

Butch swung around to see a tall, unshaven Richardson looming over him. Butch was a strong, stocky fellow but short in stature. He startled, almost falling back against the fence, although he wasn't afraid of him.

'Gidday—Butch Rogers is my name. I'm visiting farms in the area to offer a free hoof check and if you want, I can offer a substantial discount for shoeing for first-time clients.'

'Is that right? What did you say your name is ... Butch, did you say? Oh yeah, I heard you've been the local blacksmith for thirty years. Is that right?'

'Sure is. I suppose you think I'm just drumming up business, but I like to have a good rapport with all the locals. I offer the best rates for miles around here.'

'Fair enough. Have you time, today? I'll get those horses into the stalls if you like.'

'Sorry mate. I'll have to book you next week sometime. By the way—I noticed that wound on the young black stallions shoulder. It's infected, mate. You really should get that seen by the vet as the infection can affect the muscle and he could end up lame.'

'Oh, okay. I'll get that seen to. What day can you come next week?'

'How about Friday? I have a whole day free then.'

'Great. I'll see you out that gate—darn thing the latch keeps jamming.'

Butch couldn't believe he actually spoke to the culprit who stole Mack's stallion. Richardson waved him off while Butch was feeling a little guilty that he was about to report him to the police. He couldn't wait to get home to ring Mack and Jessie.

Mack came off the phone to Butch and tried hard to control the large teardrops that oozed from his eyes. It didn't work. With a huge sigh, he let go of the bottled-up tension he'd been harbouring all these weeks of waiting and praying, deeply missing the friendly young stallion to whom he had become so attached. He had spent hours training Zoro so that he became easy to manage and was a fine workhorse for the farm. Wait till he tells Cole.

Once he had composed himself, he rang Cole and asked him to join him and go to the police and then retrieve Zoro and bring him back in his horse truck. He also let Jessie know what they were doing.

The next day, the two men sat at the local police station showing the officers the photos of Zoro's branding and every photo and video clip that Mack had of him. Cole was there as a witness as he had photos of him when newborn and one of him being branded.

The police accompanied the men to Richardson's farm and arrested him for theft while Cole and Mack loaded Zoro into the truck and took him home.

The first thing Mack did when Zoro was in the truck was to phone Jessie. 'Please, can you come, Jessie? I'm really worried that the wound might turn into septicaemia. He should have had antibiotics ages ago.'

'Sure, no problem. I'll be there as soon as I can. I'll just pack my treatment bag and be off.'

At last, Jessie had found a way to return Mack's rescuing gesture by making sure she healed that bad wound on Zoro's shoulder. 'Thank you, God. I knew you'd come through for me and find me a way to settle scores with Mack. You know how much this means to me.'

Jessie sang in a high voice all the way to Mack's farm with her windows wide open. A farmer driving past with his truck window wound down called out 'beautiful!' and tooted at her.

For the next few weeks, Jessie visited Zoro every day to observe the result of the antibiotics she had given him. Of course, there was plenty of time for her to get to know Mack really well and a strong friendship began to blossom.

Chapter Eight

Today was Jessie's first proper day off in months. Since she'd taken on the extra task of visiting Zoro each day to attend his wound, she'd found no time for herself to unwind.

More snow had fallen in the nearby hills and completely covered the mountain tops. She was grateful for the old potbelly stove for burning wood. It stood in the corner of her lounge, but it had gone out during the night although the lounge was still warm from the remaining embers. She'd been so tired the night before that she'd forgotten to top the fire up before she went to bed.

She flopped into her lounge armchair and was trying to decide what to do for the rest of the day when she heard banging.

Who would be visiting her, apart from Hope? She hadn't said anything about dropping around to see her. The banging became much louder, so she got out of her chair to check the door. As she stood up, she almost jumped out of her skin. There was a tanned face and leather Stetson filling the frame in her window.

'Mack! I wonder what brings him here,' she muttered on her way to open the door.

'I'm not too early, am I? Happened to be just passing on my way back from the General Store to pick up some hard feed for my sheep. I've had some heavy snow in some of my lower paddocks and they need extra feed.'

'No, it's not too early. I've been awake since dawn. I got a bit cold when the Pot Belly went out. Please … come on in. I'll put the kettle on.' Jessie stopped at the mirror in the hall to push her hair into place but it was unmanageable. It needed a trim, and she hadn't had the time to go into Glenorchy to the only hairstylist for miles. She appeared dishevelled.

Meanwhile, Mack was struggling to get his boots off and his socks were wet. Jessie glanced at the wet socks. 'Here, bring them by the fire. I'll just stoke it up again. Put them on this rack and they'll be dry by the time we've finished our tea.'

'Actually, the reason I'm here is to ask if you'd like a load of wood. I've heaps of pines on my farm, and I can cut some and bring a truckload over if you like. That's in return for all the care you've given Zoro.'

Jessie was uncomfortable with his offer. In her mind, she was no longer in debt to him after caring for his horse. But she needed the wood.

'That's very kind of you but I'll pay you for it.'

'No, I won't have that. Please let me do it, Jessie. It's no trouble, honest. On one condition though—that you make me one of those to die for blackberry pies you gave me to try when you first moved here, remember?'

'I don't have any berries though. They are summer fruit.'

'No, but I have—I collected plenty from up on the farm last summer and froze them. I eat them occasionally with ice cream. It's a pity it's not blackberry season right now. Look … I promise you I'll take you out berry picking next summer. There's a great spot not far from here.'

'I'll look forward to that when I can get a break. I'll be back in a few minutes—I'll just pour the tea.'

Jessie scurried into her bathroom and quickly brushed her hair. She desperately wanted to change her old worn-out track pants and tee-shirt and put on something more eye-catching, but it would be far too obvious and Mack sat waiting patiently for his cup of tea.

She carried the tray of tea, a plate of muffins she had made the night before and tomato sandwiches into the lounge.

'Ah—fresh baking. How do you find time to do all that as a full-time rural vet?'

'Oh, I usually bake a batch of muffins each week to take in the car on my visits. I take a couple of them and some fruit. That gives me enough energy for the day.'

Mack wolfed down a sandwich and took a muffin.

'Mmm, they taste good. Blueberry, my favourite—oh yes, I knew there was something I wanted to tell you.' He took a large bite of his muffin and then took some minutes to clear his mouth. He continued, 'the crook who stole Zoro—that bloke Captain Richardson—he isn't really a captain any longer, though he used to be when he was in the British army. He's one of those pretentious people who like to pull rank as a civilian. Anyway, he's going to Court next week. The police have plenty of evidence to charge him. This will implicate poor Joel as he'll have to give evidence that he branded Zoro and that one of the Kaimanawa horses was a sire. He'd mustered them legally when they were running wild.'

'Wow! That's pretty heavy, isn't it? Poor Joel having to go to Court. Hope doesn't need all that worry about her father when she's about to have a baby. It's due anytime now.'

'It won't be a problem for Joel. He has given the police plenty of evidence and I'm also a witness. I took part in the muster when we captured Zoro's father. It'll be a storm in a teacup and all blow over pretty quickly. Just you wait and see.'

'Hold on, that's my telephone. Sorry, but I'm on call so I'll have to take it.' Jessie handed Mack another muffin then hurried into the small room she'd made into an office. She picked up the phone. It had an exclusive business landline number. Most of the calls came directly from the Vet Cooperative's Call Centre.

'What! Really? Of course, Cole, I'll be right over.' She put the phone down and hastened back into the lounge.

'I'm sorry Mack but I have to rush away. It seems that Hope has gone into labour and the midwife is miles away at another birth. Cole doesn't want to call the rescue helicopter unless they're sure she's in proper labour and he's asked if I could examine her. They know I've delivered babies when I did a short stint as a paramedic.'

'Really? You'd better go then. I'll shift my truck out of the driveway, and I'll be letting you know soon when I can bring that load of firewood over to you.' He leaned on the front door post pulling on his knee-high leather boots after having already grabbed his socks from the fireplace.

Meanwhile, Jessie had picked up her black leather medical bag and said goodbye as she raced into her vehicle. She called out through her window, 'I'll phone and let you know the outcome later tonight. Thanks for the offer of the firewood.' She gave him a warm smile and his face just lit up. He lowered his Stetson at her as she drove off while he walked to his truck with a spring in his step and a radiant grin that wouldn't leave his face.

Chapter Nine

Jessie's Land Rover made its way through the light dusting of freshly fallen snow down the long driveway to Dart River Ranch homestead. Cole was waiting for her on the front porch and rushed out to greet her, his eyes seeming to jump out of his head with angst.

'Quickly, come as fast as you can. Her waters have broken!' he bellowed before Jessie has opened the vehicle's door. Cole rushed forward and grabbed her medical bag, almost dragging her up the steps by her arm. She could hear Hope groaning loudly down the hallway. She hurried into the room where she lay sprawled across the bed, her face twisted with furrowed brows as though she was in a torture chamber. Hope burst forth, 'I'm certainly relieved to see you!'

'I'll have to examine you to see how far you are then I can attend to this pain of yours.' With that, Cole left the room.

'Let me know when you have finished,' he called behind him as he shut the door.

Jessie finished her examination and opened the door to let Cole back in.

'Have you been in a warm bath yet like your midwife advised? Heat is a great pain reliever in childbirth. Let's get you into some warm water.'

'Anything to kill this pain!' Hope bellowed.

'Come on,' Jessie said, tugging on Cole's arm. 'You need to fill that lovely claw bath of yours right to the brim.'

'Won't the baby drown in there?' Cole's eyes almost popped out of his head. He started to hyperventilate.

'She's not fully dilated by a long shot. You are going to need to calm down, slow down your breathing so you can help your wife,' Jessie spouted.

Cole helped Hope get into the bath. She slumped into the water and lay there like a beached whale while Jessie popped a rolled-up towel behind her neck. She took a packet of Epsom salts from her pocket and threw some into the bathwater.

'I'm sorry—I can't administer nitrous oxide gas or give you Pethidine injections. I'm only qualified to use these with animals.'

'Her midwife lent her a TENS machine—you know ... it sends some kind of electrical impulses to the skin to help with pain relief. But we've forgotten how to use it.' Cole darted back into the bedroom and pulled the machine out of a cupboard while Hope lay in the bath groaning, but not as loudly as when Jessie first arrived.

'Oh, really?' Jessie leaned over to inspect the machine.

'I know exactly how it works. I would have used it in the first place had I known. But the warm water has certainly made a big difference.'

Almost two hours later, Jessie helped Cole get Hope back onto the bed to review her progress again.

'It won't be long now, Hope. Your baby will soon be on its way,' said Jessie, squeezing her hand.

Cole filled her a hot water bottle to hold then as she lay on her side he carried out the massage that he had so often rehearsed at the ante-natal class in Glenorchy.

An hour later, having examined Hope again, Jessie announced that the baby's head was crowning. 'I can just glimpse your baby's head. You're in the second stage of labour.' She called Cole to come back in and repeated it to him. Before long, Hope was screaming and pushing her baby out with each contraction until a strong, healthy baby boy lay across her abdomen after Jessie had cut the umbilical cord. Hope lay motionless with exhaustion, as she had been in labour for some time before Cole had rung Jessie. As she held her newborn close, Cole hovered gently, his long arms around them both.

Myra, Hope's mother had been eagerly waiting around to help. Cole handed the infant to her to wash, dress, and wrap in the shawl that Hope had made for him. His bassinet was ready. Jessie dealt with the afterbirth and Cole helped to wash his wife with Myra's help.

'Do you have a name for him yet?' Myra asked?

Cole looked at Hope who nodded her approval. 'Bertie—it's a name we both like. I suppose people will think his proper name is Albert, but it's not. It's going to stay as Bertie.'

Myra's face lit up. 'Oh, you've named him after my father!'

It was just a coincidence that Cole chose the same name as her grandfather, but Hope said nothing.

'I know he died before you were born so it's nice you have named Bertie after him, even though he was known as Albert, not Bertie.'

Cole winked at Hope and when Myra looked the other way he whispered, 'Leave it, no harm in letting her think that.'

Hope looked around to see Jessie still hovering over baby Bertie, 'I don't know what we would have done without you, Jessie,' said Hope. 'The midwife had intended to be here but she was called out to another emergency birth.' She wiped the beads of perspiration from her forehead with the back of her hand. 'Are you sure you're in the right occupation, as you were marvellous?'

'That comes from delivering all those lambs with Dad during my youth. I've had a good teacher.'

'Thank God you'd done a paramedics course. Or I could have been giving birth to a calf!' Hope managed to laugh as they both cracked up at that image.

'I hope you'll stay and have dinner with us over at our house,' said Myra. 'Cole can probably manage for a while and Hope just wants to sleep.'

'Sure—thank you, I will. I'll just examine Hope again and make sure everything's in order then I'll be right over.'

After she carried out that procedure and helped Hope put her baby on the breast, Jessie made sure Cole was able to cope and left the three of them alone. She was glad of the break, as it had been challenging for her, quite different from delivering four-legged animals and it had certainly boosted her confidence.

Jessie excused herself straight after her meal and couldn't wait to get home to phone Mack with the great news. Or was there perhaps another reason her heart was pounding as she got in the door and picked up the phone to ring him?

***

She struggled to control her breathing when he answered.

'Oh, hello, Mack. You wanted me to let you know the outcome of Hope's labour. She gave birth to a strong, healthy baby boy at four o'clock this afternoon. I stayed there to help clean her up and her parents invited me for dinner. Now I'm bushed—almost as exhausted as Hope is. Oh, by the way, they have named him, Bertie.'

'Wow! I'd say you are some special kind of vet that can do midwife stuff as well as look after animals. Very impressive.' Jessie went quiet. Her cheeks began to burn with embarrassment.

'Well ... catching up on our earlier conversation today. I said to give me a call when you want me to bring the firewood over to you. I hear we're in for a cold winter and we may get some heavy snow around here before too long. You'll need that fire.'

Jessie came off the phone and crashed onto her couch. The fire she'd lit in the morning was still burning as she lay there dozing. She imagined cosy evenings sitting in front of a fire with heavy snow outside with a fat cat lying on the hearth and enjoying a visit from Mack—letting his charming voice lull her into oblivion. She quickly shook herself out of her fantasy putting such idle thoughts out of her mind. Why would he be interested in a woman vet? Any relationship she'd had up until now had never lasted. The men were afraid of commitment. Maybe they just didn't like vets. Would Mack be any different? The men she had met in the Waikato had appeared to be after a dolly bird and she certainly wasn't anything like that. She'd been a bit of a tomboy in her pursuits, but she dressed like a lady when she did ever dress up. The thing is she just wasn't desperate for a man, although she'd been thinking lately how lonely it could be in such a remote place.

Chapter Ten

Mack had been struggling to make a viable income from his hundred acres in Glenorchy—it just wasn't sufficient land to make it work for him without a secondary income. If only he could have joined forces with his grandfather, and it saddened him to think of past regrets. Perhaps he could try him once more—really convince him that he is now a passionate and skilled farmer in all the rudiments of sheep and cattle farming as well as proficient in breaking horses, thanks to Joel Grey.

It was the end of a long day as he finished hammering in the barn he had been transforming into a new home. It was taking shape thanks to the recent help of a few church members who assisted him with lining the walls. He had some regret over buying a new barn for his animals and keeping the old one for a home that was poorly insulated. But with extra help from his church friends, he'll complete his new dwelling in time for the worst of the winter so his stock will have shelter in the storms.

He drove his quad bike down by the river to bring some sheep into the barn ready for collection the next day. They were off to the meat works. His border collie, Bluey, from the litter of Joel Grey's dog, Casey was the best sheepdog Mack had ever seen and had become his close friend and companion—just like Zoro.

Mack had a special way with animals, unlike other farmers apart from Joel Grey. It was a great attribute to have in a high country farmer. Bluey took no time at all jumping on the back of the quad bike and rounding up the paddock of sheep which Mack had chased through the gate down towards the barn where for pick-up the next morning.

Once he'd enclosed them, he checked the water levels and pellets in the troughs.

When Mack had finished feeding and watering the flock, he drove alongside the paddock where Zoro grazed. The animal saw him coming and trotted towards the gate. Looking down at the horse's shoulder, Mack could see that his wound had completely healed and offered him a carrot.

He loved working Zoro on the hills. He was a sure-footed animal and intelligent. Mack always rode the high country extra carefully on the quad bike. He didn't trust the machine on the steep, rugged slopes and usually only used it in the lower foothills.

He leaned over the fence looking straight at Zoro. 'What do you think of working on a large high country station, my boy? Can we handle it? The old man will probably say no again—but what if he says yes?' With that, Zoro pushed him hard in the chest with his head playfully and stood staring at him. It was as if he was saying yes—at least, that's what Mack was thinking. He decided to make one last attempt at trying to get hold of Walter and that evening he wrote him a letter.

The next morning Mack was sad to see his mature flock of sheep being sent off to the meat works. This was something new for him and he had regrets at cutting their lives short. It was so different from being a sheep shearer. But he convinced himself that farmers have a great role to play in feeding and clothing families and communities. He saw it as a necessity. No room for human emotion. One thing was for sure—he was going to be a humanitarian farmer and take care of his animals. Now there were fewer sheep to muster, the farm seemed kind of quiet although Mack still had a few hundred cattle. He hadn't yet built up his stock levels to a viable level on his hundred acres.

Chapter Eleven

Walter Reed had almost finished for the day. He'd been in the office with Aron Bendon his Station Manager discussing how to replace him. Aron had just resigned after thirteen years of managing Reed Station in the Dart Valley. His pregnant wife was near her time and so he'd decided to move them nearer to her family and a smaller station where he wouldn't be working such long hours. He planned to be able to enjoy some family time.

Walter had been about to tell him that he was also pulling back on account of his health and that Aron was going to have a lot more responsibility.

'This is no game for an old fella like me, Aron. This is the life for a young man. I don't know what I'm going to do as there aren't many young folk around here, let alone strong, young Station Managers.'

'Gee, I'm really sorry, Walter, but I've got to put my family first. I always told them I would. My wife, Sally is going to have twins and will need some help.'

'I know—I get you. But what am I going to do? I've such a substantial station here, I need a good manager.'

'You'll have to advertise. People all over New Zealand will see the advertisements. Doesn't have to be someone from around here.'

'And I've got to do all that interviewing and stuff. I'm past all that.'

'Well, I'm not going for a month. I'm sure I can help you with all that. We can interview them together.'

'I'll get going now. Don't bother getting up.'

'Actually, it's time for my afternoon nap in my hammock, so I'll follow you out onto the veranda.'

As the sun sank deep behind the mountain range, Walter waved to Aron who was on his way home to the station hand's cottage a mile down the road. He slid into his hammock on the covered veranda and pulled a piece of notepaper out of his pocket after putting on his dusty spectacles. He squinted then removed them, wiping the dust off with the sleeve of his Swaandri and placed them back on again. Even then, he struggled to see the details on the paper—

Mack Reed
RD Dart River Valley
Phone 03 123....

Walter grimaced then pulled his glasses off briskly. He let out a loud sigh. 'Darn! Stupid paper.'

The notepaper had got wet in his pocket when he'd been hosing out some stockyards and half the phone number was illegible. He struggled out of the hammock and walked into his kitchen where the light bulb was flickering. 'Huh! That confounded thing needs replacing already!' He pulled open a drawer and took out a writing pad and pen and then sat back at the dining table. Before the kitchen light went out, he quickly scratched a quick note, wrote urgent on the envelope and placed the letter inside.

Dear Mack

*****

Mack couldn't believe his eyes when he tore open the envelope he'd received later in the week. His heart raced. He could feel his pulse pounding in his temples and wanted to yell out and tell the world about the possible breakthrough.

'Thank you, God. I knew you wouldn't let me down. I've been patiently waiting for you to act and now you're finally coming through for me.' Mack had the first-hand experience of God often coming through in the eleventh hour.

What his grandfather intended for him was an enigma. Will they get on together? He was busting to ring and tell Jessie. Instead, he waited until he had spoken with Walter.

Sleep was elusive that night. He had stoked up the wood burner before going to bed, but the bone-chilling cold still penetrated him. The large, corrugated iron barn was hot in summer and cold in winter. Although the building was insulated, the internal walls were not finished. It wouldn't be long though, as his church had promised him a working bee would be there at the end of the month.

After tossing and turning for an hour, he got up and put the kettle on to make a hot drink. He sat in his armchair with his mug, fantasising how life could be on a large station. Is this his dream come true? An hour later his head started to droop, and he almost spilt the remains of the Milo drink when he jolted awake. Half asleep, he put the mug in the kitchen and got back into bed.

He prayed, Please, God, grant me the serenity to accept the things I cannot change

Courage to change the things I can, and the wisdom to know the difference.

With that ... he fell into a deep, peaceful sleep.

***

Jessie walked into the General Store almost knocking over the whole magazine stand with her bulky, leather shopping bag. She was in a hurry to gather her fortnight's supply of groceries before she started her working day.

She bent over to pick up the magazines she'd knocked to the floor. As she replaced them on the shelf, one, in particular, caught her attention—the new edition of the Australasian Veterinary Journal with a photo of a mobile veterinary clinic.

'Mmm, just what I need,' she muttered as she hauled the overloaded bag of supplies onto the counter.

'Goodness! You need a packhorse for that lot. Mind you, I won't complain. You've become a cherished regular customer of mine. I'll help you out to your vehicle with it if you like.'

'Aw, thanks, Mr Barnaby. I don't want to wear myself out before my rounds. I have a few farms to visit out this way and thought I'd do it all at once.'

'Just call me Barney—everyone else does. Though my first name is John, I've become rather partial to Barney.'

Jessie sensed the warmth in his voice. He was like most of the locals—friendly and helpful whenever possible, except for a miserable minority.

'Are you taking the magazine, Miss?' He pointed to the one she still held in her hand after she'd paid for the goods.

'Oh, stupid of me. I forgot about that. Yes, I'll take it.'

'Tell you what. You can have this one on me this time. Perhaps my old cat may need you someday and you might give me a discount.'

Jessie beamed, revealing a mouth full of well-cared-for teeth while Barney helped her out to the vehicle with her groceries.

'Thanks, Barney. I'd better get on my way. See you in a fortnight.'

He waved and went back inside the store.

Jessie fossicked around on the floor below the passenger seat. She'd brought a chilly bin for her meat and dairy products, although the outside temperature was getting cold enough to keep it cool.

Looking at her diary, there were three farms to visit— the first one being McKlintoch's Red Deer farm.

***

Doug McKlintoch called out roughly to his farm dog to get out of the way as Jessie approached his old Queenslander homestead. Doug stomped over towards Jessie's vehicle. She hesitated, not knowing where best to park. She glanced over towards the red-faced Scotsman who stood stiffly with his burly arms folded, eyeballing her. 'Over here! Park next to the shed, woman,' he shouted.

With that onslaught, a warm flush of blood rushed up her neck to her face. She was livid at being yelled out by the rude farmer when he'd never set eyes on her before. She wanted to turn around and take off back down the rough, stone driveway, as he didn't deserve a house call. But she had a responsibility towards the animals which were all under her care, just as most of the farm animals in the area had been previously under Max's care. This was her lot, and she had to either get used to it or go back to being a small animal vet in the city. She banished the thought immediately.

'Sorry, Mr McKlintoch. I didn't see you waving at me as I drove in, and I certainly wasn't aware you had planted fresh grass seed over there.'

His frown relaxed as he beckoned her to follow him around the back of the house to a small enclosure with a high wire mesh for treating the stag.

'It's his front leg on the left side there.'

'Can I get inside? I mean—is he tame enough to approach?'

'Of course, you've no worries there. This one likes a good scratch under the antlers, but you need to keep watching how he moves his head and keep your face away from them.'

'Well, I have to sedate him, anyway. If you could get him ready for me please.'

Jessie dived into her bag to take out the sedative injection she had already prepared.

Within minutes the over-towering animal had gone down and Jessie quickly went to work cleaning and stitching the leg.

'These stitches will just dissolve in a few weeks. I'll be back and check the wound then, and in the meantime, you'll need to keep an eye out for any infection.'

In no time at all, Jessie had packed her bag up and after making another appointment to return, she started walking back to her vehicle, not wanting to stay a minute longer.

'By the way—how long are you filling in for Max? When are they getting a permanent bloke out here?'

Jessie couldn't get away from the insensitive farmer quick enough. He was the worst she'd met so far, of all the mean spirited, misogynistic farmers. She had already come across several but that wasn't really a lot considering the size of the Glenorchy community. Most of the farmers she'd met had been kind and supportive of her new role. But the ones who weren't, made her life a misery.

'I'm sorry to disappoint you, but I am it! And you'll have to get used to me, I'm afraid!' she huffed.

Red-faced, she stomped towards the Land Rover. She roughly threw her bag onto the passenger seat and climbed in fighting the surging anger that choked her. When she started the engine, about to drive off in a fury, Doug hastened towards the driver's door.

'Wait—I forgot to say thanks for helping out ... I should have asked you in for a cup of tea. My wife is away up north visiting the grandchildren ... otherwise, she would have invited you in.'

The choking feeling around her neck seemed to subside after he showed her a more human side. He didn't ask her in, to her relief. She wasn't sure about him—a vulnerable young woman with a lonely farmer in such a remote area.

'That's okay, I have to move on. I've no time for cups of tea.'

While driving to the next farm, she prayed for the grace to accept the ignorance and male chauvinism of these high country farmers. They were victims of generational brainwashing. She was determined to win them over and become as well accepted in her new community as Max had been.

***

The next visit went a lot smoother than the previous one. The farmer had a herd of Angora goats which he had reared himself. One of the nannies had an udder infection which Jessie had been treating with antibiotics. She needed to check it regularly.

As she drove up to the farm, she started to imagine that if she had a mobile clinic down on the flat in Glenorchy, some of these farmers could transport their smaller

271

animals to the clinic. That would save her from having to make many long trips in one day to the remote high country farms. She would definitely do some investigating on that subject.

The goat farmer, Bob, although not over-friendly did not treat her badly. He just never smiled and appeared to have no sense of humour. But this time, as she said goodbye, he handed her a bottle of goat's milk and a lump of feta cheese wrapped in muslin as she started her engine. His wife, Alma ran a small cottage industry of products made from goat's milk as well as using their wool which she sold to craft shops in Queenstown.

It was after nine in the evening by the time Jessie had finished her rounds. She'd spent far too long with Bob and Alma and hadn't even eaten. She headed back down the Glenorchy-Paradise Road towards home—BANG! Her vehicle swerved off the road, skidding on the loose stones and coming to a halt in a small ditch. Although she wore a seatbelt, the impact had winded her. She sat in her seat clutching at her chest, trying to recover from the shock. She stretched her neck sideways. 'Ow, not a whiplash as well,' she cried out.

She stumbled, almost falling when she opened the driver's door to take a look at the vehicle. 'Oh no, why now?' She glared at the rear tyre that had gone completely flat. As she looked closer, she could see a large nail poking out of the rubber.

'Dear Lord, this is unbelievable. Why do these things have to happen at night?' She spoke almost angrily as if she was admonishing her maker for allowing it to happen. But that wasn't in her nature to hold resentment towards God.

She shone the torch on the Carphone on the dashboard, picked up the handpiece and dialled the Vet Call Centre.

'I'm stuck on the Glenorchy-Paradise Road, just past the Priory Road turnoff heading south. There's a nail in my tyre and it's pitch black out here. Can you send someone to help me?'

The Call Centre Operator asked her to hold on while she looked down the list to see which farmer lived close to Jessie's location.

'It looks like Sam Grimsley is closest to you. I'll call him and send him over to you.'

Oh, no, thought Jessie. He was one of the nasty members of the High Country Farmers Association who was Doug McKlintoch's buddy and who'd also given her a hard time.

'Is he the only one nearest to me? Is there anyone else as I don't think he'd be too keen if you called him out at this hour?'

Time was flying by and Jessie was aware that most farmers go to bed early. It must be at least nine-thirty now and hardly anybody would be still up.

'No, sorry, Jessie. There is Jerry Lynes and his wife is ill. I can't phone him.'

Perhaps she should have contacted Mack. He would always help her but this time, she didn't want him to think she was just a helpless female. Or did she have too much pride?

'Oh—okay, then. It will just have to be Sam,' mumbled Jessie though the speaker.

'I'll stay on the radio until he arrives if you would rather,' said the operator. 'I'll let you know if he's unable to help you. If I can't get hold of him, I'll find someone else, or I'll phone the local police constable if there's nobody available.'

'That's kind of you, but I think I'll be okay ... except for the batteries on this Carphone that are going flat. I'll just keep the door locked. The locals say that nothing happens out here.'

When she hung up the receiver, she sat in her vehicle looking out across at the Richardson mountain range in the distance. Although it was dark, the snow-capped peaks glistened, boasting pastels of pink and purple in the light of the full moon. She carried a camera in her vehicle to snap the spectacular scenes in and around Glenorchy whenever she could and wanted to jump out of the car to snap this one but she pulled back. There was an eeriness that existed in the dead stillness of the night as she noticed formidable shadows dancing in the reflection of the mountains. Suddenly she caught a glimpse of a small light flashing in the distance coming rapidly towards her. Her heart pounded and missed a few beats. She froze in her seat. There could be all kinds of weird people wandering around out here.

She fought back her wild imagination and tried to cast unsettling thoughts out of her mind by whispering a short prayer. After that, a thought came to her. Mack, I'll call him. Let's face it—this is an emergency—he shouldn't mind.

She picked up her Carphone again and tried to get hold of him but there was no reception. The batteries had run out.

'Oh no! Not now please, God.'

She'd forgotten to recharge the batteries the evening before. Up until now, she'd always recharged them with the charger in her office before going to bed each night just as Max had instructed her

She tried not to panic and before she broke out in a cold sweat, the advancing small light had suddenly become large as bright headlights suddenly dazzled her. Within an hour, to her relief, a noisy truck pulled alongside her, the vehicle's lights blinding her. The driver wound down his window and Jessie did the same.

'Jessie, the vet, isn't it? Just heard from the Call Centre to say you're in trouble.'

'Ah ... not exactly in trouble. I have a puncture and can't see to repair it.'

Sam muttered something under his breath and shifted his truck so that the headlights shone on her vehicle's wheels.

Jessie stepped out and pulled her spare wheel from the back. Sam grabbed it and rolled it towards the rear wheels.

'I don't think we've met,' she murmured, hoping to break the ice.

'That'll be right. I bring my smaller animals to the clinic in Closeburn and Robbie Byrnes comes out here to my farm whenever I need him. I haven't had any need for your services.'

Jessie swallowed the lump in her throat and coughed. Her blood pressure rose at his obvious discrimination of her—frustrated by her sense of defeat at that moment. She prayed for courage and determination to rise above it as she was definitely going to have to do that if she wanted to continue practising as a vet in the high country. If only she had a sign, a sure indication from God that this was her calling. Her veterinary friends and colleagues had made it clear to her that in order for her to function well as a remote high country vet it would have to be a divine calling. Otherwise, it would just be too hard.

It didn't take him long to change the tyre. 'I'd be getting myself an extra spare if you plan to continue running around out here at night. You wouldn't want to be stranded. Lucky I came along, eh?'

'Yes, you're right. I'll make sure I do that. I'm so sorry to get you out here at this time of night. Thanks a lot.'

He fitted the damaged tyre back into its space on the back of the vehicle. 'Well, there you are, all done. I suggest you get this one repaired as soon as possible. In fact, even the one I swapped it with is not too great, so make sure you get onto it.'

He rubbed his hands together as if to clean them, wiping them on his overalls.

Sam was being respectful, contrary to his convictions about female vets. Jessie started warming to the old fella in a way she'd not thought possible after their first meeting.

'Thanks again. I owe you. Let me offer you some free vaccinations or consultation sometime.'

'Mmm ... I'll give it a thought. You'd better get off now. I'll follow you until you get nearer Glenorchy, just to make sure that tyre's going to be alright.'

Jessie accepted his offer and guessed he had a touch of humanity. Perhaps he too could change. She would have to pray for him—another grumpy farmer to add to her prayer list.

She wiggled her neck. Thankfully the pain had settled. She hadn't sustained a whiplash but was shaken. Stranded on an isolated road in the dark, alone for almost an hour. It won't happen again. God forbid!

Chapter Twelve

Mack knocked on the old solid oak door. He rubbed his hand over the unusual knot in the wood that gave the gnarled door a rustic appearance. No one came. He knocked harder this time. He was sure he had the right day. He glanced at his watch—he was dead on time. He heard the pounding of hooves nearby and turned around. A horseman who appeared to be one of the station hands trotted towards him.

'Gidday, mate—Mack, isn't it? Your grandfather's expecting you. He's on his way. Ben's the name. We had trouble with one of the water bores that got blocked with ice. He said to show you into his office. You can wait there.'

The horseman flung himself out of the saddle and tied his chestnut mare to the railing in front of the dated, wooden colonial homestead that needed a coat of white paint. Mack followed him up the steps and onto the porch where Ben shook off his high leather riding boots and Mack followed suit.

'Take a seat in here. He's just along the track in his truck. I'll leave you to it if you don't mind. There are some young steers up the back I need to shift, and a couple of our station hands are at the Agricultural Show today. Can I give you a beer?'

'Oh, no, thanks mate. I'm okay. Don't drink the stuff—it doesn't agree with me. Catch you another time.'

By the time Ben had unhitched his horse and cantered off, Walter had stepped out of his truck and headed for the office. Mack rubbed his abdomen as if to relieve the knot the tension had caused—the stress of the build-up to this special day he had hoped and dreamed of for years. Take a deep breath ... keep on breathing, he kept telling himself.

The sight of the tall, frail-looking farmer with blond turned grey hair and weathered skin that looked like an old leather handbag made his eyes smart. He fought back the uncontrollable moisture oozing from his eyes.

'Mack! Thanks for coming.' Walter lunged forward to shake Mack's hand with a strong, firm handshake that impressed him.

'Stay seated. Can I get you a beer or coffee, maybe?'

'Thanks, but I don't drink ale. I'm okay thanks. I had a coffee before I left home.'

'Well ... let's get down to the brass tacks. I guess you are wondering why I've asked you here ... well, it's not exactly for a social visit. It's hard for me to say but I need some help.'

Mack fixed his gaze on the aged man's face—a profile that told a thousand tales of times past. He saw that his estranged kin was lost for words and attempted to rescue him.

'Sorry, do you mean with the station or you personally?'

Mack's thick eyebrows curled, and a furrow formed in his brow. He spoke with a croak in his voice.

'This place, of course.' He pointed towards the green rolling hills. 'All two thousand acres of it. You see ... my health hasn't been good for the last few years, and I've been struggling. I have a great Station Manager—Aron is his name, but he has resigned. His wife is about to produce twins and he needs to help his family. He's moving to the McKenzie country to work as a leading farmhand on a small sheep station.'

Mack's heart gave an extra beat. 'Oh, really? What are you going to do? It's a big job for you on your own.'

'I've got four station hands. but none of them is manager material. I've heard through the grapevine a great deal about your farming skills and capabilities. I'm hoping you might be the right man for the job. Let me see those bits of paper you've brought me.'

Mack dived into his leather satchel and pulled out a Manilla folder full of documents.

'As this is one of the smaller stations in the area, you would actually be a head shepherd as well as Station Manager. I can still manage the books, but I'll eventually need to employ a bookkeeper.'

It's strange he doesn't mention anything about Dad or why he hasn't been in touch all these years. Mack's throat had dried up. He struggled to swallow while forcing himself to relax and breathe as he thrust the file into Walter's hands. Five minutes later Walter handed it back to him while he sat painfully still for every minute.

'Right, follow me. I'm going to take you for a drive. I can't show you the whole station, but you will be able to get a good idea of the size and capacity of the station. I'll introduce you to any of the workers if I see them. You've already met my leading station hand, Ben. You can always rely on him.' Walter's gruff, commanding manner irritated Mack. Would he be able to tolerate this cantankerous old farmer? He would have to win him over somehow. Still, he's waited so long for such a break-through he will just have to practise some long-suffering with God's help.

After a busy morning seeing most of the station, either by truck, horseback or by farm bike, Mack returned to the homestead overwhelmed. Walter shook off his gumboots at the front door while Mack pulled off his leather boots and followed Walter into the lounge. Walter offered him a seat while Mack looked around at what appeared to be a time-warp of memorabilia on the walls and scattered about the room. These were photographs and artefacts of Mack's great grandfather, the gold miner before he purchased Reed Station. The black and white photos impressed Mack.

'Ah yes—you wouldn't have seen any of these I suppose. I don't think your father has any.'

'No, he hasn't. I've never seen them before.'

'Take a look over here.' Walter walked over to the fireplace and on the wall was a large photo of what appeared to be Reed Station when it was first purchased and a substantial white colonial mansion that no longer existed.

'Wow—that must take you back. I guess you'd be able to write a book about that heritage. It's very interesting.'

'Yeah well ... your father never took any interest. But there's a book over here that one of the Historical Trusts has published. It has a lot in there about the Reed family history. You must take a look sometime, but first of all, we need to get back to brass tacks. I want to know what you think and more so how you feel about managing a station this size. I'll be around still to help you out and advise you as long as the old ticker keeps going.' He winked at Mack who sat on the edge of his seat, eyes wide.

'To be perfectly honest with you, I'm completely blown away by the awesomeness of this place. It's amazing and it would be a huge privilege for me to manage this for you. I'm a bit dumbfounded by your offer.'

'Oh, forget all that palaver. Are you willing to take it on or not?'

His curtness upset Mack. He tried to stretch his neck muscles to ease the tension caused by his grandfather's abrasiveness. Why is he so abrupt? What has made him so hard and rigid? A smile would crack his face.

'Absolutely, without a doubt. When would you want me to start?'

'It would have to be pretty soon, as Aron is staying for a month to orientate you before he leaves.'

'That's no problem, I'll start next week. I'll have to work with Aron part-time while I'm winding up my own property. I need to sell the cattle and sheep I have left and once I've settled in here, I'll sell the farm. Then there's my stallion, Zoro. He's my workhorse.'

'What about bringing the stock over here? Load them up on a truck and the station can buy them from you. Just write down how many animals you have and their details. I'll let the accountant know. I don't handle that side of things.'

Mack sat wringing his hands—the tension in his neck beginning to cause pain until Walter walked over to him and put out his hand. Mack took it eagerly as Walter shook it hard. After this act of humanity, Mack was able to relax.

'Wow, that's a really generous offer—thanks very much. The cattle are healthy and almost fat enough for the meat works. The sheep are merino like yours and will make you proud.'

'It's time for a good feed. My house-keeper, Bessie, usually cooks a hot meal at midday but it will be a little late today. The station hands also partake in a meal in the other dining room. I think lamb hotpot is on the menu today. Come on, I'll have to introduce you to her.'

'Mmm, it sure smells good. Thanks for everything ... um, I don't know what to call you?'

'I'm your grandfather, aren't I? You call me, Grandad, okay? But whatever you do, don't start calling me gramps.' Walter almost broke a weak smile.

The two men had broken the ice. They wandered down the long hallway to the old farmhouse kitchen where Bessie was waiting for them. Walter introduced Bessie to Reed Station's new manager then led him to the dining room. He seated Mack next to him at a long solid oak table which had been attractively laid with all the attributes of farmhouse cuisine including old world bone china. Once again Mack's eyes starting to smart with salty moisture which he forced back.

This was a long-awaited answer to prayer and the joy in his heart that bubbled over was indescribable. This was the first day of a whole new chapter in his life. But where did his friend, Jessie fit in? Had she now disappeared into insignificance? Only time would tell.

Chapter Thirteen

A Month Later

The snow had thawed on the foothills surrounding her home but remained on the mountain tops. It was an awesome sight as Jessie went hiking alone high up onto the ridge near her home. It was a fresh morning early in spring as she stumbled up the well-trodden rough track to the top. From there she was able to look over the surrounding farms and in the distance, she could see as far as Paradise and Mount Earnslaw. Spring and autumn were her favourite seasons. In spring she loved to watch the birds come to life after a long hard winter as they fluttered about searching for seeds.

She sat on a rock with her eyes fixed on the tender green leaves on the Poplar trees. A wave of nostalgia came over her—memories of pencil-shaped Poplars that lined the paddocks on her parents' farm.

For the first time since she had arrived in Glenorchy, she was fighting pangs of homesickness. Minutes later, as she fixed her gaze onto the majestic snow-capped mountains and watched a large Kea bird flying overhead, she remembered what it was that kept her there. The mountains had called her once and right now they continued to pull at her heartstrings again. The nostalgia for Bethlehem soon left her, as she set off down the track towards home.

As she tugged at her boots at the front door, she was sure she heard the phone ring, then stop. It was her usual day off and the Call Centre would divert her business calls. It didn't ring again. She knew Hope and Cole had gone to a horse breeder's convention in Queenstown and wouldn't be back till late that night. Oh well, she thought. If it's really important, they'll phone again.

She still needed the wood fire and managed to get it going with the small pile of wood she had left. The load of firewood Mack had delivered to her was running out and she would still need another load to last her through spring. It got pretty cold in these parts and heating the whole house with a small electric heater was too costly. Perhaps she should give him a call and pay him a visit as it had been some time since she'd last heard from him. He'd told her he was busy with his renovations and taking stock to the auctions. But Jessie thought he had gone unusually quiet.

I know—I'll pay him a surprise visit and take over some of my Apple Crumble he likes so much. She rallied around looking for a dish for the dessert she had frozen and packed it into a basket with several fresh muffins. She had always baked on her day off and she'd made this batch early that morning.

The thought of visiting her friend, Mack, put an extra spring in her step as she busied herself trying to coordinate her denim jeans with the right woollen jumper. She tried on a tomato red, soft Cashmere top that contrasted perfectly with the blue denim. Next, she pulled on the new tan suede boots with high heels—the pair she'd brought home from the General Store earlier in the week. It was one of her few opportunities to wear them, as her social life was lacking in Glenorchy.

She climbed into the Land Rover that she now owned, thanks to Max. He had offered it to her for a most reasonable price on his return from holiday, as he and his wife had agreed to upgrade their vehicle. The Land Rover was just right for Jessie. It even had plenty of room in the back for her to be able to sleep when staying overnight in Queenstown, once she'd got rid of the doggy smell. It was something she'd always imagined driving.

As she carefully veered around the icy corner towards Mack's driveway entrance, the vehicle almost skidded as she slammed her foot on the brakes and screeched to a standstill next to a large sign on the gate. With her hands frozen on the steering wheel, her eyes narrowed as she leaned her head towards the windscreen.

There in front of her stood a sign that read, "Farm for Sale". *Why hadn't he said anything to me about this?*

The poached eggs and bacon she'd eaten earlier started swimming their way up her gullet. She willed the sick feeling away and drove hastily through the large puddles along the driveway towards Mack's homestead. His old tractor was parked next to the animal barn. She climbed out of her vehicle and looked around. There was an eerie silence as she glanced the extensive rows of paddocks. There was not an animal in sight. Usually, she would hear the barking of a working dog, and Zoro, his horse was usually in the front paddock next to the home. Mack had always kept him close by since the stallion's abduction, but she couldn't see him anywhere.

He wouldn't just suddenly leave without telling me. What's got into him? Mind you, I've been so run off my feet lately and haven't had time for anyone. Perhaps it was he who was ringing me. She knocked on his front door then went around to the back. She even wandered over to the large animal barn and still nothing. All the animals had gone. Stumbling on hard green cowpats, she raced back to

Mack's homestead that appeared to be completely renovated—the first time Jessie had seen it in months. When she peered through the windows, her heart sank and that same sick feeling came over her. All of Mack's household contents had gone. The place looked bare except for scanty items of furniture. He's moved away and without a word. What on earth happened? I must get home and phone Hope and Cole. They'll know.

Why was she feeling so upset? She asked herself. They weren't in a relationship, just good friends, or so she thought—or was she in denial about her real feelings? Her eyes smarted as she drove bleary-eyed back to her cottage whispering a prayer to ask God to shed some light on Mack's disappearance.

***

Cole answered the phone. 'Hi, Jessie. Haven't heard from you in a while. Hope has phoned you a few times.'

'Oh, really? I had no idea. That makes me think I really have to buy one of those flash Phone Mate answer machines.'

'Bertie's been missing you,' he laughed. 'He's put on so much weight. Hope took him to the Plunket Nurse in Glenorchy this week.'

Jessie loved to hear about little Bertie but she was busting to say what she had phoned about.

'Um … I've been trying to get hold of Mack as Zoro's vaccinations are due soon. I've just been to the farm, and it appears to be for sale. There's a large sign at the gate and there's no sign of any animals. His home is bare too.' Her voice quavered even though she tried hard to stop it.

'Oh, no. Mack said he would phone you and let you know. I'd assumed he'd done that.'

'He should have contacted me through the Vet Call Centre. They could have located me on my radio phone.'

'I expect he didn't think it appropriate if it was a personal call.'

'Where has he gone?'

'To work for his grandfather who offered him the job of Station Manager.'

'Wow, really? On that two thousand acre farm! That's so amazing. Did he sell all his stock?'

'No, his grandfather bought the stock and Mack's using Zoro as his workhorse. Why don't you go out there and see him? You said you need to vaccinate Zoro. Hold on ... I'll just get the address and phone number. You can decide if you want to phone first or take pot luck and drive out there.'

Jessie's hand shook as she scribbled the address.

'I ... suppose so. Thanks, Cole. Is Hope able to come to the phone for a quick word?'

'Oh, sorry. She's taken Bertie into Glenorchy for his vaccinations. Pity you can't give them.'

'Ha, not likely. Anyone can deliver a baby but I have to be certified to give people vaccinations.'

'I'll tell Hope you called. Maybe she can call you later this evening for a girl's chinwag,' he chuckled.

It had been an eventful day but not a relaxing one as Jessie had anticipated. Later that evening she rearranged her diary to fit in the visit to Reed Station in Dart Valley the next day. There were some other horses in the area to vaccinate so she thought she may as well do Zoro too. Fortunately for her, she had been able to build up quite a large clientele in the district not too far from her home. Before she settled into bed that evening, the phone rang. She almost jumped out of her skin then remembered Cole had said he would get Hope to call her. It was her, and the two chatted until late catching up on all their girly news.

'Well, I really think you need to go to Reed Station tomorrow,' said Hope. 'Mack has done a quite a bit of sheep shearing here for my father in the last month and said he had tried to call you a few times to let you know he was moving. Just go and surprise him. Let me know how you get on. And by the way—can you help with a bit of babysitting this weekend? We've got a wedding to attend and you're so good with Bertie. Or would you rather we ask one of the older girls from church?'

'Sure, I'll do it. I'll call you later in the week to confirm.'

'And to let me know all the juicy gossip about Mack.' They both laughed. The phone call lifted her spirit. Her face glowed and excited expectation infiltrated her soul.

Chapter Fourteen

Spring started to announce its arrival. The sun forced its way between her bedroom curtains, falling on her shoulders as she soaked up its warmth while she was dressing. There was an eagerness in her heart today. She was keen to hear all about Mack's wonderful new role as Station Manager, but more so, how he was getting on with his grandfather. It would be a dream come true for him. It annoyed her that he hadn't been able to get hold of her by phone. He wasn't the kind of man who would leave her guessing. She wondered if she should put the Apple Crumble she had baked for him into the chilly bin with the lunch she'd packed for herself. But what if he wasn't there? She'd only have to bring the dish home again. She decided against it. Anyway—perhaps he had more interesting things to think about than her Apple Crumble. She quickly banished the idea.

By lunchtime, she'd finished the visits to both the smaller farms on Glenorchy-Paradise Road. She stopped her vehicle in a pull-in by the Beech forest, her preferred spot where she found peace and tranquillity. It reminded her of the horse-treks she used to take with her friend, Hope before she had married Cole. Now their lives had changed so much—Hope with a baby and herself a busy vet.

She unwound the car window and focused her gaze on the forest where they used to see the wild horses come down to the lake to drink and remembered the time they had seen a mare with her foal. She would love to have her own land and keep a few horses, as she grew up with them. How she missed those times, but Hope had said she can ride their horses any time she liked.

She was distracted by what she thought was a black horse. Or was it just that she'd been daydreaming about horses? No, her eyes did not deceive her. Near the lake by the entrance to the extensive red beech forest, stood a tall black horse drinking at the water's edge. Its sleek coat glistened in the sun and it appeared oblivious to a group of picnickers sitting at a table nearby. She wanted to go over and take a photo but knew that by the time she drove over to the horse, it would be gone. This wonderful memory will just have to stay in the back of her mind for safe-keeping.

Glancing at her watch, it was time to visit Reed Station. The sandwiches she had bolted down seemed to stick in her throat as the anxiety built at the thought of driving out there uninvited, but it was now or never.

***

As Jessie was about to turn into the long driveway that led to Reed Station, she turned on the windscreen wiper to clear the thick layer of dust that had settled on the window when a vehicle had driven passed her through a puddle earlier. The water made it worse. Now it was just a muddy mess, and it blurred her vision. This is the life of a rural vet, she reminded herself. She stopped the vehicle and pulled out an old rag to give it a good wipe then climbed back into the vehicle.

She drove on up to the nostalgic colonial homestead minus the picket fence. Climbing roses would have suited that style of home, she imagined. There was an old hay baler in one corner and Mack's Ute parked nearby.

290

She banged on the oak door. The house-keeper opened it and said, 'Well, well. It's the first time I've seen a woman on this station, apart from myself … not for many years. Bessie's my name. What can I do for you?'

'Hello, Bessie. My name's Jessie. I'm the new vet and I'm looking for Mack. His horse's vaccinations are due.'

'Oh my goodness. You're the one they've been chatting about. Mack has tried to get hold of you. He'll be pleased to see you, as he's worried about you. His grandfather, Walter has had some concerns about one or two animals this week and hasn't got around to calling the Vet Cooperative yet. Come on in,' she said as she directed her into the lounge.

'Mack is on his horse below that ridge up there by the pine trees. A steer fell into a creek and he's had to free it. He hasn't taken his radiophone with him as he said he wouldn't be away long. Walter should be around somewhere mending fences. He's not far away either as he usually comes in for lunch and hasn't eaten yet. He'll be on his quad bike somewhere.'

Jessie smiled while she observed the robust friendly woman, someone she could warm to easily.

'If you don't mind, I'll have to keep going. I'll go and look for them. How far can I take my vehicle up there?' Jessie asked.

'Most of the way up that track, and when you get to the first long wooden gate, you can go through it, but you'll have to go by foot. Mack will be across that paddock over there just before the creek. It's a bit of a walk, mind you, but when you see Zoro, his horse, you'll be in the right place. Or maybe it'll be better to wait here until he comes in.'

'Oh, I'll be fine. I've strong walking boots and I need the exercise. I spend a lot of time in my vehicle.'

'Please come back with him for a cup of tea,' she said, retying her apron.

Jessie thanked her for the directions and got back into her vehicle. She drove slowly up the dirt track that led to the large wooden gate that Bessie described. The track was longer than she had imagined which was understandable as she was only used to farms the size of her father's four hundred acre farm. The paddocks on a station this size were huge in comparison.

'Ah, this must be the gate,' she muttered as she stopped suddenly. She scanned as far as her eye could see and there was no sign of Mack. She got out and wandered up and down the track searching again full circle. Nothing. She was afraid to drive on in case she got lost in the maze of numerous side roads and tracks between vast paddocks. Then something black caught her eye on the opposite side in the distance. She got back in the vehicle and drove as far as she could until she found a gate on that side and got out. It was a black horse, and it appeared to hang its head over something lying on the ground. She grabbed her medical bag, put her Stetson on her head, and started walking. As she drew closer after a five-minute walk, she recognised the horse. It was Zoro without a rider. 'Oh no, it's not Mack lying there, is it?' She spouted, loudly. The horse seemed to be nudging what appeared to her to be a man lying on the ground. The stallion was gently licking and butting him with his head. But the figure definitely wasn't Mack. As she hurried towards the scene, she saw an elderly man lying on the ground. Zoro towered over him licking his face and hands repeatedly trying to keep his body warm. The horse then started rubbing his head up and down Walter's body. There was snow on the surrounding hilltops and the ground was still ice-cold for late spring.

Jessie rushed to the man's side then patted the horse's nose. 'Thank you, Zoro. You've been trying to help him.'

As she examined the lifeless man he moaned. From her examination, she ascertained that he'd likely suffered a stroke.

She dived into her medical bag after turning him on his side to help his breathing and then tried to use her radiophone. There was just a lot of static. She had to get assistance. 'You stay here with him, Zoro. I'll go for help.'

Before she went off, she'd realised that the hay that covered the aged man's body was not from the farmer carrying it, as there was no bale anywhere near. She'd seen one by the open gate when she had raced over to him. It must have been Zoro who had gathered the hay from there and spread it over the victim's body to keep him warm.

She bent over and gathered up the loose straw that had fallen off when she had turned him onto his side and covered his torso and legs with it.

Jessie guessed that the old man was probably Walter as the tools on the ground next to him were reminiscent of fencing tools.

She raced back and alerted Bessie who was able to radio one of the station hands to find Mack. Bessie then contacted the doctor and the air ambulance.

Jessie hurried back in her vehicle to Walter with a rug that Bessie had given her and waited until Mack turned up. As she ran across the paddock with the rug, Zoro was still standing over Walter like a sentry on guard. He was licking every bit of skin that was exposed on Walter's body. The horse whinnied softly when Jessie returned and nudged her arm gently as she covered Walter with the rug. He groaned then opened his eyes and stared at her, trying to speak, but his speech sounded garbled.

'Hello, Walter. I'm Jessie the new vet. I'm also a friend of Mack's and I think you've had a stroke and we're getting help. The air ambulance from Glenorchy is on its way, but the doctor will get here first.'

She placed a cushion she'd carried from her vehicle under his head. He tried to talk again with disjointed speech. 'Just you rest and try not to talk. You are going to be all right.'

Five minutes later, Mack arrived on a quad bike with a station hand sitting behind. He ran to his grandfather's side.

'Goodness me, Jessie! What brings you here—just in time? You've saved my grandfather.' He leaned over Walter and grabbed his hand. 'What happened to him?'

'It's not me you need to thank … it's Zoro, here.' She patted the horse on the neck and let him lick her hand.

'Your faithful horse guarded Walter closely and kept him warm by spreading hay on his body. He's amazing, an angel. Unusual for a stallion. I think your grandfather has had a stroke, but I can't say for sure.'

Just at that moment, another quad bike with two men on it turned up at the gate. Mack rushed over to let them in. It was one of Mack's station hands with the doctor who raced to Walter's side. Within a short time, he confirmed the patient had suffered another stroke.

The air ambulance, a shiny red helicopter landed in the paddock next to Zoro's field. Before long, Walter was on his way to Queenstown Hospital. Mack stayed behind to manage the station.

'I should have taken my radiophone with me, but I was initially only going to help a steer stuck in a fence then I ventured further up the track on Zoro to check some other stock,' said Mack, as he and Jessie walked back to her vehicle. 'When I dismounted to take a look at some of my steers, Zoro took off down the track towards his paddock. He'd never done that before. I realise now that he knew something was wrong with Grandad who had been repairing the fence in Zoro's paddock. That's his quad bike over there.' He pointed to the track next to the paddock.

'That makes him a pretty special kind of stallion.'

'That's for sure. He surely saved Grandad's life. I won't go off without my radiophone again, though, I can assure you.'

'It's not me you need to assure.'

Mack climbed into Jessie's Land Rover. She drove him back to his homestead.

'What brings you here, anyway? I've tried to call you several times to let you know Grandad asked me to manage Reed Station, and I have put my farm up for sale,' Mack asked.

'I know. Cole told me and so did Bessie. I'm sorry, but I've been so busy and often don't get home until late. Next time, just phone the Vet Call Centre at the Co-op. They'll locate me. By the way—Zoro's vaccinations are due. That's why I'm here, just in case you've forgotten.'

'Oh, that's right. I knew they were due sometime soon. It's a bit much for you today. Thanks so much for helping Grandad. You came just in time. I'd appreciate it if you come again soon to vaccinate Zoro. You can always leave phone messages with Bessie.'

'I'll come back next week. I need to go home now. Give me a call when you want me to come back and do the vaccinations.'

'Aren't you going to come in for tea or coffee? We can have a good catch up.'

'Sorry, I really need to get going.' She couldn't get rid of the reasoning going on in her mind that if he genuinely wanted to see her, he could have called the Vet Call Centre and left a message.

'I'll be in touch soon. Zoro obviously recognised you,' said Mack. 'He'll look forward to seeing you.' He glanced at her with a sheepish grin. She tried to read between the lines. He was probably feeling guilty, but perhaps he had meant it.

Jessie was shaken up by the events of the day. She'd looked forward to a grand catch up with Mack and it had really turned to custard. Part of her had wanted to accept the invitation to stay for afternoon tea but the ordeal with Walter was exhausting. Her feet were aching, and she was sure she had pulled her calf muscle when she ran across the paddock with the blanket, tripping on thick tufts of grass and uneven ground.

When she arrived home, she tugged off her boots and crashed on her bed. She lay there thinking about the day's events and said a prayer for Walter. She prayed for healing—Please, God, restore Walter to good health again. Have mercy on poor Mack as he has only just begun to unite with his grandfather. Let him be able to have a relationship with him that he has always longed for. Amen.

Chapter Fifteen

Three weeks later, the hospital discharged Walter in good shape after a mild stroke. He had regained his speech and apart from some residual weakness down one side of his body, he walked with a limp. Mack was sure it was a miracle, and the old man showed determination to help him run the station again.

Bessie had her work cut out running around after Walter more than usual. She kept a good eye on him making sure he followed the doctor's orders.

Early one evening, Walter sat under the awning of the veranda drinking tea from his beloved worn out mug that Bessie had handed him. He was discussing the future plans for the station with Mack who was enjoying a bottle of Bessie's new batch of ginger beer.

'I want you to hold on to this station, and maybe one day, if you have a family of your own, they might just be interested. I don't know how much longer I'll be active, with my health the way it is. You need to get yourself a wife to help you keep the place going.'

Mack turned and gaped at him as he picked up his glass. He spluttered, almost choking as he swallowed. 'There aren't many women in these parts who are still available, Grandad.'

'What about the young lassie who came to see me in hospital—that young vet you've been talking about? I was away with the fairies a bit when she came to see me, but I remember she was the one who found me. A lovely girl she is. She'd fit in well up here, don't you think?'

Mack cleared his throat and scuffed his boots under his seat back and forth. 'I haven't really given that any thought— I've been so busy. I don't think she would be interested, and if I marry, it will be for love and not a business proposition, Grandad.'

Walter's neck reddened. He went quiet for a moment.

'Sorry, Mack, I didn't mean to embarrass you. I should mind my own business. I just worry about how you will cope with this place on your own if I croak.'

'It's okay. We have reliable station hands and there's Bessie of course who has been here for years. She has part-time cooks she can all on if we have a lot of workers to feed. The ranch hands can pay for a hot meal which Bessie organises, but they often look after themselves.'

'I can also ask experienced farmers like Joel Grey and Cole Rigby for advice. They don't have such an extensive property as we have, but they are some of the most skilled and notable farmers around here, according to Max, the vet who recently retired.'

'If you say so. Sounds like you have plenty of confidence, that's for certain. I'm sure you'll do just fine.'

'Hope you don't mind, but would you be able to give me a quick rundown of the history of Reed Station? I can't remember the chain of events leading up to you living here.'

'That's a good idea. Could you top up my mug first, please? We might be in for a long session. His eyes smiled at Mack.

'No problem, Grandad.'

While Mack took the mug into the kitchen, Walter's countenance changed. He started pulling at his fingers and wringing his hands. When Mack trundled onto the veranda with a fresh mug of tea, Walter was sitting at the small café table tapping his fingers. Sadness clouded his facial features.

'Good strong tea. Bessie's brew is always stewed—just how I like it. Now, you want to know all about the Reed family history.'

Bessie came out to the veranda.

'I think you'd better come in for a short nap before dinner, Walter.'

'Not now, Bessie. I'll be in a bit later. I think Mack and I are in for a lengthy session.'

Bessie got the message and scurried away.

Walter rubbed the nape of his neck then began—'Our ancestors had become wealthy during the Otago gold rush in Arrowtown. Some years later they purchased Reed Station. I met your grandmother, Hazel, in the McKenzie country near Lake Tekapo, where she grew up on a sheep farm. We married in the Church of the Good Shepherd near the lake. I worked as a farmhand on her father's farm. Several years later, following a severe drought, her parents lost all their livestock, and eventually their farm after they had gone bankrupt.'

'Wow. That's a hard blow. Where did you both go after that?'

'We came here as I inherited Reed Station at that time. Your grandmother and I had considered having a large family but conceived only one son, Len, your father.'

Walter looked around for his jacket which he found on the railing and put it on.

'It's getting a bit fresh now the sun's going down.' Mack rubbed his arms and shuddered. 'I'll just duck inside and put a jumper on.'

When he returned, Walter continued.

'The Reeds had been able to keep this station in the family for generations until your father had rejected my offer to help me manage it, heading off to university in Wellington instead.'

'I'll bet that was a lump of disappointment for you to swallow, your only son abandoning you in a way.'

'We'd had major arguments about his future plans upon graduating from university, but he was headstrong. When he moved to Wellington to set up a lucrative export business, he fell in love with your mother. You know the rest.'

'Do you mind talking about my grandmother? I never got to meet her.'

Walter drew in a long breath then continued.

'Hazel had missed out on seeing both you and Meg, as she died of complications of pneumonia during a hard winter when were snowed in. There was no time to get her to the hospital in Queenstown. I lived alone on Reed Station and isolated myself from the rest of the family after she'd gone.'

'That's so sad, Grandad. I wish I'd met her. But none of this was your fault.'

'I still think I need to make amends. I'll find a way to make it up to all of you. Just give me time.'

Large globules of water kept hanging on the end of the old man's nose. He pulled out a large wrinkled handkerchief and blew his nose like a foghorn.

Mack turned away and wiped his eyes with his sleeve.

'I suppose I should be getting back inside. Bessie rules me with an iron tongue sometimes.' He managed to laugh.

'Wait, Grandad.' Mack took his arm to stop him. He wrapped his arms around him. 'Thank so much for sharing all of this with me. I had no idea what you've suffered. You don't have to do it alone any longer.'

Walter squeezed his hand. 'You're not only a good shepherd, Mack. You're a top grandson. We're in this together.'

'I'd better start winding down too. I've got help some of our shepherds tomorrow to bring the sheep down to the woolshed. Shearing season has commenced.'

***

After he'd eaten his meal that night, Mack picked up the phone and called Jessie.

'I'm sorry I never got around to dropping off another load of firewood with my farm selling and everything. We've plenty of old pines up here so I can still do it in time for next winter if you remind me.'

Jessie leaned over her office desk rubbing her eyes and unwittingly yawned down the phone. 'Oops, sorry. I'm not bored, just really tired. Thanks for the offer. I'll put it in my diary for next autumn. I can come next Monday to do Zoro's vaccinations.'

'That suits me—but make it the afternoon if you can. Some contract shearers are coming tomorrow and they're leaving Monday morning. I need to sort out their wages before midday.'

'That'll be fine. See you Monday afternoon.'

Jessie was delighted. Perhaps she might get to spend a bit more time with Mack than she did with the last interrupted visit. Her social life was almost non-existent, and she had not yet made many friends in the area.

She went back into the kitchen to continue to prepare her meal. It was a fish pie she'd made from cans of smoked fish and mashed potatoes from her own vegetable garden.

She opened the oven door and checked that the breadcrumb topping had browned. It was ready to serve, and she'd developed a hearty appetite after a busy day running around the countryside in her car. The green peas on the cooktop were ready. As she picked up the spoon to serve her meal, the phone rang again. 'Oh, not now,' she

301

uttered. She hurried back to her office and picked up the phone.

'Jessie, sorry to phone you at this time. I need to talk to you about something urgent that has cropped up.' It was Hope's father, Joel. There seemed to be an urgency in his voice. It sounded strained and croaky. Not his usual self.

'How about popping around tomorrow when you finish work—or another day if that doesn't suit?'

'Oh … okay. Is there a problem?' Jessie didn't usually get phone calls from Joel. She'd helped him out with foaling several times, but apart from that didn't visit his home that often. She would usually be with Hope and Cole for meals or babysitting for them.

'Not with me there isn't, but something has come up with some local farmers—look, let's not discuss it on the phone … dinner tomorrow?'

'If you don't mind, I won't stay for dinner. Need to do a heap of paperwork at home. I'll be over around five if that suits. It'll be a hectic schedule tomorrow on my clinic day at the surgery in Closeburn.'

Jessie put the phone back on the hook. Suddenly she'd lost her appetite. She didn't like the sound of Joel's voice. I had a negative tone that spelt trouble.

She'd been so hungry when she'd walked through the door after work but now the fish pie and green peas no longer held their appeal. Or was she worried for nothing? Instead of putting the food into the fridge until the next day, she served herself a small helping and forged her way through it after reheating it under the grill.

***

It had been a long and hot day with the inland temperatures around mid-twenties Celsius. Unusual for early December. Jessie had spent the morning with Robbie Byrnes assisting him with surgery on some of her own patients. She then had to drive up a long and dusty road towards Mount Judah to check the wound of a female dog she had spayed in the clinic the week before. The owner was elderly and make the trip to Closeburn.

I don't understand why people who don't drive, live remotely. They are so dependent on others.

The dog owner's neighbour dropped the dog off at the clinic on the day of the surgery and Jessie returned it to its owner after treatment.

The sheer stress of so much driving to patients in isolated areas and her weekly clinic in Closeburn exhausted her.

If only there was a clinic, she had access to in Glenorchy. She didn't have the finances to build one as she had plans to buy a home of her own.

There had to be another solution. It was easier for Max to manage when he was the remote vet, as he always had an extra colleague to help cover him until the last one resigned.

Vets in this area were as scarce as hen's teeth, especially experienced clinicians. Now Jessie was the only one north of Glenorchy and as far south as the Closeburn district. The trip took more than an hour on loose metal roads.

Perhaps she should raise the issue with Mack when she goes to give Zoro his vaccinations. Or even with Joel too.

Chapter Sixteen

Jessie loved driving down the long entrance to Dart River Ranch and to catch sight of Bertie toddling around the front garden. There was a wire fence between Hope and Cole's cottage and the large homestead that Hope's parents, Joel and Myra owned. But Cole had built an ornate, white picket fence around their humble home to keep Bertie safe. This time, Hope was on her front porch with Bertie. She waved out to her.

When she arrived at Joel's front door, Jessie knocked with trepidation, fearing what he was going to say. She couldn't guess what it was, but from the tremor in Joel's voice when he had spoken to her on the phone, she knew it wasn't good news.

Myra answered the door. 'Oh, Jessie—come on in. Joel isn't far away. He has been expecting you. I'll go out back and call him.'

She ushered Jessie into the lounge and then went back into the kitchen to put the kettle on.

Jessie sank into the armchair and sat plucking at the fluff on her shirt-blouse. Nervously she started twirling a strand of her sandy coloured hair with her index finger then sat tugging on it. The house cat spotted her and must have sensed her lack of composure. It started rubbing its soft coat along her shins, giving her a degree of comfort.

'Jessie, good to see you. Glad you were able to come at such short notice. I know how busy you are.' Joel stood there looking more serious than usual giving her a half-smile.

'Not as busy as I'd like to be. At least, not in these parts—I haven't been getting as many calls from the Vet Co-op the past few weeks. I really thought by now that business would be thriving, seeing that I'm the only remote vet in the area.'

Joel gave a nervous cough. He didn't sit down this time.

'Look—I think it might be better if we go into my office if you don't mind. We have a few ranch hands working close to the house today. They often use the bathroom and I'd rather give you some privacy.'

Jessie followed him into the office while Myra hovered around offering them some refreshments.

'If you don't mind, just a glass of water would be fine, thanks.' Jessie smiled at Myra who brought in a jug of water and glasses. Joel closed the door after her.

Joel had been like a second father to Jessie since she had moved down South. He was always jovial around her and had given her much encouragement whenever she was treating his animals. This was the first time she had been ill at ease with him—or perhaps she was just over-reacting.

He sat back in his seat, crossing his feet and clasping his hands together on his lap.

'Well, Jessie, I don't know how to broach this issue as I believe you're going to find it distressing, but please bear with me and don't for a moment think that I agree with any of it,' he spouted.

Jessie's muscles in her jaw tensed. A surge of adrenaline raced around her body as she prepared herself for the worst.

'I have just attended the committee meeting of the High Country Farmers Association. We meet quarterly and this week's meeting was a real eye-opener. They had been discussing the new remote vet, namely you, and what they had to say was not awe-inspiring, to say the least.'

'Oh no! What do you mean?' Jessie's forehead puckered as she started biting her lip.

'There are some hot-heads amongst them, mostly farmers who have been in the area for decades and who hold prejudice against female professionals like you, no matter how clever or skilled you are. In fact, I was so offended by their behaviour and the derogatory way they spoke about you, I almost walked out. But instead, I stayed till the end to defend you.'

'That is so mean. What have I done to deserve all this? Please—be honest with me, Joel.'

'I am being honest. The thing is, in the end not one of them was able to make an incriminating report about your professional or clinical conduct. It all stemmed from an absolute abhorrence of any females working in the capacity of a vet in any situation. A lot of these farmers see women as domestics, either hanging out nappies on the clothesline or cooking the meals for their station hands. Occasionally some of their wives work on the farms with them but it is not that common. They are there to back up the men in a domestic capacity. But that's not how folks brought me up on the farm.'

'Nor was it like that on my parents' farm. My mother and I used to round up the sheep and cattle along with my brother, so we didn't need to hire farmhands. Sometimes we employed a house-keeper at a particularly busy time but my mother was not a doormat.'

'Well then—these men will have to learn a few home truths. We need to find a way for you to show them you can match the skill of any vet between here and Queenstown, including Max. I know your worth and they need to know too.'

'But if the whole province is against me, how can I succeed? Anyway, who are these men, this vigilante? Please, Joel—just tell me who the ring leader is and I'll avoid them.'

She gulped down half a glass of water then cringed as she realised how loud it sounded—indicating her agitation.

'I think it's a case of them avoiding you and telling the Co-op to send them another vet. They have to pay the extra travel expenses that the other vets will charge though so it's a case of the "cutting off the nose to spite the face".'

'Who is the one who has instigated it? Is it old Mr Greeson? He was pretty grumpy last week when I visited his farm. He had half a dozen cows I had to take serum samples from, and he was so negative, complaining about all his neighbours including me. He wasn't even interested in holding the animals still to help me do my job properly. I was glad to leave there.'

'No ... it was that Scotsman McKlintoch on the deer farm. He was the main one stirring the pot. He has a real big chip on his shoulder.'

'Of course, I should have known. He was that unpleasant man who yelled at me and gave me a few really nasty looks.'

'Everyone around here knows he is Master of the Hunts. He thinks he's a cut above the rest of the community because of the first-rate horses he bred.'

'What am I to do? This is my livelihood. He might turn them all against me. Perhaps I should move.' She drooped, placing her elbows on her thighs and resting her face in her hands. Her head was thumping as though it was about to explode. She was sure her blood pressure had risen.

Joel saw the deflated look on her face. It was obvious it exasperated her. 'No—don't think like that. You mustn't take on board their rubbish. They are just blowing hot wind. You must detach and I'll get my buddies in the area to bring you influence.'

'I don't know. It will be hard to believe I will ever break into this community.' All Jessie wanted was her own father to pray for her just as he used to when she was still living at home. She found it hard to lift her head as though they had drained her life force from her.

'Jessie.' She looked up, responding to Joel's gentle voice.

'Let me pray for you and ask God for guidance in this situation. In fact, I'd like to ask for a breakthrough in such a way that this community of farmers will not only accept you but also honour you as a clinician in your own right.'

'Oh ... okay then, thanks.' She bowed her head as Joel prayed an articulated prayer that seemed to emulate her father when he used to pray for her. It made her relax and her confidence returned. She turned to Joel with a heart full of appreciation. This time she could smile without forcing it and Joel's sympathetic facial expression had sufficient warmth to soothe her soul.

Chapter Seventeen

Jessie arrived home from her visit with Joel, off-loaded her bags in her office, and crashed on her bed. She didn't bother to remove her boots, as she was drained—still upset from the negative feedback she'd received from him, even though he told her to ignore it.

The attack on her personal and professional reputation had left her reeling. She'd worked hard at building up her credibility in this remote, rural community and had done everything possible to become integrated, but it had been futile. What chance did she have now of building up her veterinarian practice with this vigilante mentality determined to undermine and discredit her? In spite of what Joel, Cole, Mack, and even Walter Reed had said in her favour, she'd begun to lose confidence in herself.

Right now she wished she had her little cat from back home to comfort her. The fat, fluffy, ginger animal always knew when she was hurting, and at times like this, she would bury her face in the cat's long bushy fur until it had soaked up her warm tears. But this time, there was no furry comforter, just her eiderdown saturated by the continual flow of droplets as she sobbed her heart out.

She spoke out loud to her creator—'that's it, God. You said that you would be my comforter and protector, but I can't take much more of this. I've decided that, if I encounter one more case of bullying from those mean-spirited farmers, I'll toss the towel in and head back to the Waikato to do a job without my heart being in it, just going through the motions—if that's what you want me to do, God, I will.'

Later, having slept a little, she awoke glad to be home after the long intense session with Joel. She sat at her dining table staring at the walls wondering if her dream of being a high country vet had now been shattered. She was exhausted from all the pent-up emotion and hardly had the energy to get up and prepare a meal. She'd completely lost her appetite. Suddenly floods of tears soaked the tablecloth where she sat sobbing her heart out again. How can she go on like this? Perhaps she had made the wrong decision about taking the role of a remote vet—or any kind of vet in this area, for that matter. She roughly blew her nose and tried to compose herself so she could think. She wondered if she'd misheard God speaking to her heart in her prayers when she was back in the Waikato and had prayed hard for guidance before she took the job on. What a mess. Perhaps she should talk to Mack about it. He might be able to help her shed some light on the unpleasant predicament in which she had landed herself.

Her heart was almost breaking at the thought of having to give it all up—the mountains, the lakes, as well as her best friend, Hope. Of course, there were other friends such as Mack too. She suddenly remembered she was due to visit him the next day but first had to visit a sick animal not far from her house—a miniature horse that was lame. The farmers were kind people and the last time she had visited them they had treated Jessie with respect. The woman had even given her a brown paper bag full of freshly baked muffins. Tomorrow will be a relaxing day she decided, as she ran a bath full of bubbles.

✦✦✦

The next day the visit with the elderly couple was a complete change from dealing with the handful of obnoxious farmers in the area. These humble people who bred tiny horses were a breeze. They fussed over Jessie and esteemed her highly. This time they invited her to stay for lunch after she'd taken care of the horse.

The cute animal was lame from a deep bruise which Jessie ascertained had been caused by the last dumping of snow in the spring. Its hoof had probably become impacted with ice, she had told them. Because the horse had no shoes, the bruise had become worse while trotting on the stony tracks around the farm when the grandchildren came to ride him.

'It will need rest, and once the swelling has gone down I'll check it again to see if he is ready to be shod. The shoes will protect his feet.'

After a pleasant lunch, Jessie said farewell and zoomed back onto the main highway heading towards Reed Station. She began rehearsing what she wanted to tell Mack. As she veered around the tight corners, a hare shot out under the vehicle which swerved, skidding several metres on the loose metal. It came to a halt in the long grass at the side of the road. Her hands, still glued to the wheel were shaking. She gasped. The impact had forced the air from her lungs. Relieved to discover she'd avoid hitting the animal that had skittled into the bushes she knew it was wrong to swerve to avoid them.

Ten minutes later she'd regained her composure and managed to drive her vehicle out of the long grass and back onto the road.

What a day, she thought. She hoped nothing else would go wrong for the rest of the week. It was a welcome sight to see the attractive colonial homestead belonging to Walter Reed but now Mack Reed lived there too which made it even more inviting.

She drove into her usual parking area at the side of the house and was greeted by Mack's border collie, Bluey. He stood next to the vehicle greeting her with a friendly yelp as she rolled down her window to say hello, the dog placed his paws on the window ledge.

'Get out of there,' called Mack. 'Sorry about that. He knows better than to do that.' He walked forward and helped her inside with her bag.

'Have you got time to come inside for a cool drink first? Bessie has just opened a new batch of ginger beer, her special recipe.'

'Ah ... sure. Thanks, I'd love to.'

They sat at the dining table and drank the ice-cold, invigorating beverage while they caught up on all their news. While Bessie loomed in the background, Jessie was not yet ready to tell Mack her sad story about her rebuff from the anti-female-vet brigade, she called them.

After their short catch up on all the latest local news, Mack carried her bag as they wandered over to the stable where he had penned Zoro.

'You know he's a very special horse, Mack, especially after the incident with your grandfather. He appears to have extrasensory perception or something. Either that or he is exceptionally intelligent. Perhaps he can be used to help others to heal someday. It's worth thinking about.'

'I like that phrase you used—extra what? Anyway, I think he has that.' They both chuckled as they entered Zoro's pen.

After she gave the horse a full examination to check his fitness for the shots, Jessie administered the vaccinations. Later on, Mack invited her to sit on the veranda for a rest to recover from her incident with the hare that she'd reported to him.

As they both sat on the bench staring out at the acres of paddocks on the horizon, Mack asked her how she'd been doing since her last visit and whether the business had started to build up.

'I've been referring my mates to you through the Vet Co-op, so hopefully, that might help.'

'Thanks, Mack. I really appreciate it. Most of them tell me if you have referred them to me. They are the decent ones worth having on my books. Not like some of them.'

'Oh that's good—but what do you mean? Are you getting some unpleasant clients out here?'

'Unpleasant is too kind a word for certain farmers around here. I would say outright nasty, in fact.'

She couldn't withhold it any longer and just caved in. She squeezed her eyes to try to hold back the unwanted tears, but they started to slide down her face, the salt stinging the cracks in her dry lips. She tried hard not to sob heavily but her emotions threatened her.

'Oh, no, what's happened. Who has upset you? Tell me, Jessie. What's been going on and maybe I can help.' He placed his arm across her shoulders then pulled back, not knowing what her reaction would be.

'I've noticed that a bunch of local high country farmers have intentionally not requested my services, in fact, not for months. The usual clients on Max's books have not wanted me to visit their farms.'

'Perhaps they've had no need for a vet for some time.'

'No, that's not true. They have deliberately been avoiding me, Joel Grey told me yesterday. They discussed my plight at the recent meeting of the High Country Farmers Association and several of them were caustic about having to put up with a female vet. Joel said they had not one bit of evidence to back up their argument and he fought for my defence.'

'Ridiculous old fools,' Mack snorted. 'Who on earth do they think they are? Those men are just deeply entrenched in narrow-mindedness and prejudice and haven't moved on—and times are changing.'

'But that doesn't mean they have to be nasty and unwelcoming. No one can change them after all these years and I'm afraid they will turn more and more farmers against me.' She sniffed loudly then blew her nose just as noisily on her handkerchief. Mack handed her another glass of ginger beer that Bessie had put out on the veranda earlier for them.

'I think maybe I might have to move away. It's just too hard managing this whole area by myself, driving miles each day along rough, windy, and dusty roads to ungrateful bigoted men who despise me.'

'Would you like me to pray with you? I don't mind, honest.'

'That's okay, don't worry. Joel prayed with me yesterday. I just needed to offload it.'

'It sounds like a regular case of bullying too. Look, Jessie, let me tell you about a similar experience I had as a young lad starting out on farms. That's when I first worked as a sheep shearing contractor. I was not your run-of-the-mill, beer-swilling, rugby-mad contractor like many of them. I was a shy, sensitive guy back then and kept to myself a lot. I was ostracised for not drinking or hanging around the girls in bars. They used to single me out and often start a fight with me just for the fun of it. Some bullies would even take credit for the sheep I had sheared.'

Jessie went quiet. For the first time, she was able to see Mack's soul, his real self.

Mack continues, 'I toughened up and learned how to box and even learnt some martial arts. I also went to a sheep shearing expert to learn great skills that won me awards. The worst thing was that some of them were abusing the sheep—badly. So much that some poor animals had broken eye sockets and head injuries from being kicked or battered with tools. A few of the shearers even stole wool or the odd sheep and sold them on the side. I became a whistle-blower.'

It sickened Jessie to listen to this, but he was drawing an analogy to what was happening to her.

'Men in positions of power abusing weaker, vulnerable ones,' she uttered. Her eyes widened, and she fixed her gaze on Mack's face as he continued with his story.

'One bloke deliberately provoked and picked a fight with me. He came off second best. That was the last time they ever went near me. I didn't run from it. You have to show them you aren't afraid. I've heard stories of excellence about your work, Jessie, so never doubt yourself.'

Jessie was speechless. She admired Mack for sharing something so personal and just sat still, soaking up every word.

'Look, Jessie. I want to share a verse from the Bible with you that changed my perception of the situation, a scripture that gave me hope and courage and made me realise that God understands. It goes like this ...

This is what the Sovereign Lord says: 'Should not shepherds take care of the flock? You eat the curds, clothe yourselves with the wool, and slaughter the choice animals, but you do not take care of the flock. You have not strengthened the weak or healed the sick or bound up the injured. You have not brought back the strays or searched for the lost. You have ruled them harshly and brutally. I am against the shepherds and will hold them accountable for my flock. I will remove them from tending the flock so that the shepherds can no longer feed themselves. I will rescue my flock from their mouths, and it will no longer be food for them. For this is what the Sovereign Lord says; I myself will search for my sheep and look after them. As a shepherd looks after his scattered flock when he is with them, so will I look after my sheep. I will rescue them from all the places

315

where they were scattered on a day of clouds and darkness.'

Jessie had not heard Mack speak like this before. She was speechless after he spoke those words from the Bible, trembling from head to toe.

'How are you finding the workload at present?' Mack asked.

She composed herself. 'The Co-op should have replaced the other vet who had shared the province with Max. Now Max has gone that just leaves me. I mean … they haven't even provided me with a clinic.'

'There has never been a clinic here, but we've certainly needed one.'

'I read about those mobile surgical units in the United States and even Australia that they use in remote areas like this. Perhaps I need to try that as one last solution to the problem. I've been thinking—instead of buying myself a house of my own, I could purchase a small bus and turn it into a mobile, fully functioning clinic. Then many of the clients with smaller animals can bring them to me. I'll also be able to carry out minor surgery in it instead of having to travel all the way into the one near Closeburn. If that doesn't work out, I'll just have to pack up and head back to the Waikato, as my old boss will give me my job back again any time. What do you think?'

Mack's face dropped. Suddenly his countenance took on a sombre serious expression. He scratched his head and started blinking nervously.

'Oh, Jessie. I'm sure it won't come to that. I do rather like the idea of the mobile clinic but not having to forfeit being able to have your own home. I know how hard you'd been saving for that. And those pompous fools at that meeting … I believe Max had about fifty high country farmers on his books and there is only a handful who are behaving badly.

You continue to prove your worth as you have been, and they'll fade into insignificance. You mark my words.'

Jessie wasn't convinced but trusted Mack's opinion. She was a lot happier now that she'd offloaded it.

A truck roared down the driveway and came to a halt in front of the house. It was Walter who had been driving and appeared to have had a full recovery from his minor stroke.

'That's a surprise to see Walter driving already. Is he okay now?'

'He's fine. No trouble with his legs, just one arm is a little weak and his speech slightly slower, but the doctor said he will probably completely recover. He is looking forward to seeing you. By the way—I forgot to tell you that Grandad, and I have reconciled and forgiven each other. He seems to be a changed man and comes to home church with me now and then.'

Jessie's heart leapt. It was amazing news, something that really uplifted her.

'In fact, he wants to invite my family to share Christmas with us and he suggested that you might like to come too, seeing you saved his life, he told me. What do you think?'

Jessie couldn't believe her ears. She was on a roller coaster ride with so many emotional ups and downs and a boost.

'I'd love to—oh, hi there,' she addressed Walter who walked towards her with his face beaming, showing a whole set of new dentures after the last set had been broken during his fall.

'What a nice surprise to see you, Jessie. In fact, I think I owe you for saving my life out there in the field that day.' He put out his hand and shook hers, hesitating before he released it. 'It seems that I am in your debt.'

Her face flushed. She wasn't used to such flattery.

'Oh, it wasn't me who rescued you, it was Zoro. You'd been lying flat on your back when I arrived and had been covered with hay. I guess Zoro had scattered it over you to keep the cold out.'

'You're right. The last thing I remember was carrying a small bale of hay into the paddock, but that would have been where the gate is, a long way from where I fell. He's an unusual champion, that stallion, unlike any I've ever seen—but you ran to my aid I hear and got help.' He turned to Mack. 'I hope you talked to her about Christmas. It's only a few weeks away.'

'Yes, Grandad, she's coming.'

Walter walked off into the kitchen and the wry grin stayed on his face while he handed Bessie the groceries he had brought back from the General Store.

Jessie drove off down the driveway back onto the main road, and her smile never left her face until she arrived home.

Chapter Eighteen

After a hectic day and her visit with Mack and Walter, Jessie's feet ached. Her toes burned inside her new leather boots that threatened to blister her tender feet. She sat up and tugged at them until they dropped onto the floor then sat staring out of the window. She was trying to remember the scripture that Mack had so eloquently poured forth to give her encouragement. She picked up her Bible and found the verse which she read out loud. Then it came to her— just as Mack had responded to his bullies, she would become bold too. God was on her side, and he would give her the inspiration and help she needed to come out on top.

She was startled by the phone ringing in her office. She didn't want to answer it as she'd planned to start reading the new C. S. Lewis novel she'd brought home from the tiny Glenorchy library the week before, but she was on call for the next twenty-four hours. She answered with a flat tone in her voice. It was the Vet Call Centre.

'Who? McKlintoch you say, from Priory Road? I didn't think he wanted me to go back there. He doesn't like female vets. Can't you ask one of the vets in Closeburn or Queenstown?' Jessie raised the tone of her voice, vehemently opposed to going to his farm.

'I have tried everywhere. There are vets off sick with the bug that's going around, and some are away on holiday. You appear to be the only one left. One of Doug's best hinds has gone into labour and needs help urgently.'

Oh yes, that has to happen to me of all people. He doesn't deserve my help. She wanted to explain the situation about his bullying but knew it would sound strange over the phone.

'He said the hind is having twins and has some complications. You are the only one left to help.'

'Are you sure he said, twins? It's very unusual for red deer to have twins.' Jessie's heart sank even further.

'He certainly said that, and he asked for someone who is skilled in delivering them. I said you had safely assisted many cattle, horses, sheep, even twins during birth, but not deer. I told him not to worry as deer usually give birth unaided in the wild.'

'Please let him know that it will be me attending the birth. I'm sure he'll refuse.'

'I've already told him you are his only option. You don't have to rush as she has only just gone into true labour, he said.'

Jessie knew she's been bludgeoned into agreeing to go and help her enemy as she saw him. But deep down, she figured that somehow this might be the way to win this man's admiration. On the other hand, if it all turned to custard, she would abandon ship and leave the beautiful south—heartbroken, of course.

***

She wound her way along the rough, loose metal road to the deer farm. She saw a logging truck pelting towards her. In an instant, she swerved to the side into the long grass to let him pass —CRACK! A large stone shattered her windscreen. 'Stupid fool!', she yelled as she stepped out of her vehicle, almost in tears. She went around to the back of the vehicle and took out a dustpan and brush to clear the shattered glass away from the inside of the car and placed it in a paper bag she had in her glove-box. If only she'd noted his licence plate number but was too shaken up. She had a much more important agenda.

This was one of the drawbacks of living in Glenorchy. She had to get used to the potholes and stony roads. No lovely tar-seal, like some parts of Queenstown.

Shaken up and discouraged, she stepped back into the vehicle and made her way up to McKlintoch's farm.

Doug McKlintoch paced up and down the path in front of his house waiting for Jessie as her vehicle swerved into the driveway and screeched to a halt, almost knocking him over. Bad start, she thought. She scrambled out of the vehicle almost falling over and pulled her medical bag off the back seat.

Doug, over six foot high, stood erect—his form looming over her, far too close for her liking. She got a whiff of the perspiration that ran down his tomato coloured temples and dripped off the end of his nose.

'Hurry, woman! I don't know what to do with her. I'm at my wit's end and I don't want to lose her. She's my prize breeder— you'd better get this right!'

'Sorry—I got a stone in my windscreen, and it shattered.'

'Is that right? Let's get this job done first and we'll worry about that later.'

He panted his way along the track with Jessie in close pursuit to the barn where the hind was still on her feet. Jessie kept thinking of the difficult twin births she'd assisted with her father's cattle and although she'd never attended the birth of twin red deer, she'd gained plenty of experience and confidence with birthing farm animals. Though she'd never had a bully standing over her intimidating her.

She placed her medical bag on the thick layer of hay in the corner of the pen. Doug was still panicking and started to annoy her.

'Can't you see she's in trouble? Hurry up and do something! She's been pacing up and down for an hour now.'

With that, she looked him in the eye as close as possible and spoke firmly. 'Look here, Doug ... I'm an experienced vet and have successfully delivered twin calves and breeches, some of them from large Highland cattle. Do you think the Vet Co-op would have employed me as a remote vet to high country farm animals if I was incompetent? Either you put your trust in me and let me do my job without harassing me, or I'll walk away right now!'

The sharpness of her tone and the accompanying threat was enough to cause him to teeter backwards. He slumped down onto a stack of feed that lay at one side of the pen and wiped away the sweat from his brow with his sleeve.

'Right you are,' he stammered. 'I'll leave you to it, lass. Let me know if you need anything.' He pointed to a steel bucket of hot water and a bottle of disinfectant for her to clean her hands and arms. A clean towel lay next to it. After scrubbing up, Jessie donned her long rubber gloves and examined the animal. A few minutes later she reassured the nervous farmer.

'I think this fine mother is going to do quite well without too much intervention. I'll just stand by and give her a helping hand when necessary. She's in normal labour but with twins, it's going to take a while. It's incredibly uncomfortable because of the pressure of the two babies, and that's why she's pacing up and down to relieve it—not because she's having complications.'

'Is that right? So where's she at then?'

'I'll have to help her along gently, but we should start seeing the hooves and head of the first one soon, by the look of her. But I may need to give her some assistance with the second one. They can be a little tricky.'

'Thanks for that. I'll slip inside to ask my wife, Jill if she'd make you a cup of tea.'

'Thanks, I'd love one.' Jessie let out a deep breath of relief to have him out of her presence briefly.

His prickly demeanour had changed to one of angst. He hurried inside the house and called out to his wife Jill who, in a short time brought them a tray of tea and chocolate biscuits. She placed it on a shelf near the action and walked away quietly and left them to it.

Contrary to Doug's overreaction and incorrect presumptions, the hind experienced no great complications except that the birth of the second one took longer than the first.

By eight o'clock that night, the second of her two healthy calves had been born. Jessie had eased it out of the birth canal and Doug placed it where its mother could reach it to start cleaning it and bonding. Both the twins had both arrived safely.

Doug and Jessie left the hind in peace to continue bonding with her twins and wandered over to the house. Jessie was exhausted from the build-up of nervous tension and the farmer's face was as white as a sheet.

He wouldn't stop thanking and praising her. 'You don't know how grateful I am that you came out here. No one else would come, and the Call Centre told me you were quite reluctant because I'd caused you so much grief recently.'

Jessie just nodded and said nothing, still shaking from all the stress of the challenging day she'd had.

'I know it's late, but please come inside. Jill has kept some supper for you, as she knew it would be a long night. Please, Jessie. I need to talk to you before you go and then I'll take a look at that windscreen.'

Was this the breakthrough she'd hoped for? Perhaps he really was human after all. Anyway—she'd worked up quite an appetite and her stomach was screeching out for food.

'Oh, thanks, I will. Have you some clean water for me to wash up with?'

He ushered her to the outside laundry where she could clean up properly. While she was out there, she heard Doug through the kitchen window on the phone to one of his colleagues saying how great the new vet was and what a wonderful job she'd done with assisting the delivery of the twin fawns. Jessie knew that the word would spread and at last she would be able to relax. She silently thanked God.

When she sat at the table eating the beef hot pot and drinking hot chocolate, Jill made her feel welcome by inviting her to be a guest speaker at the Country Women's Institute meeting in the new year. By the end of the evening, Jessie knew that they would become friends.

While Jill was busy in the kitchen with the dishes, Doug sat in the lounge with Jessie, trying to make amends.

'Look—I know I've been a thorn in your side and have misjudged you ... I'm sorry for all the trouble I caused when I hardly knew anything about you. I realise there's no excuse for my bad behaviour, but many of us old boys on the farms out here have lived on our family farms for generations. We've never had female vets, let alone women managing farms. But I realise now we'll just have to adjust to changing times, and you have proved to be a pioneer in your own right, Jessie. Please forgive me for the pain I have brought into your life. I'll be telling a different story to the committee of High Country Farmers—in fact, I'll draft a letter to them tomorrow.'

Jessie didn't know what to say. She was moved by his confession and just managed to utter, 'Thank you for trusting me. I'd better get on the road now.'

'Wait, a moment—I have something in my shed that might make do until you can get your windscreen fixed.' He turned the light on in the shed and had to wade through a lot of stored items to find a windscreen cover. Eventually, he brought it back onto the porch to show Jessie.

'What do you think of this?' he asked, wiping the dust off with a cloth.

'Oh, that's superb. I've never seen one of these before.'

'Good, let me take a look at it. Hop into your vehicle and drive it closer to the porch to catch the light.'

Jessie did what he said, and in less than half an hour he had the plastic cover firmly in place. Jessie was over the moon, and instead of seeing him as her enemy, her perception of him had rapidly changed into a gentle giant towering over her.

'I hope you have full car insurance, as they usually cover broken windscreens, and you certainly need it out here.'

'Yes, I was advised about it by Max before he left. It's all taken care of, thanks again. I am so grateful for your help. Let me know how the twins get along, and if you have any problems, please phone the Call Centre to get me out here as soon as you can.'

She poked her head into the kitchen. 'Bye, Jill. Please let me know when you want me to do that speaking engagement. I'm off now.'

Doug and Jill waved her off from their porch as she tooted, driving out onto the highway into the dark abyss with the security of her radio-phone hanging on the dashboard. No lights for miles except for the bright headlights of her vehicle and the wide eyes of the odd opossum that stopped momentarily on the road then shot to the side as she passed. She barely believed what had taken place—but tonight was the beginning of a whole new exciting chapter of her life. Only a week ago she had thought she may not have been mentally strong enough for this demanding and challenging work out in the middle of nowhere. But God did for her what she was not able to do for herself. And now it was evident that she wouldn't have to leave the mountains and her friends whom she held dear. She was here to stay.

But for now, she had to contact Mack's mechanic to book her windscreen in for repair. He had been able to get her a good discount with this mechanic. Although it was unlikely, she would try to get it fixed through New Year.

Right now she had greater fish to fry and Mack was her priority at this time.

Chapter Nineteen

Jessie stood in the mirror tying then retying her lilac scarf. She wanted to wear it with her white short-sleeved cotton jumper and mauve skirt, but the way she draped the scarf around her neck just didn't look right. She hung it back up in the wardrobe then walked over to her dresser, lifting the lid of her cherished wooden jewellery box that played the tune of The Sugar Plum Fairy. One by one she sifted through the pile of necklaces to find one that suited her outfit.

'Ah—here it is, just the right one,' she uttered, standing back in front of the mirror, struggling with the clasp on the necklace of synthetic amethysts. They contrasted well with her mauve skirt and blue eyes.

The necklace had sentimental value, as her parents had given it to her for her twenty-first birthday and she had always cherished it.

She was a little guilty that this would be the first Christmas that she hadn't spent at home with her folks, even though she had promised them instead that she would see the New Year in with them and her brother. She had planned to stay for a week if the Vet Co-op could get someone to fill in for her.

Mack insisted Jessie arrive early on Christmas Day so she would be able to meet his family before Christmas lunch. She had some trepidation about being in the middle of strained family relations, and even if Walter was willing to forgive and forget the past, the family may not be so full of grace. Nevertheless, she was a guest of Mack's and would support him through it as a loyal friend.

***

Mack's border collie, Bluey was the only farm dog that was allowed to run around the house. He was treated as one of the family, as he had been more than a working dog. He was to Mack, a beloved friend. Mack had always let him inside the house, although at Walter's place he had to stay outside at night and sleep on the veranda. He had his own special kennel outside Mack's bedroom door that led onto the long, wooden deck. Unbeknown to Walter, now and then during the winter, Mack would sneak him into his bedroom to sleep on his mat—only when Bessie was away visiting her family, as she would blow the whistle on him if she knew. The other farm dogs were in warm kennels several metres away from the farmhouse.

As Jessie drove up to the house, Bluey ran out to greet her as usual but knew not to jump up on her vehicle. She glanced around at the two strange cars in the driveway and guessed they must belong to Mack's family. She sat with the engine running, not knowing where to park. She didn't want to park far from the house as she had a large Pavlova with cream sitting on the seat next to her in a plastic cake carrier and imagined herself tripping and sending the thing flying, or worse still, smashing it down the front of her skirt.

Mack caught sight of her and rushed forward, waving at her.

'Hold on!' he called as she wound her window down. 'Over here, next to the house. I'll shift the quad bike.'

He jumped on the bike and moved it away from the house.

'Sorry, I should have moved it a lot earlier to make way for all the vehicles.'

She stepped out and went to the passenger door to reach for the Pavlova.

'Here—let me help you with that. It sure looks good. The family have come with cakes, but no one has brought one of these. Christmas isn't the same without one.'

'The strawberries are from my garden, by the way.'

'Ah, yes. Hope and Cole told me you've got green fingers. Come inside and meet my family.'

Jessie tried to ignore the hard knot forming inside her stomach and the tension in the back of her neck, as he said that. She followed behind him into the kitchen, as he placed the Pavlova on the sideboard.

'Let me pour you a drink before we go into the lounge. The family is all in there. Some have brought wine, and I made a large punchbowl. I've also got Bessie's ginger beer in the fridge.'

'Punch would be fine, thanks.'

'I'll tell you all about the new relationship my grandfather has with my family. It's a miracle. Thanks for your prayers, by the way. Let's talk later on. They arrived yesterday evening, and after lunch today, Grandad is taking them on a tour of the station.'

They carried their beverages into the lounge where there appeared to be a congenial atmosphere, much to Jessie's surprise after all the negativity she'd heard.

Mack's parents, Len and Helen stood up out of their chairs, as Jessie entered the room, followed by his sister, Meg and her husband, Joe, which unnerved her. She loathed being the focus of attention, as they moved forward to shake her hand.

'Well—we finally get to meet you,' said Helen softly, giving Jessie the sweetest smile. Jessie was taken in by the warmth of her eyes. She would easily take a liking to her. Len, who had given her a hard handshake, almost too hard for her liking, had sharp features and appeared to be a typical detached businessman in his manner— far removed from Mack who seemed to take after his mother, even in appearance with her thick, wavy hair and high cheekbones.

Jessie was overcome by the pressure of suddenly having to relate to Mack's family all at once. They bombarded her with questions about her vet role in a remote area. The women couldn't take their eyes off her.

Meg went with her mother to organise the dishes to go on the table. Walter sat in the corner chatting to Jessie about the favourable feedback he'd heard from his farming friends about the way she'd assisted Doug McKlintoch's prized hind deer giving birth to twins. Mack caught up with his brother-in-law, telling him about the successful working merino sheep station he now managed.

Walter had given Bessie a few days off while his family were staying. She'd gone to stay with her own family in Cromwell.

'Mack, would you mind slicing the ham and turkey for us,' Meg asked, nodding at Mack. He raced into the kitchen like an obedient child and after slicing the ham, took it into the dining room, and placed it on the table as Meg directed him. 'Joe, please can you bring in the turkey, please? It'll need cutting up too.'

Jessie's eyes almost stood out on stalks as she saw the size of the enormous turkey.

'Grandad, would you mind blessing the food for us, please?' asked Mack, while Len and Helen looked at them both somewhat taken aback. As Walter prayed and gave thanks for the food, he also thanked God for the restoration of his family. Then surprisingly for Mack, his father joined in and gave thanks for Walter and Mack and all that God was doing in healing their relationships. Helen followed suit too, but Joe and Meg remained quiet, appearing a little embarrassed. Jessie gathered that the rest of the family had accepted God into their lives but perhaps Joe and Meg weren't quite there yet. She and Mack would have to keep praying for them.

Christmas lunch was a joyful occasion as Jessie carefully observed the interaction between Mack and each member of his family. She liked the way that he appeared to thrive in a family setting—just as she had done with her own family back in Bethlehem. After they rested, the guests all decided to walk off the first course. They saved Jessie's Pavlova, Meg's cheesecake and Mack's fresh fruit salad for later on. Walter offered to take the family on a tour of the station in his truck.

***

Jessie and Mack were busy in the kitchen putting the dishes away after the main meal, while Mack's family readied themselves to go on the farm tour.

'They'll be at least an hour or longer doing that tour with Grandad. That's how long it'll take to show them all the farming operations. Let's go for a walk down by the river? It's going to be a warm afternoon so we'll get a pleasant cool breeze off the water.'

Jessie looked at her shoes which were unsuitable for stumbling over animal dung and rough ground.

'Oh ... I'd love to, but I didn't bring my walking shoes, sorry.'

'Ah, no need to worry. We can just sit out on the veranda until they come back. I should have phoned you to ask you to bring them.'

Jessie rolled her eyes and banged her hand down on the bench, annoyed with herself that she'd removed the spare boots from her vehicle that she usually carried with her. She had taken them out to clean them and forgotten to put them back.

'Are you okay—what's wrong?'

'Just annoyed that I haven't got my spare boots in my Land Rover. I'd love to come for a walk along the river.'

Mack placed the baking dish he was holding back onto the oven top and grabbed her arm. 'Wait here a minute ... what size are your boots?'

'Size eight. Woman's size, that is.'

Mack raced down the other end of the house where his family were staying and called out to his sister. He explained the situation to Meg, and she handed him a pair of trainers. He hurried back to Jessie. 'Here, try these on, I think they should fit. She and Joe are going to take my Ute and follow the others on tour.'

The shoes fitted perfectly. 'Come on, let's go. Make the most of the time they are away. They're taking off now.'

The water level of the river was still high, even in December, as there had been a few random dumps of snow the last few nights. The water was a beautiful turquoise, full of glacial flour—the fine-grained silt that created the colour.

'I love seeing this. You only see it in the south. It's gorgeous,' Jessie said as she stood staring at the water.

At the side of the river was a small group of apple trees with ripe fruit. Mack reached up above his head and plucked a red apple and handed it to Jessie.

'Try this—it's one of Grandad's prize varieties that has been in the family for generations. It's crisp and sweet.'

Jessie started munching on the fruit then picked another one, slipping it into her pocket.

'Come! I want to show you an amazing view.' They kept walking alongside the river until Mack stopped to point to something standing in the clearing by the pine trees. It was a horse—a beautiful golden Palomino watching them from a distance. It whinnied softly.

'Wow! Where did you get that? It's gorgeous ... a mare, isn't it?' Jessie pushed a branch of an overhanging young poplar tree aside to get a better look.

'She is your Christmas present. I had my eye on her when I saw her amongst Joel Grey's herd and asked him to keep her for you. I saved up and paid Joel off while I was still on my own farm. I waited until you had purchased your own grazing as you had planned, but you can graze her here for now.' Mack's smile stretched across his face as he looked back at Jessie and saw her eyes were full of tears—tears of joy. She turned and wrapped her arms around him squeezing him tight. 'How did you know I wanted one so badly?'

'Hope told me you had to leave your own horse, Rusty behind and how heart-broken you were. I put her in this paddock so that you wouldn't see her from the house, but she can't stay in here and demolish all Grandad's apples.'

'But what about Walter? What does he think about me grazing her on the farm?'

'I think he might not be too fussed when he hears about the second gift I have for you,' he said with smiling eyes.

'Oh, no, I haven't given you yours yet? It's in my Land Rover. I didn't want to do it in front of everyone today. I planned to give it to you before I went home.' Jessie turned to look at Mack, and for an instant, he had left the spot where he was standing. She watched him stoop down to the ground as if he was searching for something.

'Ah, here it is!' He had dropped something in the grass and his face had turned the colour of beetroot. Jessie approached him.

'What was it you dropped?'

He stayed on his knees.

'Are you okay, why don't you get up?'

'I dropped your other gift—well, actually it's not really a gift, it's a ... goodness, Jessie will you marry me?' he managed to blurt out, trying to remain upright kneeling on one leg on the rough, uneven ground.

Jessie stood stunned, her mouth and eyes wide open as if she couldn't believe what she had just heard.

'Yes, yes, of course, I will!'

He managed to pull the sparkling diamond ring out of the small box and slip it onto her slim ring finger.

'Sorry—I know it's kind of clumsy, but I wanted to surprise you and give you a lift, as I know you've had a stressful time of it with the McKlintoch business and hacking it out here alone. It's a harsh area for women on their own.'

Jessie was speechless. When Mack kissed her with deep passion, time froze—and the Palomino didn't take her eyes off them.

'Thank you for going to all this trouble, Mack,' said Jessie as she drew breath.

Mack searched her face with his wide hazel eyes.

'I hope you'll be happy living up here. We'll have to discuss it all with Grandad and see where he wants us to live. The homestead is big enough for all of us if you don't mind living there.'

'It's wonderful, I'll be very happy to live there.'

'But we need to discuss a date for a wedding. I was hoping in six months. That'll give you time to let your folks know and arrange for them to come down.'

'I suppose that sounds okay, but I need time to think about it.'

'Of course, I don't mind. But it would be great if we could let my folks know we're engaged, while they're still here.'

'Of course'. She turned and started walking towards the horse in the distance.

'I'll have to find a name for her, or does she have a name already?'

'I was going to leave that up to you', Mack said, as he approached them both.

It was as if the Palomino knew Jessie already. The mare shook her head and bumped her affectionately. Jessie reached into her jacket pocket pulling out an apple which Chantilly took from her.

'Here you go, girl. I'll be back to ride you soon—just you wait and see. We're going to be good friends. You're gorgeous.'

'Her name is Chantilly, delicate like lace and sweet like cream,' Jessie said, as she reached forward and rubbed the mare's nose.

'You can come here and ride her whenever you like. I'll take care of her until you are living on the station. It looks like Buster, our house cat has also taken a liking to you, the way she follows you around the house. Come on—we'd best be going back. Let's talk again tomorrow. I've got to go into the Farmer's Depot in Glenorchy to pick up some dry feed. I'll drop by late afternoon if that's okay with you.'

'That sounds like a good idea, as we need to talk about some things.'

'Are you ready for our announcement to the family? It's now or never. We don't have to confirm the date with them just yet.' He elbowed her and took her by the hand, leading her carefully through the long grass. Even though it was comforting to have her hand in his, it was a major adjustment to share her life with a man when she'd been self-sufficient for so long. Perhaps it was time to let go.

Chapter Twenty

The family had already gathered in the lounge when Mack and Jessie turned up. Before dessert was served, Meg and Joe were offered a beer by Walter while the others drank the rest of the chilled punch that remained.

'Well, what did you think of Reed Station? Was it big enough for you?' Mack asked his family, his eyes darting towards each of them. 'It takes a while to get around, doesn't it?'

Len answered first. 'It has certainly developed a lot since I lived here. We didn't have a dam in those days or solar power. Nor did we have those high-tech irrigation systems. The conifer trees you have as windbreaks were only saplings. You've certainly built the station up, Dad.'

'Well, that's what I'll continue to do while I can, thanks to good farm managers such as Aron and now, Mack. That's something I'd like to talk to you about—the future of Reed Station. Perhaps later this evening. Let's get into this food.' Jessie ascertained that the subject was uncomfortable for Walter to talk about and probably wanted to choose the right moment, after she'd gone home, perhaps.

Jessie's Pavlova, Bessie's traditional Christmas cake and the cheesecake Meg had bought, went down well. The women continued to sing Jessie's praises about her exceptional baking skills while she handed the plates around and sat down

'You'll make someone a great wife someday, lassie,' muttered Walter loudly, winking at her and making her cringe even deeper into her chair with the unwanted attention.

With that comment, Mack took it as his cue.

'Actually, we have our own announcement to make—Jessie and I have some news for you all.'

Everyone at the table sat holding their dessert spoons dead still and stared saucer-eyed at Mack then at Jessie.

'Jessie's accepted my hand in marriage today while you were touring the station.'

Their mouths changed from gaping holes to wide-brimmed smiles, especially Walter's. They all stood up and rushed up to congratulate them.

Walter, who was sitting between Mack and Jessie, immediately welled up with emotion. He leaned over and whispered with a croaky voice, 'I hope you aren't going to leave me now, Mack?'

Mack looked him in the eye. 'Not if I can bring my bride here and we can both share the house with you,' Mack whispered back to him.

Walter almost burst into tears of joy. A broad smile stretched across his face. 'Let's celebrate with some champagne!'

Mack grabbed his arm. 'Oh, Grandad, Jessie doesn't drink alcohol.'

'It's alcohol-free champagne from Cromwell, made from the finest white grapes.'

After they drank the champagne that Walter had kept for a special occasion, the family said their goodbyes to Jessie and excused themselves. 'We've had a big day and Walter wants us up early to tour the other half of the station. We'll be looking forward to seeing you at your wedding,' said Mack's mother, as the guests all went off to their rooms.

Jessie was overcome by all the excitement and wanted to have some time on her own to assimilate everything.

'I think I'd better get off now too. I'm a bit weary after today's activities. Can you come to my place for dinner tomorrow? We can talk about our plans for the future.'

'Sure can. I think it would be good to have some time on our own.'

'Come to my Land Rover and see what I got you for Christmas,' she said like an excited child.

Mack followed behind her and waited while she ducked into the back of the vehicle and pulled out a large package wrapped in red shiny paper. She handed it to him. 'Open it, please—before I go. It's something you had said you wanted.'

He opened the parcel on the roof of the vehicle and as the paper fell away, a black leather strap appeared then another. A brand new bridle presented itself.

'Wow! A brand new bridle for Zoro. His current one is completely worn and I need one for the dressage event in the next show. Thanks so much.' He leaned over and kissed her, this time taking even longer than he did when he had given her the engagement ring.

He slowly inspected the classy, black leather bridle with brass fittings designed for show events.

'This looks expensive. You shouldn't have. Perhaps you might like to keep it and use it on Chantilly.'

'Oh, no. I want Zoro to have it. He'll look gorgeous in this. Please take it.'

'I love it and so will Zoro. That's kind of you.'

'I'll be getting off now. I'll see you tomorrow. We have lots to talk about,' she said as she pulled herself up into her vehicle.

'I look forward to it, and I'll bring a load of firewood over. We need to make sure it'll last until you leave the cottage.'

He leaned through her open window to steal another kiss before she shut her driver's door then stood and waved her off.

As Jessie drove out onto the main road, she was surprised at how light the sky appeared. It was getting late. The sun had just disappeared behind the mountain range but a full moon lit up the road—a huge silver moon that appeared to smile at her. Tonight the stars appeared brighter than she'd ever seen before and she began to feel as though it had all been a dream, and she would wake up and find that none of it had actually happened.

As she opened the front door to her home, she realised that perhaps in six months' time she would no longer be coming home to an empty house—a bare property with no pets or a beloved horse. Her reality was soon going to change.

She sat in her armchair looking at her new sparkling engagement ring. Adrenaline rushed around her body at the thought of phoning her parents with the news. Then she decided to leave the phone call and surprise them at New Year with the good news.

Mack had slipped a photo of Chantilly into her hand before she had left Reed Station that day. It was as though it was a kind of magnet to encourage her to go and live at Reed station. She quickly shrugged off that random, suspicious thought, as she believed that Mack had much more integrity than that.

Tomorrow she would discuss with him how she would manage her veterinarian business while living on the station. Would he be expecting her to give it up to help her with farming? That was something she would need to clarify.

Jessie had worked up unwelcome anxiety about Mack's pending dinner date. She'd hoped it would be a relaxing romantic evening but now it seemed to have tension-building issues hovering over it like an ominous cloud. She prayed for peace of mind and courage to change the things she can, to be able to remain a strong independent woman as Mack sometimes unwittingly took charge.

***

That evening, Walter sat with his family in the lounge ready to have that discussion that he had hinted at having with them earlier—the subject of the future of Reed family estate, now that Mack was managing the station.

He got up out of his leather armchair. 'Anyone for a cold drink, or hot chocolate if you'd, rather?'

'Come and sit down, Grandad. I can get that if they want one. I thought you wanted to talk to us about the estate,' said Meg, as though she had an invested interest in what was going to happen to her share of the family inheritance.

'Yes, you're right. I'd better get onto that.' He took a worn-out handkerchief from his pocket, blew into it loudly and then stuffed it back into the pocket of his gabardine trousers.

There was quietness in the room. Joe began crossing and uncrossing his legs and Len sat erect clasping his hands together. Helen just peered out the window watching the large moon as it bobbed up behind the mountains. It was a clear, cool night, and the stars were sparkling diamonds—something city dwellers wouldn't see.

'You know that I wrote and told you that Mack has been managing the station since my longstanding Manager, Aron left. He has been a Godsend since my health has deteriorated and has shown himself to be competent and skilled in all aspects of sheep farming. Therefore I'm handing over the control of my estate to Mack with

340

provision for Meg, a portion set aside for her on my death if the station is still making a profit.'

'I thought you had told me last night that the Trust was set up in such a way that it would always be kept as a working farm and would not be sold off,' said Len, frowning. 'That's why I had said I wouldn't want to benefit from the estate.'

'That's right. It will never be able to be sold off. That is stipulated in the Trust, but my will makes provision for Meg to even things out as Mack will continue to be Manager of the station.'

Mack just sat there watching the body language of the family members Walter had been addressing.

'That sounds okay to me. But what about you, Meg—are you happy about the situation? We don't want any red herrings thrown into the water later on.' Len nodded his head at her.

Meg gave her father an austere glance, frowning so much her nose-bridge wrinkled.

'I have another option you may not have thought about, Grandad if you want to make things equal between me and Mack.'

'Oh, I see ... go on.' Walter leaned forward resting his arms on his thighs and stared at her intensely.

'I have been thinking about how great this location would be for an exclusive country lodge. I could build one on the station. How do you both feel about it?' She bit her lip as she glanced at the men.

Mack, by this time also sat on the edge of his seat.

Walter spoke first. 'Absolutely no! I will never entertain the idea of running a tourist business on my station. This has been a sheep station for many generations and will not change. But Mack and I have another solution to the disparity in equity that you might have seen. Mack—you explain it.'

He glanced at Mack and nodded, giving him the go-ahead to talk, then sat back, clasping his hands like Len. He stared at Mack, waiting with tight, thin lips, ready to listen to him backing him up.

Mack's cheeks turned red. He undid the top button of his shirt as if it would make his breathing easier.

'I've been trying to sell my hundred-acre farm, as you already know. It has been on the market for several months now, but I've had no bites. That's mainly because of its remoteness. It will of course suit the right buyer, a local farmer. Nevertheless, in order to make my takeover of Reed Station fair to you, Meg —I've decided to gift my farm to you so that you'll be able to create the enterprise you want. The building which I have turned into a substantial farmhouse used to be an enormous barn and it's very solid. It will provide you with a good start. You can turn the land into grazing and lease it for locals who run out of feed. That will give you a supplementary income to support your project. What do you think Meg … Joe?'

Meg was speechless for a minute. She sat there looking at her feet with a clenched jaw trying to work it all out.

'I think it's a pretty good offer, my girl,' said Walter. 'You can decide to run your boutique farmstay that will probably attract holidaymakers or keep it on the market and sell it as a farm.'

'And I know you can get resource consent for the farmstay if you do go ahead, as my neighbours got one when they applied. But they sold up and moved away to Queenstown instead,' Mack added.

'Wow! I'm having trouble taking it all in. Joe and I need to discuss it first. What do you think, darling? Are you sure you want to leave Dad's business?' Meg asked Joe.

Len interjected quickly before Joe was able to say anything.

'Joe will have to have something to do when I retire at the end of this year. If you don't want to take over my company in Wellington, I'll sell it. If you are interested, I could be involved in the business side of your farmstay, just as we have already discussed. I just didn't expect to be doing it in such a remote area but I already feel the challenge. I think it'll be great.'

Mack was relieved that, in spite of the conflict and tension caused by Walter's decision to hand the station over to him the family meeting had a positive outcome.

'Perhaps we should all think about the propositions Mack and I have made this evening. Let's get together again tomorrow so that we can come to some sort of agreement before you all head off back to Wellington,' said Walter

They nodded in unison and went off to their bedrooms while Mack sat with Walter swapping feedback on how the evening went.

'Do think they were really happy with the solutions we came up with? I mean—you know your family better than I do now. We have become estranged all these years. What do you say, Mack?'

'I think Meg looked excited about the prospect of owning her own farmstay, and for years she has talked about how suffocating it was living in the city. It was Joe I was more worried about. I can't see him giving up the corporate business world to live in a remote rural area. But then again, I had no idea my father had decided to retire this year either.'

'Well, our prayers have been answered, Mack. God had made a way where there seemed to be no way. Let's pray about the meeting tomorrow and for Meg and Joe— that they will also come to know God as we know him.'

They bowed their heads and prayed that the outcome would be in God's hands.

Chapter Twenty-One

The next day, Mack arrived with a Ute full of firewood. As he approached Jessie's front porch, a delicious smell emanated from the house. She held open the front door.

'Hi there—by the smell of that lovely aroma wafting out the door, I'm sure I'm at the right house.' He removed his Stetson and pulled her toward him, kissing her more fervently than before.

'I'd better remove my boots before I come in.' He yanked them off and walked inside displaying his grey woollen socks full of holes. 'Whoops! You weren't supposed to see these,' he said, his neck flushing suddenly.

Jessie wondered if it was a hint for her to take them and offer to mend them. Then again, she barely had time to take care of her own clothing while she worked long hours as the area's only vet. What will he expect of her once they are married? This issue kept playing in the back of her mind. Perhaps he would ask her to stop her vet practice after the marriage. Was she having second thoughts? If not, why was she feeling so vulnerable?

'Come and sit in here.' She directed him into the lounge. 'It's cosy and warm with the fire going.'

'Mmm—I smelled the macrocarpa wood as I drove in. I have another load for you out there. How about I unload it for you first, before it gets dark?'

'Um ... okay, I suppose it's best. Let's have a coffee first though. I've got the kettle on and dinner will be a while yet.'

They sat and spoke small talk in front of the fire with their coffee then they both went out to the Ute. With the help of a wheelbarrow, they managed to unload and stack the wood just in time before the sun disappeared.

Minutes later, Jessie lay back in Mack's arms on the couch, trying to ignore a large toe poking through a hole in one of his socks. She chuckled.

'Something amusing you?' Mack poked her in the ribs.

'It's just your toe staring back at me. You sure have big toes.'

'Well, that's because I have a big heart!' They both laughed.

Jessie was almost lulled to sleep by the warmth of the fire and the strong, muscle-bound arm draped around her.

'Sorry,' she said as she suddenly pulled herself away. 'I'd better rescue dinner before I fall asleep.'

'Can I help?'

'No, honestly, there's nothing to do except dish it up. Do you mind if we eat here on our laps? I'll give you a tray.'

'Sounds very cosy to me. In fact, nice and relaxing. Just the mood to discuss our plans for our new life together.'

They both sat savouring the chicken and thyme hotpot with the poultry that Joel had given her on one of her visits. She only kept her own chickens for their eggs.

'Mmm, I hope this is a sample of what goodies I can expect when we are married. I'll have to sack Bessie and take you on as a cook.' He loved teasing her and this time she gave him a sharp elbow in his ribs.

'Ow! Okay, just joking. I know I'll have to keep Bessie on.'

'I need to talk to you about my vet practice—how I'm going to run it once I'm living on the station. I'm not sure what to do. I'll be too far away from Closeburn to be able to use the clinic there for minor surgery and other clinical procedures.'

'That's what I wanted to talk to you about. Do you remember we'd had the discussion about the possibility of you running a mobile clinic? You can buy a bus and have it fitted out as a minor surgery clinic and run your practice from Dart Valley. You won't need to buy a home now, so you can invest the money in the clinic.'

'But what about my clients on the other side of the lake in Kinloch?'

'I heard that Robbie Byrnes wants to extend his practice and offer more services south of Glenorchy. You can talk to him about it, in fact, discuss it with the Vet Co-op first. I'm sure they'll agree to you covering the whole of the Dart Valley out to Kinloch which is closer to home. That is a big enough area for you to manage on your own. If you withdraw your services from practising south of Glenorchy, they will have to find another vet and Robbie will do it.'

'It sounds good in theory. Where are these buses you are talking about?'

'In Queenstown. I can take you there when you get back from visiting your folks.'

'By the way—what was the outcome with your family, if you don't mind me asking? I mean Meg's request to set up a boutique farmstay on Reed Station?'

'No, I don't mind telling you, as it will affect you.'

He got up and took his tray and Jessie's out to the kitchen and came back and sat down.

'Grandad refused to entertain the idea. Instead, Meg and Joe have decided to take over my farm and set up the farmstay there. They'll use the land for local farmers to graze dry stock or they can lease it to a farmer. They may fence off a few fields as a mini-farm for guests to get close to animals. Meg has been keen to run ponies for children.'

'Meg with horses? I thought she was just a city girl.'

'Actually, she has been an experienced rider but not in the style that you and I are accustomed.' Mack knelt down to stoke the fire.

'Really—how's that?'

'They've been well-heeled, very well off. In fact, one of the elite couples in Thorndon. Meg has kept a few horses in stables there that she rents and has attended hunts with high-brow people in Wellington. I suppose one would call her a snob. But she had a few back problems and sold her horses several years ago.'

'Ah—so she's not the proverbial city slicker that I thought she was. I can see why she would want to keep horses then as a kind of compromise.'

'Yeah, she sounds pretty keen and my family support their move to my farm that I have gifted to her.'

'Oh, that sounds wonderful. How do your parents feel about the boutique farmstay?'

'They aren't bothered as my father has decided to retire this year. He has a lucrative business to sell and an upmarket home that will fetch a high price too. He and Mum are going to move to a small coastal town, probably to Nelson.'

'That's marvellous. It all appears to have gone smoothly then. What you thought was impending doom actually has worked as a blessing. Everyone is happy. See—I said that if we trust him, God will do for us what we cannot do for ourselves.'

They managed to get off the subject of the Reed family property and their finances and put the focus back onto themselves and their own future.

Mack pulled Jessie closer as she snuggled up to him. 'I was thinking that it might be snowing heavily by June or July. Don't you think we should plan the wedding later, perhaps in spring?' she asked.

'Actually, I was thinking of the same issue, only not about delaying it because of the weather but bringing it forward. What do you think about getting married in late April? I know it will be autumn, but it will less likely be snowing heavily then and the weather is still stable,' said Mack.

'Goodness, that's in four months. I hope we can be organised then.' Jessie sat up erect and looked at him.

'I'm sure we'll manage, and we can hold the reception at Reed Station. Bessie will be a great help. I'll pay for your folks to come down and your brother, Tom as well.'

'Are you sure? I'd love that. But first I need to tell my parents all our news and let them have some input. They'll want to meet you first. Perhaps you can manage to tear yourself away from the station for a weekend,' said Jessie making him aware of her own needs too.

'I was hoping to invite them down here. There's plenty of room for them at the homestead and Grandad would like to meet them too.'

'I'll ask them when I go back home next week. I have lots to tell them and they are going to be a bit staggered, I would say.'

'Let me take you to the airport ... Monday, isn't it that you're flying out?'

'Yes, it is. Are you sure? I can ask Hope or Cole if they can take me.'

'No, honestly. I can use the trip to pick up some supplies in Queenstown. What time is your flight?'

'Eleven o'clock.'

'I'll be at your place at eight-thirty. That should give you enough time.' He flicked his wrist and looked at his watch.

'Great Scott! I didn't realise it was so late. I've got an auctioneer coming early in the morning to conduct a stock sale. I have to get the sheep penned up before he comes. I'd better get to bed.'

He kissed her and pulled her up on her feet, placed his Stetson on his head and walked towards the door.

'Leave me your holey socks. I'll repair them for you, and you can give me any others that need darning. I don't mind, honest I don't.'

'Really, are you sure? I don't want you to think I'd be wanting you barefoot and pregnant as soon as we're married.' He laughed.

Jessie swiped him with a sock then threw them into the laundry tub, while Mack pulled his boots onto his bare feet.

'I'll see you on Monday. Thanks for the firewood. I really appreciate it.' Jessie squeezed his hand, and Mack grabbed her around the waist and held her tight. 'I'm going to get used to these hugs really quick,' he said, winking at her as he turned and walked out to his Ute.

After he drove off, she had a sense of deep anticipation that was new for her—something she hadn't experienced all the years that she'd been alone. But now her hard-earned independence was starting to wane, and she was rapidly getting used to having affection and emotional intimacy fill a void in her life. She looked forward to Monday, the hour's drive with Mack to the airport. She already started fretting about having to fly to the Bay of Plenty and leave him behind. Her life had certainly changed.

Chapter Twenty-Two

The trip from Glenorchy to Queenstown Airport was pleasant—especially with the handsome, rugged chauffeur who was well-dressed in his blue and white check shirt and light brown suede trousers. Jessie was sure she could smell aftershave this time. The one that her father used to wear when he took her mother out for the evening. Her father, Wyatt was also a romantic. "Paco Rabanne"—that was the brand her father used. Fresh and spicy like cinnamon and vanilla. Expensive taste for a merino sheep farmer, she thought. Today Mack was clean-shaven and had his hair slicked back. Not with Brylcreem, but attained by a good brush.

He drove at a leisurely pace so he could talk. 'I have some news for you—something that will put a smile on your face while you're away.'

'Oh, really. What's that?'

'I told Grandad about you wanting to run a mobile vet clinic from Reed Station once we're married.'

'You shouldn't have told him that, as I haven't even got a vehicle to do it with.'

'No, wait. When I told him what your plan was to modify a minibus and turn it into a mobile clinic, he took me out to the large barn that he keeps locked all the time. He told me it was full of old vehicles and tractors that he doesn't use any more. You will not believe what was in there. A beautiful minibus that he had bought and turned into a motor home with the intention of travelling around when he retired. He had purchased it before he got sick the first time when he employed Aron as Farm Manager. It has been sitting in the barn unused ever since. It's a bit dated but in perfect condition.'

'Wow, that's amazing. Is he going to sell it?'

'No, he wants you to have it as a kind of engagement present—no strings attached. He has seen the need for a mobile vet clinic for years out here and feels he is contributing by giving it to you.'

As Mack turned to look at Jessie, large blobs of tears ran down her cheek.

'I can't believe how blessed I am. What a lovely generous man. Please tell him I'll be thrilled to be able to use it.'

'I have a good friend in Queenstown who is a mechanical engineer. He could probably modify it for you.'

'I can't wait to see it.'

As he waved to her from the departure lounge, she wished he was coming with her to meet her parents. Now she would only be able to describe him—his character and his appearance. Especially his character which was the most important aspect of Mack that she needed to focus on.

***

Prue and Wyatt Lee were overjoyed to see their daughter walk through the airport's arrival gate. Her mother rushed up to her, almost knocking her over with excitement.

'It's been far too long, Jessie. I almost forgot what you looked like. Goodness, how you've grown up so quickly. You're a mature woman now.' Prue kept fussing over her.

'Where's Tom? I thought he would be here too.'

'Your brother has had to watch the farm while we're away. There are ewes lambing right now and can't be left. He has almost finished his agricultural degree by distance study. We're so proud of him and your father has made him farm manager now that he is almost retiring.'

'That's marvellous. I knew he would do well. Anyway, Dad, where is my hug?' she asked, lurching forward at him as he wrapped his arms around his daughter. His smile didn't leave his face during the entire walk to the car.

'Wait—what's that on your finger?' her mother asked, as they were almost at the car. 'It's not what I think it is—or is it?'

Prue grabbed hold of Jessie's hand and stroked the diamond ring.

'Yes, I'll tell you about it in the car on the way home.'

As Wyatt swung onto the highway heading home, Jessie told her parents about Mack and how their relationship had developed. She went into great detail about Reed Station and her plans to operate her veterinary practice from there.

By the time they'd arrived at the farmhouse, Jessie had told the story about McKlintoch and how she'd finally won the battle for her credibility amongst the farming community

That evening, Jessie turned in early. She was shattered after the week's events. She looked forward to staying up to celebrate New Year's Eve with her family the following night, but right now she desperately needed sleep.

***

As Jessie snuggled into the bed that had always been hers, a strong sense of nostalgia soothed her. She realised that she'd missed her folks' farm and home. What troubled her was her mother's reticence about her being engaged to a high country farmer, so far away in such a remote place. Jessie really wanted her parents' blessing but now she wasn't sure that she was going to get it.

She recalled the conversations that had taken place earlier that evening. She had spoken to them about the events that had led up to Mack proposing to her and they didn't look happy. Prue had a constant frown and her lips were pursed. Wyatt kept looking down at his feet. Unlike him, his mood was flat. Tom had gone to bed early after working with the ewes all day, but he was the only one who appeared elated with the news of Jessie's pending marriage to a South Island sheep farmer. Tomorrow she would have to win them around, especially on New Year's Eve.

***

Jessie and her family didn't do much for New Year's Eve except go to the local beach to watch the fireworks display. Wyatt wasn't keen on fireworks except under strict control far away from the animals. The display had been put on by the local Lions Club and Jessie found it impressive considering Bethlehem was such a small community.

When they arrived home from the display, Prue made hot chocolate for everyone, and they all helped themselves to freshly baked raspberry muffins and sat around the lounge chatting.

Prue brought up the subject of Jessie's plan to settle in Glenorchy and Wyatt took part as well. Tom did not want to interfere with Jessie's decision he told her earlier and took himself off to bed. 'Happy New Year, all of you. I think I'll turn in now. The lambs have worn me out the last few days.'

Jessie knew he was allowing his parents to have a good talk to her—the issue that needed discussing before she returned to Glenorchy.

Prue started first. 'I don't understand why a young woman like you would want to drive up and down on those dusty rough roads in an old beat-up truck to grumpy farmers, as you had described over the phone. And it can't be safe for you driving around those roads late at night visiting farms out in the sticks—not safe at all.' Prue's voice shook, and she appeared upset on the verge of tears. 'And Dart Valley is extremely remote, we've heard—miles away from anywhere, and there's nothing there. Not the life for a woman.'

'But that's what I've been doing ever since I moved there. I'm used to it now, and the vehicle is a sturdy, four-wheel-drive Land Rover, not beat-up at all. Anyway—Mack's not keen on me doing that anymore. He wants me to just focus my business on the Dart Valley area and not south of Glenorchy. The Co-op will have to find another vet for there. His grandad has a minibus that he had planned to use as a motor home before he had his first stoke. But after he suffered another stroke, he kept it in storage in the hope that he would one day be able to tour around in it. When Mack told him I was going to buy a minibus to use as a mobile vet clinic, he said to Mack he would like to donate it to my vet practice, as there's a desperate need for a mobile service in the area. Mack's engineering friend is going to modify it for my use.'

Prue cupped her head in her hands and Wyatt slumped back in his chair with his arms folded tight.

'But remember that time you told me you had a flat tyre late at night and had to sit in your vehicle in the dark until some grouchy farmer turned up—the one who was a trouble-maker like that Doug McKlintoch.'

'I told you —I won't do that once I'm married. They'll have to get someone else to do the call-outs at night. Please, both of you. Come down to Glenorchy and see how beautiful it is, and you'll change your minds. Dad, you've got to see how such an enormous sheep station runs. You'll love Walter. He'll show you around and Mum—you and Bessie will get on so well. You can both fly back there with me this time. At least then you'll get to meet Mack's family before we are married.'

'We'll discuss it and let you know by the end of the week. We need to think about it. You'd better get some sleep, as you've had a big day travelling up here,' said Wyatt.

That night, Jessie was disturbed instead of being relaxed in the bed of her childhood. She really needed her parents' blessing and now was unsure if she would get it. The last thing she would want to do is to cause them pain. She was desperate.

Dear God—I don't know what I would do if I don't get my parents' blessing. Please speak to their hearts and persuade them to come back to Glenorchy with me. I know they'll love Mack and Walter. Perhaps we can all meet up with Mack's family in Wellington on the way too.

Jessie had pangs of guilt making such a request to God, as she knew he wasn't there to be used as some kind of Santa Claus. But she had a close enough relationship with him and knew he was loving and full of grace and would not want to withhold granting her hearts desires, not unless it was going to cause her harm.

***

At the end of the week, Jessie was all packed ready to return to Glenorchy. She'd accepted that she would be travelling alone again. Up until now, she'd decided that her parents were not showing any interest in her marriage to her high country farmer in the Southern Alps. But to her delight, she discovered she was going to be flying back to Queenstown with Wyatt and Prue in tow after all.

They had surprised Jessie by saying that they had considered it carefully and had decided to keep an open mind. They also suggested she phone Mack to arrange for them to meet up with his family in Wellington on the way. That would involve two flights, and they offered to pay for her flight tickets to both airports. This marriage was already turning out to be a costly business, Jessie had decided, but these family details were important for her future happiness with Mack. But what if none of them gets along or they have a clash of personalities? The thought of it was too much for Jessie to bear, as she had always enjoyed a close and loving relationship with all her family members for whom she had much respect.

Chapter Twenty-Three

Tom stayed home to look after the ewes and lambs on the farm in Bethlehem. He relished the extra responsibility since his father had been preparing him to take over the farm once he decided to retire.

Mack had managed to arrange for his sister, Meg to collect Jessie and her parents from Wellington Airport. They were greeted with warm smiles as Meg and Joe met them at the arrival gate. Jessie sat squashed between Meg and her mother in the back of the car, while her father sat in the front talking about the state of the economy with Joe.

Jessie overheard her father saying to Joe that he was trying to decide whether it was time for him to retire. Why didn't he tell her that instead of her having to hear him tell it to a stranger?

Her parents' retirement was well overdue, she thought. They'd had children late in life and were both in their sixties.

'What will you do? I'd say it would be a wrench to give up farming after all these years,' said Joe.

'I had thought of selling the farm, but my son, Tom is keen to keep it going. He has almost finished his Agricultural Degree and is very up with the play. But I don't know what we'll do if we retire.'

Jessie sat half-listening to Meg chatting about her exercise and dieting routines while trying to catch on to every word her father was saying to Joe about their farm.

Joe tried to look cool driving his shiny, black Rover around the corners of Oriental Parade with a suntanned forearm leaning on the window frame. Jessie focused her gaze on the fancy Ray-Ban glasses he was wearing.

'I've invited my parents over for dinner so you can meet them before the wedding,' said Meg to Wyatt and Prue. 'They'll love to hear all about the Bay of Plenty, as we had a few holidays in Tauranga several years ago.'

When they arrived at the two-story home in Thorndon, Jessie was blown away by their assumed wealth. The ostentatious home had a tennis court and swimming pool. How can a couple who live like this think that they can survive in a remote area like Glenorchy? Mack had told her that Meg and Joe had not wanted to have children. She said that they had far more important things to do with their lives. Jessie kept her opinions and concerns regarding this, to herself.

Jessie and her folks barely had time to relax before Mack's parents Len and Helen arrived and introduced themselves.

Later on, during the evening, Joe brought out all kinds of cocktails after a substantial meal, but he'd forgotten that none of them drank alcohol.

Meg explained to Jessie's parents that her brother, Mack had gifted his farm as her share of Walter's estate. Their grandfather had bequeathed it, in trust, to his grandchildren. Meg said that she and Joe were planning on turning the large home and ten of the one hundred acres into an exclusive boutique farmstay, but they were in a quandary about what to do with the residue of the ninety acres of grassland. Joe said that they might put sheep on it.

'You're an experienced sheep farmer, Wyatt, so I hear. What do you think I should do—do you think it could work?' asked Joe.

'I think it would be too big a job trying to run an exclusive farmstay which is a lot of work, as well as manage ninety acres with sheep. Even if you just used the land for grazing for another farmer, you would still need to maintain the fences, keep the weeds down, and fertilise the soil. There is also water to consider. Walter told me about the major droughts they've been getting in the last few years. You'd be better off employing someone to manage it for you and graze cattle on there, not sheep.'

Joe sat on the edge of his seat, leaning on his knees and rubbing his chin with his index finger. He didn't say anything for a few minutes, and then Helen passed around the cake she'd baked for them. Wyatt remained pensive and appeared to be mulling over the problem Joe was asking him to help solve.

Mack's parents stayed out of the discussion about the change of ownership of their son's farm. They preferred to keep their opinions to themselves, and Len had suffered enough heartache over family farms.

Joe lifted his head and turned to Wyatt who now sat awkwardly eating his cake with the dainty silver fork Meg had handed him.

'Wyatt—it's just an idea, and I may be barking up the wrong tree. But you mentioned you'd like to retire soon and take a step back. You said that your son, Tom is close to being able to manage your farm for you. What do you think about the idea of managing a smaller property such as our farmlet in Glenorchy? You can help us draw up a lease and manage it as grazing for other farmers. We will give you a good wage and we can build a separate dwelling for you and Prue to live in.'

It was as if someone had dropped a bomb. Everyone stopped what they were doing and stared open-mouthed at the two men. Jessie found her head spinning, as it was all moving too fast. She wasn't married to Mack yet and now all this was happening. But if it all worked out, she realised it would be a good thing. It seemed rational and logical, as her father was an exceptional sheep and beef farmer —but to imagine city slickers like Meg and Joe owning and running a farm seemed ludicrous.

This time Len spoke up. 'Think carefully, both of you,' he said nodding at Meg and Joe. 'It will be a huge upheaval after living here in the city and having everything at your fingertips. Not that I begrudge Wyatt and Prue managing your property—they are seasoned farmers and are used to living that way. Just discuss it carefully amongst yourselves before any of you make any commitments.'

Len was talking like a true businessman, and he'd been a good one at that. He was a level-headed man, much like Mack who was a chip off the same block. Jessie sat thinking how Len and Helen might be quietly feeling left out at the thought of all their family living in a remote community far away from them.

***

The next day, Joe spent hours taking Jessie and her family on a tour of the city by car. They returned home exhausted. He'd given a long and detailed history of every notable building in Wellington. Jessie was delighted they were only staying two days and couldn't wait to get back to the pure mountain air.

During the evening, they all took part in discussions about farming practices and the upmarket farmstay that Meg envisaged running. Jessie's mind was in another sphere. She imagined being married to Mack and having her parents living nearby. She wanted to see her father managing a small farm without having all the worry and responsibility of owning the business. But what if they move down there and find they don't like it? She would feel so bad.

'Don't you all think we should wait until you've had a look at Glenorchy to see if you like it there—I mean because it is so remote? I love it there, but you have to make sure it's what you really want and whether you can handle that isolated lifestyle.' Jessie was uncomfortable bringing it up, but she knew it had to be said, no matter how much she would want to have her family living down there with her.

'Well said!' Prue uttered, having not said a word the whole time. Jessie guessed that her mother was also facing the dilemma of considering how good it would be living so close to her daughter, and on the other hand, how remote it actually was living in Glenorchy.

They all agreed to wait until her parents had spent their holiday at Reed Station. They said that before their return to Bethlehem, they would decide. Tom would have to be happy with the arrangement too.

***

Mack had missed Jessie intensely but didn't let on when he picked them up from Queenstown Airport. She introduced her parents then did her best to fill in the gaps in the lack of conversation as the Ute left the airport. She also guessed that her parents, especially her mother still had reservations about Mack, mainly because of the distance he would create between her and her daughter.

'Wow, look at that view! I had heard that the Glenorchy-Queenstown Road has some of the best views of Lake Wakatipu.' Prue rolled down her window to gape at the spectacular sight of the snow-capped Remarkable Ranges. The bright blue backdrop of sky cast a colourful reflection onto Lake Wakatipu. 'Can we stop for a photo please, Mack?'

'I sure can. It's beautiful, isn't it? One of the things that keeps me here. Wait—I'll pull over into this rest area along the road.'

Prue fumbled around in her handbag for her camera.

She stepped out of the Ute and walked to the concrete barrier, snapped her photos then stepped back into the Ute.

'That's why they call New Zealand Land of the Long White Cloud. See that long cloud that follows the mountains right along the Lake. When I used to travel south for my sheep shearing contracts, I often travelled along this road at sunrise. It was a majestic sight,' said Mack.

'That's so awesome. The scenery is breathtaking,' she replied.

Prue had shared something in common with Mack—a love of God's beautiful creation, part of the country's God-given heritage.

'There's lots more where that came from, Prue. Wait till we show you the mountains and lakes around Glenorchy.'

'Careful, I might just start to enjoy it,' she said, her eyes smiling at him. Even Wyatt leaned over her shoulder, gazing at the view. He appeared awestruck.

'Wait—we'll just make a little side tour.'

'Where are you taking us?' asked Jessie, tugging on his shirt sleeve.

'Ah, this is a little surprise for you too.'

As they drove along the lakeside towards Wilson Bay, Mack veered off to a side road. Jessie hadn't noticed the name on the road sign.

'What have you got up your sleeve?' she asked.

'Not long now, just wait and see. Wyatt, you're going to enjoy this one. It's right up your alley.'

The street led to another long private dirt road that wound its way through golden hills with dry yellow grass from the drought during this unusually hot summer. It appeared even more remote than Dart Valley. Mack drove slowly as sheep began to appear on either side of the road and before their eyes a lake suddenly appeared. Lake Moke popped up like a mirage, set against the yellow pinnacles. It was as flat and smooth as ice and the reflection was so perfect it looked like an artist had painted the background.

'This is unreal. What is this place?' Wyatt asked as Mack pulled over near the lake.

'This is called Ben Lomond Station—thirty-three thousand acres of grassland running seven thousand merino sheep and a few hundred cattle.'

'Well ... I've never seen a working farm this size in my life.' Wyatt just sat and scanned the peaks. 'Which one is Ben Lomond?'

Mack pointed to the mountain as he drove the Ute a little further.

'Look at the horses!' Jessie cried out, pointing at the horses at the side of the lake. 'Would they be wild?'

Mack laughed. 'No they aren't. They are working horses. Well looked after, aren't they? You can book a horse trek here on the Moonlight trail.' He turned the Ute around and headed back along the dusty road.

'Sorry, folks but the sight-seeing tour is over now. I have to get going as I have a few things to get ready before the morning. I have a stock agent arriving at eight.'

The mood in the vehicle was relaxed for the rest of the trip. Mack gave Wyatt a detailed rundown of the history of Ben Lomond Station and how it works. Prue was mesmerised by the awesome views of Lake Wakatipu, especially the range of blues in the reflections, repeatedly winding down her window and taking photos. Jessie sat back in her seat praying silently that the cordial relations between them would continue to flourish.

When they arrived at Jessie's cottage, Mack helped them with their suitcases and Jessie put the kettle on. He'd been looking after Jessie's house while she was away and unexpectedly placed a roast in the oven for her and her folks. Jessie had given him a spare key.

'Oh, wow! I didn't know you can cook. Especially as Bessie does all the cooking.' Jessie thought this was a real bonus in a prospective mate.

'Ah, not the case—sorry. Bessie cooked it early this morning and all you have to do is heat it in the oven.' He winked at Jessie and tugged her hair playfully while Prue whispered in her ear, 'No such luck! He's a farmer.'

Jessie was much more relaxed being back in her own home with her parents. She had not been at ease at the home of Meg and Joe, although they were kind and hospitable. Their lifestyle was so different from that which Jessie was accustomed.

Prue and Wyatt settled in and made themselves at home. After Mack returned to Reed Station, Prue told Jessie that her father had been quite taken aback by seeing the enormous Ben Lomond Station that was just minutes out of Queenstown. That trip seemed to unite the two men, a big plus for Jessie. And she could tell that her mother was impressed by her tall, rugged sheep farmer. They had hit it off well, she thought. Now to get both her parents to Glenorchy and see if the intrigue still draws them.

Before her parents turned in for the night, her father stopped to say goodnight.

'Before I forget, I want to give you this.' He pulled something out from behind his back. He handed her a cardboard box that had her name scribbled on the lid. She lifted it off and looked inside. There was her old straw rodeo hat and hidden underneath lay a pile of her satin, horse show rosettes and leather awards that she had won at rodeos.

'I thought you might still want them, and perhaps they'll be a little reminder of the good times you had growing up on our farm in Bethlehem.'

'Oh, Dad, that's sweet of you. Thanks for remembering to bring them down. That's the hat you bought me after I had won my first prize. I'll never forget—honest I won't.'

Prue overheard and walked into the hallway. 'I think he's really saying he doesn't want you to forget him.' She smiled, kissed her, and headed off to bed.

Jessie hugged him tight and walked into her office, making the excuse she had to finish some paperwork. She was trying to blink away the tears that forced their way down her cheeks at the thought of her father missing her more than she had expected.

Chapter Twenty-Four

The day after Wyatt and Prue had arrived in Glenorchy, Jessie drove them out to meet Walter who was waiting for them to arrive. He had put on his best clothes—probably the only set in his wardrobe and Bessie had left a casserole in the oven for them and gone out for the day. He paced up and down the veranda, waiting to greet them as they walked up to the front steps. He had even Brylcreemed his thin, grey hair.

Jessie rushed up and hugged the old man with whom she had bonded and was like a grandfather to her. He bared his new dentures in an overly full smile as Wyatt stepped forward to shake his hand, then Prue. He still hadn't got used to the new teeth he had made for him after his fall.

'Where's Mack?' Jessie asked as she quickly scanned the inside of the house.

'He won't take long. A ewe caught its head in the fence and he's gone to help it out,' said Walter as he ushered the entourage into his lounge.

'Mmm, something smells good through there.' Prue pointed towards the kitchen.

'Oh, that's my house-keeper, Bessie's beef casserole and I can guarantee it will be a hearty one. Can I get you a cup of tea or coffee? Or home-brewed ginger beer?'

'Oh, Grandad, let me.' Jessie jumped to the rescue. Since her engagement to Mack, Walter had asked her to call him Grandad.

He sat proudly talking at length about the history of Reed Station, how he had modernised the farm and built it up. Jessie was thinking about how insignificant his two thousand acres was compared to Ben Lomond Station.

Wyatt was intrigued by Walter's summary of the Reed family history and how he had single-handedly built up the station without the help of his family. Walter also went on to say how Mack had been his God-send and had come to his rescue. He told him how he had quickly shown himself to be a worthy successor to Aron, his previous Station Manager.

Jessie heard Mack's boots clunk as he tossed them into the corner by the front door.

'Oh, here's Mack,' she said gleefully, in the hope that he would rescue her from trying to keep a harmonious atmosphere between them. But she didn't need to. Her future seemed to be sealed in concrete already.

'Sorry to hold you up. I'll just go and wash up,' said Mack as he poked his head in the door.

'How about we eat after that, then you can take Wyatt and Prue on a Cooks tour of the station?' Walter nodded at Mack.

'That would be wonderful, Mack,' said Prue.

The substantial meal was followed by rhubarb and apple pie, with fresh cream from a neighbour's cow.

'Dear me, I hope I can still walk around after that lot!' Wyatt pulled at his leather belt and let it out a hole or two. 'Ah—that's better. I can breathe now. Tell Bessie I might take her on myself.'

Prue pulled a face of disapproval at him, playfully.

Jessie sat in the back of the Ute with her mother while the men chatted in front. It all went smoothly as if it was meant to be, she thought.

Half an hour later, as they were standing on the highest part of the station looking at the view of the expanse of paddocks and sheep, Prue turned to Jessie with a serious look on her face and spoke quietly. 'Mack and Walter are lovely. But the farmers in this area who have lived for years on these stations all their lives, have grown up with the remoteness and isolation. So different from where you grew up in the Bay of Plenty on a small farm near town. Are you sure you can live here like this? You'll only be able to do your grocery shopping once a fortnight, or even monthly. There's no doctor, and it takes over an hour to get to Queenstown on that metal road.'

Jessie clenched her jaw tight. Was her mother about to put the damper on her new life and, in spite of enjoying her stay, refuse to give Jessie her blessing? Perhaps her father thinks the same way. She watched him in deep conversation with Mack who was proudly pointing out notable aspects of the geography as far as Mt Aspiring National Park. To Jessie, her father appeared to be quite taken in by the enormity of it all and perhaps, not only interested but also impressed by the high country farmer who would soon become her husband.

'Jessie—I think we should take them up into Paradise and let them see the Red Beech forest in Mt Aspiring National Park. You don't have those up north, do you?' Mack asked Wyatt.

'No, I don't think so. We have English Beech trees but they aren't the red variety.'

'Well, our Red Beech is a native. It is abundant in the Mt Aspiring National Park as you'll soon be able to see.'

As they drove onto the Paradise-Glenorchy Road, they crossed a small river bed that was full of schist, a rock with blue-green hues that is quarried in Paradise.

'That is Arcadia Station over there and behind it is Diamond Lake.' Mack pulled up so that Prue could take more photos.

'That's where my friend Hope and I have ridden to on horseback. Isn't it beautiful?'

'Wait until I take you further up here. I can show you an amazing view of Mount Earnslaw. The weather is really mild for this time of the year. We can get out and have a walk around so you can photograph it.'

When they arrived at the spot that Mack was referring to, a flock of ducks appeared in front of the Ute.

'What funny looking ducks. They're goose-like. What are they?' asked Prue.

'They are called Paradise Ducks. The ones with the black bodies and white heads are the females and the males have green-black bodies,' said Mack as he continued driving up to a knoll near a clump of Beech trees.

'I thought that this place was called Paradise because it is like heaven here,' said Jessie, wide-eyed.

'No—that's what everyone thinks. It is named after these ducks.'

They stepped out of the Ute. 'Oh, that's a pity,' said Jessie. 'Because it really is paradise here. I didn't see as much as this on horseback. It seems different seeing it this way, and Hope and I didn't ride as far as this.'

'Wait until you see the view from up there,' Mack said, pointing at the grassy knoll. 'Are you happy about walking up there, Prue? It's only a short walk, but it'll be worth it.'

They followed Mack in single-file up to the top of the knoll. It was a wind-still warm day and not a cloud in the sky. As they reached the top of the small hill, there in front of them was a spectacular view of snow-capped Mount Earnslaw. Prue was mesmerised.

On the drive back to Glenorchy, Mount Alfred came into full view again.

'I've climbed that one—remember I told you I went up there with Mack, Hope, and Cole?' She elbowed her mother to jog her memory. 'That's the time that I slipped into a crevice and poor Mack rescued me.'

Mack turned his head and smiled at her.

'It was pretty difficult too, I might add,' said Mack, winking at Jessie.

'Oh, so you have been quite a hero in your day,' said Prue, beaming at Mack.

'Well, everyone. What do you think of Glenorchy? A touch of heaven, isn't it?' Mack chuckled as he came to the end of his tour.

Walter had been lying down resting when they arrived back at Reed Station. He got up and offered to make them a pot of tea.

'Sorry, Grandad, we're off out again. We've been invited for dinner with the Greys at Dart River Ranch. I'm sure their invitation included you.'

'Please thank them for me. I feel a bit tuckered out today and would rather stay home if you don't mind. I hope I see you, folks, again soon,' he said, glancing at Prue and Wyatt.

'Of course, they will. There's our wedding, remember?' Jessie looked at him with a querying glance, wondering if he really had forgotten about the wedding.

Jessie's parents said their goodbyes and Mack said he would follow them over to Dart River Ranch in his Ute.

***

Joel and Myra Grey hadn't seen Jessie and her family since she had left Tauranga to live in Glenorchy. They had more to do with them when Jessie and Hope went to the same school. That was many years ago.

Joel and Myra made a big fuss of them and before the meal, Joel took Wyatt on a guided tour of Dart River Ranch. Wyatt returned with a smile on his face and plenty of questions to ask Joel about running the ranch.

Prue was busy being entertained by little Bertie and finding out from Myra how she had found living in Glenorchy after leaving Tauranga. Hope took Jessie to the stables to see the new foals.

It had been a positive and uplifting evening and Jessie was more optimistic than she had been when her parents first arrived. Perhaps they had changed their minds, and she now had a concrete future in Glenorchy. But they still had a few more days to go.

Chapter Twenty-Five

On the way back to Jessie's cottage, her parents were quiet, probably fatigued after the grand tours that Mack had taken them on. He had organised with Wyatt to show them around his own farm, the one he had recently gifted to his sister. They would have to do that the following day as Mack had too much to do on the station after all that. It had been a whirlwind break for them down south. There was so much to see and do in such a short space of time. But Wyatt had a particular interest in wanting to see Mack's farm.

They were waiting at the gate of Jessie's cottage on the dot of eight the next morning, as the sun poked its head above the Richardson Mountains. The trees in the foothills were covered with a changing landscape of autumn trees—a myriad of pastel hues of orange, red and yellow.

Mack arrived rearing to go, wearing tan suede pants and blue and white check Swanndri. He climbed out of the Ute to greet Wyatt and Prue and helped them into the back of the vehicle.

'It's a bit chilly this morning when that southerly wind blows, even when the sun is shining. It's good you've brought jackets, as you might need them up on the ridge.'

Jessie climbed in next to Mack and kissed him on the cheek. As they drove to his farm, she placed a hand on his knee and Mack pulled her closer to snuggle up to him.

'Strap yourself in Jess. Here, let me help you,' he said leaning over with one hand, fumbling for the safety belt's port.

'It's okay—got it.' Jessie plugged it in then placed her hand over his weathered fingers.

As Wyatt and Prue were busy in the back talking about the different ranges of mountains they could see and naming the high country stations that they passed, Jessie took the opportunity to talk with Mack.

'We haven't had much time together with all this going on, sorry,' she said to him, screwing up her forehead.

'I know. I've missed you too. Never mind, they'll be gone tomorrow—shush.' He shook his head back to indicate her folks might be listening.

As they drove down the long driveway towards his old farm, a wave of sadness rolled over Jessie as the land appeared abandoned and neglected, although Mack had put a flock of sheep in the paddocks to keep the grass down. They got out of the vehicle and wandered down the path towards the house. Weeds were growing between the cracks in the footpath and at the front of the house thick cobwebs had meandered their way across the kitchen windows.

'It's sad to see no one living here after you've worked so hard to get it looking nice and homely,' said Jessie.

She turned to her parents. 'You know that this house was originally a massive barn that clever Mack skilfully turned into a lovely home. Can we go inside to take a look, Mack?' She pulled on his hand.

'Yeah, sure. I'll just grab the key. It's in my Ute.' He walked back to the vehicle while in single file they wandered around the perimeter of the house. Wyatt stood on the veranda looking out at the paddocks and scanned as far as he could see.

Mack showed them inside the house and then asked Wyatt if he would like to come with him on the quad bike he kept in the barn. He wanted to show him the rest of the farm while the women sat in the house talking about interior décor.

'Do you think Meg and Joe will be able to make something of this place, Jessie? It's a big house and the ground here is flat enough for them to extend it. But I just wonder if they will find it a mighty wrench after living in the city.'

'I think they'll be okay, Mum. Mack and Walter are family and they aren't far from here. Our church will probably help them, but it will be good if we can get them to come along to fellowship with us first.'

'Perhaps if your church helped them out here, they might warm to the idea of going to church. If they aren't churchgoers, it will have to be easy-does-it.' Her mother spoke wisely. She was always the one in the family who was the most level-headed.

'Mack told me that they are believers but have fallen away and haven't been to church for years. Mack and I have been praying for them, but Mack is concerned over their apparent materialism— that they won't be able to tear themselves away from it.'

The men arrived back on the quad bike and Wyatt appeared as happy as a sandboy flashing his off-white teeth. Prue rushed at him before he could get through the door. 'Well, what did you think of it?'

Wyatt brushed the mud from his boots and stood in the doorway re-adjusting his trouser belt. 'It's marvellous, so fertile. It's got all this flat land here, but if you go up on the ridge you'll see green, rolling hills that belong to the property. It's ideal for what Meg and Joe want to do,' he said.

'I'm sorry, but I can't make you a cup of tea or anything before we go, as I've emptied out the place,' said Mack with a sheepish grin.

'We can have one when we get back home. You've done enough for us, Mack,' said Prue, rubbing his shoulder with her hand.

'When you come down for the wedding, Meg and Joe will be here. That's if they can sell their own house by then,' said Mack.

'Mmm,' said Wyatt. 'That's going to be a great adventure for them. Wouldn't it be good to be young again?' He looked at Prue.

'What do you mean?' she asked. 'You've already been there and done that.'

'I mean taking on an enterprise like they are. It's a real challenge and sounds exciting. I don't know how they'll get on if they can't find anyone to manage the farming part of it. They have a perfect property here for sheep or cattle and it would be a pity to let it run down.'

'What about you, Wyatt, will you think about it?'

'I'm not sure. Prue and I will have to discuss it with Tom and see what he wants to do. I can't just abandon my own farm. It's something we'll all have to pray about, isn't it, Jessie?'

'I can ask our prayer team from church to pray if you like. They would be happy to do that, I'm sure,' Jessie said, uncertain if living on this property was the right course for them to take.

'I'll have to get you back home, as I have a few things to do before the day finishes. Hope you don't mind.' Mack rattled his keys in his pocket as a hint and made his way to his Ute with the others in close pursuit.

As they walked down the path, Wyatt kept looking back over his shoulder while Prue stopped to take photos.

'It's kind of sad to think we are leaving tomorrow,' Prue muttered in the back of the Ute. 'Time has gone far too quickly.' The corners of her mouth turned downwards as she pressed her face against the car window.

Was she actually imagining living here? Jessie wondered.

Chapter Twenty-Six

Over a month had passed since Jessie's parents had visited. Mack arrived to take Jessie out. They took off walking along a track on the Richardson Mountains overlooking the Rees Valley, talking about wedding plans on the way up the track.

'I can't believe it's March already. We are supposed to be getting married soon. It's gone so fast, and we aren't even prepared. So much to organise. How are we going to do it all by then?' Jessie asked, pretending to pull Mack up the hill.

'I know what you mean. We've both been so busy since your parents visited, and our feet haven't touched the ground. Don't worry— we'll work it out somehow.'

'Isn't that a lovely sight?' Mack pointed to the mountain range that appeared golden in the slowly setting sun.

Jessie stopped still to let the last rays of the sun gently warm her bare, swanlike neck. 'Have you heard my parents' news? I thought Meg and Joe would have told you. Mum phoned last night.'

Mack stared at her. 'No, what news?'

'Dad has accepted their offer to manage their pastures which will be leased out to farmers for grazing dry cattle. Meg and Joe are going to have a minor dwelling built for Mum and Dad which they will lease from them. It all seems to be happening very quickly so Meg and Joe must have been quite persuasive, seeing that they had seemed so convinced that Glenorchy was too remote.'

Mack stopped and pointed to a large flat rock. He led Jessie by the hand and urged her to sit down on it next to him.

'Let's stop here for a rest—it's all a bit sudden I guess. To be perfectly honest, I didn't really think your folks were that keen. Now we really will have to settle down together, won't we?' He looked at her and gave her waist a tug.

Jessie suddenly realised what the repercussions of all this would mean. It started to hit home what a great upheaval it would be for her parents to leave their own farm and start all over again in Glenorchy. What if we did that and our relationship with Mack breaks up or we don't end up getting married? She ruminated.

'I agree. I think it's all a bit rushed too,' murmured Jessie, pensively. 'Perhaps in view of all this, we should postpone our wedding until they come down. It would be better, as they should be settled in by then. What do you think?'

Mack shrugged his shoulders. 'I don't know. It's perhaps something you need to talk to your folks about again and find out exactly when they're planning on moving down. I think they may need more time to work it out.'

'I agree, I'll phone them tonight and let you know.' Jessie hauled Mack back up and urged him to get walking, as she wanted to take some photos of Mt Earnslaw from the top of the high ridge. When they reached the top, they saw the young farmer tenant waving to them from below as he repaired a fence by the entrance to the station.

'It's good he and his wife let us walk up here whenever we like. I've done a bit of contract work for him and we're good mates now,' said Mack as he waved back.

When they reached the edge of the ridge, Jessie took out her camera and got to work taking photos. 'I'm doing this for Tom, because he may not get the chance to come down here for some time yet while he is attached to my folks' farm,' she said, removing her sunglasses.

They sat down again, this time on an old log. Mack pulled out a chocolate bar and shared it with Jessie.

'Here—this will give you the energy to walk back down.' He chuckled.

'Don't you think it kind of complicates things that Mum and Dad are moving down here permanently because I've moved here? I feel for poor Tom running our farm on his own. And it all sounds so concrete. What if they get here and don't like it?'

'I think you're jumping to conclusions. Trust God—we've already prayed about it and now the outcome is in his hands.'

Jessie was aware that Mack didn't want to rock the boat when the wedding plans had been heading in the right direction.

'It's just that I'll feel really bad if they make a mistake and have to move again if it doesn't work out,' she said.

'It's the same for you and me. There's always a risk involved in commitment, and you can be in exactly the same boat. Just wait and see what they say when you phone them. I'm sure it'll be fine.'

Nothing more was said. The weather was warm, and Jessie was in her element as Mack walked the rest of the way with her hand in his, now and then giving it a gentle, affectionate squeeze. He showed a chivalrous streak by helping her over a stony stream or a rugged part of the path.

When they arrived back at the cottage, Jessie left her boots at the front door and waited for Mack to do the same. Instead, he took her in his arms and kissed her warmly, while still standing on the front porch.

'Sorry, Jessie, I've got to get back. I've been away all afternoon. I need to talk to Grandad about one of the irrigators that seems to be playing up. I won't be there when the mechanic arrives tomorrow, and he will have to handle it. Give me a call later and let me know how you get on with your parents.' He started to walk briskly towards his vehicle as Jessie followed behind.

'Oh, that's a pity. I have a chicken casserole in the slow cooker that should be just about ready.' Dashed hope sank to the pit of her stomach like a sack of potatoes.

'That's kind of you, but I told Bessie to keep me a meal.'

He placed his Stetson back on his head and climbed into his Ute.

As he drove off, Jessie was stunned. Had she said something during their walk that had changed his mind about her, perhaps? She realised she spouted on far too much about her parents not liking it in Glenorchy and the possibility of her relationship with Mack breaking up. Why didn't she keep her big mouth shut instead of verbalising her apprehension and wait until the process unfolds a little more? She thumped the dining table with a closed fist. 'You've done it again and put your foot in your mouth.'

Her voice still quavering from her upset, she picked up the phone and rang her mother.

'Jessie, lovely to hear from you. How are your wedding plans going? I had intended to call you tomorrow.'

Jessie turned her head to the side and coughed to clear her throat.

'Hi, Mum. We've got a lot to organise and think we might need more time. We may postpone it until spring to give you time to come down here.'

'Oh, really? I thought you might be all settled on Reed Station by the time we move. We were hoping to rent your cottage when you move out on your wedding day. I wanted to ask you to talk to your landlord.'

'Why is that? Aren't you moving onto Meg's property now?'

'Yes, we are. They are shifting down here next month and have already found a local builder to start on the chalet where we'll be living. It should be ready by the time you get married. You don't need to postpone your wedding for us.'

Jessie hesitated, trying to get her head around it all.

'Mack has tried to share his faith with Meg and Joe but they seem to be far away from God. That's just my concern if you are going to be living on their property.'

'Well, we are just going to have to pray hard for them. Perhaps that's the reason your father, and I have been led to move onto the farm with them. God will change their hearts—just you wait and see. Even if it takes years, he will succeed.'

Everything seemed to be moving so fast, but she didn't want to dampen her parents' plans.

'If it's convenient, we'd like to stay with you until you move onto Reed Station after you are married. Please speak to your landlord first and let me know if he'll transfer the tenancy over to us.'

'Sure, Mum. I'll phone him tomorrow. It'll be nice to have your support for the wedding. I just hope you'll be happy down here. Otherwise, I'll feel really bad if you aren't.'

Prue continued to reassure Jessie that she and Wyatt both desired a change and Tom needed the responsibility, as he had become a man. She prayed a short prayer over the phone and hung up.

As Jessie was about to leave the office and walk into the kitchen to put the kettle on, the phone rang again. Why would her mother be phoning her back?

'Jessie—it's Mack. Have I caught you at a bad time?'

She was taken aback that he was phoning so soon. It must be urgent.

'No, not at all ... is everything alright?'

'Ah ... yes ... sort of. I have a confession to make ... you see I really did want to stay for dinner when you asked me in but when I kissed you I had stronger feelings for you.'

'What do you mean—that's normal, isn't it?'

'What I'm trying to say is ... the kind of feelings that are best left at the doorstep. I was caught off guard because of the fun time we had on the walk today. I respect you and our mutual agreement to wait until our wedding day.'

'I'm so relieved to hear you say this. I was so worried I had said or done something to put you off me. The thing is ... I feel the same way about you. I have loved you so much ever since you pulled me out of that crevice on Mount Alfred.'

'You're a darling. Why do you think I kept asking Hope or Cole when you were coming back to Dart River ranch again? I can't stop thinking about you. We've got a lot to talk about and to plan.'

Jessie perked up after that conversation with Mack and the next day they discussed their wedding plans together as they didn't want to put it off any longer. They decided to plan for late April, that time of the year when the snow caps on the mountains make a perfect backdrop for photos and the weather is still warm enough for a garden party reception. If her parents moved in with her, that would make life easier—then after she moves to Reed Station, they will be able to stay in the cottage. Perhaps this is all part of God's plan. She stoked the fire and gave it no more thought until the next day.

Chapter Twenty-Seven

Lance, Jessie's landlord was more than happy to give the tenancy over to her parents. He and his wife, Mary had both met them during their visit to Glenorchy and they got on well. After Jessie had let her parents know, she phoned Mack.

'That's great news, Jessie. All sorted then! Oh, by the way—Meg rang me last night to say that Briars Property Development will start the build on your parents' cedar chalet next week. It should be ready in a few months. They are moving down in a month. Their house is on the market but may take a while to sell.'

'Well, that's all settled, then. It's kind of exciting, I suppose.' Jessie caught herself, realising how that must have sounded.

'You don't sound so convincing, but you just wait and see— everything will fall into place. I have a good feeling about it all.'

***

It has been a long, hot summer, and although autumn had arrived, it was unusually warm.

Wyatt and Prue piled into Jessie's Land Rover ready to drive out to Meg and Joe's new property, Willow Park. They appeared excited, as the outside shell of their new chalet had been completed—an attractive, Swiss-style chalet with a concrete path leading to it at the back of the boutique farmstay. Meg and Joe had already moved into their home. They'd arrived earlier than expected and were hard at work outside clearing away weeds and shrubs ready to create a new garden.

As Jessie drove up to their house, Meg stood up and waved. Instead of her chic, elegant Hartley's attire, she wore faded denim jeans, black tee-shirt, and muddy gumboots. Her hair was in disarray.

'Mmm, maybe she is cut out for rural life after all,' Prue muttered to Jessie.

'It's possible. She said she always loved holidays in the country, so who knows? It may suit her.'

Prue and Wyatt were over the moon about their home taking shape. It was far enough away from the lodge to give them plenty of privacy.

Afternoon tea with Meg and Joe was on the agenda. After they had finished, Joe took Wyatt up to the back of the farm to discuss their plans while the women looked at Meg's décor books for ideas for the farmstay. With Prue and Jessie in tow, Meg did the rounds of every room in the large house then led them out onto the patio where they sat and chatted until the men returned.

'I went to my first Country Women's Institute meeting a few days ago. It was not what I expected. I thought they just sat around showing off their knitting and preserves, but there were some speakers—professional women discussing the changes going on in women's roles in farming and local politics.'

'That's nice, dear. I'm glad you're getting involved in the community. We all need support, and you can make some friends there.'

'I'm not so sure now. I may have upset some of them. When I told a few of the women about my boutique farmstay, they frowned and murmured amongst themselves making me feel really uncomfortable. The speakers had been talking about their opposition to all the housing development that has been going on in the area— farmers being offered large sums of money to have their farms subdivided into smaller properties. I wish I'd never told them. I was just trying to drum up some publicity for our new venture.'

Prue, who had been a long-term, staunch member of the Bethlehem branch of the Institute, pulled a straight face and bit her lip.

'I'm sure they'll warm to you once they get to know you better. Maybe if you show them your farmstay and invite them around for afternoon tea, they'll become more accepting of you.'

After the tour of the property, they were all busy on the trip back home, chatting about all that was going on with Meg and Joe's farmlet.

***

Jessie terminated her employment with the Vet Co-op a month before the wedding. It had not taken long for them to find a replacement this time, much to her delight. Some farmers who lived near Reed Station had told her they would continue to use her services, particularly her private mobile clinic.

Everything appeared to be falling into place, just as Mack had suggested, thought Jessie. This was only the beginning, and they had a long road ahead before their new lives in Glenorchy would show promise.

Chapter Twenty-Eight

April arrived faster than Mack and Jessie realised, and the weather remained dry apart from snow on the mountaintops. They'd planned a simple country wedding on Reed Station, and although they had tried to keep the guest list to a minimum, it just seemed to grow. There were so many local people they couldn't leave off the list.

Tom had arrived the night before. Cole and Hope had driven to the airport in Queenstown to collect him off his flight and Cole kept him busy showing him around their ranch after they arrived home.

Jessie's parents stayed with her at her cottage and Meg invited her folks to stay at Willow Park. She wanted her father to help set up her business accounts before they returned home to Wellington. He was the one with the tax accounting skills.

All the ladies, including Jessie, were hard at work helping Bessie the day before the wedding, preparing the colonial homestead which the men had whitewashed. The crimson carnations and mauve cineraria were in full bloom and the women had cut many of the blooms and placed them in a bucket of water ready to be made into bouquets and posies mixed with white gypsophila. They laced miniature dark red roses together to form a chain to drape around the railings on the veranda.

Walter had made sure his station hands would be able to sit at a table and share in the wedding breakfast, as they were part of the family. It was a way that Walter showed his gratitude for their long-term loyalty.

After dinner that evening, Prue was busy in her daughter's bedroom sorting out her bridal gown and accessories. Jessie had arranged for one of the local farmer's wives to arrive early on her wedding day to fix her hair. Everything was running to plan.

'Tom—while you're here for the next few days, it would be a good idea to ask Walter if he'd give you a tour of the station. The sheer size of it will blow your mind,' said Wyatt, tousling his son's hair with his hand.

'Sorry everyone, but I'm having an early night. I've got to get to bed,' said Jessie, walking into the lounge to kiss her father.

'Night, night, sleep well.' Tom called out from the hallway. 'I'm turning in too.'

Prue was in Jessie's bedroom doing a last-minute check of the crème, Chantilly lace bridal dress, and headpiece of white satin flowers. Jessie startled her. 'Ah! Don't creep up on me like that. Just making sure you have everything ready for tomorrow.'

'Sorry—thanks, Mum. I'm exhausted. Need to get to bed, as we have to be there by eleven. The Pastor will be starting the ceremony at twelve.'

'No, you can't let Mack see you until the wedding. Meg, Mack, and Joe will be able to set everything up and Bessie will be there too. Your father is going to drive us there in time for the start of the ceremony.'

'Aw, thanks, Mum. You're an angel. I'll see you in the morning.'

'Wait—let me say a wee prayer before you go to sleep.' Her mother sat down on the bed next to her. She took her hand and asked God for guidance and protection and that everything would go smoothly for Jessie's special day.

***

The station hands set up a large marquis and trestle tables which Bessie covered with long white tablecloths. She and a few other ladies placed mini, dark red roses in small vases. It was not a formal affair. Most celebrations in the area were usually laid back and involved the whole community.

All their neighbours and church parishioners had offered to bring food and started slowly arriving, taking the food into the house for the women caterers to prepare to put out on the tables later.

Pastor Johanne waited in the front garden by the lily pond, while the guests sat patiently waiting to see Mack and Jessie appear.

As they all looked around to see from which direction the bride and groom were arriving, the sound of a horse clip-clopping down the track drew the attention of the crowd. At the same time, beautiful music wafted in the breeze towards the guests who looked around to see where it came from. It was the harmonious tune to the wedding song I Will Always Love You. It emanated from the veranda as Walter walked out the front door playing the fiddle. He was dressed in a sophisticated woollen, marine blue suit with a navy tie. His thick grey hair had been washed and styled. The guests stared open-mouthed as he continued to produce awe-inspiring music.

Suddenly, as if from nowhere, Mack appeared on his beautiful black stallion. Zoro walked steadily towards the bridal party and stopped by the Pastor. Mack was wearing the same style of suit as Walter, who stopped playing and stepped up beside him as best man.

Zoro appeared to be showing off, with his tail swept up in a blue band. His mane had a blue ribbon braided through it. The animal just stood there as still as a queen's guardsman. The black horse contrasted with the backdrop of snow-capped mountains in the distance. He was harnessed in the new black bridle that Jessie had gifted to Mack.

It was the first time that Mack had heard his grandfather playing the fiddle. He had simply not expected to feel so overcome with the emotions that flooded his mind and his eyes with salty tears. He had not known that Walter could play like this, as he had had told him he had stopped playing after his first stroke some years earlier.

***

Wyatt and Prue had furtively arrived in the Land Rover with Jessie in the back and stopped around the back of the barn. They were busy helping her to make a surprise appearance on horseback. When she was ready, Prue went over and sat next to Helen and Len on the seats provided for the bridal party and started chatting to them. She was wearing a pink and grey, flared chiffon dress with a tight bodice, and carried a pink clutch bag.

As suddenly as Mack had appeared, a stunning golden Palomino carrying a radiant bride appeared from out the back of the barn with Jessie sitting side-saddle. Her dress, made of exquisite Chantilly lace fell elegantly in layers covering the saddle and the side of her mount.

The well-preserved saddle was one that Walter had kept in the barn all these years in memory of his wife Hazel. He'd offered it to Jessie for the wedding and spent hours polishing it up and shining the silver buckles for her.

390

As Chantilly approached the gathering near the homestead where the guests were seated, Jessie was suddenly distracted by a bright blue object amongst the guests. She caught sight of Meg who was walking down the steps of the house simultaneously as she was arriving. She stuck out like a sore thumb, standing on the lawn preening herself in a royal blue, satin dress and white, stiletto-heeled shoes. Her long, blond hair was swept up and on top of her head was a large, flat, blue disc, a hat that appeared as a flying saucer covered in blue netting to match her dress. There was another layer on top with several miniature flying saucers hanging over the brim. It was a though she was trying to look like one of the Royals.

Jessie sat open-mouthed. Meg was trying to steal her thunder. Joe appeared to be embarrassed, pulling at his tie, and running his fingers through his hair. He pulled on Meg's arm, trying to get her to sit down.

With Wyatt at her side, Jessie urged Chantilly on towards the spot where Mack and Zoro waited. Wyatt held the horse's cream coloured bridle and reins which matched her dress. He had come to give his daughter away. Chantilly threw her head in the air as if to make a statement then came to a halt next to Mack, who sat still in his saddle staring at her and beaming from ear to ear.

He leaned over and squeezed her hand. 'You look radiant, a real picture in all that lace on top of Chantilly.' Mack lifted off his dark brown leather Stetson and bowed at his bride.

Chantilly's mane had been intricately braided in a pattern that resembled Chantilly Lace with miniature dark red rosebuds interwoven. Her tail had been decorated in the same fashion. The guests started photographing the amazing spectacle before the horses became restless.

At last, the Pastor started the ceremony with Hope standing alongside Jessie as Matron-of-honour and Wyatt on the other side. Walter now stood next to Mack as his Best Man holding onto Zoro's bridle.

The guests were entertained by a little pageboy—Bertie, Hope Rigby's son. He stood next to Mack's faithful dog, Bluey on the bottom step of the veranda wearing dark blue pants with a midnight blue waistcoat and red velvet bowtie. Bluey sat patiently, showing off a similar red bowtie.

Bertie held a small, red velvet cushion that housed the rings. He was pleased as punch that he played a part and stood there babbling baby talk. His father, Cole supervised him while the guests laughed. The small boy leaned over to place the cushion on the step and as he went to sit down on it, Cole snapped up the rings in a panic. That brought forth another outburst of laughter while Bluey gave a loud howl like a coyote and joined in.

It was a simple but powerful event with a strong message. The Pastor preached about the power of love and forgiveness. Walter's eyes stayed moist for almost the whole of the wedding ceremony.

The event was doubly emotional. With their final tying of the knot, Walter and his grandson, Mack had healed a long-standing generational feud with Jessie's help.

Jessie and Mack had both agreed when they had been planning their wedding, that they would write their own vows. Of course, they had to get Pastor Johanne to look them over so that he was in agreement. When they each read out the words they had written, they were said with deep sincerity as they looked into each other's eyes.

After Pastor Johanne had announced them, man and wife, Mack lifted Jessie off Chantilly's back carefully so that she wouldn't damage her delicate lace dress. He pulled her close and kissed her more passionately than ever before until the Pastor nudged him to say that the ceremony was over, as he wiped the steam from his spectacles. When

Jessie looked at the crowd, she saw that what had taken place had brought tears to many eyes.

Mack stopped Jessie from walking off so that he could get a good look at her. Even though the Chantilly lace she was wearing had matched the colour of her mare's coat, she had stood out beyond description. She had grown her thick, flaxen hair a bit longer for her wedding and Walter's neighbour had styled it for her and set it in long ringlets. Her cheeks were rose pink because of the anxiety she had experienced during the ceremony, but her facial colour also contrasted with the colour of her dress. On her feet, she wore dainty, flat, cream-coloured satin shoes. A far cry from the heavy leather boots she wore each day to work.

She had always wanted to get married on horseback, a quirky dream of hers and it had come true. Mack was her Lancelot, and she was his Guinevere. He pulled her close again and kissed her neck.

Tom had offered to take care of their horses before and after the ceremony. He was proud to be of service to his sister that day. He had dressed smartly in the same attire as Walter and Mack. The station hands also joined in with the guests for the rest of the occasion, eating, drinking, and accepting Mack and Jessie's hospitality.

One of the guests managed the roast lamb-on-spit and Tom proudly handed around refreshments. Bessie provided last season's ginger beer and there were some fine Marlborough wines for those who wished to partake. Seats lined the walls of the marquis that had been ornately decorated.

Several women started to go back and forth into the house and out to the trestle tables bringing an abundance of savoury dishes to go with the roast meat. This was followed by rich desserts fit for a king, such as Black Forest Gateaux, Chocolate-pineapple cheesecakes, Pavlovas covered with strawberries and cream, huge chocolate logs and trifle.

Joe, as the master of ceremonies, headed up the toasts after he had read out the telegrams. They raised their glasses as Joe spoke— 'To the bridal party and our supportive community for making this such a happy and memorable occasion for Mack and Jessie, that it has turned out to be.'

At the end of the toasting, they were entertained by a singing telegram that had arrived for the bridal couple in the form of an Elvis Presley impersonator singing Crying in the Chapel. For Jessie, this was the highlight of the wedding reception.

The emcee announced the cutting of the cake that sat on the Sweetheart Table. The four-tiered cake had been made by Jessie's mother, Prue—a traditional rich, dark fruit cake with imitation miniature purple roses. On the top tier of thick Royal Icing, stood a bride and groom on horseback.

Walter handed Mack and Jessie his late wife, Hazel's elaborate silver knife to make the traditional first cut of the cake. Hazel had been an accomplished cake decorator and Walter had kept it as a memento. Jessie and Mack placed the first slice on a plate and fed each other a mouthful with small forks. Prue then took over and gathered up the top tier—it was a tradition in her own family to freeze this until it was required as a Christening Cake for a firstborn child or a first wedding anniversary.

The rest of the cake was left to a couple of young people to hand around to the guests after the bride and groom had each taken a slice to the bridal table.

***

There was still a chill in the air, and instead of the dance being held outside in the marquis where they had been eating, Mack decided they should move into the big barn.

His station hands had put up the coloured lights around the inside walls earlier that morning to brighten it up and placed more chairs borrowed from the church to put around the dance floor.

Of course, Walter provided the dance music along with one of his ranch hands, an accomplished musician like Walter who played the piano accordion.

Jessie watched her brother, Tom closely when he was dancing. She knew it wouldn't be long before some sweet girl would whisk him off his feet and marry him.

Meg gave a few performances demonstrating her trained, angelic voice, once again soaking up the limelight.

'Remember I'm still waiting for that last dance that I didn't get at Hope's twenty-first birthday party or her wedding. I've been waiting ever since.' Mack cupped Jessie's face in his hands as she melted.

'You're kidding, aren't you?'

He kissed her softly and kissed her again.

'No, really. I was thoroughly disappointed when I was trying to impress you way back then. I had to wait a long time for you to return to Dart River before I could try to win your heart.'

Jessie's face turned pink. 'I'm sorry. It wouldn't have been on purpose. I think I was called away to help Myra prepare the supper at her twenty-first, then forgot you were waiting. As regards her wedding, you just weren't quick enough off the mark. Someone else beat you to it!' They both laughed.

'Well, I'll never have to wait again, will I?' He chuckled. 'Let's dance the night away.'

'You know something ... all our prayers seem to have been answered. It's amazing isn't it?' Jessie wrapped her arms around his neck as she danced and snuggled into his neck.

'It does seem we've been in God's will, even when it didn't feel like it. So, what do you think—will you be staying on in remote Glenorchy, grumpy farmers and all?' He poked her in the ribs and smiled.

'I can't imagine going back to town. It appears that this is my divine purpose. You and I can make a real go of it. Let me help you run the station, and I'll work at my vet business part-time. Once my mobile clinic is up and running, I won't be doing any more after-hour calls, now that they have a new on-call vet.'

'Really, that's great news. A husband and wife partnership. You'll have a heap of work to do caring for our own farm animals with a thousand merino sheep, four hundred cattle, dogs, and horses—then there's me, of course,' he said, his eyes gleaming playfully. 'Oh, don't forget Grandad too.'

'That's what I realised. I'm rather looking forward to it. I made up my mind after you gave me Chantilly, that I can now do what I've always been cut out for—that is, working on the land. I miss it … I miss riding.'

When the music stopped at the refreshment interval, Mack took Jessie's hand and led her outside to look at the sky. It was so clear it seemed as though she could reach up and pluck the sparkling stars like diamonds from the heavens. The brightness of the imposing silver moon gave the illusion of being able to warm her, on this crisp, autumn evening. She shivered. 'I should have wrapped my shawl around my shoulders. I left it inside.' She rubbed her hands up and down the top of her bare shoulders.

'Come and sit down over here. I'll keep you warm.' He pointed to a wooden bench at the side of the barn. He took off his jacket to reveal a white shirt with long sleeves. 'I'm lucky I've got a thermal under this. Here—this will keep you warm.' He wrapped his jacket around her shoulders.

'Do you hear that? It's someone else playing the fiddle.' Jessie was leaning over peering through the entrance to the barn. 'It's the Pastor—he can play too. He's playing a tune so that Grandad can dance. Take a look.'

Mack leaned over Jessie to see Walter dancing with Meg. Then he saw his parents dancing next to them.

'It's one of Grandad's favourites called, My Heart Will Go On, the Titanic theme.' Large globules rolled down Mack's cheeks. 'It's hard to believe that it took our marriage to break the icy hearts of my family and dissolve the feud that has kept us all apart for so many years.'

It's just as you told me that time when I was about to give up—when all the odds seemed against me. You quoted that verse from the Bible— 'But seek first God's Kingdom, and his righteousness and all these things will be given to you as well'.

***

The honeymoon on Coronet Peak zoomed by far too quickly for Mack and Jessie. It was Walter's wedding present to them. He had even booked them into a honeymoon suite in a fancy Swiss chalet.

Not far from there was Arrowtown, a favourite place of Mack's. That's because it exhibited many photos and articles about Mack's ancestors in the little museum there. He loved the fact that a sheep shearer called Jack Tawa first found gold in Arrowtown.

They could only spare a week away from the station, as they couldn't leave Walter with all the responsibility. They had asked Wyatt and Prue to help out, although the station hands were reliable and responsible. At least Jessie's parents didn't have to go all the way back to the Bay of Plenty, as their chalet was already completed and they had settled into their new home. Tom had returned to the farm in Bethlehem and was coping well.

Chapter Twenty-Nine

They were at last settled in at home on the station. The snow was now low lying and the view from the veranda of their homestead was spectacular. The newlyweds sat on the wooden seat looking out at the mountains. The pinnacles glistened in the late afternoon sun, which cast a myriad of pastel hues over them with shades of pink and mauve.

Jessie pulled her merino shawl tighter around her shoulders as Mack slipped his arm around her slight waist and pulled her closer.

'You know—when you were having all those awful ups and downs trying to break into the farming community, I have to say, I did despair a few times. I thought you would shoot through never to be seen again. I'm so glad you stayed.'

She leaned over and kissed his cheek. 'It wasn't me who kept me here. God did for me what I couldn't do for myself. He put the desire in my heart and gave me the strength and courage to overcome.'

'I know he did. He certainly made a way where there seemed to be no way. Look at how everything has come together.'

They continued to sit watching the changing horizon as the sun was going down. Jessie Reed had become a high country station manager jointly with Mack, and the new on-call vet had already started work. Now she would be able to help Mack run Reed Station, as well as work part-time running a few clinics each week. She had it all—the handsome farmer, her family around her and the mountains. Jessie had been so blessed, and she was determined to make a real go of it. The high country was her home, and she was here to stay.

Chantilly appeared at the fence watching them.

'Oh, okay Chantilly, I'm coming'. Jessie picked up the bucket of oats she had ready for her on the veranda and turned to Mack.

'I can see what you or someone has written on her cover. That's sweet of you.'

As she drew closer, she read the words painted on the horse's cover—*Jessie Reed—just married*!

She looked back at Mack who sat on the veranda grinning. Chantilly whinnied and nudged her with her head as if the intuitive animal knew exactly what was going on. Jessie's heart melted. It was as though her life was just about to begin all over again.

THE END

MACK THE GOOD SHEPHERD

Copyright Patricia Snelling
First published in New Zealand 2019

Contents
Chapters 1 – 27

MACK THE GOOD SHEPHERD

Chapter One

Summer 1982

Mack Reed lolled on the timeworn couch, weary from another day with the shearing gang. He'd been up since five working with his musterers, bringing sheep down from the rugged hills into woolshed holding pens ready for the contractors. Mack was always hands on and today he'd spent most of the day demonstrating to agricultural students his own unique shearing techniques. By late afternoon, he was exhausted but pleased with himself. He'd shorn three hundred sheep single-handed. Together, the crew had handled two thousand sheep. It was tough and dirty work.

This year, the shearing gang brought their own shedhands and cooks. His grandfather, Walter's long-serving housekeeper, Bessie had always done the cooking aided by her domestic staff, but now things had changed, and she didn't mind at all.

Mack took the cushion out from behind his head and puffed it up with his fist. When he placed his head back on it, his mind raced, robbing him of peace thinking about his sister, Meg. She'd got herself into a tangle. Things had become worse at home, and it looked like her marriage was on the brink.

As he lay there pondering current events, a deep sense of gratitude about his own life stirred within him. He was now the manager of a high country merino sheep station and married to the sweetest woman he knew.

When Mack had first arrived in the remote farming community of Glenorchy, he never imagined he would be a catalyst for changing lives. He'd initiated the healing of a long-standing feud between his father and his grandfather, Walter, who had previously alienated himself from his whole family.

Mack's father, Len, had shown no interest in farming, even though he'd been born and raised on Reed Station. This two- thousand-acre station had been in the family for generations, and that trend had almost ended when Mack rejected the idea of farming during his youth. After a long stint travelling overseas and casual employment on an extensive ranch in America, he soon came to relish farming life. He became a skilled shepherd and when he returned to New Zealand, he spent several years in the South as a contract sheep shearer. Eventually, he journeyed to Glenorchy where he wove his way into his estranged grandfather's life and in time, became the manager of Reed Station, gifted to him by his grandfather.

When Jessie Lee, an adventurous, young vet from Waikato moved to Glenorchy for work, Mack couldn't believe how blessed he was when she walked back into his life. They'd first met at her friend, Hope Rigby's twenty-first birthday and again at her wedding and longed for the opportunity to see her again.

His dreams became a reality when Jessie moved to Glenorchy to set up her vet practice. After they married, Jessie shared the running of Reed Station on remote

Routeburn Road, with Mack and his grandfather, as well as operating her part-time vet clinic from a custom-built bus.

Mack now had ownership of a vast station, but his sister had been left out of their grandfather's estate. To make things equal between himself and his city-slicker sister, he'd offered Meg his small farm holding in the Dart Valley—one hundred acres to do with as she wanted. She could now fulfil her dream of operating an exclusive boutique farmstay.

Meg arrived in Glenorchy full of grandiose ideas. She disrupted the community with her outrageous plans, especially the members of the Country Women's Institute thus alienating herself from them.

Mack had deep regrets that he had invited Meg and husband Joe to live in Glenorchy and felt responsible for cleaning up the chaos.

Chapter Two

Mack startled at the noise of Jessie's mobile vet bus as it rumbled down the driveway. Springing off the couch, he rushed to the bathroom to splash water over his face, which was covered with dust and sweat. He slapped on his sun-baked jaw his Paco Rabanne aftershave that Jessie had given him last birthday. Pulling his boots on, he raced back outside to give his wife a hand in with her gear.

'Mmm.' She planted a full kiss on his sunburnt lips as she stepped onto the veranda. 'Good to see you're working hard at keeping some romance alive, love,' she teased.

'It's the least I can do to cover up the grubby day I've had today. It's so dry out there and the sheep were kicking up a dust storm. I hope we get some rain tonight to calm things down.'

'Perhaps you should jump straight in the shower.' She walked past him straight into the office to drop off her Carphone with Mack in tow.

He offloaded Jessie's day bag onto the office desk and walked back out onto the veranda. She followed him out.

'Anyway—what sort of day have you had? You were going to get a new client from Kinloch. You told me this morning.'

'It went well.' Jessie sunk into the well-worn wicker armchair while Mack sat back onto the couch that stank of dog.

She continued, 'They brought me their pregnant Kune pig to check over. They've started breeding Alpacas and want me to come out to Kinloch to look them over. The wool is sold to an exporter in Canterbury ... are you okay, Mack?' Jessie had noticed he'd gone quiet as she bent over and yanked off her boots.

'You're looking awfully sombre. Is there something you're not telling me?'

'Let me take a shower out back if the staff aren't using it. I'll tell you about it later.'

'Good. While you do that, I'll take a hot bath before dinner.' She shot into the kitchen to pour a glass of water, gulping it down.

When Mack stepped into the shower, he remembered the bathroom fitters were arriving the next day to install the new shower in the staff quarters. He'd have to drop around to let them know before they fell asleep after a hectic day mustering.

He finished showering, dressed and wandered back outside.

Jessie caught sight of him going to the front door. 'Where are you off to?'

'I won't be a few minutes. I have to let the staff know the bathroom fitters are coming tomorrow.'

'Oh, yes. I'd forgotten about that.' She shut the door behind him.

Mack was exhausted as he trudged along the path to the staff quarters. Their tired yet compact bungalow had recently been renovated on the inside, but he could see paint flaking on the external walls. He sighed—another job to do.

Up till now, the station hands had always used the spare bathroom in the homestead. Mack and Jessie both preferred a shower, except now and then Jessie enjoyed soaking in the old cast iron claw bath. With so many people using the water supply, it often dried up, especially in a drought. They decided it was better for everyone if the staff had their own separate water tank and shower box.

The station staff ate in a dining room at the back of the homestead and their food was cooked by Bessie who called on an assistant cook when required. She'd been a Godsend to Jessie who operated a private, mobile vet practice and helping Mack run the station. They couldn't have done it without Bessie who had a live-in position and was treated as one of the family.

Mack knocked at the door of the station hands' bungalow. Coran, a tall, lean man, in his twenties, greeted him. He was still dressed in his black woollen singlet and flannel trousers and Mack turned his head away as the shepherd opened the door, thinking he could do with a clothes peg over his nose.

'Sorry mate, you must be dog-tired. I forgot to remind you that the bathroom fitters are coming tomorrow.'

'That's no problem. I wrote it down and I'll make sure I use the bathroom before I turn in. I'll let Ben and the others know in the morning as they're sleeping.'

'Right, you are. I'll see you tomorrow.'

***

Mack had wanted to catch Ben to tell him what a great job did as Head Shepherd. Although Mack had relinquished that role, he himself would always be a high-ranking shepherd despite that. He and his grandfather had elected Ben to take over that position, now that Walter had semi-retired. The young man had come from another large station, with experience in high country shepherding.

Further along from the staff quarters for the shepherds and musterers was a similar-aged building to the staff bungalow, but much shabbier. This was a lined, corrugated iron bunkhouse for the contract shearing gang. The kitchen had a fully functioning oven and electric hob and in the corner stood a sizeable fridge. Mostly, the shearers ate high-calorie meals and used their own cooks.

Mack thought he'd have to talk Walter into updating the contract shearers' accommodation as well. As Station Manager, he should have the most say. *Who knows how long Grandad is going to be around and I'll have to make all the decisions once he's gone.*

***

Jessie dressed and entered the kitchen with a turban-shaped towel on her head. While she stood over a saucepan stirring beef stew, Mack crept up behind her. He leaned over, kissed her neck then gave her waist a squeeze with both hands.

'Let's eat,' she said, serving the re-heated vegetables onto the plates followed by steaming beef.

She poured Bessie's home-brewed ginger beer into the glasses while Mack took the plates and placed them on the quilted placemats. They'd been handmade by Bessie, which she'd gifted to them on their wedding day.

'Where's Grandad—is he eating with us?'

'No, he ate earlier and went to his room. Says he needs an early night and is listening to the radio. He helped us with drenching today.' Mack pulled a piece of paper from his pocket, squinting in the poor light as he read the message.

'Bessie left a note to say it's her day off tomorrow and she'll be staying overnight with her friend in Cromwell. She'll be back late afternoon tomorrow and has left us a smoked fish pie in the fridge in case she's delayed.'

While they ate, Jessie was aware Mack had gone unusually quiet again. She glanced at his face—the deep furrows that had formed recently.

'Come on, out with it! Stop bottling up. Remember, we promised each other on our wedding day not to stuff our feelings down or withhold worries from each other. What's bugging you, Mack?'

'It's... ah... it's Meg. Her life's a complete mess and something needs to be done before it falls apart—but I don't know what.' He rubbed his eyes, trying to relieve the tension.

'Why—what do you mean?'

'I spoke to my mate, Larry, from Young Farmers who lives on Priory Road. He says she's been telling his wife and the other women at the Country Women's Institute that she has applied for resource consent to sell off ninety acres of land for property development.'

'What? But my folks live on their property,' cried Jessie. 'I can't get the point of them moving down to Glenorchy from the Bay of Plenty so Dad could manage their farm. What was she thinking of throwing my folks off the land? And I'd like to know what Joe thought, too.'

'I don't know. The last time I saw him at the General Store he was looking rather frazzled and now I understand why.'

'But would she actually be able to do that?'

'I suppose she can. Before I handed the land over to her, my previous neighbours had Resource Consent to subdivide—but only into five acres lots—not a subdivision, as Meg puts it. She appears to have brought chaos into our lives, just when everything has been going smoothly and God has been good to us.'

'Look, Mack. Let's both pay Meg a visit and try to talk sense into her. I mean ... if there are three of us, including Joe, trying to convince her she's going off the deep end, maybe she'll listen.'

'We could do. Why don't you phone your folks and ask what she said to them? She shouldn't be mouthing off to other people about her plans when your parents will be the ones most affected by it. It's your father's livelihood at stake.'

'I realise that. I'm sorry, Mack—I know she's your sister, but she is inconsiderate placing them in that predicament.'

***

Jessie went into their office and picked up the phone. Her mother answered.

'Hello, dear. It's been a while since we chatted. I was going to phone you tomorrow on your half day.'

'That's okay, Mum. I need to ask you something, as we've had some unsettling news. Have you been to the Country Women's meetings recently?'

'Oh, no, not for a few months. I've had too much to do around here and the last trip back to Bethlehem made me miss a meeting, too. Why, what's the problem?'

'It's hard to talk over the phone. It's about something that Meg is getting up to—something that may affect you and Dad.'

'You mean, her highfalutin talk about putting in a swimming pool for the guests. It won't really worry us, though.'

'No, Mum, not that. She's been telling the women at the meetings that she has applied to the Council for Resource Consent to subdivide ninety acres of farmland that Dad manages. Her intention is to sell it to a developer for housing.'

There was a momentary silence.

'Mum, are you okay? I'm so sorry to have to break this news to you. Wait till Dad finds out. You'll have to tell him, and he'll be devastated.'

'When did Meg think she was going to drop this bombshell on us? Or were we going to be the laughing stock of the community when everyone knew except us? Your father will be livid.'

'Look, Mum. Mack has suggested we all go together and talk to them on my afternoon off tomorrow. Why don't you and Dad come with us to find out exactly what's going on? Meg should have approached you first.'

'She's the landowner. We're just tenants who manage the land.'

'You pay for the lease of that house, for goodness' sake! Doesn't that count for anything?'

'I'll talk to your father tonight and we'll meet you tomorrow. Arrange a meeting with Meg, and you and Mack stay afterwards and have some dinner with us.'

'Mack and I will pray for you all tonight, Mum. If we hand it over to God, he'll direct our paths.'

When Jessie got off the phone, her heart sank. *If I hadn't come to Glenorchy and married Mack, my parents would not be in this predicament. Although Meg's actions are irrational, I'm partly to blame.*

Chapter Three

Mack and two shepherds had spent another day in a dusty sheep race, drenching hundreds of ewes. His grandfather still worked with the animals but mainly did odd jobs around the farm. Since his last stroke, he'd become frail, and his muscles had wasted. He enjoyed getting around on his quad bike and overseeing the running of the farm, although he had a reliable farm manager in Mack. The old man could still repair the odd fence and feed the stock hay from his old John Deere tractor.

Today Walter spent the morning with Mack who took his dog, Bluey to direct the sheep into the stockyards where the station hands stood ready with their drench guns. When they'd finished for the day, the two men relaxed at the dining table, drinking stewed tea.

'Bessie won't be back until late this afternoon. She left a pie in the fridge made from those tins of smoked fish you like. Jessie and I are off to a meeting with Meg and Joe about an important issue they want to discuss—I'll tell you about it when we get back. Bessie should be here before we arrive home and if not, just hoe into the pie without us.'

'I think I'll have a nap before that—I'm tuckered out. It's hot for this time of the year and draining.'

'Okay, Grandad—I'll see you later. I've got to get freshened up and meet up with Jessie. She's going straight to Meg's on the way back from Kinloch after her home visits.'

***

Jessie arrived at Meg and Joe's farmstay. As she drove her Land Rover towards the gate, she saw an obtrusive new sign that had been erected on a post that read, *WILLOW PARK*. Mack's Ute was parked to the side as she arrived in the driveway. He'd arrived just before her, and out of her side mirror, she glimpsed him walking towards her vehicle. He banged on her car's roof.

She rolled down her window. 'What are you doing wandering around out here?'

'I wanted to wait for you. I thought we could walk around to your parents' place first and rehearse how we're going to approach the issue with Meg.'

'Sounds okay to me, but what if Meg sees us first and invites us in?'

'I'll make some excuse—don't you worry about that. Come, let's go.'

They walked in single file along the separate pathway at the rear of Meg's home to the chalet at the back where Jessie's folks lived. Pru saw them through the kitchen window. She opened the door, waving her hand, directing them inside.

'Come in, quick. I need to talk to you before we go over to see them. This is nerve-wracking, to say the least—especially living right next door. It's a difficult predicament and likely to cause division between us.'

Wyatt walked up behind her. 'Come on, everyone—let's not stand in the kitchen. Take a pew in the lounge and we'll let you know what we think about this whole crazy situation. I don't suppose it's worth offering anything to drink, as I'm sure Meg's going to do that.'

He showed them into the lounge and offered each a seat.

413

'We knew nothing about Meg's intention to sell off the land to developers. Perhaps it's best you talk to her, Mack and say what a serious impact it will have on this farming community if prime agricultural land is ripped up for housing. There's enough of that going on in Queenstown, and we don't need it here.'

Mack sat on the edge of his seat, as though he was about to take off. The fire in his belly was irrepressible.

'You all know how hard I've toiled on this land to make it arable. I worked my fingers to the bone to convert it into top quality land capable of nourishing first-rate livestock. When I handed it over to Meg, I trusted she would keep her word. She'd agreed to operate the farmstay on ten acres and keep the remaining ninety fenced off as grassland. I feel betrayed by her.' Jessie moved closer to him on the couch and placed her arm across his shoulders.

'She's just a city woman trying to make her way in a place that's alien to her. I don't think she understood the ramifications of the whole proposition you made to her. She is just one-eyed, following a pipe dream,' said Wyatt.

'Yes, I know that, but we'd better get her to stop dreaming before she wakes up to a nightmare one day. She's getting into a minefield, turning the entire community against her. Council Resource Consent issues are a time bomb waiting to go off,' said Mack.

'So—will you try to talk her out of it when we go next door?' Wyatt nodded at Mack as he got up. 'Pru and I are the ones most affected here, never mind the community. We left our farm behind in Bethlehem to help them out. If I'd known they would do this, I'd never have considered leasing a dwelling on their property and becoming their farm manager. Now we'll have to move.' Wyatt spat out his words like a car misfiring.

'Let's all just calm down a minute. Perhaps we need to hear Meg first and then try to reason with her. Tell her that if she wishes to stay in the area long term, she's going to need the support of her community. They could make it bad for her business,' uttered Pru who hadn't sat down the whole time. She walked to the hall mirror to check her hair, straightened her blouse collar, and joined them back in the lounge.

Mack had grown to admire Pru and knew her to be a fair mediator. Perhaps his mother-in-law was talking sense.

'I suppose you're right. She may feel threatened if we go in with all guns blazing and then dig her toes in. It'll be interesting to see what Joe has to say when we bring it up in front of him.'

'Are we ready?' asked Wyatt. 'I need to know where my future lies as an employee here. I'll certainly be confronting her on that one.'

'Ah... ah. Now that's exactly what we don't want to be doing. We ought to be taking a care-fronting approach, not a confrontational one. Please tread carefully.' Pru looped her arm in his to hold him back.

Mack and Jessie led the way followed by her parents. As Mack approached the door of Meg's home, she opened it before he knocked. 'Oh, come on in. I've just put the kettle on. Joe is in his workshop—I'll call him.' Her voice shook as she called out to Joe.

Mack picked up on Meg's discomfort. She showed them into the lounge to take a seat and cleared her throat, which Mack knew she did when socially ill at ease. As a young girl, whenever she was in trouble she would twitch her nose.

'Oh, here's Joe.' Meg relaxed when she heard a thud on the front porch. Joe pulled off his heavy boots and smacked them hard on the top step to remove the mud. 'I'm just going to clean up. Give me a minute,' he called back to her.

'All having tea or perhaps a cold drink?' she asked. The teapot in her hand trembled as she placed it on the serving trolley.

'Tea please,' they said in unison. Meg went back to the kitchen for a plate of cakes and placed them on the trolley.

'Before you say anything—no, I haven't had time for baking and yes, these ginger gems are from the General Store.'

Mack could never remember his sister baking, and it would be a miracle to see it now.

'What brings you all here?' Joe's left eyelid twitched. 'Meg said that you've heard that she's applied for Resource Consent to sell off some land. We don't even know if it's going to be possible—and I tell you now, none of this was my idea!' Joe's face contorted. He pouted, causing his forehead to pucker.

'Humph!' Meg retorted with eyes like steel balls aimed at Mack. She shot around the room, poking the plate of cakes under the nose of each guest.

Once she was seated, Mack broke the chilling silence by speaking first.

'Meg, we just want to discuss your reasons for selling the land. Wyatt has been toiling this soil to make it suitable for grazing heifers. The farmers, with whom he is contracted, pay a hefty price to you because of his efforts.'

Meg twitched her nose again and glared at Mack who knew his sister well and was aware she'd be annoyed with him for bringing it out into the open.

She looked at the floor, pulling at loose hair around her ear. 'The farmstay is not really working as I expected. The tourists are mainly from overseas, and the feedback has been that it's too far from town and there's nothing for them to do here. I thought it would be well-sought after. And then there have been problems with the neighbours. I've had a busload of tourists stay recently and when I held a garden party for them one night during summer, the locals came knocking on our door complaining about the coloured lights and music.'

Jessie found her voice. 'Why did they complain—was it too loud? And how could the lights do any harm?'

She and Mack had been praying for Meg, that she would settle down and change. They'd been trying to encourage her to come along to their chapel, but she'd resisted.

Meg continued, 'It startled the animals, they said. Some women told me to go back to where I came from.'

That was the first time Mack had heard her say this and felt sorry for her. 'Well, that's pretty harsh and uncalled for. Who was this woman?' He had a powerful urge to suddenly defend her.

'I can't remember her name. I think she's married to the butcher next to the General Store.'

'Mmm, I think I know who you mean. Look, Meg—you just have to rise above these things. You can get that reaction in any neighbourhood, even in town. You don't need to sell up and clear out because of it.'

Meg bristled. 'Then there are the women at the Country Women's meetings who have formed an outright clique. I don't like them.'

'Did you do as I suggested that time and invite them for afternoon tea? That would certainly break the ice,' asked Pru, with a softness in her voice.

'Ah ... no, I just didn't get around to it.'

'You could tell them about the horses you kept at your stables in Wellington and the shows and contests you've been involved in. I'm sure they would be interested. You could offer to teach their children to ride.'

'But all of that will not make my business profitable, will it?'

Joe sighed, jumped up from his seat and grabbed his Stetson from the hat stand. It was one that Mack had given him. 'I won't listen to all this any longer. You tell the family your plans, Meg. You can count me out. Sorry everyone—I need some fresh air and I'm off for a walk.'

Mack heard the door slam behind him. He wanted to run after him, but he stopped short and sat back in his seat, realising that his sister needed help.

Jessie and Pru collected up the cups and placed them on the tea trolley, wheeling it out to the kitchen. They left Mack to continue trying to talk sense into Meg while Wyatt went outside to look for Joe.

Mack stood up and followed Wyatt to the front porch. 'Sorry about all this, but I'll have one last go at trying to change her mind and then we'd better leave it and let her think about what we've all been saying. Don't you want to discuss your position here, too?' Mack asked Wyatt, walking onto the veranda.

'Not yet. I want to find out from Joe whether Meg is sincere about placing Pru and me in a bad position. I'll hear it from him first.'

Chapter Four

Meg was way out of her depth and sinking fast. Deep inside Mack a sense of misplaced guilt gnawed at him. Was he mainly to blame for this dilemma by gifting his farm to this city girl who had no farming experience? Did he only make that generous offer to appease his conscience after having his grandfather's two- thousand-acre station handed to him on a platter—the inheritance which should have been shared with Meg? Mack's stomach churned as he saw his part in the conflict. There had to be a way through this.

'Look, sis, you need to understand the implications for me if you sell prime agricultural land for housing development. This kind of pasture is precious, and the farmers around here associate this farm with me as I originally lived and worked on it. You'll not only alienate yourself from them, but you'll also cause a breakdown in my relationship with the farming community and that will consequently harm Reed Station, too.'

Meg dropped her head and stared at her feet. She leaned forward, bracing her arms on her thighs and gave a loud sigh. Moments later, she sat up straight again.

'I'm not selling all the land. I'm keeping ten acres around the house and thought I might buy some ponies and small animals to entertain the tourists, but there is no point if they don't want to stay here. We do get some guests, but I expected the place would stay fully booked.'

'You don't have the expertise to do a subdivision, Meg. It could go horribly wrong—I've heard all kinds of horror stories from others who have done that.'

'I'm not doing the subdivision. A developer is keen to buy it at a high price. I just need to get the Resource Consent before he goes ahead with the sale, as it requires consent to subdivide. When I get the money from the land sale, I want to turn the farmstay into a luxury lodge with a swimming pool and tennis court.'

Mack's lungs ejected a quiet sigh as he leaned on his knee with one arm, looking sideways at Meg with an expression of disbelief. *What is she going on about now? Surely she doesn't mean this. That's why Joe was so exasperated.*

'I'll hire a shuttle bus driver to collect guests from Queenstown Airport and bring them here. Just imagine if I could get a heliport built out the back and wealthy tourists could fly in from other parts of New Zealand.'

Mack drifted off mentally while Meg continued to elaborate. *Is she being sincere with these wild ideas, or is it just a pipe dream?*

He wasn't familiar with his sister lying or being insincere, although she'd been revoltingly ostentatious at times, but he believed she meant what she said. In that case, he needed to devise a plan to stop her, something that could turn her head and fulfil her instead of this far-fetched plan.

Meg shot into the kitchen and sauntered back into the living room with a small glass of Port wine in her hand. Mack's heart missed a beat to see his sister so strung out. She'd always been well-groomed and taken good care of herself. He even doubted whether she'd run a comb through her hair that day—birds could lay eggs in it. He glanced at her nymph-like body, his eyes coming to a halt on her thin, scrawny legs. His mouth fell open at the sight of the pea sticks that were once athletic calves.

'Do you want one?' She lifted her glass in the air.

'You know I don't drink except for the odd Stout—I'm okay at the moment.'

She slumped into the two-seater couch opposite him and at first, didn't meet his gaze.

Mack was speechless, waiting for her to look up at him while she rested her arms on her knees in deep thought. Before long, she sat up and began kneading her temples.

He couldn't contain himself any longer. 'Look here, Meg. All this will not do you or anyone else any good. Please hear me out. It's as though something has got hold of you and set you on a collision course like a motorbike on ice.'

'You just sound like Joe. Can't anyone be on my side for once?'

'Oh, dear Meg. This is not a contest unless you make it a battleground. Quite the contrary. We're saying all this because we love you and don't want to see you get into trouble. If you aren't careful, you could gain an empire and lose Joe. This is driving the two of you apart.'

Meg sniffed in defiance. 'Joe just doesn't understand my concept of building an exclusive holiday resort. I don't think he was too happy about coming down here, anyway.'

Mack poured himself a glass of Meg's apple cider.

'Give me a few days. Perhaps all of us can come up with an idea that could suit everyone and create a win-win outcome.'

'No, Mack. Stop trying to talk me out of it. It's alright for you. I can see you've had your dream come true, becoming the manager of Reed Station—that's every farmer's dream. But that's not me and I have dreams too. I've always wanted to operate an exclusive resort and couldn't afford to do it in Wellington—now is my opportunity.'

'You're going to continue to get much opposition,' Mack snapped, exasperated with her stubbornness.

'They will all change their minds when they see how beautiful it will be. It may even bring some employment into the area for the farmers' wives who need to bring in an extra income. In fact, I was going to say to Wyatt that I could offer him a position as a caretaker for the grounds if he was interested. When I have ponies, they'll need care as well.'

Mack couldn't believe what he was hearing. How self-centred his sister had become. *Why did she think an experienced farmer such as Wyatt would be interested in doing that?*

'I'm going to have to get back. We've got a stock sale at the station tomorrow and I have a heap to do to get the paperwork organised. Just keep in touch. Wait—the family has arrived back.'

Mack walked outside to see Jessie and Pru approach him in deep conversation.

'Where's Joe?' He glanced around and noticed the women returned with his father-in-law, Wyatt, and no sign of Joe.

Wyatt shook off his boots. 'He came for a long walk with me and when we returned, he said he needed to take a drive up to the lake to think things over alone. He said he'd be back before we leave.'

'I've got to head home now. Are you coming, Jessie? You can stay on longer, but I've got a lot to do before the stock sale tomorrow.'

Jessie looked at Pru. 'Do you mind, Mum? I need to give Mack a hand if that's okay. I'll phone you tonight and find out what Joe's take is on this whole thing.'

Mack took hold of Jessie's arm and led her away so as not to get caught up in another dispute.

Wyatt and Pru left at the same time as Meg came to the door.

'Oh, you're all going. I didn't mean to upset everybody, but I've got to follow my heart or I'm not being true to myself. Please don't hold it against me,' she said, her voice quavering.

'Never mind,' snarled Wyatt. 'I think you and I need to have a talk tomorrow about where Pru and I fit into your grandiose plans—seeing I'm employed to manage the grazing contract and take care of the land you're selling off,' he said, slamming his Stetson on his head. 'In fact, if you don't mind, I'd like a quick word with you now, before Pru and I walk back to the house.'

'Oh, I suppose that's okay. I don't know where Joe is but come into the lounge again—I'll put the kettle on.'

Pru followed Wyatt back inside.

'No tea, thanks! We want to go home. I have a big day tomorrow digging up the gorse that has sprung up in the paddock on the west side.' Wyatt clutched at his Stetson and scrunched it in his hands as he spoke.

Meg waited until they were seated and chose a seat on the far side of the lounge further away from Wyatt and stared out the window.

Wyatt continued, 'We want to know what your intentions are with Pru and I. We trusted you, Meg, when you offered me the role of taking care of your farmland and managing the grazing contracts. You also asked Pru to help you run the farmstay. Now we both feel that you've pulled the rug out from under our feet.'

'You can continue living in the chalet. You are lessees and I wouldn't take that away from you. I enjoy having you share the property with us, but you could always buy us out if that suits you better.'

Pru and Wyatt looked at each other aghast.

'I wouldn't be interested in staying on here with twenty houses going up next to me. Nor would Pru, would you dear?' He nodded at his wife.

'No, I'd hate it, to be honest. We've lived all our married life on a farm, and therefore we thought we could compromise and leave our own property to Tom and help you out.'

'Why not wait and see how I go with the Council. If I get the Resource Consent, perhaps you might be interested in the options I offer you.'

'We'll see. You'll have to keep me informed after this. I've put much toil and strain into getting that pasture just right for you and Joe so that you can get a viable income which you are now receiving. I need to come to terms with the fact that you already wish to abandon this venture so fast. We'll be going now. Good evening.' Wyatt, without replacing his hat, signalled to Pru to go.

They whipped out the door and stomped off back home. Meg stood on the doorstep scanning far across the paddocks towards the road. No sign of Joe yet—he'd been away a long time.

Chapter Five

Mack followed Jessie home behind her vehicle, finding it difficult to focus on his driving. He felt the pressure of a tight band across his forehead and just wanted the stress with Meg to go away. Why did this dark cloud descend over his happy valley and rob him of the future he'd longed for—or was it sent to test him? If so, according to what he knew from his Bible, it will strengthen his faith and give him tenacity.

Without warning, he hit the brakes hard almost lurching into the back of Jessie's vehicle as she swerved at a hawk in the middle of the road pecking at the remains of a dead opossum.

He had followed Jessie's vehicle too close, with his mind still on Meg and her problems. He felt shaken by the near-miss and realised how much his sister's unmanageable life affected him. Jessie continued on without realising.

They both arrived back at Reed Station intact. A delicious aroma wafted out the front door as Mack stepped inside.

Bessie, their housekeeper, stood in the hallway wiping her hands on her apron. 'Where's Jessie? She didn't say she wouldn't be in for dinner. I haven't seen her return from work yet.'

'She's here—still outside unloading her vehicle. We've had a stressful afternoon visiting Meg and Joe at Willow Park, but I won't get into it right now.'

Bessie screwed up her forehead, revealing multiple creases. 'I hope it's not too serious. You sure you don't want to talk about it?'

'Nope ... ah ... here's Jessie. Do you need a hand out there, love?'

His wife, with hands full walked straight to their office to unload her bags. 'No, I'm fine. I've got what I need out of the Land Rover, and I put the rest of my gear in the bus. I'm running a mobile clinic in Kinloch—early start. Mmm ... something smells good, Bessie.'

The matronly woman stood in the doorway, beaming. 'It's ready—your favourite chicken dish.' She whipped back into the kitchen and pulled on a pair of padded gloves ready to pick up the stoneware casserole dish.

'Here—let me!' Mack called, seeing the size of the dish. Bessie stood back and removed the gloves, handing them to Mack who carried the dish out onto the dining table. Jessie came out with a bowl of salad.

Bessie traipsed into the hall and called out to Walter, expecting him to be in his room.

'Grandad's out in the workshop. I saw him as I pulled up. I'll fetch him in for dinner,' said Mack as he hurried down the steps to the corrugated iron building that housed many contraptions Walter had invented or altered.

Mack felt indecisive whether he should update his grandfather on his sister's latest farcical schemes. It could break his heart, bringing such trouble to this peaceful, hard-working community. Walter stood bent over, trying to repair an old plough.

'Grandad ... I ... um ... dinner's ready.'

Mack raised his voice a few tones higher as he stood in the doorway. 'Grandad! Dinners ready.'

The old man looked up, squinting at Mack, as the late afternoon sun caught his eyes.

'Oh, okay, buddy. I'll be there in a jiffy. I'll just wash my hands in this sink. All covered in oil, they are.'

When Mack went back inside, Jessie had lit the fire. She stood in front of it, warming her hands. Mack approached her.

'Jess ... say nothing to Grandad yet. I don't think he could take it. Let's just wait and see what happens. Maybe the Council will put an end to land development.'

'Let's pray about it tonight. It sounds such a mess.'

'Okay, sure—Bessie doesn't need to know, either,' he whispered as he saw her enter the lounge.

Walter came inside and stood in front of the fireplace, warmed his hands then joined them at the dining table.

'Did you notice the new fire surround I put there earlier? It's one I'd been working on all week. I salvaged it from the recycling tip in Glenorchy. It's pure brass and has a border collie dog on it, though it's looking worse for wear.'

Bessie dished up the casserole for everyone.

'Yes, I noticed when I lit the fire and didn't know it was one you had salvaged. I wondered where it had come from.'

The rest of the meal continued in a jovial tone. Mack and Jessie kept their pact and didn't say a word about the fact that Walter's granddaughter was on a collision course.

***

Early the next morning, the autumn sun rose over the mountains surrounding Reed Station like a giant sunflower, shedding its laser-like rays across the rolling, dew-covered pastures.

Mack, now a seasoned farmer, was always out of bed first at daybreak. Jessie was not a morning person and struggled to get out from under the warm eiderdown. It was one that Walter had given them for their wedding present, an heirloom that had been quilted by Hazel, Mack's grandmother whom he regretted not getting to know.

427

Mack leaned over to kiss her. 'Come on, Jessie. I thought you had a clinic in Kinloch this morning. I'll go out and check the oil and water before you take off.'

Jessie sat up, trying to clear her throat as she struggled to respond. 'Okay, thanks,' she croaked.

Bessie was up early and had breakfast ready. Mack came back inside, washed his hands and sat at the table.

'Morning—sorry, I'm not waiting for everyone else, as we've got a stock sale this morning and the agent will be here early, he told me. I'm meeting him at the sale yards. The musterers are bringing in the sheep right now. I believe you're giving them breakfast this morning.' He slurped at his coffee in a stoneware mug.

'That's no problem—I'm all organised. I'll have Gina, my kitchen help from next door here all morning. Have some eggs before you rush out the door.'

'You know how to take care of a man, Bessie. My wife doesn't know how well-off she is. Mind you—she could melt any man's heart with her culinary skills,' he said, winking at Bessie. 'I just hope she doesn't forget how to use them.' Bessie flicked a tea-towel at him.

He scoffed his last piece of toast and gulped his coffee. After bolting his meal, he shot out the front door.

Jessie trudged into the lounge in her candlewick dressing gown. 'Morning, Bessie. Mack said he had to fly out the door to meet the stock agent. I hope he ate something.'

'He sure did. He wolfed down a plate of eggs and bacon. I hope he doesn't get indigestion the way he devoured it. Are you ready for yours?' Bessie looked Jessie over as she placed a pot of tea in front of her. Still half-asleep, Jessie picked up her Royal Albert china cup and started pouring the tea. 'Oh, sorry, I don't think I could eat anything at the moment.'

'Are you alright? You're looking peaky, my girl.' The woman's eyes fixated on Jessie, as she reached for the milk.

'I'm not sure—I felt nauseated when I got out of bed. It couldn't have been anything I've eaten as we all ate the same food last night. I don't feel like taking the bus out to Kinloch today, but I have a couple of clients with urgent needs.'

As soon as she said that, she ran to the bathroom and came out a few minutes later, bumping into Bessie standing in the hallway waiting for her.

'You've been sick in there, haven't you? At least, that's what it sounded like,' she said, gently grasping her arm and looking her in the eye. 'Do you think you should be back in bed?'

'No, I feel a lot better now. I've felt off for the last few days, but today is the worst.' Jessie clasped her hips, arching her back.

'I'll just take it slowly and cancel the last client if it's too much. Have been feeling tired lately—more than usual.'

'Well, just get checked out if it continues. Perhaps you could visit that new doctor in Glenorchy.'

'Don't worry—I will, if it persists. Have to hurry and get dressed now, Bessie. I know you've got a handful of men to feed at lunchtime, so I'm sorry I won't be here to help you.'

'Gina is coming from next door to give me a hand. You just get on and worry about yourself. I've made you a packed lunch if you feel like eating anything later.'

'We're so fortunate to have you. Where's Grandad—I haven't seen him yet?'

'He went out early to help the men get the sheep in and took his dogs with him.'

'He's amazing, isn't he? I don't know where he gets the energy at his age.'

Jessie rushed off and dressed, gathered up her medical bag, and scurried out the front door, passing Bessie who thrust a lunchbox into her other hand.

'Thanks, Bessie. See you later.'

Just as she opened the front door to go out, the phone rang. 'Drat. Just at the wrong time,' Jessie muttered. She waited a few minutes to see if Bessie answered it, but it kept on ringing. Bessie must have gone out the back she thought and raced into the lounge to pick up the call.

It was Meg on the phone. Joe had returned home and announced he was leaving her, although she didn't sound too distressed.

'That's awful, Meg. I'm so sorry it has come to this—I'll get Mack to call you when he comes in. Perhaps he can change Joe's mind. He had a meeting with a stock agent and left early this morning.'

Jessie put the phone back on the receiver after a brief conversation and hurried out the door.

Chapter Six

Autumn

Mack sat in his armchair next to Walter, warming his feet in front of the fire. The two men were worn out. The snow had fallen in the hills and the shepherds had gathered the sheep from the steep ridges into the valley earlier. Mack and Walter herded them into the paddocks onto the flat ground, although their dogs did most of the work.

Today differed from most days. The weather forecast spelt possible snowstorms in the high country and the sheep needed to be protected. There was more shelter in the way of trees and large, open barns lower down. The temperature was unusually chilly for autumn. Mack had checked that the dogs had their covers on for the night in their kennels, as well as the horses.

Jessie arrived home late. She parked the bus in the large metal garage and came up the steps carrying her medical bag. She rushed inside like a fleeting tornado.

'Hi, love! Mack jumped to his feet. Anything outside that I can help you in with?'

'I've got a box of mandarins that the couple with the Angora goats in Kinloch gave me. Oh—and my chilly bin I took for the vaccines. Stay here, I'll go back out. You'll catch a chill after sitting in front of the fire.' She kissed him and took off back to the vehicle again. Mack ignored her courteous remark and followed her out to the garage.

Mack took her hand, glancing at the pallor in her face as the last rays of the sun peeping through the gap in the garage doors illuminated her translucent skin.

'How did you get on today—were you sick again? I've been worried about you.'

'No, don't worry, I wasn't sick, but I felt as though I was on a sinking boat all day. I'm glad I haven't got any more mobile clinics this week. By the way—I forgot to tell you Meg phoned in a distressed state. She said Joe arrived home after we left, but it wasn't until late at night. He'd been sitting down by Lake Wakatipu thinking things over and the situation there was not good. He's talking about leaving, so you'd better phone her.'

When they went back inside, Jessie went straight to their bedroom to rest while Mack dropped the mandarins off in the kitchen. He offloaded her chilly bin in the office and placed the icepack in the freezer. *Please, God. Bring healing to her body.*

He went back to check on her.

'Please don't fuss. I'm just done in, that's all. Tuckered out, in fact. I must have picked up a bug and need an early night. I'll rest awhile, then come and join you for dinner later. It's Bessie's evening off, but she left us a steak and kidney pie, which I don't think I could manage tonight. I'll poach a few eggs instead.'

'Okay then. See you shortly,' said Mack, eyeballing her for a moment. He trundled back into the living room and slipped a macrocarpa log onto the fire, trying not to wake Walter who snored loud enough to startle Buster. The ginger ball of fluff slinked off his lap and curled up on the mat.

Mack went to the kitchen and turned on the oven to heat the pie, and while it was heating he set about poaching eggs for Jessie. When the pie was ready, he looked in on his grandfather to see if he had stirred. Buster had returned to his lap, purring as loud as Walter had been snoring.

'Grandad—I've got some food in the kitchen for you. Steak and kidney pie that Bessie left us. Would you like it on your lap, or will you come to the table?'

Walter looked up with a soft smile. Mack sensed that his expression reflected gratitude for having a caring grandson.

'On my lap, if you wouldn't mind. Where's that hard-working woman of yours? I hear she was poorly this morning. Is she alright now?' He eased Buster off his lap and got out of his chair.

'No, not really ... I'm not sure. She's more tired than usual and her stomach is queasy—probably from rushing around in the cold too much. I've cooked a few eggs for her and I'll see if she's coming to join us.'

Mack met Jessie, heading along the hallway.

'I've got some eggs and toast for you ready. Do you want to eat at the dining table, or we can join Grandad in the lounge where it's warm?'

'By the fire would be good. It was cold in our room—I should have thrown a rug over my legs.'

Mack brought the meal, placing the tray on her lap.

'I knew there was a good reason for marrying you, darling,' she said, chuckling with amusement. 'What do you think, Grandad?'

Walter sat back in his chair again, sitting up, waiting to be served by Mack who had gone back out to the kitchen.

'I'm just glad our family has reconciled, or I would have missed out on all this VIP treatment,' he said, glancing at Jessie with a warm smile.

Mack waited on his grandfather first, and once he prepared his own meal, cutting a large piece of the pie, he joined the others. 'You just can't beat Bessie's fluffy pastry—sauce, anyone?'

He struggled to get the top off the glass bottle, but once he did, he smothered the pie until it was red with tomato sauce.

Jessie couldn't eat the eggs and took the unfinished meal out to the kitchen. 'Sorry, love. I just haven't got my usual appetite. This queasiness keeps returning. I think I'll phone the doctor tomorrow and make an appointment,' she said to Mack as she settled back by the fire.

'Oh, really? It's that bad, is it?' Mack stopped eating and frowned, discarding his light-heartedness.

'To be honest, I'm getting concerned myself. I know it's not a virus, nor is it a stomach bug. I just want to get checked out.'

'Bessie's back tomorrow. Perhaps I can go with you as my day won't be too hectic. None of the station hands are away, so we should be okay.'

'Don't forget me, young fella! I've still got plenty of go left in me yet. Remember that less than a decade ago, I was running this place. I've just slowed down a bit since my stroke, that's all.' He narrowed his eyes, and the corners of his mouth turned downwards.

'That's right, Grandad. We know that, and it's the very reason I can accompany Jessie tomorrow.' Mack stood up, rubbed his stomach and gathered up the dinner plates. 'That was a hearty feed. Anyone for a cup of tea?'

'You've done enough, lad. Let me get up and make the tea. It's the least I can do. I'm not decrepit yet.'

Mack and Jessie laughed in unison.

'Sooner we find out what's ailing you, the better.'

'I'll ring first thing in the morning and after I phone a few clients, I'll take the rest of the day off. Turning in now, sorry—might just read for a while. Goodnight, Grandad.'

'Night, darling. You get a good sleep. It's amazing what that can do for a person.'

'I'll be coming in an hour. I've got some bookwork to do after that stock sale,' Mack said as she bent over to kiss him.

Jessie took herself off to the bedroom while the two men stayed in the lounge for a chat.

'It's a bit of a worry, Grandad. Hope she's got nothing serious. It's unusual for her to be poorly, as she's pretty tough. Working on the station keeps her fit when she's not running her vet clinic. She does plenty of walking up those hills with the dogs just to get exercise when she's not riding Chantilly.'

'Don't you call her Chantilly Cream anymore?'

'Jessie only calls her that when she's showing her. Around here she's just Chantilly.'

'Look, mate. I've been thinking maybe that Jessie could be … you know … in the family way. It's possible, isn't it?'

'We hadn't planned it right now, but I suppose it's possible.'

'It's just that I can remember when your grandmother was pregnant with your father—we didn't know, being young and naïve—much younger than you and Jessie, anyway. She was expecting for months before we had any idea. It was a right fiasco when we found out. The doctor was miles away, and we were living with your grandmother's parents in a small house.'

'Really? How would you feel if she was expecting a child, Grandad? Could you cope with the patter of little feet in this house? And what about Bessie—she might not cope?'

'I would be over the moon. It has been a lifetime since little ones have crossed my path—and Bessie is besotted with her own grandchildren. They live so far away so she doesn't get to see them much.'

'Perhaps we are jumping to conclusions and making undue assumptions. We'll know more tomorrow.'

Walter went off to his room while Mack sat staring into the fire that was fading. The glowing embers were hot enough to keep the winter chill at bay. He relished the heat and let it saturate him as it penetrated his muscles, relaxing him. Buster returned to the room after leaving it earlier when the heat from the fire became too hot. The overweight ball of ginger fluff rubbed himself against Mack's legs, then dumped his body onto his companion's socked feet like a sack of potatoes.

Mack drew comfort from this four-legged friend's uninvited presence. He became mesmerised by the occasional frenzied flames that shot up from the embers, desperate to save themselves as though they knew that death came, then cold.

Could his grandfather be on the right track? It would be beyond his wildest dreams.

Before he turned in for the evening, he went into the office to phone Meg. There were two phones in the house. One in the lounge and a private extension in the office. He didn't want Walter to pick up the drift of the conversation and worry him. After speaking to Meg for at least thirty minutes, he came off the phone perplexed. This was another thing he had to deal with as well as a sick wife. Meg confessed Joe threatened to leave her and return to Wellington if the trouble in the valley continued following her selfish plans to destroy prime agricultural land. But Meg was determined to build her exclusive country resort at the expense of wrecking the farmscape. Joe needed to understand that this was her one opportunity to fulfil her dreams.

Mack hung up the phone, exasperated. He couldn't believe how self-centred his sister had become ... at least, more than usual.

She was even prepared to lose her marriage for her irrational pursuit of a pipe dream.

He prayed that God be his guide and direct his thoughts, asking for healing for his wife and wisdom for Meg to make the right decision to save their marriage. *God, please make a way where there seems to be no way through for Meg and Joe.*

He decided not to tell Walter about the conversation he had with Meg, but he would tell Jessie when she felt better. His mind was troubled, but the prayer calmed him.

Chapter Seven

Jessie sat next to Mack in a waiting room the size of a shoebox. The clinic was still in the old building, but the construction of the new clinic was underway at the south end of town.

'It's stuffy in here,' muttered Jessie, her geisha-like face resting on her hand as she dug her elbow into her thigh.

'He shouldn't take long, the nurse told us. Sounds like a baby has just had a jab by the sound of that screaming.' She walked over to read the name on the doctor's door, stretched her back a few times and plonked herself back on the seat.

'The name on the door is Doctor Joshua Douglas. Joshua is a Biblical name, isn't it? Douglas is Scottish.'

'Yep. Grandad said his folks knew Grandma's family in the Mackenzie country. Apparently, he's a widower—his wife died of leukaemia.' Mack flicked his wrist to look at his watch.

'Oh, no. That's so sad, poor man.' Jessie glanced along the corridor as the woman with the baby ducked into the bathroom opposite.

'Jessie Reed. You can come through now.' A nurse in a starched white smock called along the passageway pointing to a door. 'Just go into this room—the doctor is waiting for you.'

Mack sat in the waiting room while Jessie went in and closed the door with the nurse in tow. He glanced at his watch again, scuffing his shoes backwards and forwards. He jumped out of his seat, glaring at the door of the doctor's room then sat back down again. The magazine lying on the table with a showy Ute on the cover looked inviting. He picked it up, flipped through the pages a few times then slapped the magazine back on the table and started wringing his hands. When he saw Jessie enter the bathroom a few minutes later, he noticed she came out with a small plastic pot, which she handed to the nurse before knocking and entering the doctor's room again.

Mack wondered what was going on. *Perhaps it was much more serious than I thought. It's all taking so long.* He saw the nurse return to the doctor's room soon after Jessie had gone in.

Finally, Jessie opened the door and walked down the corridor towards him, red-faced and agitated.

'Come outside—I'll tell you the news.'

Poker-faced, she walked out towards the Ute. Mack felt a rock hit the pit of his stomach. *Something's wrong*. He opened the passenger door for Jessie, then hurried around to the driver's side and got in.

'Congratulations!' Jessie cried out. 'You're going to be a father.'

Tears streamed down her cheeks. Mack wasn't sure whether they were tears of relief or joy, probably both. Moisture appeared on the stubble of his face.

'What? That's awesome news—it's so hard to believe— are you pleased about it?'

'Pleased? I'm ecstatic! Honestly, I thought something much more serious was wrong with me. I'm already two months pregnant, so it's going to be a Christmas baby. In fact, the doctor said there's a chance of me having twins as they are on my side of the family.'

'Awesome—let's get home and tell Grandad. It'll put years on his life.'

Mack kissed her, placing his hand on her abdomen momentarily then started the engine and drove off, his face beaming all the way home.

***

They arrived back at the homestead as Walter headed down the track towards the house in his truck with Bluey on the back. On seeing Mack's Ute in the driveway, the dog flew off the truck and bounded up to Mack's vehicle. It was as though he knew something, as he wasn't usually this excited when his master arrived home.

'Gidday boy—you seem pretty excited. You're going to have a wee mate to play with now.' Mack jumped out of the vehicle and dashed around to assist Jessie.

'Hold on—pregnancy doesn't make me a cripple—I'm only two months along. Really, Mack—you'll have to back off. I'll be working right up to the end unless I have complications.'

'Shhh—here comes Grandad,' Mack whispered. 'We have to make it a surprise. He's been worried about you but suspected you might be pregnant. Let's tell him—and Bessie will be blown away by the news too.'

'Hi, Grandad. Are you coming in? It's pretty icy out there. The wind is coming off the snow on the pinnacles. Let's get inside.' Jessie looped her arm through Walter's as they walked up the steps.

'Bessie will have the fire going. I want to hear all about your visit to the doctor.' Walter's smile had lost its lustre. The strain showed on his lined brow as he followed the young couple inside the house.

Sure enough, the fire was roaring with the brass guard in front. Bessie trotted along the hallway to greet them. 'Just in time for my minestrone soup. That'll warm you.'

'Hi, Bessie. We'll be there in a short while. Mack and I need to discuss something with Grandad in the lounge first,' said Jessie.

Walter sat in his tatty armchair while Mack took a seat on the couch next to Jessie with his arm around her.

'How bad is it?' Walter asked, wide-eyed. 'Tell me the truth,' he said, as Buster jumped on his lap. Walter sat back as the animal turned in circles until he curled up in a ball.

'The truth is ... you're going to be a great-grandad in seven months' time ... our Christmas present to you.'

Walter took off his glasses and pulled out a large handkerchief. Since his last stroke, he had trouble controlling his emotions he once told Mack. This time the floodgates opened and poured down his cheeks onto Buster's face. The cat shook his head, trying to remove the cold droplets that buried themselves inside his furry head.

Walter got up and lifted the cat onto the hearth mat in front of the fire then shuffled over to where Jessie was sitting.

'Congratulations, lass,' he said, kissing her forehead. 'In fact ... both of you, well done!' He patted Mack's shoulder. 'Would you mind if I tell Bessie—she'll be ecstatic?'

'Of course, you can tell her,' Jessie replied.

Walter left the lounge to look for Bessie. In a short time, he returned with her, carrying two bottles of sparkling grape juice.

'Here are the glasses,' Bessie gushed, following close behind Walter. 'I believe congratulations are in order.' She placed the glasses on the coffee table, then threw herself at them both to give them a mother hug and opened the bottles. Mack poured the beverage into the glasses.

Walter's eyes stayed moist, and he didn't stop smiling.

Jessie clasped her midriff. 'I hope this morning sickness goes away soon. I can't take time off work at present with a heap of urgent visits to make. But it's a drag working when I'm like this.'

Mack's lips puckered as he gazed at his wife. 'Why don't you call the Co-op and ask if the on-call vet can fill in until you're feeling better.' He stood behind Jessie, massaging her neck and shoulders.

'That's a good idea. I haven't called on him yet. I'll ring now.'

Jessie stood up, rubbing her lower back, then wandered into the office. She returned to the lounge directly, flashing a broad smile.

'He's available for the rest of the week, as things have been quiet for him. Thank the good Lord for that!' She flopped into an armchair, stretching her legs out on Walter's footrest.

'I'm having my first ultrasound scan in two weeks. The doctor said I'll be able to find out what gender the baby is.'

'Are you sure you'd want to find that out?' Bessie asked.

'Absolutely—I think it would be awesome,' Mack blurted.

'Me too. I can't wait,' said Jessie.

'Let's hope you have a strapping big son to help you run the station in your old age.' Walter winked at Mack.

***

After bringing in some firewood, Walter followed Bessie's suggestion and took himself off for a rest.

Jessie stood up. 'I'm going outside now to feed Chantilly her oats. I'll put her winter blanket on and take her to the barn. There's bad weather coming.' She hesitated. 'What about Zoro—do you want me to put his cover on too?'

Mack got up and looked out the window, peering at the dark clouds above. 'He's already wearing his blanket. I put it on him this morning before we went out. I'll bring him down to the barn, but I'll help you, first, seeing you're not feeling that great.'

'I'm not unwell! Most women get morning sickness for a few weeks during the first trimester. It's easing, the further along I am, so please don't fuss over me. Doctor Douglas said I can keep riding for the first three months. The tiny baby is protected by my pelvis, he said, but to be more careful in the last six months. There's no protection if I fall and the jarring when trotting could cause problems.'

'Don't tell me that. Now I definitely will fuss over you now!'

They strolled over to the large shed to get Zoro's bridle and a halter for Chantilly from the rack. Jessie placed the tack into the quad bike's crate and climbed onto the seat behind Mack. When they arrived at the horses' paddock, Jessie climbed off and approached the gate, calling out to Chantilly. Although the horse was a fair distance away, she pricked up her ears and whinnied, followed by Zoro who echoed her. Both of them cantered over to her.

'If you give me a hand to tack up, I'll ride Zoro and lead Chantilly back to the barn. You take the bike back first so they don't startle and I'll see you back there,' said Mack, letting Jessie through the gate first.

'I can ride back with Chantilly and lead Zoro—I don't mind,' said Jessie as she slipped the halter on her horse.

'Let me take them. Chantilly may not be used to leading another horse behind. It's not worth the risk.'

Mack was aware he was more protective of Jessie than she appreciated, but he wanted to avoid accidents at any cost. He could still remember the time Hope Rigby had a riding accident, sustaining a head injury. She'd been hospitalised over a month and had suffered a bad concussion for a long time afterwards. *I will not risk my wife and child having a riding accident like that.*

After they'd settled the horses in the barn and given them a feed of oats and lucerne hay, they shut the large sliding door and strolled back to the house. Mack stole a quick cuddle with his wife while walking back to the homestead with his arm around her waist.

'I'd best make the most of this—I won't be able to get my arm around you soon.' He laughed, pulling her closer.

Jessie elbowed him playfully. 'Hey—when are the builders coming to renovate the barn? We could do with those stables already and I thought they would be here before the winter.'

'It's too late now. They rang last week, sorry. With all the concern about you being sick, I forgot to tell you. They've been delayed—some kind of hold-up over materials being shipped to Queenstown. Now they won't be able to start until winter is over as it'll be too muddy. I know it's a jolly nuisance, but we'll just have to keep them both in the barn. They'll be okay together.'

'What about the stockmen's horses? Will they house them in the new stable-barn too?'

'I think it makes sense for all the horses to be kept together. That way, we can all monitor them ... I mean, during the cold months.'

'That's a good idea. We'll have to work out how many stalls we'll need for that purpose. I think eight—four on either side will be good. Let's go inside—it's freezing out here.'

Mack picked up a couple of logs for the fire from the stack at the side of the house and carried them in. Jessie went straight to the bathroom to freshen up.

'No sign of Grandad, Bessie,' said Mack, as he met her in the kitchen. 'I need to talk to him.'

'He has just got up and went out the back to feed the chickens. I guess he'll be in soon. Looks like the weather's about to pack up.' Bessie bent down with a brush and pan to sweep up the mess on the fire hearth.

'Oh well, I suppose it is late autumn. We can't complain as we've had a great summer.'

'Doubt your winters will ever be the same again. I hope you'll have a bonny child to brighten them up—can't wait to find out if it's a boy or girl when you have your scan.'

'Well, whatever God has planned for us will be the right one—boy or girl. No expectations.'

Jessie walked back into the lounge, catching the drift of their conversation. She pursed her lips and set her jaw in an act of defiance against generational patriarchal tradition.

'Precisely—that's what happened to Hope when she had Bertie. Her husband, Cole, was dying to know if he had a boy to help him on the ranch, I guess. But any girl could fill those boots. I don't know what all the fuss is about having a boy if there is a farm involved. Hey, here's Grandad.'

Mack turned to his grandfather. 'Hi there, Grandad. We've got a few things to talk to you about regarding the new stable-barn. Let's go in and sit by the fire.'

Chapter Eight

Winter

Jessie's Land Rover rumbled down the long driveway that led to Dart River Ranch where her friend, Hope and husband, Cole lived in the cottage next to her parents' ranch house on the road to Paradise. The vehicle barely avoided an oversized puddle. It was the remains of an all-night downpour the night before. Jessie thought it uncommon for this time of the year when there was usually more snow than rain.

Hope and her son, Bertie waved from the veranda. Jessie had been like an aunt to the boy since the day she delivered him during Hope's emergency childbirth.

As she walked up the steps, she opened her canvas bag and pulled out the wooden pickup Walter had made for Bertie in his workshop—the one he'd been working on each afternoon. After she'd handed it to the child, Hope invited her inside.

'Oh, wow, Aunty Jessie,' the child blurted with a lisp, struggling to get his mouth around the letter J in her name.

'It's red, like daddy's pickup.'

Jessie glanced toward the shed where Cole's red Chevrolet was parked. 'That pickup is still as shiny as when I first came to stay with you on the ranch. I asked Grandad to replicate it as much as he could.'

'He's done a pretty good job. Does he have a lathe?'

'Yes—he spends hours in that huge workshop of his. I'm glad Bertie likes it.'

'What do you say to Aunty Jessie, Bertie?'

'Thank you—I love it.'

He took off inside and started playing with his new toy in the hallway while the women seated themselves in the lounge.

'Sorry—Cole can't join us today. He's busy with the farrier with a couple of horses that need new shoes.'

'That's okay. How is the breeding program going?'

'Really well. We've got some new stallions Dad and Cole trucked down from up North. One is an Appaloosa and the other a Quarter Horse.'

'Oh, really. I'd love to see them. Are they in the stables?'

'Not normally during the day, but because it's been pouring with rain, Cole brought them down and put them in the stables last night. We could look after a cuppa—if you want.'

They sat drinking tea and eating fresh scones that Hope had baked. Bertie couldn't leave his new truck alone and carried it around the house. 'I'm gonna show my daddy when he comes. He'll like it 'cos he has a pickup like this one.'

Jessie smiled and placed her hand on her frontal bulge.

'Has he started kindergarten yet?'

'Kind of. There isn't a proper one in Glenorchy, but the school has a room at the back that has been set up for preschoolers and they've employed a teacher. There are volunteer parents to help them, and it only runs half a day. Bertie has just started, but it's a bit of a hassle driving him there each day. He only goes three days a week. That's enough for him and one of the mothers drops him home afterwards. Anyway—what's the news you have for me? I'll bet Chantilly is in foal.'

Jessie sat on the edge of her chair. 'Better still—I'm almost three months pregnant.'

Hope got out of her chair and threw herself at Jessie, almost knocking her off the edge of her seat. She wrapped her arms around her. 'At last! I've been waiting for you to have a baby, so Bertie will have a playmate.'

'My first scan is tomorrow.'

'Hope you're going to ask what gender the baby is.'

'Sure am. Can't wait—but either way, I'll be happy so long as the child is healthy.'

'Bertie will be four by then, so he will just have to be like the bossy older brother or sister around your new one. He's already commandeering his pet goat and dad's dog.' They both chuckled.

After spending the rest of the afternoon looking at the new stallions, it was time for Jessie to drive home.

'I've still got that pregnancy sickness which I thought would only happen the first thing in the morning, but it comes in the late afternoon too. Perhaps I should go home and lie down. Pity, as I was hoping we could both go riding, before I get too big.' Disappointment was etched all over Jessie's face.

'It's unfortunate you don't live close enough to ride Chantilly to our ranch, or for me to ride to Reed Station.'

'I don't think it's safe for me to ride such long distances on my own. Perhaps it's something we may have to put off for a while. Pity there are no short cuts across other farms.'

'You could ride one of our horses and we could go out to Diamond Lake, just like the old days.'

'I'm so used to riding Chantilly now—I'm not that keen on riding other horses—not even Zoro.'

The two friends said their goodbyes and arranged to meet in town at the tiny café next to the General Store for coffee and cake sometime, before the new baby arrives.

Jessie arrived back at Reed Station happier after seeing her close friend. Mack was waiting for her back at the homestead.

Bluey almost knocked her over as she struggled up the steps with her medical bag in one hand and a blueberry pie in the other that Hope had given her.

'Hi sweetheart,' Mack said, throwing himself at her as she walked through the doorway. He was overly concerned and found it hard to conceal it. 'Here—let me take those for you.'

'Thanks, darling—I'm just fine. I'm going to have a long hot soak in the bath before dinner. Mmm, smells like Bessie has a roast chicken in the oven.'

'You're right—I'll take the pie to her. If you're up to it later, I want to chat about something that has cropped up. But if you're too tired, we can leave it until tomorrow.'

'No, I'll be okay. If you need to chat about something, we can do it after dinner. Remember—we have an early start in the morning for my scan at Queenstown Hospital.'

Jessie took a bath while Mack sat in the lounge with his grandfather. Walter stretched out in front of the hearth with the fire roaring, wiggling his toes and revelling in the heat. He shamelessly bared his two big toes on both feet that protruded through the holes in his threadbare, grey woollen socks. Buster shifted from the hearth mat and crawled under Walter's legs, but before lying down again, spent several minutes licking the old man's bare toes to the bone.

'Cut it out, Buster! That tickles.'

Mack sat back in his armchair, amused by the entertainment.

'Have you heard anything from Meg lately? I was thinking of popping over there some time. Is Wyatt doing okay with renting that grazing?'

Walter had put Mack on the spot. He knew he couldn't lie, so he had to think of an answer that would not place him in a predicament.

'Meg is pretty much all over the place at present, Grandad. She doesn't know what to do with her acreage and wants to develop the land so it can produce more income for her.'

'What do you mean by develop? Doesn't the grazing fetch enough? I thought she would do alright with that and the money from the Bed and Breakfast lodge.'

'Look—she keeps having grandiose ideas, then changes her mind. I really don't know what she's doing—it's best to talk to her.'

By the time Jessie had got out of the bath, Bessie had dinner ready on the table. Mack brought in the heavy dish with the chicken and placed it next to a platter of roast vegetables.

'Come—let's eat,' Mack called out to his grandfather as Jessie entered the dining room. Bessie joined them when they started their meal.

When Mack and Jessie had finished eating, they took their cups of tea to their bedroom. Mack couldn't contain himself any longer—he had a burden to offload. He dropped like a sack of potatoes into the armchair next to the bed. Jessie sat on the bed dangling her feet listening intently.

'While you were with Hope today, Meg rang and sounded distraught. She said they've been granted Resource Consent to go ahead with the property development for around eighteen, five-acre blocks. There is a restriction about building on the steeper hills so that can still be sold off as grazing.'

Jessie reached for her hairbrush. She pulled the tie from her ponytail and began brushing her hair. 'And she's still going ahead, even though most of the town will be against her. So why is she distraught?'

'Joe can't cope with it and warned her if she continues to pursue this path, he'll walk out. Well, today, that's just what he has done after Meg received approval for the housing estate and phoned the developer to meet and talk business.'

'What? Do you mean he has left her?'

'Yep. He took their flash Rover and left Meg the old Hillman she bought at an auction recently. He's driving back to Wellington.'

Mack sat forward, resting on his forearms, his cheeks drawn inwards. He was far from his usual bubbly self.

'Oh, no, poor Joe. I feel sorry for him. This was a marital disaster waiting to happen. Where will he stay? Their house is still on the market.'

'Thank God it hasn't sold. Meg had far too high a price on it. At least Joe can live in it until this mess is sorted. He told me, the day after we visited, that he'd been made an offer to join the new owner of my father's business as a consultant. He'll probably do that now.'

'We'll have to ask our church to put them on the prayer chain, Mack. This is serious and it will break Grandad's heart.'

'I know. I just can't bring myself to tell him. Oh, Jessie— why has it come to this? Your poor parents—what are they going to do?'

Jessie slid off the bed, walked over and caressed Mack's shoulders.

'I know—it'll be so stressful for them to have to uproot themselves again. I don't think Mum will want to move away now that I'm having a baby.'

'Let me talk to Grandad. Maybe they can move into a cottage on Reed Station. That way, you'll have the support of your mother to help with our new child.'

'That's a wonderful idea, Mack. Shall I ask them if they'd like to do that? I could phone after I have the scan. Mum wants to know the outcome, too.'

'Your poor folks. They were just trying to help Meg and Joe out.'

'Let's pray for them all and then I need sleep—I'm done in.' Jessie took Mack's hand as she sat next to him on the bed while he prayed.

Mack thought he was at fault for not intervening when Meg had offered Wyatt the position of Farm Manager on her land. What a mess this turned out to be. He prayed for protection, wisdom and guidance for each one of them.

Although Meg's situation had the potential of robbing them of joy, they both fell asleep peacefully and woke refreshed to a new day full of promise.

Chapter Nine

Mack drove Jessie's Land Rover to the hospital, as it was far more comfortable for long trips than his Ute. He relished the trip to Queenstown along the Glenorchy-Queenstown Road, soaking up the immensity of the Remarkables—the mountain range that stretches from Mount Aspiring National Park to Queenstown.

There was not a breath of wind. The glass-like surface on the lake projected a myriad of pastel hues cast by the mountains across the water.

'Isn't this idyllic?' he said to Jessie. 'We're so blessed to live in such an amazing spot.'

'I agree but keep your eyes on the road. There's black ice and people speed around these tight corners.'

'You're right, and I have precious cargo aboard.' He narrowed his eyes as he gazed straight ahead.

When they arrived at the hospital, they didn't have to wait long. Jessie had done all the required preparation and was ushered in for her scan on arrival. Mack could accompany her into the x-ray room. The technician rubbed gel over Jessie's abdomen, moving a transducer up and down her skin while she watched a screen. Jessie and Mack could see it, too.

'Is everything okay?' Jessie asked, screwing up her face, as she craned her neck sideways to see the screen.

'I'm just locating the baby now. Hear that?'

In an instant, there was a strong heartbeat.

'Hmm ... just a minute,' the woman muttered.

'What's wrong?' Mack asked, sucking air into his lungs at the same time. He grabbed hold of Jessie's hand.

'I think there is another one.' The woman leaned forward, straining to get a better view.

'What do you mean?' Jessie's voice quavered.

'There's another baby in there. You're going to have twins.'

Mack's mouth dropped wide open, baring a mouthful of white teeth.

'What! That's fantastic, isn't it darling,' Jessie spouted, staring at Mack who sat there in the same position, with eyes like a goldfish.

The technician rolled the wand across Jessie once more and stopped. 'Would you like to know the sex of your babies?'

'Absolutely!' They cried in unison.

The woman pressed a few buttons on the screen as they watched intensely. 'You have two decent sized boys in there—see?'

She showed with her hand the various anatomy of each baby.

'All finished now.' She wiped the gel from Jessie's skin and took her arm as she climbed off the table.

'Could you sit here while I check the scans? I'll only be a few minutes.'

The woman assisted her into a chair and walked off down a corridor.

'Wait until we tell Grandad ... and Bessie. Mum and Dad will be thrilled and so will your parents.' Mack wiped his eyes roughly with his sleeve and sat staring at Jessie's bump in her abdomen. 'Just imagine two babies growing in there.'

'I can't wait to tell my parents. That'll give them a boost with all this negative stuff going on with Meg and Joe. They definitely will have to come and live on Reed Station now.'

The technician returned. 'You can get dressed now. Just throw the gown in the basket in the changing room. You can go after that and your doctor will get the report in a few days.'

They walked to their vehicle with Mack holding Jessie's hand, leading her down a cracked, concrete path to the carpark.

'It's icy today. I can't take the risk of letting you slip.'

'I'm not an invalid, Mack, but I get your point. The footpath must have iced over last night. Let's hurry and get in the car—it's freezing out here.'

Mack pulled out of the carpark then hesitated.

'I thought we could stop for a coffee at that great café on the other side of town near Closeburn.' He leaned forward to turn up the heating in the car.

'I've got another idea. Why don't you go to talk some sense into Meg and tell her what we've come up with as a solution to her problem, and I'll visit Mum and Dad to see if they'd like to move to Reed Station.'

'That's a great idea. Your news about the twins should cheer them up after all their disappointment with Meg and especially the idea of living nearby to help with their grandchildren,' said Mack.

'Maybe this is divine intervention so we can all work in together as an extended family,' said Jessie, relaxing back into the seat.

***

Jessie ambled along the path to her parents' chalet, while Mack disappeared inside Meg's house. She'd seen him arrive and held the door open for him.

'Coming to rescue your wayward sister, are you?' She gave him a wry smile. 'It's all a bit of a mess, isn't it?'

Mack guessed she'd been crying, by the dark rings around her eyes and puffy eyelids. *Rare for Meg to break down. She is usually pretty stoic.* 'Well, I can't just leave you in the lurch. Jessie and I have come up with a few suggestions that might ease your burden.'

Meg hadn't offered Mack a seat, so he barged in and slumped into one of her sleek, leather armchairs. She followed suit and sat in the chair opposite.

She pointed at the cabinet where Joe kept bottles of wine and whisky—remnants of their high society lifestyle in Wellington.

'Pity you don't drink as I'd ask you to have a glass of wine with me.'

'No, thanks. I'd love a coffee, though.'

'I've got some percolating—I'll bring it in.'

While she was in the kitchen, Mack glanced at a pile of papers sitting on the coffee table—sale and purchase papers all drawn up ready to sign. He bent over the documents to look for her signature, but the dotted line was bare.

Meg returned with a tray of coffee mugs and chocolate cake.

'Here—have some cake. I don't know if you'll like it. I bought it from the General Store yesterday and it's nothing like your Bessie's baking—or Jessie's for that matter.'

'Sorry, but I couldn't help seeing the sale and purchase papers for your property,' Mack muttered, as Meg reached down and grabbed them.

'Oh, yes. I wanted to tell you about it—the council will only allow the land to be subdivided into five-acre allotments and this property with the house can be divided into ten acres. That's what I want to do.'

Mack sat bewildered about her behaviour. *Her husband has just left her and she's babbling on about property development.*

'Meg! I'm here to find out what's happening with you and Joe, not your land. What's going on?'

'Joe had an offer a while ago to work as a consultant for the new owner of dad's old company. He couldn't accept it because of our move here. He is upset by all the opposition from the community over my interest in property development. I mean ... he didn't have to stalk off like that. I couldn't bear to turn my back on all this.'

She stared at the ground, then pulled out a handkerchief to wipe her nose. Mack glared at her as she folded her arms on her lap with a belligerent expression on her face.

He remembered how she had always respected him when they were young and how close they'd been.

'But you haven't considered Joe in any of your plans—or Jessie's folks either. This has been all about you, and to be honest, I think you've become incredibly self-centred. I'm disappointed in you.'

Meg pulled her head up and burst out crying. Mack was about to continue when loud sobs interrupted him as she pushed her face into her hands. She blew her nose, making a sound like a foghorn. Mack waited until she'd calmed down, then walked over and put an arm around her.

'Look sis—I don't know why or how you've got yourself into this predicament, but Jessie and I want to help you sort it out and restore your marriage. You do love Joe, don't you?'

'Yes, of course, I do. I just can't understand why he won't accept my point of view.'

'Perhaps he's asking himself the same question. Have you ever put yourself in his shoes? He gave up a successful career and stately home in Wellington—not to mention all his friends—to come to a remote and rugged area to live off the land, which is totally alien to him. I feel sorry for the guy.'

Meg tried to pull herself together.

'You gave me a hundred acres, and I wanted to put it to good use. You know I always dreamed of owning a resort, just as you always had your heart set on managing a high country station.'

'Yes, Meg, but not at the cost of hurting others. You've got it all wrong. Listen to me.'

Throughout this, Mack dearly wanted to tell Meg she was going to be an aunt twice over, but he had to pick his moment. It would have to wait—or not. He had an idea.

'Meg—Jessie is pregnant. We've just come back from the hospital where she had her first scan. She's two months along already and going to have twins,' he blurted, then waited for her reaction.

Meg stopped her snivelling and sat bolt upright, pushing her hair out of her face. Her eyes had doubled in size as she suddenly perked up.

'What? Congratulations! Why didn't you let me know she was pregnant? I wouldn't have worried you with all of this.'

'We didn't want to break the news when Joe had just walked out. That would have added to your pain.'

'I feel so foolish now—I'm sorry. As you can see, I haven't signed the papers for the sale. I don't know what to do. What ideas did you say you had?'

'Now that we are going to need support with two babies, Jessie is going to ask her folks if they'd like to move to Reed Station. That way, her mother can help with the twins if she chooses. Her father may be interested in assisting me to run the station. Grandad is pulling back a great deal these days.'

'Oh, that's a pity—they don't have to move out. They might change their mind now that there won't be a housing development taking place. Where will they live—in the house with all of you?'

'We have the small cottage that Aron, my predecessor had tenanted with his wife—it's still vacant. Grandad was going to rent it out to our new Head Shepherd, but he has moved into a house down the road.'

Meg looked down at the ground. Her face took on another strained appearance.

'I'll talk to them tomorrow and see what they'd like to do. I need to make amends to them somehow.'

'I've got an idea. Someone at the High Country Farmer's meeting mentioned that Dan Hislop, your neighbour, needs more land. I thought Wyatt could ask if he wants to rent grazing from you or he could make an offer to buy the remaining ninety acres. If you hold on to ten acres for your own animals, you could keep horses.'

'Oh, good heavens. It does seem a better idea than having twenty houses going up around me. That would make everything straight forward and I'll have the money to put into the resort too.'

'Land of this quality is valuable around here and fetching high prices. Let me talk to Dan to see if he's willing to make an offer.'

Meg got out of her chair and lunged at her brother, enveloping him with her arms.

'Thank you so much, Mack. I thought I could work it out on my own, but it has got out of hand.'

'Well, that's what families are for. Jessie and I may have some other ideas to help you but first things first. Let's get this land sold, and I want you to promise to keep the communication open to Joe. We want to see this marriage restored.'

Meg stared at her wedding ring and pulled at it. 'I'll do my best.'

'I'm going next door to take Jessie home. Do you mind if I share with her parents the conversation we've just had?'

'No, not at all. I'll see them in the morning. Please tell Jessie I'm sorry about all the grief I've caused. I'll be in touch with her.'

Chapter Ten

Walter had already finished eating and kept the rest of the evening meal in the oven for Jessie and Mack. Mack walked into the lounge with his meal on a tray and perched next to Jessie who sat back eating with her feet elevated on a stool.

'Hi, Grandad. Thanks for keeping our food warm.'

'I can't go off to bed not knowing the outcome of your scan. I'm waiting for your report—is everything alright?' He craned forward to listen, almost crushing the cat on his lap.

'Don't you have any ideas about leaving this world just yet. We're going to need your help around here with this extended family on its way.' Mack winked at Jessie who beckoned him to continue.

'Don't keep me hanging. Well, what is it—a boy or a girl?'

'Peter and Paul, Grandad,' said Jessie, beaming.

'What ... what do you mean—are you having twins?'

'Yep, that's right. I'm just joking about the names, but I have two boys in here.' Jessie patted her belly.

'I'll need you to train them to be good shepherds, Grandad.' Mack threw him an infectious smile.

The old man rubbed his eyes. 'This is more than an old man could ask for at my age. You two are so blessed.'

'They will be a blessing to you also, Grandad,' said Jessie.

'Just wait till Bessie hears this news. She arrived home earlier and went straight to bed—all the driving tired her out when she visited her family today.'

Mack and Jessie spent the rest of the evening discussing with Walter their plans to bring Jessie's parents onto the station.

Walter yawned loudly, rubbing his eyes. 'I think that will work out well. The cottage is all kitted out, so they should be at home there. Aron had even landscaped the small area out front, so it should be easy for them to maintain.'

Jessie smiled. 'Thanks, Grandad. I can't wait to show them their new home.'

Walter gave Jessie a loving glance. 'We are family, after all and need to look after each other.'

She got out of her chair, walked over to Walter and wrapped her arms around him. He caught his reading glasses just in time.

'No need for all that sentiment, girl. Any decent person would help in this situation.'

Mack joined in, 'Thanks, Grandad—stop trying to be so modest—you're a proper champ.'

'You just don't realise I have ulterior motives. My friends in the Bay of Plenty said that Wyatt has great shepherding skills and sound farming experience. He has been a long-standing member of the Federated Farmers meetings there and is well known. I think he's going to fill the gap for me when I can't oversee the running of Reed Station any longer—even if it's only in an advisory capacity.'

Jessie patted Walter on the shoulder and sat back in her chair. 'Mum seems to have got on well with Bessie— perhaps she can be of help to her as well.'

Walter nodded at Mack. 'I think we're all going to be a great team, despite Meg's foolishness and short-sightedness. She has been on a collision course for disaster, and you just curbed it. It's best for Jessie's parents to stay well clear for now.'

Jessie got up to rush off to the office. 'I'll call and ask if they'd like to check out the cottage tomorrow. I can't wait to have them come and live with us.'

***

Jessie sat in her vehicle the next morning looking at her work schedule. She had two visits to make near Dart River Ranch where Hope lived. It had seemed ages since she'd visited her friend whom she had phoned the night before to warn of her arrival. Life had just been too hectic, but she had so much news to share.

Mack and Walter had already left the house to meet up with the stockmen to bring the young heifers down for Tuberculosis testing. The agricultural technicians would soon arrive from Queenstown, and Jessie didn't need to be there.

Her farm visits were over by midday, and she was eager to visit Hope who had lunch ready for her when she arrived.

She sat at the dining table with Bertie sitting next to her. He attended kindergarten daily, but today Hope kept him home for Jessie's visit.

His mother handed him a slice of brown bread coated with a thick layer of peanut butter.

'Come on, Bertie. Show Aunty Jessie how well you can eat all your lunch.'

'I want milk,' he uttered, pouting

Hope frowned at him. 'Please! Ask nicely, Bertie.'

He looked at Jessie with a wry smile, licking peanut butter from his fingers.

'Milk please, Mummy.' He shot another glance at Jessie. 'Bertie's going to have a sister ... aren't I, Mummy?'

'Shush—eat your food!' Hope's face turned the colour of her pink blouse. 'He's excited as he overheard me telling my

463

mother that he's getting a sister, but he wasn't supposed to tell anyone yet. Yes—I'm expecting number two.'

Jessie's eyes lowered to Hope's abdomen while she patted her own. 'That's awesome news!'

'How did your scan go? Do you know what you're having yet—boy or girl?' Hope stared at Jessie, waiting for a reaction.

'That's what I came here to tell you—I'm going to have twins.' Hope's mouth dropped open. 'What—really? How far are you?'

'Almost five months. I thought my baby would be a playmate for Bertie, but he will have one of his own. My twins are both boys, so Bertie will have mates.' Jessie started pushing on her bulge. 'Here, feel this—one of them is kicking.'

The girls sat entertaining themselves, trying to identify the different body parts of her unborn twins.

Bertie came off his seat and leaned over Jessie, staring at her abdomen. 'Aunty Jessie—can Bertie feel your tummy too? Please—let me touch the babies.'

'Of course, Bertie—let me show you.' She took his hand and guided it to the spot where the strongest kicks could be felt.

'Well, now—how far along are you, Hope? You've been keeping your news quiet.'

'Sorry, Jessie. Like you, we've been so busy and have had little social life. We wanted to wait until I had the first scan before announcing it. I'm expecting a baby girl in November.'

'That is so amazing—my twins are due in December! We could have them at the same time. I hope you don't have my midwife, especially if we are in labour at the same time.'

They both chuckled.

'Let's go out onto the veranda.' Hope carried toys out for Bertie with Jessie in tow. The boy sat down happily while the women continued to talk.

'I was thinking our local mobile vet could deliver my baby. What do you think—it was you who brought Bertie safely into the world without a problem?'

Jessie could see by the look on Hope's face that she was serious. 'You're joking of course. That was an emergency, and I don't think I'd like to be in that position again. You just stick to your midwife.'

Hope's smile turned upside down. 'If you insist ... who is your midwife?'

'I'm under that new Dr Joshua Douglas. He is a General Practitioner who does obstetrics.'

'Oh, I see. Mmm. I heard that he's pretty dishy—a bit of *eye candy*,' Hope teased, becoming animated again.

Jessie was quick to defend herself. 'He knew Walter's family back in Lake Tekapo apparently and I heard he's a good doctor, so thought I'd check him out.'

Hope continued, 'My other news is our stud is flourishing and I'm now involved with Cole in the breeding program full time instead of running riding courses—I've no time for that. It's a pity, as there's no other riding school or holiday program around here.'

Bertie entertained them with dance moves to a musical duck while Jessie told Hope all about the drama that Meg had created. When she had finished her synopsis of the situation, she burst forth.

'You've just given me an idea to help Meg! She's an experienced rider from Wellington—I've seen her trophies. For a while, she was a riding instructor, so maybe she could start a riding school at Willow Park. What do you think?'

'The only time I've met her was at your wedding, and it's hard to imagine her as an equestrian. Perhaps Dad and I could help her get started—you know Dad is a horse whisperer.'

'Yes, I know and so are you—he taught you well. It would be great if Meg goes along with this, but you won't be able to do much with another baby on the way. Mack can train horses, and he was taught by your father, too.'

'Remember, I have Mum living next door to help me. I didn't give up anything after I had Bertie—I've had to reduce my hours, that's all. I only recently stopped running the riding courses and holiday program to help Cole with our business.'

Jessie sat ruminating about Meg, twirling a lock of her hair around her index finger.

'I suppose Meg could run a holiday camp. She has a huge lodge that is often empty at low season. There are eight double bedrooms that could fit bunks. She could turn that massive barn of hers into bunkrooms for the kids and keep one for stables.'

Hope reached for Bertie's hand as he was about to take off down the steps. She planted him back down on the veranda.

'What a superb idea. I remember when I took my horse to various camps in the Bay of Plenty, there was one that was unique. An oversized barn had been converted into bunkrooms surrounding an inside arena. It was so special going to sleep with the nostalgic smell of hay and horses emanating through the wooden bedroom doors.'

Hope stood up again. 'I don't mind meeting up with Meg to help her get started. Let's move down onto the steps so I can watch Bertie if he wants to play on the lawn.'

Jessie couldn't wait to get back to Reed Station to discuss her ideas with Mack. Or should she call by Willow Park and discuss it with Meg now? She had already answered her own question. It was time to smooth things over.

'Sorry, Hope, but I'll have to get off now as I've got a heap of things to do. Thanks for lunch—it's my turn next time.'

She hugged Bertie and Hope and hurtled along the long driveway in her vehicle onto the main road. Her heart raced at the thought of seeing Meg turn her life around. *Was this an answer to prayer?*

Chapter Eleven

Jessie loved the scenic drive along Glenorchy-Paradise Road, passing the majestic Richardson Mountains on one side and the Humboldt Mountains on the other. The late afternoon sun disappeared quickly behind the mountains. *Before long, it will be dark. Perhaps I should have come another day.*

When she pulled into the space near the front door, Meg's face appeared at the kitchen window, then pulled back. Jessie couldn't help noticing ivy-like weeds smothering the footpath to the house. The outside of the home appeared tired and neglected. *Is this the beginning of the decline, as it looks like she hasn't been managing here on her own since Joe left?*

The windows needed a good clean and Jessie thought how unappealing the entrance to the *so-called* boutique farmstay would be for the tourist who would expect an exclusive country lodge or something more welcoming.

'Jessie! Come on in. I wasn't expecting you, but it's good to see you.' Meg pulled at the loose wisps of hair that dangled down her forehead, trying to sweep them back up again.

She wore no makeup—unlike her Wellington days when she would decorate herself like Cleopatra. Now it was obvious to Jessie her life had become unmanageable.

Jessie's eyes quickly scanned the lounge, spying the cobwebs hanging from the bookshelves and dust that coated the furniture. It was a far cry from her home in Wellington that was so pristine one could eat off the floors. She grimaced—*why did she allow herself to plummet so low?*

'Sorry that it's a bit late in the afternoon … I was just passing.'

'I'm glad of the company … coffee? I've just percolated a fresh lot or you can have tea if you'd rather.'

'What about that fruit tea you gave me last time I visited?'

'I've still got some of that—it was raspberry. Back in a minute.'

Meg brought back a tray with a stoneware mug of coffee for herself and a china cup with tea for Jessie.

'I hope you don't mind, Meg, but I've been thinking of ways to help you rise above the um … difficult situation … you've found yourself in.' Jessie really wanted to say it was a situation she had brought on herself but stopped short.

'That's kind of you. Can I pass you a gingernut biscuit?'

'Yes, thanks. If you don't mind, I like to dunk these in my tea.' Jessie was aware Meg would see that as common, but she couldn't help herself. She continued. 'My friend, Hope, whom you met at my wedding is an accomplished rider like you and, until recently, has been running a small riding school for children who slept in a fully insulated barn on hay bales. A few kids with asthma stayed inside her folks' ranch house.'

Meg screwed up her face. 'Sorry … what are you getting at?'

'Now that Hope is expecting another baby and engrossed with their Stud, she has stopped running the horse camps and riding lessons. The closest one is on the other side of Queenstown near Cromwell. Perhaps Hope and her father, Joel, can help you set one up here. Apart from them both being horse whisperers, they can give you good advice and

Mack or Wyatt might help, too.' Jessie kept her eyes fixed on Meg's face.

'I suppose that could work. It would supplement my income after selling the land, as long as I could get regular clients.'

'It was popular amongst the school and university students, and the tourist industry is already taking off in the area. You can provide horse treks just as she did—and riding lessons. Riders visited their camp from all over the South Island. I'm sure it will do well as Glenorchy is becoming popular.'

Meg sat silently for a few minutes. 'Come and look at the ten acres I'll have at my disposal.'

'I'd love to look around as it appears as though it hasn't changed since Mack lived here. Can I look at the barn over there?'

'Okay, let's go.' Meg went to get her boots, which were on the doorstep where Jessie had left hers. She burst forth, 'Oh, I forgot to tell you—my neighbour, the farmer who lives on the boundary of my property has made an offer to buy the ninety acres from me. Apparently, Mack phoned him and said I was looking for a farmer who would only use the land for agriculture.'

'No, I hadn't heard—but good old Mack. He's such a dear, isn't he?'

Meg gave her a lopsided grin. 'Yes, he's been a good brother, even though he has been a thorn in my side lately. I suppose he has become my rescuer.'

They arrived at the oversized corrugated iron building that resembled an American barn. Meg tried to slide the heavy door open, but it wouldn't budge.

'Here—let me have a go.' She moved aside as Jessie pulled and shoved to no avail. 'Do you have a piece of wood or something that we can use to push the latch? It appears to have seized up.'

'I know—wait. I've got a heavy screwdriver in my toolkit at the back door.'

Meg returned with her tools. After a bit more wrenching and a great heave from both women, the door opened.

Jessie pinched her nose. 'It stinks of horses in here. You don't have any on the property, do you?' Her eyes squinted from the sun's rays that penetrated the skylight above.

'No, not yet. Wyatt and Joe just rode the quad bikes as Wyatt kept all the pasture for grazing cattle. It must be from Zoro when Mack used to shelter him in here on a cold, winter's night.'

'Well, I think this would be ideal for accommodating children during holiday camps. It's really warm in here and it's in good condition.'

'Where will the ponies go during the winter? This is designed for animals, and they'll need shelter during the cold months.'

Jessie appeared to be in deep thought and walked back outside.

Her eyes scanned the estate. 'Where is the boundary of the ten acres you are holding onto?'

'It includes all those paddocks at the rear of the house right up to the treeline by the road and it's all fenced.'

'So that takes in that huge implement shed too. What do you keep in there?'

'It's empty. I've been trying to think of a use for it.'

Jessie's face lit up. 'I've got just the answer! I suggest turning it into an arena with a bunkhouse. You're not still planning on building a swimming pool and tennis court, are you?'

'I was going to do that. Let's go back inside and talk again.'

Once seated in the lounge, they continued their discussion.

'Look, Jessie—I had presumed that Joe would cool down and change his mind. When I last wrote to him, he replied I was going overboard with the exclusive country lodge idea and the housing development. He doesn't trust me and says that if he comes back, I'll probably start some other hair-raising scheme, and he called me self-centred and ostentatious!'

'Do you love him? If so, maybe ask him what he would like to see happen. That'll be a change from you always having to be in control, if you know what I mean.'

Meg walked into the kitchen and left her visitor sitting there. She called out, 'Just putting the kettle on again.'

Jessie sat on the couch trying to make herself comfortable, wondering if she overstepped the mark then stood up. 'Don't go to a lot of trouble. Just a cup of that fruit tea I had earlier will be fine—no biscuits for me, thanks.'

Meg lowered a tray with the tea onto the coffee table and sat down. Jessie picked up her cup and returned to the couch.

'Please Jessie … let's keep chatting … I've been bottling up all this time and need someone to talk to.' She poured tea for herself from a floral porcelain teapot.

'I know I'll have to give up the idea of the exclusive country lodge. It was my pipedream—but if I want Joe to come back, I'll need to consider his needs too.'

'What does he want to do?'

'He'd rather we did something that would be of service to this community … I mean … the land was a gift through the generosity of my family and perhaps we can show charity to others too, he said.'

Jessie leaned over and touched her hand.

'He wanted me to re-evaluate my plans, and that's why I agreed to sell to the neighbour.'

'Maybe you have to show him you are already doing it. By opening Willow Park as a pony camp, you are giving a service to the community.'

'I think you're right—it's a marvellous idea, Jessie. I'm sure Joe will go along with it. The funds I was going to use for the swimming pool and tennis court can be spent on the arena and the barn accommodation. I'll talk to my builder and get it underway.'

Meg's whole countenance changed. The furrows in her brow became shallower and colour returned to her cheeks. She stood up and wrapped her arms around Jessie.

'That's it! I knew deep down there was another solution to my dilemma. You and Mack have saved me from myself. I can't wait to get my new enterprise started. Oh, and congratulations on your pregnancy. You are going to be the best mother ever!'

'Thanks, Meg—but it's not Mack and me—it's God who is guiding you in the right direction and I think he sent me here to talk to you.'

'I'm realising it—but I'm still grateful you put yourself out. You're a kind sister-in-law.'

***

Back at Reed Station, Jessie went into great detail about her visit to Meg and their talk about the pony camp.

Mack placed the last of the dinner plates in the dish rack.

'You're a champion. How did you manage that?'

'I think she was desperate, and I arrived just at the right time.'

'It's a great idea of yours, Jessie. It couldn't have come at the worst time as far as availability for us both, though. We're going to be too busy to help her on her feet.'

'Hope said she'd give a hand once her baby has settled in. Having children doesn't seem to incapacitate her. I suppose

473

having twins is quite different, but I can help in an advisory capacity I told Meg.'

Mack grabbed the tea-towel out of her hand. 'Let's sit down in the lounge. Grandad has turned in already.'

He went in and sat down next to Jessie. She nestled into him.

'I'm going to ask Dad to give her a hand as Hope's father is in demand on their ranch at present. You don't need him around all the time, do you?'

'No, I can spare him at the moment. Now, you need to get your feet up. Bessie left us some of her fruit cake in the fridge—would you like some?'

'No thanks, not at the moment.' She stretched herself out, leaning against Mack. 'I want to make the most of riding Chantilly before the babies come and so I'll take her for a ride tomorrow.'

Mack frowned and looked hard at her growing bump.

'Are you sure it's okay to do that—it won't hurt the babies will it?'

'No, I'll only be walking her and keep close to the tracks. I'll let you know where I'm headed and take a radiophone with me.'

Later in the evening, Jessie stood in front of the bathroom mirror, staring at the bulge that had grown twice the size since she had first discovered she was pregnant. She muttered a brief prayer before going off to bed.

'Surround these babies with a hedge of protection, God, and help them grow up in the knowledge of you.'

Chapter Twelve

Summer

Willow Park Pony Camp became a great hit in Glenorchy. Children arrived from all around the South Island, many of them bringing their own ponies by horse truck. Meg kept the fees low to include children from families on limited incomes. Mack and Jessie saw a great change in her as she became less self-centred and more focused on how she could help others.

Wyatt and Pru settled into their cottage on Reed Station and Wyatt assisted Meg with the horses a few days a week. She found local volunteers and paid staff to help her run the pony camp.

Great changes took place at Willow Park, beginning with the implement barn that was transformed into custom-built rooms with stable doors that opened into simple bunkrooms. These encircled an inside arena, just as Jessie had described to Meg when she'd first suggested pony camp to her.

A few of the regulars to Willow Park were children with special needs. One was a girl with Asperger's called Bonny and the other, a boy with Down's syndrome, called Daniel. They were always accompanied by their carers.

Circumstances meant that Bonny's parents were forced to sell their farmlet, which meant the pony, which had been the love of Bonny's life, was taken away. She hated living in the city and became depressed, but with financial aid from the Asperger's Association, she could attend Meg's camps regularly and responded well.

***

This weekend the camp was full. There were children sleeping in the custom-built barn and those with special needs slept inside the lodge accompanied by their carers. Meg slept inside in the residence and there was Charlie, the caretaker on-site who acted as a security man and lived in the chalet.

On sweltering summer days, the children played in the swimming hole—a natural spring near the main residence which Meg had previously wanted to use for a swimming pool complex.

One evening, when Meg sat in front of her television in her private living room, her solitude was interrupted by pounding at the door.

'Who is it?' she called, reluctant to pull herself away. She was watching a video she'd put on for the evening, sitting back in her armchair with her feet up.

'Sorry, Mrs Wilds,' a timid voice erupted from outside the door. 'Daniel is sickening for something. He's covered in spots and running a temperature. What should I do?'

'Hold on—I'm coming.' She lifted the dinner plate from her lap, gave a loud sigh and hurried into the kitchen. After placing her meal in the warming drawer of her oven, she attended to the carer.

Meg glanced at Daniel who moaned and kept asking for cold drinks. The red spots on his face and torso looked familiar.

'His sister has recently had chickenpox. Do you think that's what it is?' asked the carer.

'I guess it is. I'm not a medical person but I've worked with a lot of children, and I recognise it. You'll have to keep him away from the others and give him plenty of clear fluids.'

She went out to the kitchen and brought back a jug of lemon and barley water. 'Pour Daniel a glass and keep up the fluids. It will help bring his temperature down. I'll phone Doctor Douglas. He's always on call for Pony Camp— it's an agreement we have. I'll be in to see you once I've spoken to him.'

Doctor Douglas took no time at all in arriving at Willow Park, which was ten minutes from his home in Glenorchy village. When Meg opened the door to him, a tomato red flush shot up her neck as a radiant smile beamed across his face.

'Oh, Joshua—how nice to see you. Thank you so much for coming after hours. Come this way.' Meg hesitated in front of her hall mirror, checking her hair on the way down the passageway. She pulled the loose strands behind her ears.

Meg spoke to Daniel's carer. 'The diagnosis that you and I had deduced was correct. I suppose I'll have to call his parents tonight. It's a pity that they've brought him all the way from Arrowtown.'

'Chickenpox is not serious. He could convalesce here, but he'll have to be isolated from the rest of the children, as it's highly contagious,' said Joshua.

'I'd better ask his parents to come and collect him.'

'Yes, it's probably best.' His gaze fixed more on Meg's blue eyes than on the boy.

'He'll be so disappointed. He was looking forward to being here,' said his carer.

Meg followed Joshua into the hallway. 'Have you eaten, Joshua? I have a Beef Lasagne I cooked tonight and there's plenty left over.'

'That sounds enticing, and I don't have any other house calls, so that is a yes from me.'

Meg phoned Daniel's folks and arranged for them to collect him. 'They'll collect him in the morning,' she said as she sat Joshua down in the lounge. She went to the oven to dish up the food.

'I hope you don't mind eating on a tray on your lap, Joshua. That way, we can sit in front of the television.'

'Not at all—we should do this more often,' he said as he switched on the video they agreed to watch. 'You must come and have dinner with me one evening. Honestly, my cooking won't kill you.' They laughed and sat enjoying the video together for the rest of the evening while now and then Meg checked on Daniel.

Her guest's voice was a distant clatter, as she seemed oblivious to his conversation and what she was getting herself into. *He's just a good friend, and it beats eating on my own* she kept telling herself.

***

The twins were not due until the end of the month, and the intense weight pressing down in Jessie's pelvis caused her to waddle like a duck.

During her pregnancy, she had kept a close bond with Chantilly and gave the horse a treat instead of her usual feed. She trudged into the recently built stable-barn and fetched the pellets in a bucket, which she carried to the quad bike and placed in the crate. Standing next to the bike, she supported her bulging abdomen with both hands and heaved herself onto the seat. This time, she rode at a snail's pace tensing at every bump along the track to Chantilly's pasture.

The horse was on the far side of the field when she stepped off the bike with the bucket and just as she was about to call out to Chantilly, she let out an almighty, 'Nooooo. Ow!'

The bucket of feed dropped to the ground and spilt everywhere.

Jessie leaned forward, grabbing hold of the wooden gate panting, then stumbled back to the quad bike to pick up the radiophone, but there was nothing but a crackling sound. The dark storm clouds overhead interfered with the signal.

She groaned once more, holding her belly and slumped onto a hay bale next to the gate.

When she tried the radiophone again, it continued to crackle. 'Darn thing! Why don't they make things that work in an emergency?'

She tried to stand but crumbled back onto the hay bale again. 'Please God—let this not be labour pains. I'm far too early and there's nobody around. I don't think I could make it back home on the quad bike.'

Jessie sat with her face in her hands, wondering what she would do if this was labour, and the thought distressed her. A familiar sound startled her. It was the sound of a horse's hooves pounding the earth.

With all her life-force, she bellowed, 'Help! I'm over here—help me!' Waving her arms in the air.

When she scanned the dirt track, an outline of a black horse appeared. Within seconds, the animal stood before her with its mount.

'Jessie! What on earth are you doing on the ground? It's getting a bit late in the day for this, isn't it?' Mack had come at the precise moment.

'I've been getting strong cramps in my belly—I hope it's not the babies coming, as it's far too early. You'd better call Joshua and get him to come out here pronto, and then you'll have to take me back on the quad bike.'

Without a word, he raced over to the gate and led Zoro through into the field. He removed his saddle and bridle and let him loose. 'I'll be back for you, buddy—I've gotta help Jessie first.'

'The horse whinnied and took off across the field.'

***

Back at the homestead, Jessie lay on the bed with Mack sitting next to her.

'Joshua's on his way and I called your mother to ask her to be on standby—just in case. Fortunately for us, your doctor doesn't live too far away.'

'How was it that your arrival was so timely—did you hear me yelling out?'

'No, it had nothing to do with me. It was the same scenario that happened when Grandad collapsed with a stroke in the field when Zoro instinctively knew something was wrong.'

'What do you mean, Zoro?'

'I couldn't control him in the western sector by the old windmill when he got the bit in his mouth, and no matter how hard I tried, I couldn't stop him galloping down the track to you. Somehow, he knew you were in trouble.'

'Wow—he's better than a tracker dog. I should have thanked him before you let him loose.'

'It's okay, he'll understand. He has the mind of a human, almost.'

'Owww! Here it goes again. I'm sure I'm going into labour.'

'What can I do for you? Wait... I hear a vehicle.'

Before long, Bessie had the doctor by the arm, directing him down the hallway to where Jessie lay.

'Hello there—my goodness, you're a lot bigger than when I saw you last. Has the midwife been to see you recently?'

'Not for a while. I told her I'd stayed under your care, seeing you specialise in obstetrics and that you would deliver my baby.'

'Let me look at you.'

Bessie left Jessie and Mack with Joshua.

'You can stay while I examine her if you like. Is that okay, Jessie?'

'He can if he wants.' She nodded her head at Mack.

'No, thanks—if you don't mind, I'll just wait at the door. I'll come back in when Joshua has finished, Jessie.'

'Could I please wash my hands?'

'Of course. Follow me.' Mack led him down the hallway to the washbasin in the bathroom.

On his return, the doctor opened his medical bag and took out some instruments, placing them on a clean towel on the side of the bed. Before long, he completed his examination.

'I have finished here. You are in early labour, but it's not critical except you need to be in a hospital. Mack—please phone the rescue helicopter. I'll need to talk to the paramedics, as your wife will have to be transported to Queenstown Hospital.'

'It's too early for this, isn't it?' Beads of moisture were visible on Mack's forehead.

'Not at all—it's common for babies to be born a few weeks early or late. It's just because twins can offer a few more challenges. Being so isolated out here, it's not the best place for her to be.'

'I see—will she be alright?'

'Everything is perfectly fine and she'll be placed in a facility with all the right equipment.'

'She was hoping for a home birth.'

'That may have been possible with one baby but not with twins. I'm sorry—I did tell her that.'

After Mack had made the phone call, he handed the phone to Joshua who advised the staff about Jessie's condition.

Mack went back into the bedroom to reassure her. 'I'll go with you and I'll phone your folks first to ask for their help.

Wyatt could give Grandad a hand on the station and your mother might help get things organised for when we bring the babies home.'

Mack loathed the unwanted panic churning inside him. His chest felt tight when he held his breath in stressful circumstances. He quietly reminded himself to breathe. He sat on the bed caressing Jessie's flaxen, wavy hair.

'Would you like your mother to come with us?'

'No, I need to her to help get the room ready for our babies. She knows what to do—we've already been over it. Is she coming over now?'

'Yes, she said she'll be right over.'

Before the helicopter departed from Reed Station, Pru had arrived and primed her daughter on everything she needed to know and to do once she got to the birthing unit.

'I think it's more important for Mack to be at your side during the birth than your mother. I'll be needed when you bring the twins home and Bessie is looking forward to supporting you too.'

'Thanks, Mum—I'm so glad you're living next door—oh, no—here it comes again. It's getting stronger!'

'Well, the helicopter is just in time then, isn't it?'

Jessie tried to talk between catching her breath with the strong contractions.

Mack packed their bags and gave instructions to Walter about farming agendas for the next few days.

'You can hand most things over to Ben to manage—and make use of Wyatt, Grandad.'

Walter nodded in agreement as he stood next to Bessie on the veranda. They waved them off as Pru drove Jessie and Mack to the helipad in the Land Rover to meet the helicopter. It landed on a field next to the house.

Joshua checked the helicopter that it had everything needed for a birthing emergency and saw them into the air.

He declined an invitation to stay for afternoon tea by Bessie. Before he stepped into his car, he had a quiet word with Mack.

'You have a wonderful sister, if I might say so, and she is mighty spunky running that camp by herself. I had an interesting evening with her recently, did she say?'

'Um ... no, she said nothing.'

'I had to pay an after-hours visit to a sick child, and she invited me to stay for a meal. A most enjoyable evening and I look forward to paying another visit—if you get my drift.'

Mack was horrified. He didn't think Meg would do something like that—entertaining a male friend so soon after her husband had left the bed. He knew Meg wouldn't do anything to violate her marriage to Joe while they were still working things out, but he was disappointed that she allowed herself to be tempted.

'Please don't be the instigator of more mayhem in my sister's life, as she's a married woman to a man she loves. Her life is complicated right now and the last thing she needs is an illicit relationship.'

Joshua leaned on his car with one hand, still holding his medical bag in the other. His face resembled that of a young child being scolded by a parent.

'I mean no harm—I'm a widower and don't get to spend time with a lovely woman—that's all.'

'It's really none of my business, but I know how impressionable my sister is. Just tread carefully, that's all.'

Joshua kept a leash on his emotions, shook Mack's hand and went on his way.

Chapter Thirteen

December 1983

The twins were born at midnight two weeks before Christmas, a month after Hope Rigby had given birth to a baby girl. Two rowdy, bonny baby boys emerged without complications, one after the other following a long labour. They both had a thick shock of dark hair, like their father.

Jessie lay almost lifeless. The uncharacteristic pallor in her cheeks gave a translucent, deathly appearance. Mack sat at her side, holding her hand while the midwife busied herself around him, checking her blood pressure and heart rate.

'She needs to rest as there was more blood loss than expected, but it shouldn't impede her recovery. We are monitoring your babies at present, but you will see them before long.'

'Aren't you going to bring them in here?'

'We just have to wait until the paediatrician gives them a full examination as they were under stress during the labour.'

'Oh, I see—will they be alright?' Mack sat wringing his hands while moisture formed on his temples.

'From my observation and the comments of the obstetrician, I think they are fine. Don't fret, Mr Reed— you'll see your boys before long.'

Jessie roused, tugging on Mack's coat pocket. 'What's all this about my babies—where are they? I want to have them here next to me.'

The midwife approached her bed. 'Please don't worry, Mrs Reed. Your babies need to spend a short time in the Neo-Natal Unit to be examined by the paediatrician before they can be brought into your room. You all had a bit of a rough time, and they're exhausted just like you.'

'Oh, no—I was hoping to start feeding them.'

'You just get some rest. There'll be plenty of time for that and believe me, you're going to need your energy.'

Within a short time, both mother and father closed their eyes and fell asleep. The midwife left Mack lying back in the armchair he had at his disposal next to Jessie and left the room.

***

A week later, the sound of crying babies echoed across the valley at the homestead on Reed Station.

'Breakfast is on the table,' bellowed Bessie down the hallway.

Pru poked her head around the door of the nursery and called back. 'We're almost there, thanks, Bessie. The babies are almost settled.'

Mack came out of the master bedroom in his pyjama pants and headed straight for the bathroom. He washed and returned to the room, stopping at the door of the nursery.

'Thanks so much, Mum, for coming over so early each morning to help. If it wasn't for you, I wouldn't be able to manage the station, honestly.'

'That's okay, Mack. I get a lot of pleasure from this. I'd forgotten what it was like, but it soon came back to me. You get on out there—Wyatt is helping you today, I believe.'

'Yes, I'll make the most of it, too. I think he's going to Willow Park next week to help Meg with a few of the ponies that need shoeing. The Blacksmith's going to be there.'

Mack hurried back into the room and within minutes sat with a mug of coffee at the table, bolting down the fried eggs and sausages Bessie had put in front of him.

'Jessie shouldn't take long. She's just settling the babies with Mum.'

Bessie sat down at the table and hurriedly ate her own breakfast before the others arrived. 'I've put a lunchbox in your saddlebag at the front door, Mack. I know you're going to be away all day and not home for lunch.'

Mack stood up, wiped the butter from his lips and kissed Bessie on the cheek. 'You're like a mother to me—what would we do without you? Thanks for looking after us all so well.'

Bessie wiped her hands on her apron and beamed at him. 'Go on with you. Stop being so soppy, you big softy.'

Bluey rushed up the steps to meet him as he walked out towards the barn where he kept his quad bikes. The frisky animal jumped on the back while Mack attached the saddlebag, taking off along the track in a cloud of dust on this parched summer day.

***

Christmas day was a simple affair, as everyone was too tired to celebrate in their usual way. The family performed their own church service in the homestead.

Walter dressed in his Sunday best and read from his vintage Bible. They all sang Christmas carols and at the end of the service, the octogenarian prayed for the health and strength of Jessie and her babies.

Mack had invited Meg, but she'd declined to attend and arrived shortly before lunch. He was disappointed that she

486

wasn't ready to join them in giving thanks to God. *What will it take to humble her?* He asked himself.

The family couldn't sit at the table and eat together as they were constantly disrupted by Jessie having to feed the twins on demand.

'Sorry, everyone—just help yourselves. I'll eat after I've put the boys down for a nap.'

Mack could see from the dark shadows under his wife's eyes and her sallow complexion that she was exhausted. 'You aren't doing that on your own—I'll help after you've fed them.'

When they'd finished their meal, Bessie sat next to Pru and Wyatt, catching up with all their news.

'Where's Tom?' Bessie asked. 'I hope he's not having Christmas on his own.'

Pru's face took on a sombre expression at the mention of Tom. It was their first Christmas without him.

'No, but he's in excellent hands. Recently, he got engaged, and his fiancée's parents invited him to join them. He's coming down here for New Year.'

After Jessie finished feeding the babies, she wandered back into the lounge with Mack in tow, each carrying a child. Walter sat back in his chair pensively watching all the comings and goings. The twins were only a few weeks old, and they were the best Christmas present an old man like Walter could ever have. He just couldn't stop staring at them.

'Do you want to hold one of them, Grandad, before they go to sleep? They said at the hospital not to take them out in the community and hand them around to others in case they contract a bug—but apparently, it's okay within the family home.'

While Mack sat with Will, Jessie wrapped Oliver tightly in his delicate woollen shawl that Pru had knitted.

'Just stay there—I'll bring him to you.'

Walter sat holding the child as if the tiny baby was a tinsel ball. He was mesmerised. 'I can't remember what this one is called—in fact, I can't distinguish one from the other yet.'

'That one is called Oliver, and his brother is Will. If you look at his nose, it's turned up—unlike Will's, which is long and narrow.'

'Ah, so they aren't identical twins.'

Mack interjected, 'No, Grandad. We couldn't do that to you. They're going to keep you busy enough without having to work out who's who.'

The baby in his arms relaxed and didn't stir.

Jessie sat next to Meg who didn't appear interested in holding the twins.

'How are things going with you, Meg? Is the pony camp working out?'

'Yes, it's going better than I thought. I had a few children with special needs who came to the camp. One child with Aspergers is going to be coming regularly at weekends. Her parents have received a government subsidy as the equine therapy has transformed her so much.'

'Wow, that's great. Perhaps it may be something you could specialise in—equine therapy for children with disabilities.'

'I don't think so—not while I'm alone. I've employed staff, but it's not the same as having a husband working alongside me.'

Mack overheard and wanted to say that she shouldn't have chased him away, but he kept his mouth shut.

Meg turned to Mack across the room. 'Actually—I want to ask you something, Mack. I remember the story you told me about Zoro being a special horse and that he intuitively knew there was something wrong with Grandad. To add to that, Jessie told me today that Zoro had rescued her when she went into labour. He's an unusual horse and I think he may help this child who has shut down, according to her parents.'

'What child is this?' he asked.

'Bonny—the girl with Asperger's.'

'What do you want Zoro to do?'

'I wondered if you wouldn't mind trucking him over the weekend that Bonny comes to stay next. I'm hoping she can spend time with him, perhaps grooming him and leading him around to see if she can bond with him. By what you've told me, I'm sure Zoro will reach her.'

'That's an unusual request but I can see where you're coming from, Sis. I think I could arrange that—when is she coming?'

'At the end of January, during the holidays.'

'It's good you're going to have Mum and Dad stay in the chalet for a while. What time are they arriving?'

Meg looked at her watch. 'They said they'd be here by dinner time around six and I have some food prepared for them. It's a mighty long trip and they'll be exhausted. Mum said they'll be over to visit you all tomorrow.'

Mack looked forward to seeing his parents who were travelling from Nelson. It was going to be a full house, but family life was the one thing that Mack thrived on and he was going to make sure that his boys would grow up in a loving environment.

They were disrupted by Oliver suddenly letting out a roar.

Walter quickly handed him back to Jessie. 'This is where I leave off. I think he's wet and I'll opt-out of that one.'

Jessie and Mack took the babies into the nursery. Within a short time, there was silence. Jessie could finally sit down and eat her meal.

It had been a long and tiring day for Bessie. The rest of the family offered to help clean up the kitchen and give her the rest of the afternoon off.

Meg showed her change of heart by washing the dishes and tidying the kitchen before she left to go home. 'Tell Mack I'll call him tomorrow,' she said to her grandfather.

Walter stood up as she walked towards the front door.

'Wait! There's a heap of food in the fridge here. Take some with you. I'll cut some ham and turkey for you. I got extra in with so many people coming and going.'

'Thanks, Grandad. I'll just take a few things to add to my lot. I'll bet Mum has piled the car to the brim with food as usual.'

After Meg left, Pru and Wyatt took their leave and went home. That just left Walter in the lounge alone. He sat back with his berry wine and counted his blessings.

'Thank you, God, for our beautiful baby boys and this loving family that you have given me. Please keep Len and Helen safe on their long journey to join us so that they can complete the circle.'

Chapter Fourteen

New Year's Eve

Len and Helen settled in at Willow Park, and Len spent time during the week tidying up Meg's accounts, although she did have a tax accountant. He wanted to make sure she ran her business efficiently. Helen spent most of her time driving backwards and forwards to Reed Station to spend time with the twins.

'I told Mack we'll be over there again tomorrow,' said Helen. 'I think it would be a good idea for him and Jessie to have some time together tonight. Jessie's brother, Tom, has arrived for a few days, and she'll want to spend time with him too.'

Helen brought a stoneware pot with a roast chicken to the table, with Meg in tow carrying an enamel dish of baked vegetables.

'Yes, I suppose it will be a full house. We could have a quiet evening here, I suppose,' muttered Meg.

Helen started laying the table. 'I expect Jessie will be worn out by the end of the evening with two babies.'

'Where's Dad? Does he know dinner's ready? I'll go outside and get him. I think he has bonded with one of the Kaimanawa ponies from Dart River Ranch.'

Helen winked at Meg. 'That's unusual—he's not into horses much, but perhaps he's softening in his old age.'

'I guess he is,' Meg chuckled as she stood by the front door where she could see him grooming one of the miniature ponies.

She walked over to him. 'Dinner's ready, Dad.'

He turned around, smiling. 'His mane seems to be in a tangle. This one likes me, I think.'

He followed her back to the house. 'Would you like to go for a drive down to the lake with me after dinner? It's such a beautiful day and we could have a bit of father-daughter time.'

'Sure, Dad. We have had little time together lately.'

***

After the meal, Len stood ready to take his daughter out for a drive. 'Come on, Meg—we'd better get going so we can make the most of daylight saving. I'll drive if, you like.'

He kissed his wife on the cheek and hurried out to his vehicle parked in the driveway. Helen stayed behind to work outside. She'd got friendly with the animals and enjoyed feeding the chickens each evening. In the week she'd been staying with Meg since Christmas Day, she'd planted a garden bed full of petunias and snapdragons and the front yard was an array of bright colours.

While her father drove out to the lake, Meg couldn't stop chatting to him about her pony camp and what she'd done to the property since she'd subdivided it. He pulled in at a rest area beside Lake Wakatipu as the sun faded behind the Humboldt Mountains.

'I'm concerned about you, Meg. You probably don't want me to broach the subject of your marriage, but Joe is a good man and deserves a chance, and I think you made it impossible for him.'

Meg went quiet. The corners of her mouth dropped south, and the deep crevices returned to her brow. She'd been avoiding any discussion about her marriage during her parents' stay.

'He gave up a lot to give you what you wanted, and you appeared to throw it back in his face. When you lived in Thorndon, he worked hard building a future for you both. He even made a new life in Glenorchy, despite having never lived in the country before. What's happening now about your marriage?'

Meg opened her passenger window and stared out at the lake. She wouldn't look at her father who continued to shoot sideways glances at her.

'He can come back at any time he likes—it was he who left me, remember? I wrote to him and told him I didn't go through with the housing development and sold the ninety acres as pastoral land to the farmer next door.'

'Was he pleased about that?'

'Yes ... at least I think so. He said I could have left things as they were and shouldn't have considered throwing Wyatt and Pru off the land and out of their home. I don't think he can forgive me for that.'

Meg started sniffing and pulled out a handkerchief and then turned her head away to wipe her wet cheeks with a sleeve.

'It was pretty disruptive for everyone, Meg, but I can see that you are trying to make some drastic changes. Does Joe know all about Willow Park and the pony camp?'

'Yes, I told him in the last letter I wrote. He said it won't be long before I start another impulsive scheme and refers to me as a bull in a china shop.'

'Oh, I see—he still sounds angry. What does he want to do about your marriage?'

'He says he might come down and see what I'm doing after the camp has been running a while.'

'Why don't you start going to church with Mack and Jessie? You could make some new friends there and find some support.'

'I'm fine—thanks, Dad. I have a few friends in the community and the local doctor has offered me support.'

'Oh, really—what kind of support?'

'Mainly with the children when they need medical care, and he plays tennis with me. Joshua is his name, and he's a widower.'

'Do you think that's wise if you are trying to mend your marriage?' Len's voice croaked. He coughed to clear his throat.

'We are just friends, and I meet all kinds of people through the camp like him. I've made connections with some parents who drop their children off here.'

'I suppose you know what you're doing. Just be careful and guard your heart. Single people are vulnerable, and you don't need any more complications.'

'Isn't that view marvellous?' Meg pointed at Lake Wakatipu with the mountains in the distance, creating an artist's backdrop for a painting.

Len got the message and said no more until they arrived back home.

***

Helen met them at the front door. 'Ah, you're back! Let's sit on the patio and see the New Year in. Bessie gave us a bottle of the award-winning fruit champagne from the Marlborough Sounds. I'll get it out of the fridge.' She took out the bottle while Meg followed her father onto the patio carrying a platter of crackers and assorted cheeses she'd bought at the market.

Helen chatted incessantly while handing around the snacks she'd prepared while they were away.

Len passed Meg the bowl of cashew nuts. 'Isn't it gorgeous down by the lake? I love sitting there staring at the Humboldt Mountains—especially when they are covered in snow.'

'Yes, this place certainly grows on you. I can understand why people want to come and live here.'

'I'm tempted to stay longer, but we have to get back to Nelson. Your father is giving a presentation at the Businessmen's Association there.'

Meg found her tongue. 'I thought you'd retired, Dad.'

'You're right. I need to pull back and having fun.'

Helen placed a cheesecake on the table and started slicing it.

'No word from Joe about coming for a visit, Meg?'

'I'll get some plates.' Meg hurried off to the kitchen. When she returned to the patio, she glanced at her mother. 'No—I would have told you if he was coming,' she snapped.

Len darted a disapproving glance at his wife. For the rest of the evening, no more was said about Joe and Meg's marriage.

At midnight they all kissed and hugged each other, reiterating the usual *Happy New year* then Len and Helen took themselves off to bed while Meg stayed outside a little longer.

She sat on the patio staring at the neighbour's cows grazing in the paddock next door, illuminated by a full moon. Len and Helen had left her alone, as she appeared to be in another world interrupted by the occasional Morepork in the trees above.

***

Tom was in his element spending January on a high country station. Becoming an uncle to twin boys had also given him much joy as he took turns rocking the babies to sleep when the women weren't fussing over them. Even Walter competed for his share of cuddles and snuggles.

495

Jessie placed baby Will on the couch to change his nappy. 'When are you going back home, Tom?'

'I can only stay until Tuesday. I've got a shearer arriving with his gang, including a small team of shedhands, and I have to be there.'

Jessie finished changing Will and handed him back to Tom.

'It's a pity you couldn't bring Amanda, your fiancée down for New Year.'

'I'll bring her down next time—she's in Australia with her family visiting her brother.'

'That'll be good. Will she be able to the cooking for a gang of shearers when you're married?'

Tom glared at her. 'No, I wouldn't do that to her.' He glanced at Jessie again, then saw her winking at Mack and relaxed.

'Where are you getting married? You could always have a ceremony here, can't he Grandad?'

Walter had been nodding off to sleep in his armchair. 'What's that—another wedding?' he stammered.

'Don't worry—Amanda has already arranged it at her own church, which we both attend. We're planning the reception garden party on our farm—just like the one you had here.'

Pru came to life suddenly. 'Good idea—when will that be?' The woman's eyelids sagged after days of sleepless nights helping Jessie with her night feeds.

Tom looked around for Jessie as the baby started whining. 'We're not in any hurry—still just thinking about it.'

'That's wonderful, Tom, but don't leave it too long,' she said, winking at him.

Jessie supplemented the hungry babies with milk formula. 'Why don't you top him up with some of this, Tom? I've just warmed it.' She handed him the baby's bottle. 'You can get some practice, as you'll have one of your own one day.'

Pru had been rocking Oliver off to sleep. 'Shall I tuck him into his bassinet?'

'Yes, please. He took all of what I had and some formula, so his belly is full,' said Jessie.

'Have we been keeping you up, Grandad?' Jessie teased Walter. 'I hope you think it's all worthwhile having us living here with you.'

Walter pulled himself together. He stood up and tousled Jessie's hair. 'I couldn't think of any other way to spend my old age, my girl. This is more than I could hope for.'

'I'm going to put the kettle on if anyone wants a cuppa.' He wandered through to the kitchen.

Wyatt sat chatting with his son until Walter arrived back in the lounge with the teapot and cups on a tray. 'Help yourself, everyone.'

'Tom and I are taking up your offer of spending tomorrow working with you on the station, Mack.'

'Thanks a lot. It's going to be a hectic day—we have shearers arriving and need to bring the young hoggets off the hills to the woolshed for crutching to prevent fly strike. We have shepherds, of course, and the dogs do the work— but I'm talking about thousands of sheep.'

'Wow, that's a lot of sheep compared to our farm,' Tom said, glancing at his father.

'Yep, sure is. That's not counting Mack's three Angus bulls and two hundred Angus heifers.'

Tom rubbed his hands together. 'It'll be a terrific experience.'

'You're right, son. It's going to be an eye-opener for you. Mack's going to give shearing training to students from Lincoln University Summer School. He has won several Golden Shears awards and will show you some good tips.'

It was a hive of activity on Reed Station. Not only were there second and third-generation, Reed family shepherds, but in Jessie's family there were also second and third-generation shepherds too. And now they were one big, blended family. What more could a man ask for? Thought Mack as he helped himself to tea after offering his wife a cup.

Chapter Fifteen

Mack was relieved that the hectic Christmas and New Year period was over. The family had all dispersed and returned to their home towns. He and Jessie relished the quietness in the house and Pru had left them to it, as she was eager to get back to her own bed.

The day had come for Mack to take Zoro to pony camp for Bonny to ride. He and Meg had promised her this, and they wanted to give her a real farming experience.

Zoro grazed in the large paddock near the stables. He came trotting towards the gate with both ears pricked forward when Mack ambled up to the fence.

The horse licked his hand. 'Hi, fella.' Mack opened the gate and approached him with a halter. 'We're going for a ride in the horse truck today, as you've got some special work to do.'

He slipped his headcollar on and then his bridle on top fastening the cheek strap. It was as though Zoro knew he was on a special assignment as he nudged his owner affectionately. After he'd tacked up, he rode bareback down the track to the stable-barn to fetch his saddle. While Zoro was tied to the hitching rail, Mack carried the saddle to the horse truck. Within a short time, he had loaded Zoro and headed off to Willow Park.

He arrived to find cars blocking the driveway, preventing him from driving the truck through to the trailer park. As he pulled up behind the cars, Meg came around the side of the house to greet him. He rolled down his window. 'Can you ask these people to shift their vehicles? I have a horse in the truck.'

'Sorry, Mack. I forgot to let them know you'd be coming with Zoro. I'll get them to shift right now. If you put Zoro in the stable next to Toby, I'd like to tell you about Bonny. Her mother has just been and gone, and I've had an update.'

Mack's eyes narrowed. 'I'll drive down next to the stables once this car gets out of my way.' He tried not to sound pushy, but it irritated him that people could be so inconsiderate.

Once he could drive the truck down to the stables, he took Zoro out and led him into the barn next to Toby, a white pony that was docile around other males. He went inside the house to find Meg had made a pot of tea and to his unbelief, fresh scones.

'You didn't bake these, did you?'

'No, I cheated. Mum made a huge batch before she left after New Year. I keep them frozen and just heat them before serving.'

The scones were dripping in strawberry jam and fresh cream from the neighbour's cows.

'These are good—thanks, Mum,' he said facetiously, winking at Meg while catching a drip of cream on the end of his chin.

'I'm glad of a bit of a catch up with you. Have you heard from Joe—is he coming back?'

Meg's face dropped. 'I wish everyone would stop badgering me about him. I don't know what he's going to do,' she growled.

'Oh—sorry, Sis. I'm just concerned, that's all. By the way—my mate, Tony from Federated Farmers said he saw you and that new doctor fella—what's his name? He saw you having lunch with him down by the lake the other day.'

Meg put her teacup down. It clanged, almost breaking. She stammered, 'That's right, he's giving me advice and support while working with clients with special needs and has made a few house calls lately to the children.'

'Look ... I don't want to interfere, but I hope you know what you're doing. When Jessie and I came to see you that day, you said you love Joe and that you want him back—so please be careful.'

'Didn't you come here to talk about how Zoro is going to help Bonny?'

'Sure—tell me all about her.'

'Bonny has Asperger's Syndrome and when her family moved from Arrowtown to live in Queenstown, she suffered from depression after her parents made her give up her pony when they moved to the city. The horse was her best friend—her comforter.'

Mack lowered his eyebrows, creating wrinkles in his forehead. 'Really? That's pretty harsh for a young girl.'

'She comes here to ride regularly. Now that Christmas is over, she'll start coming back more often.'

There was a knock at the door. 'Come in!' Meg called out.

'Sorry to interrupt you, Mrs Wilds. We are ready to start the children in the arena. Should we wait for you?'

'Thanks, Sara. No—tell the staff to just carry on as usual. I need to sort something out for Bonny. Is she still sitting under the umbrella out there?'

'Yes—she's waiting for a visitor.'

Meg gave her a nod. 'Tell her I'll be out soon.'

'We'd better wind this up and get out there. I'd like to get Bonny handling Zoro, then perhaps she can ride him tomorrow morning. While you're here, I'd like you to go over caring for a horse with her—such as grooming, fastening a blanket, feeding, and then leading him around. If you can spare Zoro until tomorrow afternoon, I'll go over tacking with her after you've taken Zoro back to the station. She's going home on Monday evening.'

'I can give you today and tomorrow morning, but you'll have to work with her yourself after that. I'll stay here tonight and then I'll have to leave tomorrow afternoon.'

'That's okay. I have some great volunteers for the long weekend along with a few paid staff and most of them are experienced.'

Mack walked over to introduce himself to Bonny, whose face lit up instantly. 'Come with us, Bonny, to see a friend in the stable who wants to meet you.' Mack directed her to the stall where Zoro waited, and as she approached, the stallion let out a soft whinny.

When the girl draped herself over the wooden rail, the animal licked her hand. 'Hello, Zoro—my name's Bonny. Mack said you're my new friend.'

Mack held up a bucket. 'Here, Bonny, give him some of these pellets. Put them into the palm of your hand and let him take them.' Meg stood alongside her.

While the horse nibbled on the pellets in her hand, Bonny let out a squeal. 'Ooh—that tickles!'

'He loves you already, Bonny. Now I want you to give him a good brush. You know what to do—the grooming kit is over there in the box.'

Meg turned to Mack who leaned over the hitching rail listening and observing.

'I try to foster independence in the children, as many of the children have *learned helplessness* and this training enables them to become self-reliant.'

This whole new side to his sister impressed Mack. She had trained as an occupational therapist for children with developmental delays and had given it up to join their father's import company—becoming a hard-nosed businesswoman.

'He's an enormous horse, isn't he? I think he likes me, and I love him,' Bonny blurted.

By the afternoon, with her head in the air, Bonny led Zoro around the enclosed arena. The girl was tall for her age, which made the towering, black horse less intimidating.

Mack fastened the reins to the saddle and asked Bonny to walk around the arena and back again without leading the horse. As she did this, Zoro sauntered behind her and wherever she turned, he followed.

For the rest of the afternoon, Mack and Meg watched as Bonny lunged Zoro in the arena, and by the end of the day, she had won him over. The horse trusted her.

'Please, Mrs Wilds. Can I have Zoro every time I come here?'

'We'll see, Bonny—I'll do my best, but this is Mack's stock horse, and he might need him.'

'Maybe Bonny might like to pay Zoro a visit to Reed Station one weekend. If you or someone can drop her off, I can bring her back to you,' said Mack, tousling Bonny's hair.

'Good idea, brother. You're right about this horse being special.'

They watched as Bonny groomed Zoro who rubbed his head up and down her back and then licked her hand.

'Oooh,' she squealed. 'You made my hand all slimy, Zoro.'

Meg slipped her hand in her pocket. 'Here, Bonny. Give him this apple and he'll love you forever.'

The stallion behaved perfectly with Bonny. They had made friends for life.

Mack stayed overnight in one of Meg's spare rooms. He wanted to make sure Zoro was going to be on his best behaviour and didn't want to leave Meg to handle him on her own, as she wasn't used to him.

When they had finished cleaning up after the evening meal, the children went to their respective bedrooms—

some sleeping in the barn on the hay bales, a few in the lodge and the rest in the arena bunkhouse.

Later that evening, Mack sat with his sister, enjoying homemade lemonade and crackers with fresh goat cheese from her neighbour.

'Oh, no. Who's disturbing us at this hour? It's rare that I can have an evening's rest without some kind of interruption.'

The knock on the lounge door became louder. Meg hauled herself up off the sofa and opened the door.

'What is it, Carrie—it's getting late?'

A girl no older than sixteen stood, wrenching her hands behind her back.

'Sorry, Mrs Wilds—it's Bonny—she's gone.'

Meg's mouth dropped open. Her brows raised.

'What ... what do you mean, gone? Why isn't she in the room with you?'

'I thought she was asleep. I had dozed off and when I got up to go to the bathroom, her bed was empty.'

'Oh, no! Mack—help me find her!'

She turned to the young girl. 'Carrie, don't worry. She had probably gone outside because she couldn't sleep. Go back to your room. We'll find her.'

Meg tugged Mack's sleeve. 'I'll grab a torch. Wait for me out the front.'

Mack went to his room, pulled on his Swanndri jacket and waited on the front porch for her. From there, he could see a dull light emanating from the stables. *That's strange. There shouldn't be anyone out there at this time.*

Meg joined him. 'I've got the torch, but the battery is weak, and it might not last.'

'Look over there.' He pointed toward the stables. 'You didn't leave the night light on in there, did you?'

The corners of her eyes wrinkled as she tried to determine what the light was. 'No, I didn't. It is never left on unless we have a sick animal.'

'Come on, let's check it out—but first, you wait here while I look in the horse trailer park to see if there is a strange vehicle there.'

Mack shot off with the torch before Meg could reply. She shivered as she wrapped her arms around herself, watching the ghostlike silhouettes of branches catch the half-moon beams as they swayed in the breeze.

'Ah! Don't creep up behind me like that!' Meg scolded as Mack arrived back at her side in a short time.

'Shhh—keep your voice down.'

'Did you see any vehicles?'

'Nothing.' Mack heard the chattering of teeth as she spoke.

'Cold are you? Here, I've got a jumper on under this. You never seem to dress warmly.' He pulled off his jacket and handed it to her.

'Okay, brother—no need to lecture me.' She sniffed at the jacket, screwed up her nose and pulled it on. 'Where to now?'

'Follow me and not a whisper. Let's catch the culprit.'

Meg held on to the hem of his jacket as she tiptoed furtively behind him.

'Just wait here, Meg. For all we know, they might have a weapon.'

'Listen.' She put her hand up to his chest to stall him. 'I hear a horse's hooves. They're stealing one of my ponies. How can they if they've no horse trailer? Maybe it's parked down the road, or worst still, they intend to steal yours.'

'I'll stop them. You get ready to go inside the house to call the police when I say.'

Mack crept up to the side of the barn. He edged his way to the open doorway and poked his head inside then stopped short, staring in disbelief. It was as if he was hallucinating. There was a young girl wearing white pyjamas riding Zoro around the arena bareback. He lurched forward, then stalled, not wanting to alarm her.

Zoro began walking towards him.

'Halt, Zoro. You're going the wrong way,' the girl commanded, then looked over in Mack's direction. She froze when she spotted him and pulled on the rope she'd attached to Zoro's halter.

Mack approached his horse and took hold of his halter. By this time Meg had entered the barn.

'What's all this about, eh? Why are you out here?' Mack helped her climb down then Meg took her by the hand and led her away to the side. The girl appeared so stunned to be caught in the act that she couldn't find the words to say to her accusers.

Mack put Zoro back in his stall and placed some hay in his hanging feeder. He unclipped his rope and hung it back on the hook before joining Meg and Bonny.

'You don't know how worried we've been. We thought you had gone missing and were about to call the police. What were you doing?'

Bonny lowered her head then her brown, marble eyes misted over. 'Sorry, Mrs Wilds. I couldn't sleep until I'd ridden Zoro. He loves me and I wanted to keep him company out here. It's not his home and I thought he would be lonely.'

Meg put her arm around Bonny.

Mack's eyes twinkled as he beamed at her. 'He must love you a great deal to let you ride him around the arena with only a halter.'

Meg directed her towards the door. 'Come on, missy. Time for you to get to bed. Perhaps Mack will let you ride Zoro tomorrow, but we need to see you using a saddle and bridle first.'

Bonny looked directly at Mack. 'Please, Mr Mack—let me ride Zoro tomorrow. I have to go home on Monday and I won't see him for ages.'

Meg whispered in Mack's ear. 'Zoro is a lot taller than the pony she once owned.'

'Of course, Bonny, but I need to go over a few things with you on how to handle him first,' Mack replied. 'We'll do that in the morning.'

***

Mack spent the next day with Bonny showing her how to tack up Zoro on her own and by the afternoon, she was well on her way trotting and cantering in the arena. The horse connected with the girl in an uncanny way, Mack thought. *Zoro really is something special. I knew I'd chosen a unique horse.*

'I can't wait to come back next time. Please let me look after him again,' Bonny pleaded.

Mack patted her on the back. 'We'll check with your folks if you can visit us at Reed Station next time you come. Zoro will be waiting to see you.' She dashed over to Zoro's side and threw her arms around his neck before Mack led him to the horse truck.

Meg stood next to Bonny as Mack drove off with Zoro down the long driveway and out onto the main road. He tooted, as he drove past the farm, and he could see Bonny still waving in the distance on the front veranda of the house. Mack knew he and Zoro had helped to heal a broken heart.

***

Jessie managed the twins with occasional assistance from her mother, Pru who helped mostly by bringing meals that she could put in the freezer. Jessie had organised the on-call vet to fill in for her for while she was on maternity leave, but she was determined to get back to work once she could leave the babies with their grandmother—even if it was only part-time.

Jessie held Oliver in one arm and pulled back the curtain at the window when she heard Mack's truck revving next to the stable-barn. She grinned at her mother who was busy burping Will.

'Ah, good—he's just in time to help me bath the twins.'

She walked over to the window and pulled back the curtain. 'He's just unloading Zoro now.'

'Poor man. He'll be tired out, won't he? I can give you a hand to bath them.'

'No, Mum. It's good for the boys to get used to both of us handling them. We share roles in this household and I herded cattle on horseback before I fell pregnant while trying to run my veterinary business. We are equals in this marriage.'

Pru gave her a half-smile as she took a pillow-case from the pile of washing in the wash basket and started folding it after sniffing at it first. 'The washing smells so fresh after hanging in the sun with the breeze we've had today.'

A thud resounded from heavy boots climbing the veranda steps. Mack left them at the door and walked inside baring his thick, woollen socks.

'Ah! My boys are still up. Not bathed yet?'

'No, Dad—they're waiting for you and you're just in time.' Jessie lifted her head pursing her lips, waiting for Mack to kiss her. He leaned over and planted one on her mouth.

'I won't touch the babies until I clean up. Won't be long and then I'll help give them a bath.' Mack shot into the bedroom and then into the bathroom with fresh clothes in his hands.

After his shower, he arrived to assist with bath time. Once it was over, Jessie was eager to get the babies settled in their bassinettes and off to sleep. This evening, they went down without a fuss, and the house was quiet again.

Jessie massaged her neck muscles. 'What a relief—it has been a long and tiring day. Oliver had colic all morning. It must have been something I've eaten. Maybe too much garlic in that chicken hotpot last night.'

'Well, you'd better not tell Bessie that. It's one of her mother's recipes. She's a bit sensitive when it comes to critiquing her cooking.' Mack knew that from past experience.

'How about you, Mack—how did it go with Bonny—did she take to Zoro okay?'

'It was more than Meg and I could hope for. The girl and Zoro are like old friends. She took off outside last night to the stables and unhitched Zoro. After jumping on him bareback she walked him in circles around the arena in her pyjamas. Meg and I thought we had intruders in the barn when we spotted a dim light coming from there and were about to call the police. When we discovered her, we were so amazed at the sight of the two of them bonding we couldn't get angry at her.'

'Wow. What a story—it sounds unreal.'

'Remember when you found Zoro with Grandad when he collapsed in the field following his stroke? Zoro covered him with hay from the bale at the gate to keep him warm. You said he had extra-sensory perception and I think you're right.'

'Yes, and he also rescued me on the dirt track when I went into early labour.'

'You also said that one day he'll be able to help others to heal and it's already happening. Bonny is going to pay us a visit in a few weeks' time. She'll stay at Willow Park but she can come out here for a ride on the station during mustering.'

'I can't believe Meg is making provision for all this and I never thought she'd go down this track. If only Joe could see her now.'

'She doesn't seem to want to talk about him. I'm afraid that doctor of yours has turned her head and I hope she isn't on course for another disaster. I tried to warn her off him.'

Jessie lay back on the couch with her head on Mack's lap. He played with her hair, twisting it around his finger. 'I'll keep praying that the Lord will give her wisdom and a desire for her marriage to be restored,' he said as Jessie closed her eyes while Mack chatted incessantly about the pony camp. His voice seemed to lull her to sleep. He got up and looked around the room, spotting a woollen rug on an armchair. After he draped it over her, he kissed her forehead and turned out the light.

Chapter Sixteen

Autumn

Mack had been up since five bringing the sheep off the hills with the musterers and driving them into the holding pens at the woolshed. They were on horseback except on the steeper hills where it would be lethal to go by horse—then they went by foot climbing the craggy hills with their dogs and a shepherd's crook.

This year, the shearing gang brought their own shedhands and cooks. Bessie and her domestic staff usually cooked all the meals, but now things had changed, she didn't mind at all. Mack left the shearing gang in the hands of his trusty Head Shepherd, Ben.

The drought conditions on Reed Station had taken its toll. Mack guided Zoro up the track onto the jagged ridge overlooking the farm. As far as he could see around him, the high country gave a scorched appearance as though a fire had seared the terrain. The yellow-brown colour was characteristic of the Otago district, the land of extremes— parched summers and chilling, icy winters. As he looked around at the desert landscape, he could see the damage the drought had done to the hillsides.

Although they had suffered a summer drought, by God's grace the autumn rain had allowed a little grass to grow and provided extra feed for the animals. Mack and his shepherds had checked the sheep for facial eczema early that morning and there was no sign of it, although there was always a risk after a warm rain.

He was grateful the station had a fresh water supply for the animals from a few streams that crossed the land, fed by the pristine glacial waters.

Mack gave Zoro his head as the horse reached down to graze on random blades of grass he could forage at his feet. His rider sat upright, breathing in the chilly, late afternoon air which caught his breath as he exhaled.

Awe transformed his face. He squinted through the sun's glare as he peered at the panoramic spectacle before him that reached as far as he could see. The vastness of the station astonished him as his eyes welled up knowing how blessed he was to have the responsibility of managing a high country station.

Something heavy hit his stomach causing him to grimace. Did his guilt of giving Meg his own small estate still linger? He was only trying to counterbalance the two-thousand-acre station he'd inherited from his grandfather—and look at the chaos it had caused. Life was so good for him right now—a far cry from that of his sister for whom he began to have empathy. Meg's life was hanging in the balance.

Zoro flinched. 'Whoa, boy—what's up?' Mack pulled him up on a short rein as a hawk flew out from behind a towering rock and startled him.

'Come on, fella, we'd best be going back.'

He eased Zoro down the narrow track that led off the ridge into the valley. Each step the horse took he calculated on the rugged, steep hillsides. Mack recalled the time he'd received the news that a neighbouring stockman died when his horse slipped and fell, crushing him to death. He shivered at the memory. Such freak accidents like that don't happen often, but they do occur—one of the many hazards of life on a high country station and he was determined they weren't going to happen under his management.

As he glanced towards the west, the rusty, iron roof of a musterers' hut caught his attention. He would have to get it repaired. Next, he had to check the winter crops on that side of the station.

He edged his way down, urging Zoro on towards the feed shed to check the winter supplies before heading home. The gate to the paddock was already open as there was no stock on this corner of the station. The stockmen had moved them earlier in the week.

When they arrived at the shed, Mack gave Zoro a long rein to let him eat remnants of hay which lay on the ground. When he looked inside the shed his heart sank. The stock levels were at an all-time low as hay and silage were hard to source in the province.

Mack pulled on the reins to let Zoro know that his snack-time was over. He turned to head home, gazing at the extensive paddocks before him when abruptly his face changed. Something caused his eyes to sparkle and lift his spirit—it was the tender, young grass that formed a lush carpet contrasting with the bronze hills. *Thank you, God! New grass for the stock.*

He let Zoro lower his head as the animal craned his neck towards the new grass.

'Mmm. This is a blessing, Zoro, my boy. It's a good sign and so early in the year too.'

He always chatted to Zoro, like other farmers in the area, who were accustomed to talking to their working dogs or themselves in these isolated areas. Out there, these faithful friends could often be the only companionship shepherds and stockmen enjoyed—especially when they spent days in the saddle staying overnight in cold, wooden huts.

Walter had worked hard providing feed for the stock before Mack arrived at the station. When his grandfather was fitter and younger, he'd toiled maintaining crops of swedes and turnips with the help of young labourers—most of whom were horticultural students from Lincoln University. Now that the old man was unable to tend the land, Mack had employed a married couple to manage the crops.

As Zoro trotted at a slow gait towards the fields of winter feed boasting row upon row of green tops, a man and woman in matching denim overalls waved out. Pete, the supervisor turned around and spoke to the workers then walked over to greet Mack, while Pete's wife, Kathleen carried on working alongside the others.

'Hi there. Haven't seen you around for a while. How is it all going?' He removed his hat to scratch his head then pushed it back on his head.

'The twins keep us busy when I'm not out here—life's hectic right now.' He pointed at the ground. 'The crops are flourishing.'

'They sure are. Must be the warm rain we've been getting. It's mild for April. I hope it keeps up so we can have plenty of feed before the winter sets in. We're trialling kale next week.'

'Well done—we're getting low on feed, so hopefully they'll be ready in time. I don't want to have to buy another load of silage right now. By the way—you and Kathleen must visit and see the twins. Give Jessie a call soon as she'd love to see you both. She hasn't seen you since the wedding.'

'We sure will. I'd best be getting on as we've got a bit to do before dark.' He was about to walk off when he stopped short.

'Wait ... how did you get on in the Golden Shears contest this year? Did you win this time?'

'I couldn't get away this year—not with Jessie having twins. I was happy enough with second place last year, but if all the goings-on here hadn't distracted me, I could have won—sorry, I'd best be getting on now too.'

Mack waved out to Kathleen as Pete walked back to join her and the other gardeners.

It was late in the afternoon. The sun began to disappear behind the towering hills earlier in Dart Valley and it was time to get back and give Jessie a hand with the babies. As he rode out onto the dirt track, he was about to break into a canter when he thought he could see someone on horseback waving to him in the distance. Who could that be? The stockmen wouldn't have a reason to be riding over this side of the station. At least, not at this time of the year.

As the person rode closer, the sun rays outlined the silhouette of golden hair willowing in the breeze under a Stetson. The horse had been in a shadow but now it was evident it was Chantilly. Jessie waved out as she came closer. When she met up with Mack, a wide grin stretched across her face.

'What brings you here—who's looking after the twins?'

'Mum is clucking over them as usual. They aren't feeding so often now and I can get away between feeds. I just had to experience the elements and spend some time with Chantilly. I want to enter her in the Agricultural and Pastoral Show next spring. She does dressage so well.'

Mack was so glad he'd given Chantilly to Jessie for a Christmas present the year he'd proposed to her. She and the horse had bonded more than Mack had expected. They were inseparable.

'I'm glad to see you're getting back into riding. I think Chantilly has missed you—but please, be careful not to overdo it. You'll burn out and that won't be any good. You said you're wanting to return to work after you wean the boys.'

Mack caught himself. He knew he tended to be over-protective of Jessie who didn't appreciate it. He wished he'd kept his mouth shut.

'I'll know when I'm doing too much. I'm fine—really. Let's canter down the track—coming?'

Mack breathed a sigh of relief that she didn't take exception to his comment, however caring he'd intended it.

They headed off towards the far end of the paddock. Mack slid off Zoro to open the gate and let Chantilly through.

'Thanks! I catch you back at the stables.'

Jessie took off in a flash with Zoro in close pursuit cantering along the track, creating billows of dust and gravel behind them. Mack pulled back when he started eating dirt and let her go.

As they rode towards the stables, Pru stood waving from the veranda, holding one of the babies. They took care of the horses and hurried to the homestead.

'What's up, Mum?' Jessie asked, still panting.

'This little minx wouldn't go down to sleep after his last feed. He must have known you had gone.'

Mack and Jessie removed their boots and followed Pru inside.

'Sorry, Mum—I wasn't really that long. I'll just wash my hands and take him from you.'

Jessie went off to the bathroom while Mack disappeared out the back. She returned at once and took Will from her mother's arms.

'I'll try to put him down. You go off home, Mum. Dad will be thinking you have deserted him. Thanks so much for today.' She leaned over and kissed her on the cheek.

'My pleasure, my dear. Dad's taking me into Glenorchy tomorrow for lunch and to get some groceries. I'd really like to go to Queenstown, but I'll leave it for another week.'

'Before you go, I'll give you a list of a few items I need at the store if you don't mind.'

'That's fine. Have a good night.'

Mack returned from washing up and walked her to the door.

'Thanks for everything, Mum. You know we are both very grateful for all the help you give us. Take a break tomorrow. I've got the afternoon off and can give Jessie a hand with the boys.'

Chapter Seventeen

Wyatt was proud of his new pickup. It was bright red, similar to Cole Rigby's Chevrolet—a late model Ford and it was something he'd promised himself when he retired, he'd once told Mack.

As he pulled in next to their cottage, Pru caught sight of Mack returning from the cattle yards on Zoro and waved out to him. He'd been on the north side of the station working with the stockmen on horseback since dawn. They brought down the herd of young Angus steers from the foothills ready for the stock trucks to collect early the next day. He'd just finished giving them a feed of hay.

'Mack! Join us for a coffee if you've got time. We need to talk to you about something,' said Pru as she stepped out of the vehicle.

'I've got some of that milk stout in the fridge if you want one,' said Wyatt as he reached into the vehicle to help Pru carry the boxes of supplies from the General Store.

'Sure, will do—but I can't stay long. I promised Jessie I'd help with the boys this afternoon and I'm running late.'

Mack followed them both inside. He smiled and nodded as he viewed the new curtains and fresh paint. They'd both been busy renovating the cottage.

Wyatt handed Mack the stout. 'It's not really beer, is it? My folks have drunk it for years and said it was medicinal. I suppose I got into it through them,' said Wyatt.

Mack took a seat. 'Yes, it's great. Grandad introduced me to it. I'm also partial to homemade apple cider if it's not too strong.'

'Well, we'd better get to the point,' said Pru, elbowing Wyatt who sat next to her on the couch.

'When we drove towards Glenorchy this morning, we caught sight of Joe driving an Avis rental car, and he appeared to be heading out of town towards Willow Park. When we left the General Store, we took a drive down by the lake before we had lunch at that little cafe.' Pru looked at her husband. 'You tell them, dear.'

Wyatt hesitated then finished telling the story.

'I took some photos of the lake to send to Tom as he wants to show them to his girlfriend. The strange thing is— as we pulled out of the carpark, we saw Meg sitting on the park bench with Dr Douglas, both wearing tennis outfits and so I just kept driving. I know that she and the doctor are good friends.'

Pru interjected. 'I don't think Meg expected a visit from Joe. Perhaps he was going to give her a surprise visit.'

Mack raised his eyebrows. 'You're right—I spoke to Meg on the phone yesterday and she didn't say anything about Joe coming to visit.'

He took hold of his Stetson he'd placed on the seat next to him and rushed down the rest of his stout. 'It doesn't sound good to me. I'm sorry, but do you mind if I head off home? I'd better ask the family if Joe has called by or phoned while I was out.'

Mack rushed to the door with the couple in tow.

'Thanks for letting me know ... oh, and thanks for the stout. It's a good brew. I'll let you know if we hear from either Joe or Meg.'

***

Mack and Jessie had no sooner settled the twins down for their afternoon sleep than the sound of a vehicle's engine whirred in the driveway. Mack had already told Jessie about the chain of events that Pru and Wyatt had witnessed. Could this be Joe on their doorstep?

The vigorous pounding on the door echoed down the hallway. Jessie got up and peered through the Venetian blinds.

'Oh no, it's Joe, sure enough—and he appears pretty agitated. Answer the door, quick, Mack before he wakes the boys. It doesn't sound good.' She raked her hair with her fingers, pushing it back behind her ears.

Mack opened the door to Joe whose eye sockets revealed large dark rings shadowing intense, soulful eyes. He looked at Mack with relief as he stood in the doorway.

'Thanks, mate. Do you mind if I come in? Something is going on with Meg.'

Mack took his arm and led him into the lounge then Jessie stood up and greeted him with a hug. 'I'll put the kettle on,' she said, sensing the need to remove herself.

Within a short time, she returned with a tray of tea and biscuits. Moving quietly around the lounge, she placed the tray on the side table.

'Tea, Joe?'

'Please,' he answered with a shaky voice.

''I remember how you like it.' Jessie poured three cups of tea and sat down while Mack passed the biscuits around.

'Thanks, Jessie—please come and join us. I'd like your input too if you don't mind.'

Mack couldn't help noticing how thin Joe had become since moving back to Wellington. He had always been a tall, lean man but this time he looked scrawny. Even his fingers appeared to be white, raw-boned twigs.

'Gee whiz, Joe. What've they been feeding you in Wellington? You could do with a good feed.'

'Yeah, well … all this drama with my wife isn't exactly conducive to healthy living.'

Mack flashed a glance at Jessie and began kneading his neck muscles. 'I thought she may have settled down by now as we have seen she has made major changes.'

'You can say that again! You mean by changing husbands. She has hardly let the grass grow under her feet, that's for sure.'

Mack thought he would make sure they were both on the same page before he made any comment.

'Do you mind explaining why you are here? I mean … what has upset you so much … have you been to see Meg?'

Mack made sure he wasn't going to be the one to drop the bombshell. It would come from Meg. She could at least have the integrity to tell him herself.

'I've just passed through the town and stopped to buy Meg a small box of those *Roses* chocolates she likes from the General Store. As I walked towards my car, I saw a man and a woman in tennis clothes drinking milkshakes. I almost dropped the chocolates when I thought I recognised the woman from behind and then I heard a familiar giggle. It was Meg, and she appeared to be flirting with this fellow. I ducked behind my vehicle until they were further along the road and watched them cross to the other side and get into the car. I saw the vehicle veer off and turn down the road towards the lake.'

Joe's eyes began to mist over. He squeezed his eyes shut a few times as if to blink back the tears then he wiped his face with the back of his hand.

Mack tried to quell the anger rising within him and whispered to Joe. 'What did you do then?'

'I confess I just couldn't help myself as I had to get at the truth. There was an empty carpark in the church where I could wait unseen. It was a place to hide until they had reached the lake in their vehicle then I walked towards the lake.'

This is beginning to sound like a thriller, Mack thought, while Jessie remained quiet, allowing Joe to offload on his brother-in-law.

Joe gulped down the last of his tea. He coughed as though he was choking. 'Sorry—went down the wrong way.' He cleared his throat. 'I probably could have done with something stronger if I wasn't driving.'

'Sorry, Joe, but we don't have anything in the house.'

He continued. 'I couldn't believe my eyes. When I approached their park bench next to the lake, the two appeared to be real palsy-walsy from where I was standing behind the large oak tree.'

For the first time, Jessie spoke up. 'They weren't kissing though, were they?'

'No, not kissing. They were eating sandwiches together. Their obvious fraternising is enough for me to know it's time to quit.'

Jessie asserted herself, 'I think they're just good friends and companionship fills a need for them both right now. I'm sure that's as far as it goes.'

'How do you know that and how long has it been going on?' Joe's face reddened as the heat of his anger ensued.

Mack began to sense Joe's exasperation. Was he deflecting blame for his wife's indiscretion onto him for not disclosing her secret life? Even though she'd not been covert about her relationship with the doctor in Glenorchy, she'd kept it from Joe. Perhaps he should have made more of an effort to return to his wife. Mack began to see it was time to challenge Joe about his own behaviour.

'Listen, Joe. I understand you're angry and disappointed with Meg but hear me out as there are always two sides to a story.'

'You mean three sides! Fair enough.' Joe slumped forward on his chair and leaned on his knees, half glaring at Mack, looking down at his feet. His mouth curved downwards as his forehead puckered.

Mack spoke with an air of authority. 'I've spent much time with Meg analysing where she is at with your marriage. It's really not our business, but she has involved Jessie and me on several occasions making it clear she does love you and seeks the restoration of your marriage. After numerous rebuffs when she urged you to return, she just gave up.'

Joe lifted his head and sat upright eyeballing Mack.

'What are you trying to say—that she doesn't want me back now?' He sat there with eyes wide, licking his bottom lip.

'No, I'm not saying that at all. She had turned her life around in many ways, but when you refused to return to her, temptation set in. The doctor is a lonely widower and Meg is all alone on that large estate by herself, apart from the caretaker, Charlie who keeps to himself. If you work on it right now, you may be in time to save your marriage—though I'm not sure—you'll have to do some convincing and hear her out.'

'I ... I'm not sure what to think. She didn't waste any time finding a replacement. I might need to go away and think about it, but thanks for letting me know. I'll get off now and look for some accommodation.' He picked up his car keys and rattled them.

'Thanks for the tea, Jessie.'

As he walked to the door, Mack jumped up quickly. 'Wait! Why don't you stay for a while—have some dinner with us later? You haven't given me a chance to tell you about Meg's pony camp. It's doing really well and a great asset to the community.'

'Oh yeah—sounds like another of her impulsive schemes.'

Mack cringed at the sound of bitterness in his brother-in-law's voice. This was so unlike Joe to be full of resentment. He could sense the deep hurt in the man's heart.

'You need to go look for yourself. The last camp is this weekend as she closes it down for the winter to rest the ponies and the ground. Perhaps you can participate and see how rewarding it is to work with some of the children who have disabilities—she seems to have a way with them. After the weekend, she'll be free if you can spare the time to have some recreation together.'

'Thanks, Mack. It's not as simple as all that now, is it? Especially with this doctor friend of hers hanging around. I'll go find a room for the night at the hotel and sleep on it. I'll phone you in the morning and let you know where I am and what I decide to do.'

As Joe left the house abruptly and drove off, Mack realised he was embarrassed about his situation and pride had risen its ugly head.

Jessie stood next to Mack, taking hold of his hand as if she knew the anguish churning deep inside him.

'We've got to do something,' said Mack. 'We can't sit back and let their marriage go down the drain.'

***

Doctor Joshua Douglas followed Meg out onto the patio with a mug of coffee in his hand. Meg's face brimmed with delight, lapping up his attention. She'd provided him with a light meal and now they relaxed in the sun, soaking up the last days of autumn before the icy southern winter set in.

'That was a good game we had today. I don't suppose we'll get much tennis in during the winter,' said Joshua. 'The

524

grass court is abysmal. I hope the council will build asphalt courts as they have in Queenstown.'

'I wouldn't worry, as the school has a good asphalt basketball court with a net and I heard we can play there. It's only open to local residents.'

'Anyway—I've got something more important on my mind.'

'Oh dear—that sounds ominous.'

'I hope not.' He took her hand as his brown eyes gleamed when his gaze met hers.

Meg began to giggle then stopped. It was obvious Joshua was serious.

'Meg, I've been falling for you in a big way and I'm hoping you'd agree to take our friendship to the next level. I've been waiting for the right moment to ask you ... so I guess it's now. I've only just found the nerve.' He raised his brows, keeping his eyes fixed on her face.

Meg almost dropped her cup. Her mouth fell open as she pulled her hand from his grip.

'I ... sorry, Joshua ... you've taken me completely by surprise. I thought we were just tennis buddies and good friends. I mean ... we haven't really been dating or anything.'

'Oh, no, I hope I haven't scared you off—I've been falling in love with you and I thought I'd made it obvious.'

The phone started ringing just as he pulled her towards him and planted his full lips on hers. She pulled back suddenly.

'Look—this is all happening a bit too fast for me. I'm not even divorced, and I don't want to be, either.'

The phone rang again then stopped.

Joshua started biting his lip then wiped his brow.

'I'm so sorry ... I seem to have been reading too much into our friendship. Do I have a chance ... or have you made your mind up?'

The phone continued to ring. Meg stood up. 'Excuse me. I'll have to take that. I'm running my last camp this weekend, and that may be a cancellation. I'll have to get on.'

She bustled into the office, but the phone stopped again before she could pick up the receiver.

'Jolly thing. It was probably one of the children cancelling,' she muttered as she hurried back to the patio.

'I'm sorry, Joshua—I have to get ready for pony camp tomorrow and check my bookings. Can I call you tomorrow evening?'

'That's fine. I thought we could have a pleasant, relaxing evening together tonight, but I'll catch up with you then.'

Joshua grabbed his jacket and drove off, putting his foot on the pedal harder than usual, not thinking that children from nearby farms could be riding down the road. Meg stood in the carpark shaking her head as he disappeared onto the highway.

Back in her lounge a short time later, she reached up to draw the curtains when the sound of a vehicle hurtling down the driveway startled her. Had Joshua left something behind? When she took another look she could see it was Walter's truck. What would he be doing calling on her at this time of the day? Her stomach churned as she walked towards the door.

***

After knocking on the door, Walter yanked off his boots and slammed each one against the ornate porch railing to loosen the dirt. Meg held the front door open.

'Sorry, lassie, I'm coming.'

'Why are you removing the mud from your boots when you have to walk back to the carpark in them?'

Walter flashed her a wry smile exposing the fact that he'd recently lost a tooth. He didn't tell her he'd packed an overnight bag and left it in the truck.

'I'll put the kettle on, Grandad. You're staying for dinner, aren't you? There's a steak and kidney pie in the fridge I removed from the freezer yesterday.'

Walter planted himself down in the lounge on one of Meg's wicker, bucket chairs. 'Sure will, thanks. I never turn down an offer like that. You know I'm partial to steak and kidney. It reminds me of your grandmother. She used to bake one for me once a week.'

'Mine is a bit different from the usual pies. I use fresh thyme for extra flavour.'

'I'll give anything a try, my dear. But that's not what I'm here for—although I'm always a starter for home cooking. I'll get down to the brass tacks.'

Meg joined him with the tea and began pouring it.

'Oh—that sounds serious.' Her hand shook as she passed him a mug of tea before she sat down.

'What brings you here, Grandad? Is everything alright with you?'

'Nothing the matter with me, but there's a fair bit of drama going on in your life right now.'

Meg placed her cup back on the table and wrinkled up her nose. 'What do you mean?'

'Did you know that Joe is in town? He has been out to Reed Station in a right state telling Mack and Jessie his troubles. In fact, Mack was going to phone and warn you.'

Walter washed back his tea with noisy gulps and sat back in the chair crossing his legs, glaring at Meg with clasped hands.

'Sorry, Grandad—I don't understand—what's this all about? I haven't heard from Joe—at least not recently. The phone rang a few times earlier, but I couldn't get to it in time.'

'He came to Glenorchy to surprise you yesterday, but as he drove through town, he saw you fraternising with that

527

doctor you are friendly with. He was watching you by the lake.'

'I had no idea he would turn up unexpectedly. I wasn't doing anything wrong. Why didn't he approach me instead of spying?'

'He could see you were pretty chummy and jumped to conclusions. I was in the kitchen when he arrived to see Mack and overheard the whole conversation. He offloaded a heap of angst onto Mack as he thought you were having an affair.'

'Oh, poor Joe. Where is he now—is he still at the station?'

'No, he's staying in town somewhere. If you phone Mack, Joe said he would let him know where he is staying.'

'When is he going back to Wellington? He's come such a long way.' Meg stood up and paced the floor, trying to decide a plan of action.

'He flew into Queenstown and has a rental car. After seeing you at the lake, he wanted to return in the morning, but Mack convinced him to stay and give you a chance, although he's reluctant to do so. You'll have to find out where he's staying if you want to chase after him.'

Before Walter finished the sentence, Meg rushed off to her office to phone Mack. She spoke for five minutes then returned to the lounge with arms hanging limp at her sides, her eyes glazed and staring downwards.

'Mack hasn't heard from Joe yet but he expects him to call.'

'Well, we'll just have to have a good chat and wait for Mack to let you know when he hears something. How about some of that homemade pie you promised me.'

'Don't you want to get back home before dark? I'll sit here and wait for Mack's call after we've had our meal.'

Walter gave a lopsided grin. 'I hope you don't mind, lass, but I plan to stay the night if you can give me one of your guest rooms. My kit is in the truck, and I think we're in for a long talk later.'

'Oh, really? That's no problem. I'll show you to your room before dinner if you want to grab your kit out of the truck. I'll heat up the pie while you do that.'

Walter trundled back inside with his overnight bag and dumped it in the room Meg had prepared for him. She rolled back the goose-down duvet and plumped up the pillows.

'There's a wall heater on a thermostat and I've turned it on to low. The bathroom is opposite.'

'Don't fuss over me girl. Let's get this meal—I'm looking forward to it. How about some of that apple cider you keep in your fridge?'

After the meal, they retired to the lounge where Meg lit the fire.

'I think we'll need a fire from now on. That southerly wind is freezing at night although it has been lovely and sunny this week.'

Walter leaned forward in his chair pushing the palms of his hands towards the fire for a few minutes then sat back, resting his arms on his knees.

'Do you remember when I told you that I had inherited Reed Station?'

Meg sat down and stretched her legs to warm her feet.

'Yes, I do, although you didn't elaborate and told me that it was a tough life and my grandmother Hazel found it hard. That's all I can remember you telling me.'

Meg sagged as she continued to listen.

'You seem to have this fantasy that the high country life is glamorous and idyllic but you're deceiving yourself. You haven't trudged across ground when it has rained for weeks and every step you take sinks deep into the mud— when it's so cold that your eyebrows freeze over, and worst of all, seeing your prize newborn lambs or calves—

sometimes hundreds of them frozen into blocks of ice from heavy snowfalls in spring. Oh yes—and waking in the night to the piercing bellow of a prize bull lying on its back in a creek.'

Walter pulled out a handkerchief to catch a drip at the end of his nose before continuing.

'Reed Station, which was in the Reed Family Trust, was owned by my father's uncle, a bachelor who passed it on to my brother Jack, the eldest son in our family. My own parents had owned a smallholding of land in Dunedin which they used for market gardening and Dad was killed in a tractor accident. Mum died several years later in the flu epidemic.'

'When did you meet Grandma?' Meg asked with a brittle voice.

'Before I took over Reed Station, I worked as a farm labourer in Tekapo, the McKenzie country, and there I met your grandmother while joining a sheep muster on her folks' farm. We fell in love and a year later married in the Church of the Good Shepherd on the edge of Lake Tekapo.'

The light from the flames danced on his face, illuminating deep furrows in his brow as he gazed into the fire.

'Your grandmother and I lived and worked on her parents' farm until they went bankrupt as a result of a major drought. They were able to keep their house and a small block of land which they turned into crops.'

'So how did you come to own Reed Station?' By now, Meg's face appeared animated.

'I inherited it when my Uncle died. It was offered to Jack first and just as your own father had no interest in farming, nor did he and so it was handed to me by default.'

'Time for a cup of tea yet, Grandad?' Meg sat on the edge of her seat as if she was ready to dart off.

'No, wait! There's more and I want you to listen hard, Meg. You may find what I have to say life-changing!'

Meg sat back, her eyes not leaving Walter's face.

He cleared his throat then continued as the firelight exposed his frozen tears.

'The land on Reed Station was rugged, unbroken high country in those days. The roads were almost non-existent, and we travelled on the TSS Earnslaw steamship if we wanted to go to Queenstown to pick up supplies—as and when it stopped at the wharf in Glenorchy. Hazel became pregnant with your father after two miscarriages and went to stay with her parents in their humble home in Tekapo. While she remained there to have the baby, I got myself established on the station. Hazel joined me when Len was a few months old, but the remote and harsh lifestyle eventually affected her health. Life in the high country was too tough for her, and I can now put it down to my own selfish ambition and short-sightedness that I missed seeing how this was affecting her. Then against Hazel's wishes, when he was only seven I sent your father to boarding school. This embittered him so much that when he finished his schooling he wanted nothing to do with the station or me. We had arguments galore as to why he did not want to take it over which eventually made me lose my cool and throw him out. This broke Hazel's heart as she had already suffered so much—first her babies then Len and later her health. Most of all, your father was the love of her life and she never really forgave me for telling him to leave.'

When Walter finished speaking, he hung his head low and the tone in his voice matched his demeanour—flat and hollow. He sat propped up on his elbows with his head in his hands.

Meg's eyes welled up as she dived into her jacket pocket, fumbled then came out with an embroidered handkerchief to wipe her eyes.

'I'm really sorry to hear all this, Grandad. It's so sad—but you mustn't blame yourself for Grandma's death. You didn't cause her pneumonia.'

Walter lifted his head pulling a large, tartan handkerchief from his jacket pocket. He blew his nose like a foghorn then continued—this time his voice kept breaking up.

'I broke Hazel's heart even though I loved her so much—but I was hard and selfish and all I could think about was building a successful station.'

'Oh, please don't upset yourself, Grandad. That's all in the past and your relationship with Dad and the family is mended now.'

Walter looked Meg in the eye.

'Don't you know why I'm telling you this, my girl? I can see you going down the same track with Joe. From what I hear, he has been suffering as a result of your grandiose plans.'

Meg's face dropped. Her nose began to twitch as she sat back in her chair, wrenching her hands and rolling her wedding ring.

'What do you mean by suffering? He'd agreed to come to Glenorchy—I thought he liked the idea of being in the country.'

Walter frowned and set his jaw.

'You couldn't see past your own nose, to be honest, Meg. You were so focused on your own ambitions that you hadn't considered where Joe would fit into your devices and plans. He thinks you have lost interest in him and that he doesn't count anymore, just as I had made Hazel feel. Don't make the same mistake as I did, or you'll live to regret it.'

Meg's face paled. She hesitated before saying anything.

'Oh, Grandad—I didn't know I'd hurt Joe. I just thought he would rather be back in the city working as a corporate businessman than live here with me.'

'No, Meg. You drove him away and could have made him sick. If you want to avoid a life of deep regret, you need to go after him and make amends any way you can before it's too late.'

Meg stood up and walked over to the frail-looking man who had come to save her marriage. She threw herself at him, wrapping her arms around his neck.

He took her hand. 'Luckily for you, your father is the person Hazel and I made—despite my treatment of him he rose to the occasion and became a success for himself—but the guilt I've been carrying has coloured my life all this time. It's only since Mack eased himself into it that things have changed for the better, and now I have to pinch myself on occasions to believe just how wonderful my life has become.'

'I'll go and see Joe, honest Grandad and I'll try to put things right with him. Please pray that he'll forgive me.'

'It's time to sort your own life out. I've been praying for you both all this time, just as I do for the rest of the family. Now it's your turn to do something.'

'I promise you things will be different—if only I can track him down tomorrow.'

'Mack is going to phone you early in the morning after Joe has called him to say where he is staying.'

Meg rubbed her lined eyes while her translucent, porcelain cheeks screamed out for sleep.

'Hope you don't mind—I'd like to have an early night. Will you be okay? Spare blankets are in the wardrobe. I'll make you breakfast before you leave.'

'I'll be fine and don't worry about breakfast. I'll have it back at the station.'

'Thanks again, Grandad. Night-night.' She bent over and kissed his cheek, leaving him to ponder the glowing embers of a dying fire.

***

The rooster crowed earlier than usual, long before the rest of the household had risen. Bessie got up early and off out the door. It was her weekend off and this time her friends in Arrowtown had invited her to stay.

Jessie was already busy feeding the babies who'd wakened early. Mack stumbled out of bed, wandering into the nursery tripping over toys underfoot that they'd forgotten to pick up the night before.

'You're already up feeding?' Mack took Oliver from her and placed him over his shoulder. She took Will from his cot and started feeding him.

'That jolly rooster started up early making a terrible racket. He hasn't done that for ages. Didn't you hear him?'

'No—I only heard the shower when Bessie got ready to go out.'

Jessie propped Will over her knee and patted his back gently.

'She's off to Arrowtown to stay with her friend and won't be back until Sunday evening.'

Jessie looked at Mack with a compassionate gaze. 'How are you feeling this morning after such a hard time with Joe? What do you think will happen?'

'I'm feeling a bit rough. We need to wait a bit as he said he would phone and let me know what he decides this morning.'

'Perhaps you'd best get dressed, love. You may need to pay Meg a visit if Joe takes off back to Wellington and gives up on her. She'll probably spit out her dummy when she finds out.'

'Let's not think the worst. Wait for him to call.'

Mack sat at the breakfast table a short time later poking at his scrambled eggs with his fork and leaning the side of his head on one hand.

Jessie had concern for her husband who was so generous-hearted towards others. 'Coffee? It's freshly made.'

Mack lifted his head and forced a smile. 'Thanks. It's a pity all this is happening when Grandad seems to be so happy these days enjoying the twins and life in general after a difficult life.'

He reached for the strawberry jam and scooped a large dollop with a spoon dropping it on his toast. He had no sooner finished speaking when the phone rang.

'I'll get it,' said Jessie, licking her fingers and wiping them on the sides of her trousers. She hurried to pick up the phone and returned waving at Mack to come.

'Quick, it's Joe. He just asked for you and he sounds distressed.'

'Okay, tell him I'll be there.'

Mack raced into the office and picked up the phone. He kept quiet and just kept nodding his head while Jessie stood watching. From what she heard, Joe seemed to be offloading a lot more on poor Mack who finally spoke up. 'I think you're making a huge mistake if you leave now without seeing Meg and what she has achieved at Willow Park. As I said last night—I know she loves you and doesn't want to lose you.'

'Well, she didn't give me much indication of that before I left. I'm feeling too disappointed with her.'

'I think you need to search your own heart and find it in you to forgive her and then pay her a visit.'

Mack clenched his teeth and shook his head while Jessie stood in the doorway waiting for the verdict. A few minutes silence on Joe's part then he hung up.

'It's no good, Jessie—he says he's going back to Wellington today.'

'Where is he staying—has he checked out yet? Maybe it's not too late to go and talk to him again.'

'He's staying at the Glenorchy Hotel. Says he's checking out at twelve. I'm sure he's still trying to decide what to do as he probably doesn't want to lose Meg. I'm going to phone and encourage her to go to the hotel and convince Joe to stay. The ball is in her court now.'

While Mack went back to the office to ring Meg, Jessie sat in the lounge slumped in a chair, quietly praying. She heard a vehicle door closing and Bluey making the kind of racket he usually did when one of the family arrived home. It was Walter, just in time for breakfast.

Mack came off the phone passing Jessie in the kitchen as she cracked fresh eggs into the frying pan while Walter walked through the door looking the worse for wear.

'Great, Grandad—just in time for a good breakfast and then we can catch up about Meg after that. We're waiting for Joe to phone and tell me what he decides.'

'Thanks, Mack. It has certainly been a mammoth task talking sense into her, but I'm convinced she's going to ditch her doctor friend and reconcile with Joe. Let's talk after I've had time to eat and clean up. Morning Prayer first.'

Chapter Eighteen

Meg hurried into the room where her grandfather spent the night and stripped the bed. Today there was an older group arriving mid-morning and because of her predicament, Sara, her horse coach would have to manage along with the team leader.

She stood in front of the mirror tiding her hair and opened her makeup bag. Since she'd lived at Willow Park and had become involved with the horses, she hadn't bothered much with her appearance unless she accompanied Joshua on an outing. Even then, it wasn't for him but just to make her feel as though she wasn't a complete frump. The red lipstick she applied to her lips lifted her sallow complexion as she gazed into the mirror. 'That looks better,' she muttered.

A light tap on the door brought her back to reality.

Her coach stood at the front door. 'Are you there, Meg?'

'When should we bring the horses down for the first session?'

'Oh, hi, Sara—I won't be starting the class until one o'clock. Before lunch I want you and the volunteers to take the children through grooming and tacking. A few of the horses appeared to have muddy coats when I saw them yesterday. They may need washing with warm water. Use a bucket, not the hose. It's too cold at this time of year—but you know all that, sorry, Sara—I'm trying to tell Grandma how to suck eggs.' They both burst into laughter.

'I'm sorry—I have to run an urgent errand in town. I'll see you back here by one and if not, you know the drill—you're in charge.'

Meg picked up her handbag, took one more look at herself in the mirror, straightened the collar of her shirt-blouse and shot out the door. As she stepped into her car, the heel of her shoe slid on something squishy. It was horse poo. *This is the last straw—what more could go wrong today?* She crumpled forward on the steering wheel and let out a loud wail. At last, she could release her pent-up tension from the previous twenty-four hours, but in case one of the staff could see her, she held back her sobs and started the engine. Once she was on the main road, she pulled over and cleaned her shoe with an old rag. Pulling the rear vision mirror closer, she examined her wet cheeks, dabbing them with the handkerchief she had pulled from her handbag.

While driving to the Glenorchy Hotel, she rehearsed all that she would say to Joe. Will he be receptive, or would he tell her to stay away and leave him alone?

The carpark at the hotel was almost full. Not far from the vehicles was the hotel Reception with a small cobblestone courtyard out front.

As Meg walked through the entranceway, she spotted cigarette butts strewn along the sides of the footpath. She crossed the courtyard, entering the main door of the reception area and gagged. The stale stench of beer and cigarette smoke made her retch.

'Sorry about that mess outside. I could see you screwing up your face at the filthy butts. The smell comes inside here too. I'll have to find someone to go out and sweep up, as I'm too busy here at Reception. They are the tourists who have the campervans down by the lake. They come here and drink then sit outside and smoke. They never adhere to the signage that tells them to smoke out back in the designated area. How can I help you? Sorry—we have no vacancies, and Saturday is our busiest day so you need to book in advance. We're the only hotel between here and Queenstown.'

The buxom woman with inappropriate attire didn't give Meg a chance to speak and had made assumptions.

'I'm not looking for a room—I'm meeting one of your guests here.'

The woman moved her spectacles from where they perched on top of her head to her eyes. 'Oh, silly me—I should have asked first. What's your guest's name?'

'Joe Wilds is his name. He stayed last night.'

'Ah yes ... Mr Wilds has made an arrangement to check out late... midday in fact.'

'That's right. Is he in his room?'

The woman phoned and spoke to Joe. She placed the receiver back on the hook and pointed along the corridor.

'Room nine, next to the lift.'

Meg trudged along the length of the corridor. The old-fashioned paisley wallpaper caught her attention as she glanced at the room numbers, but Room Nine was not near Reception as expected. The numbers went from the opposite direction and Joe's room was towards the end of the long corridor.

As she reached the door, she stood transfixed, gaping at the doorknob. She'd already forgotten how she would greet him when he opened the door. The butterflies in her stomach caused her muscles to tighten as her knuckles of one hand tapped three times on the door. She held her breath.

The door swung open causing her to stumble backwards, losing her balance in her high-heeled shoes. A crimson flush swam up her neck to her face.

'Oh—hi Joe! Do you mind if I come in?'

'I suppose you can—you're here now,' he snapped.

The door went to close automatically before Joe held it back for her. 'Have a seat over there. They aren't that comfortable, but it's all I have.'

Meg gave him a sideways glance as she brushed past him. His face appeared drawn with dark rings around his dachshund eyes. She plopped herself into the chair and directed her gaze out the window towards the sky.

'Would you like anything to drink? There's not much here except packets of tea and coffee. Nothing cold, sorry.'

As Meg turned her eyes met his. 'Tea will be fine, thanks.'

Joe stood at the tiny alcove in the bedroom suite and turned the kettle on. 'So—what brings you here all of a sudden? I'm checking out today. Did Mack ask you to come? You know he rang me?'

'I came of my own volition, but he did tell me you were leaving today. He said you saw me at the lake with my friend Joseph and jumped to conclusions.'

Joe bristled. Meg could see his face in the wardrobe mirror. It had turned tomato red. He cleared his throat. Meg startled as he slammed the metal teapot on the tray before he filled it.

'Yes, I did see you with your fancy man. I'm not hanging around here to play second fiddle to anyone. I'm leaving in a few hours.'

He carried the tray to the desk near Meg and poured her tea, trying to remain as civil as possible.

Meg stood up. 'Please, Joe. Hear me out. You've got it all wrong. I haven't been unfaithful to you at all.'

Joe left his cup of tea sitting on the tray next to Meg's and sat on the bed, as there was only one chair in the room. Meg walked over and sat next to him. She turned to him and took his hand which he pulled away.

'Joe, I love you. You are the one who walked away and went back to Wellington—all because I'd been overzealous with my business plans. I've been so lonely and have been waiting for you to return.'

'So what's with this doctor fella? You seemed pretty chummy when I saw you.'

'He's a lonely widower and has offered me companionship, nothing else ... that is ... until yesterday.'

'What do you mean? What have you done?' He glared at her, keeping his eyes fixed on her face.

'Quite unexpectedly, he asked for a commitment—says he loves me. I made it clear I'm a married woman and do not want a divorce. We haven't even dated yet and I'm not in love with him, Joe. He's got the wrong idea, honest he has.' Meg's voice quivered. She tried to hold back the tears that formed pools in her eyes as she scratched around in her bag for her handkerchief, but Joe thrust his own one into her hand.

'It's clean—carry on—I'm all ears,' he said, his own voice beginning to crackle.

'I've never wanted anyone else but you. Please come home and see what I've been doing with the pony camp. It's a proper business—one that the whole town admires. It has helped a lot of families. Just come and give it a chance ... give me a chance.'

Joe picked up his cup and gulped down the last of his tea while Meg let her cup go cold. He took a long look at her face.

'Come here.' He wrapped his octopus arms around her, squeezing her tight.

Meg kissed him tenderly. 'You know ... it's all I've been hoping for ... that you would do this. I'm so sorry for the pain I've caused you, Joe. I just wanted to be successful, just as you and Dad were with the export company. Even Grandad and Mack are running a thriving sheep and beef station. I wanted something for myself to feel I'd achieved something worthwhile in life.'

'I'm sorry too, for being so judgemental. I never meant to hurt you, but your property development scheme would have been a complete disaster.'

Meg took his hand. 'Can we start again, from scratch?'

Joe looked her in the eye. 'I guess it's time we started doing some work on our marriage.'

'Let's get back home. I need you to help with the children today. Would you mind?'

'I suppose that's okay—I'll give it a go, although my skills are more in the business line. My suitcase is packed and I'll book out at Reception now.'

Joe had a last look around the room in case he'd forgotten something and shut the door with Meg in tow following along the passageway.

'So, I'm going to be a horsey person now, am I? Just like the old days in Wellington when I helped you with your horses in the stables. Good thing I've got experience, eh?' He winked as Meg helped him carry some of his luggage out to Reception.

'I must phone Mack when we get in. They'll be wanting to celebrate and so will Grandad. Thank you for not giving up on me.'

'We have some work to do on our relationship yet. I'll see you at home.' He stepped into the vehicle and wound the window down.

'Right, madam—here we come, Willow Park.' He winked at her as he started the engine.

Meg leaned through the window and kissed his cheek. 'See you back there soon.'

'Looks like I'm going to be your new volunteer assistant at pony camp,' He revved up the engine before careering off down the road. Meg climbed into her car and took off in close pursuit.

Within minutes she arrived at Willow Park to see Joe standing next to his vehicle with his suitcase and extra luggage propped up against the car. A wide grin stretched across her face until she remembered there was a certain person she would have to phone, right away. Her smile faded quickly forcing the corners of her mouth downwards like a sad clown.

'If you're happy to have me back home, tell your face that,' remarked Joe, in a teasing tone.

'It's not you, Joe. I'm ecstatic you're home. I have some unfinished business to deal with and it's making my stomach churn.'

'You mean about telling your doctor friend your change in circumstances. That shouldn't be too hard—just tell him the truth.'

'I'll give him a call later.'

They both carried Joe's luggage up the path to the house.

The staff had the horses lined up in their outside stalls ready for the one o'clock riding session. Sara and her assistant stood encircled by the group of riders.

Meg went inside the house with Joe to offload his luggage when he pulled her aside.

'Leave my luggage—just dump it in the bedroom. I think we need to have a good talk before you go out there. We have a few things to straighten out first.'

Meg stood still. She appeared taken aback by his directness.

'Of course, love. Let's sit down in the living room and close the door. Sara knows the drill and doesn't need me out there all the time.' Joe followed her into the lounge which was out of bounds to the guests and sat opposite Meg. He asserted himself before she had the chance to jump in first.

'I came back because I love you—but I need you to know how much you hurt me by your self-centred behaviour. You didn't once consider my needs or respect me when I opposed your grand plans and designs nor did you allow me to have an opinion about our joint ventures—in fact, it seemed they were only your projects. I didn't figure in your plans, and I don't want that to happen again.'

Meg's face turned pink. She took off her jacket and rubbed the back of her neck. Before she could open her mouth to reply, Joe jumped in, no holds barred.

'All the time you were plotting and planning, I tried to have some input, but you shut me down every time making me feel useless—disempowered. That's why I took off. I thought I had no value in your life, but I never stopped loving you. I started praying that you would have a change of heart.'

Meg's eyes glazed over. She stared at the ground, shell-shocked.

Joe continued. 'Then when I saw you fraternising with your doctor friend, it finished me—I couldn't take any more. Before you came to see me at the hotel, I thought our marriage was at an end and was ready to pack it in and head back to Wellington for good.'

Meg lifted her head and looked at him. Her eyes swam with tears as she stood up and approached him, her voice croaking as she answered.

'Please forgive me, Joe. I had no idea of the effect all this had on you and how insensitive I've been. Frankly, the way you describe it makes me sound like a selfish prat—but I'm not the same person now. God has removed my obsession to be famous or successful. I just want to help others and make a difference in people's lives.'

Joe reached out his hand and drew her close to him.

'Come and sit with me—please. I'm not trying to shame you, Meg. It's just vital that you know how it impacted me and that I can't live like that anymore—but I believe you and I can see it's unlikely you'll put me through that again. So here I am—boring stuffed shirt and all.' He enveloped her tightly.

'I hope you can bring yourself to forgive me properly, one day. I know you'll be testing the waters, Joe. But we both want this marriage to work. Let's start over again.' She kissed him on the cheek. 'We can work at it, one day at a time.'

'Don't you have a field full of children waiting for you to show up with this man of yours?'

'Oh, don't worry. I told the staff you've been working on a contract in Wellington. Now I can tell them your contract there is finished, and you'll now be part of the business—I mean our business. This is our pony camp.'

'You'd best go and get changed. The afternoon session will be over before you get started. I'll wait outside.'

Joe wandered out to the patio and sat down in the sun stretching his legs as he scanned his estate. The furrows in his brow had gone and the muscles in his jaw softened.

Within a short time, Meg appeared in beige Jodhpurs and black jacket, looking professional.

'Mmm, you look quite the part. Come on, I'll be right behind you.'

Meg wandered over to speak to Sara, her coach.

'Hi Sara, this is my husband, Joe. He'll be running pony camp with me in future.'

Joe shook Sara's hand. 'We're glad of the help today. I hear you're good with horses but don't ride— is that right?'

'Yes, I'd rather keep my feet on the ground, but I don't mind handling them. I've had plenty of experience doing that with Meg's horses in Wellington at the stables.'

'Excuse me interrupting, Sara—how are you going—are they all here?' Meg picked up Sara's clipboard with the list of children that had registered and glanced down the list.

'No, Bonny was on the list, but her mother rang to cancel as she has a cold. You'll probably get a call from her tonight. Apparently, Mack invited her to spend a day on their station, and she hopes to bring her out one weekend.'

'That's right. I'll pass the message on to Mack—we'd better get started. Are the cavaletti poles set up in the arena? I want the new riders to work on those first.'

Sara looked around to see the volunteers returning from setting up the course. 'Yes, they've just finished.'

Meg approached the staff. 'Now some of you haven't met my husband, Joe. He'll be with us for the rest of this camp, now that his contract has finished in Wellington.'

Sara flashed a glance at her sidekick, Petra, her team leader who covered her mouth to hide a grin.

Meg's neck flushed. She'd always been a private person but the fact that she'd been on her own for several months meant that Joe's sudden homecoming created a trickle of sensation amongst the staff.

Joe lifted his Stetson and bowed his head. Sara stepped in and gave the staff new instructions while Joe looked relieved as they followed the coach back into the arena.

At this final camp, there were no children with special needs so the guestrooms were empty, and Joe and Meg had the whole lodge to themselves. Occasionally a few of the younger children were afraid to sleep in the outside bunkrooms and requested to sleep inside. This weekend the camp consisted of older children who all slept in the outside accommodation in the custom-built arena bunkhouse. A few of them still enjoyed dossing down directly on the hay bales in sleeping bags.

Meg tugged on Joe's sleeve. 'Would you like to watch our first afternoon session once it's underway? Later you might like to help me put the covers on the horses for the night. We let them graze in the paddock closest to the stables and catch them again in the morning. It's too much to expect the volunteers to do it all so I always give them a hand.'

Meg's agenda was by no means hidden. She was intent on getting Joe involved with her new venture as fast as possible. That, she considered, was a sure way of ensuring he was there to stay.

Although she still commandeered, it was in a good way. Organising people was her greatest strength—that her husband well knew.

Joe draped his torso over a fence rail watching the group preparing for the afternoon session. Meg scurried down the path and stood next to him.

'Show me the way,' said Joe. 'I can remember some of the things I did to help you in Wellington when you had your horses in the stables. I might need to brush up on a few things—I'm sure you'll put me right.' He chuckled as they wandered down to the outside arena.

'Ah—yuk!' Joe's boot skidded in a pile of horse dung. 'That part of it I forgot about.'

Meg grinned warmly as he scraped his boot along the grass to clean it. Her eyes searched along the fence line. 'There's a poo bucket around here somewhere. The volunteers usually go along and scoop it up. Ah—there it is—I'll just clear it away while you join the group by the arena. If you wait over there by the gate, I'll meet up with you in a minute.'

Joe walked over and picked up the scoop. 'Please let me.'

He happily scooped up the dung and dumped it in the bucket with a small shovel while Meg looked on in her element. It looked like Joe was there to stay, and judging by his cheerful demeanour, he approved of her enterprise. As soon as they arrived at the arena, he set about helping one of the riders tighten her horse's girth.

Sara raced up to him. 'Hi, there, Joe. Meg has told me so much about you. It must have been a nuisance having to travel backwards and forwards to Wellington for your work.'

Meg arrived just in time to rescue Joe from Sara who'd put him on the spot and spun an elaborate story about Joe having to work away from home. It was the truth, but not the whole truth, and it wouldn't do any harm keeping that part quiet, Meg convinced herself.

Before Joe answered, Meg intervened. 'Joe, would you mind helping me set up the cross-rails for the jumping exercise? Sara is busy organising the riders.'

'Sure, no problem.' He willingly followed her to the other side of the arena. 'I'll bet you weren't prepared for us to throw you in the deep end,' said Meg with a wry smile.

They set up two low jumps with cross-rails.

'This is for the more experienced riders,' said Meg. 'We don't do anything too advanced. They can do that at their pony clubs. It's mainly to give them a bit of the country life for those who live in town and during the week I let local riders use the arena. They often set up a few jumps themselves.'

When they had finished, Joe took hold of Meg's arm.

'Are you going to be busy for the rest of the day? I hoped we could get some time together to talk about where we go from here.'

Meg took his hand and clasped it. His eyes met hers.

'I want that too, Joe. I'm sorry, but I have to supervise for the rest of the afternoon. The coach manages the children but I'm ultimately responsible for health and safety and need to be here—especially when they are jumping. The rest are just unqualified volunteers apart from the paid staff members, Sara and Petra.'

Joe looked awkward. 'Oh, I see—of course, you do.'

'Let's go over to the arena.'

When they arrived, Sara had begun giving her staff instructions as the program commenced, while Meg and Joe chatted at the sideline.

Meg said quietly, 'Let's go up and sit on the patio. We can watch them from there. They are in Sara's capable hands for now. As long as the crew know where I am. I'll just let her know.'

After talking to Sara, Meg hurried up to the house and brought out a jug of fresh lemonade and two glasses and placed them on the patio table.

'Good thing the arena is close by—I can see everything from here and they know where I am.'

'Thanks, Meg. I appreciate you giving up your time today— especially when you had no idea I would make a surprise appearance.'

He lounged back in the garden chair, stretching his arms out at his sides yawning, enjoying the sun.

Meg tousled his hair as she passed him. 'This is freshly squeezed lemonade with mint.'

They sat drinking their iced beverages watching the riders tackle their program. Joe's face adopted a serious look. Although the shadows around his eyes had lessened, the deep furrows in his brow were evident still.

'Meg—before I return to Wellington on Monday, I need to be certain you are fully committed to our marriage and won't change your mind again. I couldn't go through it again.'

Meg sat aghast. Her nose twitched the way it always did when she was nervous. She stood up and pulled her chair closer to him then held his hand, her stare penetrating his eyes.

'Oh, dear Joe. You have got me so wrong—to think that I would deliberately hurt or deceive you. Honestly—when you left for Wellington the first time, I was so worried you would never return. Since then I've discovered that it was my selfish ambition and self-centeredness that drove you away.'

Joe didn't stir or refute her confession while he took it all in.

'I wanted to turn my life around and prove to you that I could change but didn't know how. Mack came up with this idea of running a pony camp and use my qualifications working with children—even those with disabilities who benefit from equine therapy too.'

Joe found his tongue. 'That's good. I knew deep down that you had it in you to make a difference, and I just couldn't understand why you seemed to sabotage everything we had set before us to live a good life. Now I can see that you have changed so maybe it's time I resigned from the company and put the house back on the market.'

The two sat observing the horses trotting around the arena, listening to Sara call out her commands while the late autumn sun poured onto the patio saturating them with warmth.

Meg peered at him pleadingly with eyes like midnight jasper. 'Would you mind helping tomorrow? We are short of a side walker to accompany the new riders, as we are one volunteer down. It'll keep you fit, running next to a trotting horse and we need to keep the children safe.'

'With pleasure—I won't feel so redundant. At last, we can do something together that unites us.'

A wide smile stretched across Joe's face. He was there to stay.

Chapter Nineteen

Meg lay in Joe's arms, stretched out long on their four-seater leather couch after a light meal of beef stew that the camp cook had prepared. It was Sunday evening. All the children had left Willow Park by four o'clock.

'I'm tired out,' said Meg. 'It's healthy fatigue though, with all that fresh air and exercise running next to trotting horses on a lead. We only do that if they are novices or disabled, to encourage them to trot.'

'I'm tired out too. You're fortunate to have an experienced coach such as Sara. I'm impressed with the setup you have here, Meg. It's all so professional—you've done well.'

'Thanks honey. Would you mind putting a few more logs on that fire while I make that dreaded phone call to you know who?'

'Oh, yes, your friend, Doctor Douglas. That's most important.' Joe winked. 'Don't worry. He's a big boy and can take it.' He lay back staring at the fire then remembered Meg had asked him to put some more logs on while she made the phone call.

A short time later, she walked back into a room that was glowing. They had turned out the lights except for an old lamp and Joe was mesmerised by the flames leaping at the glass door of the Kent fire. His previous animated countenance had left him.

Meg stood in front of the fire warming herself. 'Are you okay—you appear to be miles away? It's freezing in the kitchen tonight. Good thing this camp was the last one before winter arrives.'

Joe redirected his stare from gaping at the fire to Meg.

'How did it go—I'll bet he didn't let you off lightly?'

Meg stammered. 'Oh—he was more understanding than I thought. He said he had unrealistic expectations of me and shouldn't have asked for a commitment so soon, as I wasn't divorced. I told him I was at fault for encouraging him—even though, by that, I meant playing tennis and going on picnics. I said how it must have been a temptation for a lonely man, and I apologised to him. Ultimately, we were both walking on thin ice. He seemed indifferent as if he didn't really care. Perhaps he was guarding his heart. Anyway, he said he is ready to move on.'

'So am I,' mumbled Joe. He pulled her close to him. 'I can see how you've changed, Meg. You've become humble—not like the puffed-up woman I knew before I took off to Wellington. Tell me ... what made you change your mind ... was it, Mack?'

'It was initially, but we also have Grandad to thank for showing me the way. He paid me a visit to rescue our marriage.'

'Is that right—what did he say?'

'He came here the night you offloaded our problems onto Mack and Jessie. He'd heard your distress from the kitchen and took off out the back door and drove over here to see me. I put him up in one of the guest rooms and we stayed up half the night talking. He told me a story about the way he had neglected Grandma Hazel and how his selfish ambition and self-centeredness had sabotaged his own marriage. He even attributes her ill health and subsequent death to their harsh lifestyle living on Reed Station in the early days, before the land had been broken.'

'Oh, really? Poor Walter beating himself up like that. He shouldn't blame himself—I'm sure he couldn't have been that bad.'

'He was just so intent on building his farming empire that he neglected to see how hard it was for a young woman with a toddler. Life was too harsh for Grandma in those days. She suffered, but I don't believe he was to blame for her death. He has just perceived it that way.'

'What are you trying to tell me, Meg? Was Walter trying to draw a parallel to our lives?'

'He meant that I probably neglected to see the stress that I'd put you under while chasing my own dreams—pipedreams they were.'

Joe enveloped her with his arms.

'I think you and I should think about renewing our marriage vows when I get back from Wellington. How about it?'

Meg sat bolt upright, holding both his hands.

'Really, Joe? I'd love that. How long do you think you'll be in Wellington sorting things out?'

'I'm not sure. But if you don't have any pony camps until after winter, perhaps you can get on a plane and spend some time with me in our house while it is on the market. We won't have to be there the whole time until it sells—just long enough for me to wind up my partnership in the company and sell my shares to the partners.'

'Sure. I'd like that. I'll have to ask Mack if he can take care of the horses while I'm away—or perhaps I can pay Sara and a few of the local volunteers to do that. Charlie will keep an eye on the place, but he doesn't know much about caring for the horses.'

'Why don't you ask your folks if they'll come down from Nelson for a while? They may enjoy the break.'

'That's a possibility. They have already spoken about coming down before winter sets in. I'll call them after you go back.'

'A perfect plan. I'm looking forward to our new life together, Meg. Thanks to Walter and Mack.'

'That's for certain. They are two shepherds caring for their flock. We, the family are their flock.'

'Precisely—so why don't we call them the good shepherds—just like the name of that church in Tekapo, *The Church of the Good Shepherd*?'

'Yeah, I like that. The good shepherds—that's exactly what they are.'

***

Mack opened the letter that Bessie handed to him postmarked Wellington.

'Thanks, Bessie—I think it's from Meg and Joe. I'm dying to hear how they're getting on. They've only been away for a fortnight though.'

'Oh, let me know too.'

'I'd better read it out to Jessie first. Where is she?'

'With the farrier in the stables. The twins are with Pru and Wyatt.'

'I can't linger here sorry—I've got to get back to the stockmen and work out a feed budget for the Angus cattle and the horses. Winter will soon be upon us. Have you seen Grandad anywhere— there has been no sign of him all morning?'

'Sorry, Mack. I forgot to tell you he's unwell today. Says he's been getting a few headaches. Maybe he needs to see the doctor.'

Mack's heart sank. Bessie would only mention the doctor if his grandfather was sickening for something. She always knew.

'Is he in bed?'

'Not sure if he's in bed, but he is in his room lying down.'

'I'll get this feed budget sorted out first. The supplier is coming to Glenorchy tomorrow and I can't afford to miss out and need to phone the order through pronto. I'll talk to Grandad tonight and see if we can get him to the doctor this week.'

Mack climbed onto the quad bike and disappeared up the back of the station to find the stockmen who were in one of the feed sheds.

An hour later, Mack met Jessie leading Chantilly back into her paddock. He drove up to the fence slowly to avoid frightening her horse.

'How did you get on with the farrier?'

'He thought she had laminitis in her left hoof, but I diagnosed a bad stone bruise which he later concurred. He thinks she needs shoes when I'm riding up and down the stony track. It's different if we only ride the horses on grass or soft ground. What do you think?'

'It's a good idea. You ride her up and down the track often just as I do with Zoro. That's why I've always made sure he has shoes.'

'My horse in Bethlehem didn't need them. I only rode Rusty in the paddocks and if I rode him down to the beach, we walked along the edge of the estuary away from the road. Anyway, the farrier said he'll wait until the swelling has gone down and come back to shoe her.'

Mack started to fidget. 'Look, Jess, I need to tell you about Grandad.'

'Why, what's happened?'

'Nothing yet, but I'm concerned he has started getting the headaches he used to get prior to having a stroke. Bessie said he has taken to his room for the day. We must get him to see the doctor before anything happens.'

'I hope not, poor Grandad—just when he is looking forward to seeing the twins grow up.'

'I know—but he is in his eighties and has already had two strokes. He's living on borrowed time.'

'Mack! Grandad is a tough rooster and will last many years yet. He wants to see his grandsons mustering sheep. He has great plans for them.'

***

Walter was the last patient for the day. He walked back out to the waiting room where Mack who sat patiently, ready to hear the outcome.

'Well—what's the verdict? How many lives have you got left now?' Mack stopped short, catching himself making light of it when it could be serious.

'I'm fine. No stroke looming, he reckons. Blood pressure was on the high side, but he said it is to be expected after all the upset with Meg. I didn't expect him to bring that up—in fact, by the look on his face when he saw me walk in, he expected me to give him a rollicking. He only said to take it easy for the rest of the week. I told him that Meg and Joe had reconciled, and she is in Wellington with him. He said he knew, and he just wanted her to be happy. I don't hold it against him.'

'Well let's get you home so you can rest. Those grandsons of yours need you to hang around for a lot longer yet.'

On the way back to the station, Mack stopped by Willow Park to check the horses in the paddocks. Just as Meg had instructed the camp staff before she left, the horses had their blankets on and their feed bags contained fresh hay. The staff had put them to bed for the night in the stables. Sara had organised some of the volunteers to tend and exercise them while Meg stayed in Wellington.

Walter waited patiently in the Ute for Mack. 'Come on, Grandad—let's get you home. Everything is shipshape. Meg has it all under control as usual.'

***

Jessie was back working her business part-time, driving her mobile clinic to Kinloch twice a week and one day a week in Glenorchy. She'd employed an on-call vet experienced in anaesthetics to assist her with surgery part-time. Life was hectic, coming home to boisterous twin boys after a tiring workday.

After her last client in Kinloch, she trudged to her bus, plodded up the steps and dumped her medical bag on the bench. She placed her hands on her hips, stretching from side to side, and yawned. Today had been one of the busiest in a while—mostly complicated late births of Angora goats and sheep— just before winter arrived. Now to drive home and put her feet up for a well-deserved rest. Her mother was a Godsend. She couldn't have managed without her with a veterinary business to run and the station to oversee together with her husband.

Mack had already arrived home and sat in front of the fire bouncing Oliver on his knee while Walter lay slumped in his armchair making a sound like the TSS Earnslaw steamship in his sleep.

'Hi, honey.' He screwed up his nose. 'Just in time to change this one.' He grinned at her until he noticed she didn't appreciate his teasing.

'Just joking—looks like you've had another hectic day. I'm just on my way to change him. Your mother has fed them and given them both their bottles.' Mack ambled off down to the nursery while Jessie pushed her feet into her slippers and stood with her back to the fire. Not long after, she joined Mack. They bathed the twins and put them to bed.

'Dinners on the table,' Bessie said as they walked passed the kitchen. 'I ate at midday and I'm off to my room now. The meal is all set up on the table in the crockpot. I'll see you in the morning before I leave for the weekend.'

557

'Oh, that's right. We've got that young girl Bonny coming to ride Zoro. She's arriving in the morning and going home in the afternoon. I hope she'll fit in all right. Her parents are dropping her off and they are staying at Willow Park for the night. Sara will be staying there too until Meg and Joe get back. It's only for one night so I'm sure Bonny will be okay with us.'

Bessie took herself off to her room. Walter woke just as Mack and Jessie arrived at the dinner table and shuffled in to join them.

'The old joints are stiff. It just came on when we had that drama with Joe but it's starting to settle down, now it's all sorted.'

'We have a guest to entertain this weekend, Grandad. It's that young girl who appears to have the potential to be a horse whisperer. Bonny—Meg's protégé.'

'Is that right?' Walter reached over and helped himself to a large serving of the pie. 'You'll have your work cut out, both of you.'

Mack smiled and darted a glance at Jessie.

'Grandad. We thought you might like to show her your shepherding skills with your dogs before we finish the autumn muster. She hasn't seen it before. I'll get her working with Zoro too. I'm going to let her ride him.'

Jessie passed the tomato sauce around the table.

'Is she ready to ride on the station?'

'She'll only be in the paddock by the woolshed. The shepherds are bringing the sheep down to the bottom grazing areas so they'll be safe during the snowstorms, and the ewes will be fattened before lambing. Bonny's mother says the girl wants to be a shepherdess, but I think she's a touch young to decide her future. Anyway, it will be a valuable experience no matter what she does later in life.'

'Shhh ... I think one of the boys has woken up. I'll go and check.'

Chapter Twenty

'Hi, Mack! Where's Zoro?' The bubbly girl ran towards him while he waited outside the barn. She was just as he had remembered—spirited and full of gusto as she started pulling on the sleeve of his Swaandri jacket.

Mack's eyes shot a warm glance at her mother.

'Wow, Bonny! You're rearing to go, just like Zoro. First, I'd like you to come inside to meet my wee family. Perhaps your Mum would like a cup of tea?'

'Thanks, Mack.' The woman put out her hand. 'I'm Eve. It's good to meet you since Bonny hasn't stopped talking about you and Zoro. I hear you have twin boys now.'

'Yes, we have. You're just in time before they go down for their nap. They've been up since first light. Come with me, Bonny—I'll show you your room.'

After Bonny dropped her bag in the guest room, Jessie put the kettle on for tea and introduced herself and the twins to Bonny and her mother.

The eager girl made sure they kept the time drinking tea and fussing over the baby boys to a minimum. Her constant push to get back to the barn and saddle Zoro won through. No sooner had they finished their morning tea than Pru arrived at the homestead to babysit the twins. Eve greeted Pru then sped off out the driveway back to Willow Park where Bonny's father had a day off, reading and relaxing.

'Thanks, Mum. I appreciate your help today. Now I can spend time with Bonny and Mack as I think I'm in for a unique experience. Would you mind putting the twins to bed for their nap? I'll grab our lunch boxes I packed last night and the water bottles. It could be a long day.'

'I'll get some meat out and prepare the meal. You said Bessie won't be back until late so I can help out before I head home later.'

She wrapped her arms around Pru and kissed her cheek.

'You're a gem. Bessie left a Shepherd's Pie in the fridge. We just need a few vegetables to put with it.'

'I'd better chase after that girl. Mack is getting the horses ready.'

Bonny skipped out to the stable-barn with Jessie in tow. 'There he is waiting for me!' She bounded up to the horse she knew so well and with whom she had a special bond. Zoro let out a soft whinny and when she approached, he gave her a gentle nudge with his head.

Jessie was just in time to see this special girl bonding with the horse in a way she hadn't witnessed before, not since seeing how Hope Rigby handled horses.

She drew alongside Mack. 'I think she has that special gift with horses that Hope Rigby has—a potential horse whisperer.'

'I think so too. That's why I brought her out here to see the musterers on their horses in action. Zoro recognised her straight away.' Mack approached Zoro and checked his saddle and girth.

'Now, Bonny—after I fasten his bridle over the halter, I'll help you mount using that mounting block over there.'

'I don't need one. I can pull myself on his back with my foot in the stirrup.'

'No, we don't do that, Bonny. It's hard on the horse's spine. I'm sure your coach, Sara taught you that.'

Bonny set her jaw and pouted.

'I've done it heaps of times when I had my own horse.'

'Please don't argue, Bonny. Here we think of caring for our horses. If you use the mounting block it takes the strain off his back. I'll lead Zoro over there and help you up.'

Jessie glanced sideways and chuckled at Mack's efforts to tame the adolescent girl as she saddled Chantilly.

Mack borrowed Walter's horse which his grandfather no longer used for mustering. Now that the ageing shepherd's riding days were over, university students who frequented the station would often ride him, or sometimes Wyatt worked the stock horse when Mack needed extra men on horseback.

Mack rode on ahead of Zoro in a single file with Chantilly behind. It was safer for Bonny this way, although Mack was sure that Zoro would do her no harm and Mack had attached a lead rope to his halter as a precautionary measure during the muster.

'I don't want to be led—you promised me I could ride Zoro by myself on the station.'

Mack glared at her. 'Not yet, Bonny. It's too dangerous to let you go yet. You're just observing at the moment. Once we are back in the paddock close to the homestead you can ride him free rein there. I'll lead Zoro just for now while you watch the musterers. The horses can get excited during mustering, so just watch for now.'

Walter was already down on the flat with the shepherds who'd brought the Merinos down from the hills. The dogs raced back and forth herding hundreds of sheep towards the bottom paddocks. Walter walked amongst them, oblivious to the clouds of dust billowing in the breeze. He used his shepherd's hook to steady himself, now and then stumbling on rough ground, but nothing seemed to thwart him once he was amongst the sheep with his own dogs.

Mack followed the muster back down to the low-lying paddocks leading Bonny all the way. He stopped to let her come alongside him.

'Why are the dogs chasing the sheep towards the woolsheds?'

'They aren't chasing them—they are rounding them up and guiding them in the right direction. Can you see the shepherds over there with their hooks?' Mack pointed to the rugged hills above them. 'They have walked all the way up there on those rocky crags to find each sheep and bring them down to the bottom. They can't take a horse up there.'

'Why do they have to go to the woolshed? Are they going to shear them?'

'They are going to crutch the ewes, which are the females. They'll remove all the discoloured wool and dags which is necessary before they give birth to their lambs.'

Mack wasn't keen to elaborate on the topic of mating to a twelve-year-old girl. 'We then leave them to graze in the paddocks surrounding the woolshed until spring when the pregnant ewes will have their lambs.'

Mack led Bonny down the track out of the way of the muster and once the stockmen had herded all the sheep, they brought them down to the woolshed. Jessie helped round up the rest of the stragglers on Chantilly.

Mack chose a paddock where the sheep would not be grazing until after spring. He dismounted next to the gate but still kept hold of Zoro's lead rope while he led Bonny through.

'Here you are. They won't be using this paddock today so you can now have free rein on Zoro for a while. Let me see what you can do.'

He unclipped the lead rope from Zoro's halter which lay underneath a well-oiled black bridle—the one Jessie had given him for Christmas the year he had proposed to her.

The look on Bonny's face said it all. She lit up like a Christmas tree as she urged Zoro first into a trot around the field then into a canter.

Mack held his breath then remembered to let it go. He trusted Zoro that he would not throw her off, but did Bonny have the balance and ability to ride a stock horse? Mack had seen her in action at Meg's in such a way to convince him she had special abilities, but he still felt the need to caution her as she pelted towards him.

He stood in front of the oncoming horse. 'Whoa!' He grabbed hold of the halter. 'Bonny, I don't want you to ride too fast. Just a gentle canter, please. Remember Zoro is my horse, and you need to do as I say. I don't want any accidents while you're in my care.'

'Okay, Mr Mack, I hear you. Let me see if he can still do tricks with me—watch.'

Before Mack could assist her, she sprang off the horse and stood next to Zoro. She tied a knot in the reins, placed them on the horse's withers and walked slowly in front of him. 'Come on, Zoro—follow me.' Ambling across the paddock, she turned her head now and then to see if the horse obeyed her. Zoro loped behind following her footsteps.

As Mack gazed with astonishment, another horse approached the fence. It was Jessie who'd arrived just in time to see the unusual spectacle. They both gaped at the performing duo as Zoro followed Bonny to and fro across the paddock and back again. The girl started jogging and from time to time she checked that Zoro was in close pursuit. To Mack and Jessie's amazement, the horse followed in her footsteps trotting behind her carefully as she darted to the left and right in a zig-zag fashion. Zoro never budged an inch from walking behind, heedful not to trample her.

'This is incredible, Mack. This is your reward for your hard work at trying to help Meg and Joe. If you hadn't aided Meg in turning her life around by insisting she start a pony camp, Bonny wouldn't be here today, and you would never have witnessed this. God is blessing you for being a blessing to so many others.'

'I think so, Jessie. It sure feels like providence or something.'

It was time to go. They could hear the muster approaching the woolshed. Soon the track between the paddocks would be a dusty, onslaught of barking dogs, noisy sheep, and musterers yelling at their dogs and each other.

'Let's get this young horse whisperer back to the homestead. We can't tire her all at once—there is always tomorrow.'

Chapter Twenty-One

Winter

Walter lay back in his vintage, leather armchair wriggling his toes in front of a roaring fire. His fawn, woollen socks were worse for wear. Hazel had once knitted them and each time they wore a hole, Bessie took out her needle and repaired them.

An overweight, neutered tomcat, who'd identified the pushover who often saved leftovers from the Sunday roast lamb, lay at Walter's feet.

Buster snuggled against the woollen socks that protruded close to the fire almost singeing them, while the octogenarian snored with his mouth open wide. On the opposite side of the lounge sat Jessie next to Mack, her hands moving in sequence pulling on the thick ball of wool lying on the couch next to her.

Mack picked up the wool and rolled it around in his hands. 'How's the jumper going? It looks as if it's taking shape. Pity you have to reproduce the same garment for Will. That's the only real drawback with twins—always having to double up with everything.'

'It's not that so much,' replied Jessie. 'It's just that I'm too tired to knit in the evenings after a long day running a clinic and riding on the station. I might ask Mum to do the jumper for Will, as I don't have the time. Those days are ending.'

Mack stretched out on the couch, resting his legs across Jessie's lap. 'Oh, that's a pity—just when I thought you were becoming a domesticated housewife.'

Jessie picked up a jumbo knitting needle and whacked him with it. 'Hey, none of that sexist talk—you'll never keep me in a box.'

A loud snort emanated from Walter which caused them both to erupt with laughter.

Mack stood up and reached over to a small stack of logs and placed one inside in the wood burner, while Jessie went to the kitchen to put the kettle on.

'Grandad has been sleeping so long. Do you think I should wake him? He'll be up half the night if we don't. Anyway—he always has tea at this time.'

'You could, I suppose, but do it gently. You don't want to give him a heart attack,' he teased.

Walter came to life when Jessie woke him and showed him a mug of tea and a slice of banana bread.

'You shouldn't have let me nap so long. I've been asleep for hours.'

'You must have needed it, Grandad. You spent ages in your workshop today. What are you doing out there?'

'I found some old timber to make the boys a rocking horse each for their first birthdays. It will get tricky with presents now that their birthdays are so close to Christmas.'

'That's a wonderful present to give them. They'll love them. You could call them Zoro and Chantilly—paint one black and the other gold.'

'I could do that—great idea.'

'I spoke to Meg on the phone earlier. She and Joe are getting on well. He took to the pony camp venture right off. Meg says he's right in his element,' said Mack, helping himself to a slice of banana bread.

'Pity pony camp closes down until spring in November. I don't know what Joe will do for three months, until then.'

'Meg has plenty lined up for him to do, Grandad. You know her. She has him fixing fences, feeding the horses and now he's renovating the bunkrooms before camp starts again.'

Walter laughed. 'That's Meg for you—always on the go.'

'She mentioned something I thought would give you a lift, Grandad. They want to renew their marriage vows and would like some ideas on where to do it. I said I would ask you to get in touch with her and discuss it.'

'Praise God—that sure is an answer to prayer. I'll do that—I think I have the perfect place for them.'

***

On a clear, crisp morning during a hoar frost in August, Mack and Walter ventured on an expedition to Lake Tekapo in the McKenzie country. With Meg and Joe sitting in the back of Jessie's Land Rover, they headed past Lake Wakatipu aiming to reach their destination at the Church of the Good Shepherd within five hours.

Meg and Joe were about to renew their marriage vows at the church where Walter married Hazel and where she was buried. Jessie stayed home with the twins, as she knew this should only be a Reed family affair and the trip would be too much for the babies.

As Mack drove along the Queenstown-Glenorchy highway, an orange ball of fire rose from behind the Remarkables—the mountain range opposite Lake Wakatipu. The early morning sun illuminated the feathery ice crystals formed by the hoar frost that glistened on the trees.

The vehicle meandered its way through the Lindis Valley revealing an icy wonderland. Some of the houses had their lights on illuminating the shimmering ice crystals.

Joe shivered and wrapped his arms around Meg after pulling his woollen beanie over his forehead.

'We have to be crazy doing this—it's freezing up here. Are you all right in the front, Grandad? The heating in this vehicle of Jessie's doesn't do much.'

'I'm a tough, Otago farmer—what do you expect, eh? I'm wearing my Long Johns—pure merino underwear.'

'Oh, thanks for that information, Grandad!' They all laughed.

'Doesn't it look like a fairyland down there? I've seen nothing like this before,' said Meg, fastening the woollen scarf around her neck.

Joe leaned over to pat Mack on the shoulder.

'Mack—we're ever so grateful that you offered to drive us, particularly as you're used to driving on these roads. I wouldn't like to risk driving in these treacherous conditions in unknown territory.'

Meg looked at Joe with teary eyes and sniffed. 'That's why we call him a *Good Shepherd*. In fact, both you and Grandad are just that—*Good Shepherds*. You round us up and sort us out, and you rescue and help us to heal.'

'I think we're all getting a touch sentimental. Poor Mack won't be able to stay on the road soon.' Walter chuckled.

'Grandad—during which month did you and Grandma marry at the Church of the Good Shepherd—was it winter like this?'

'It sure was. It snowed and your grandmother wanted photos taken while everything was white. I can still remember when we spotted an old, clinker dinghy upturned at the lakeside. Hazel struggled over to it in her high-heeled shoes for a photo shoot. She climbed onto the boat, dragging her wedding dress while she half froze. I might add that the photos were amazing—her long, raven-black hair against the backdrop of the Southern Alps.'

Walter sat staring out the window, momentarily transported to a time past.

'I hope your rental cottage is warm, Grandad. Are you sure it's not tenanted right now?'

'I'm certain Mack. I receive updates from the Property Manager regularly. That's why I thought it a good time to do an overnighter. It's heated and has all we need. Bessie packed a full chilly bin with enough food to last until we get back late tomorrow afternoon.'

As Mack drove the vehicle with caution through to the other side of the Lindis Pass, the road opened out. When Lake Pukaki surfaced before their eyes, Walter wiped his brow with his sleeve and started sniffing, as if he was having a quiet cry—at least, that's what Mack thought as he worked hard focusing his attention on the black ice on the road while glancing sideways at Walter. Mack felt compassion for him as the battle-weary man almost reached the burial site of his beloved Hazel and the church where the two of them exchanged vows he couldn't always keep.

'Almost there, Grandad. There's Lake Pukaki. Lake Tekapo is the next one along.'

'Right you are, Mack.'

Meg and Joe sat quietly in the back. Meg had been resting her head on Joe's shoulder dozing, but when she heard that the lakes were in sight, she sat up and leaned over Walter's shoulder, her eyes scanning the view.

'Wow! Look at that lake. Just how you described it to me, Grandad. It's turquoise-blue and milky looking.'

'Yep, you won't see that in many parts of the country. It's caused by glacial flour—the silt that flows down from the glaciers.'

'It's amazing. No wonder Grandma loved growing up in these parts.'

As they passed Lake Pukaki and around the next bend in the road, Lake Tekapo boasted a similar panorama. Scattered around the lake appeared clusters of pine trees shimmering in the sunlight with the melting ice.

As they drove into Tekapo village, Walter sat wrenching his hands.

'Right, Grandad. You'll have to direct me from here. Where's this grand cottage of yours?' Mack pulled over into a recess.

'Take that turn up there on the right and travel about two miles up. You'll see a Norfolk Pine on your right in front of a little white cottage. This used to be all farmland but now it's mostly holiday homes on small lots.'

'Thanks, Grandad. I thought Grandma's parents lost everything on their farm?'

'Farming friends purchased the farm, but they left an acre of land for Hazel's folks along with their cottage out of goodwill, as they got it for a good price. After Hazel died, I rented it out. It paid for the rates bill.'

Meg turned to Joe and whispered, 'Wow, there's still a lot to learn about Grandad. I wonder what else we don't know about him. He appears to be full of surprises.'

'He sure is one special man. This is an amazing place to re-commit our lives together—I mean, Lake Tekapo.'

Meg leaned over Walter's shoulders and strained for a closer look.

'I can't wait to see this little church, Grandad. Where is it?'

'We bypassed it on the way here. It's not far, down at the lakeside. You'll see it in the morning. The Pastor is meeting you at ten o'clock. He is the grandson of the clergyman who married us—but 3let's have a meal and a good night's sleep first.'

Mack swerved as the vehicle missed a deep pothole full of water in the driveway, pulling up alongside a well-maintained cottage with leadlight windows.

Mack, Joe and Meg piled out to stretch their legs, leaving Walter in the vehicle. For a moment, he sat still taking a few deep breaths. He wiped his eyes and stepped out.

'Where's that key? Oh yes, at the side of the house you'll see the water tank. Next to that are some giant mushrooms made of clay. They have lids you can open. The red one contains the key.'

Mack raced around to the side of the house. The ice had melted and left a muddy mess on the ornamental mushrooms in the garden. He took the key forcing it into the lock, stiffened by the hoar frost.

'Come on, Grandad. You go in first.'

Walter stood back. 'No, mate—all of you can go in and choose a room. I just need to gather my thoughts first.'

Meg placed her arm around her grandfather's shoulders and pulled him close. 'Don't get cold, Grandad. It's freezing out here. We'll get the fire on, presuming you have one.'

'That's all good, lass. Away you go, then. No one can live in these parts without a good firebox. The logs are stacked next to it, just through the living room.'

They all went inside. Walter took his time wandering around the outside of the cottage, now and then folding his arms and staring at the garden where Hazel had spent hours in a day beautifying the grounds. He pulled his Swaandri up around his neck then closed his eyes and muttered—'Thank you, God, for bringing me back here, but most of all, for what I'm about to witness with my dear granddaughter at Hazel's church where it all began.'

Mack's voice drowned out the rest of Walter's prayer as he called him to join them for a light meal.

***

Heavy snow fell during the night. The next morning, as Meg opened the door, a white carpet reached the steps to greet her as she caught sight of a rabbit hopping across the front yard. She looked up at the clear, blue sky and inhaled the crisp air—catching her breath as she puffed out her chest.

Dressed only in thick, flannelette pyjamas, she shivered. Joe crept up behind her, lifted her hair from off her shoulders and kissed her neck. She reached back and caressed his face.

'Morning, love. Where are the men—have they gone out already?' she asked.

'No, not yet. Mack's still sound asleep. I knocked and opened the door. They are both dead to the world. The spare room is full to the brim with old furniture and too cluttered for anyone to sleep in, poor Mack. Grandad's snoring is terrible.'

Joe pulled her back inside the house.

'It's freezing. Didn't you bring a dressing gown?'

'No, I forgot it. I'll grab my woollen jacket from the bedroom.'

The kettle boiled, filling the kitchen with steam. Joe found a jar of coffee in the chilly bin that Bessie had packed.

Meg returned wearing a pair of thermal workmen's socks that Joe had lent her. After buttoning her jacket up to her neck, she began fossicking in the chilly bin to see what remained after the meal they ate the previous night. Removing the eggs, butter, milk, marmalade and cheese, she reached to the bottom and discovered the large chunk of half-eaten corned beef wrapped in aluminium foil. In another small package, there was homemade bread and various tins of vegetables.

She pointed at the food she'd laid out on the bench. 'This should be enough to keep us going until we get back.'

Joe joined her at the bench. 'Good! Let's tuck into those eggs—I'll make a large omelette for all of us.' His eyes smiled at her. 'You go and sit down—there's only room for one in this kitchen.'

Before long, Mack arrived with Walter dressed and ready for breakfast and the smell of eggs cooking.

He rubbed his hands together. 'Mmm—just what I need to warm my insides. It was cold in that room last night, even with the vibration of Grandad's snoring warming the air.'

Walter swiped him with his Stetson before placing it on a side table. 'I know you would rather share a room with Jessie but I'm the best offer you have at the moment.'

'Yeah well—pity the spare room is used as storage or we could have had a room each. It really needs clearing out of all that old furniture.'

Mack silently wondered when and how that would happen, as it had been like that for years—all the old furniture Hazel had kept that once belonged to her parents was dumped in one room.

They all sat at the table enjoying some of the food that Bessie had packed for them and continuing the banter until it was time to go to the church.

Mack had not seen the Church of the Good Shepherd covered in snow. He'd only visited Tekapo during the summer holidays years ago and did not know that his grandfather had a cottage there. Meg and Joe and had never seen the church either.

The setting was an artist's canvas with the snow-covered Alps forming a backdrop to the turquoise lake and stone church at the water's edge.

As they drove up to the church, they looked aghast at the wonder of it all—except for Walter who stepped out of the vehicle with a poker face and red eyes.

Meg rushed up to her grandfather and gave him a bear hug.

'Oh, what a wonderful venue for our ceremony. Thank you so much, Grandad!'

He kissed her on the cheek. 'My pleasure, my dear. It's just a pity your grandmother isn't alive to witness all of this.'

Mack reached out to him and placed a hand on his shoulder. 'Never mind, Grandad—she is with us in spirit—in our hearts. Wait—isn't that the Pastor? We'd better get on up there.'

They made their way single file up the stony path that led to the front entrance of the church. As they entered the historical building, which was built by pioneers in 1935, they each shook hands with Pastor Paul.

Meg and Joe approached the altar, mesmerised by the breath-taking view of the Southern Alps through a feature window behind a large wooden cross. They turned around to view the décor of the inside of the church.

'Joe, look—there are Mum and Dad!'

Len and Helen stood under the archway at the front entrance talking to the Pastor. Helen spotted them and waved.

Meg's eyes streamed. Joe handed her a handkerchief to wipe her eyes, which she popped into her handbag.

Walter sat at the front of the church with Mack sitting next to him. Len and Helen joined them.

There wasn't a dry eye amongst them while the Pastor conducted the ceremony.

Meg had something to say at the end after coughing to clear her throat. 'Thank you all for being here for this amazing, memorable event. You have travelled a great distance and Joe and I want you to know that we'll be eternally grateful to you—but I want to especially pay homage to two people who made this happen—Mack and Grandad. You deserve your reputation as Good Shepherds who helped our family to heal and saved our marriage. So we have renewed our marriage vows at this church in honour of you both. Thank you for your long-suffering and never giving up on us.'

With that speech, more handkerchiefs came out. After the service, Meg and Joe mingled with Len and Helen. Outside the church, the men took out their cameras and Pastor Paul offered to take photos.

Meg kissed her mother. 'Thanks again for coming.'

Len, making sure he didn't miss out pulled her towards him and kissed her.

'You never mentioned to me that you planned to be here.'

Helen smiled at her daughter. 'Your brother convinced us to come and surprise you,' she said, just as Mack approached and greeted his parents in the same way.

'Where are you staying?' Mack asked. 'You know we could have arranged accommodation if you hadn't insisted on being independent.'

'It wasn't a problem, honestly. We're in the Lakeside Motel. It's pretty basic, but all we need. We weren't sure whether to book another night,' said Len.

'Are you still going to follow us to Glenorchy? You weren't sure when I telephoned.' Mack glanced at his wristwatch.

Meg turned to her parents. 'What's all this? Our guesthouse is empty for the rest of the winter so you can stay with us and spend time visiting your grandchildren.'

Helen glanced at Joe. 'Don't you two need to be alone—I mean—it's your honeymoon?'

He laughed. 'We've had all the honeymoons we need, haven't we?'

Meg elbowed him. 'Our chalet will soon be vacant, as Charlie, our caretaker is retiring.'

Len's brows furrowed. 'Oh! What will you do then?'

'I don't know. I'll have Joe to help me with pony camp, but there's so much to do around the property. We'll have to advertise for someone to replace him.'

Mack jerked his thumb at them, 'Let's go back to the cottage for lunch. We can discuss it over a meal. We've plenty of tucker with us. We just have to leave in time to travel in the light. It'll take five hours in these wintery conditions to get back and even then, I advise caution on these roads.'

Walter took hold of Len's arm. 'Wait, all of you! I need to do something before we go back. I want to show Mack and Meg where their grandmother is buried.'

'Of course, Dad. They haven't been here before and I came down here a few years ago. Shall we all go?' Len took the lead with the entourage in tow.

Meg looked searchingly for the multi-coloured lupins that Walter often spoke about that grew alongside the lake, but there was no sign of them.

'No lupins to put on Grandma's grave. What can I put there, Grandad?'

'No, lassie—not in this snow. Lupins won't appear until November when it's warmer.'

Walter pulled a compact bouquet of dark-red, dried roses from the pocket of his navy-blue woollen Peacoat and handed it to her.

'Here, you can place that on her gravestone.'

Mack, Len and Helen walked behind them and watched Meg while she placed the flowers on the grave. They bowed their heads while Walter prayed and after he'd finished, they stood for a moment in silence. Walter's face had lost its gaunt appearance and his facial lines softened.

He smiled as he removed from his pocket a small wooden, hand-carved cross he'd made and placed it on the gravestone.

'All is well with the world, Lord,' he muttered quietly.

Chapter Twenty-Two

'Guess what.' Mack snuggled up to Jessie in front of the fire, revelling in the stillness. Walter and Bessie had already turned in early.

'My folks surprised Meg by turning up at the ceremony. They talked about leaving Nelson and moving into the chalet at Willow Park now that Meg's caretaker is retiring. Mum wants to spend more time with her grandsons. They said they've missed out on seeing them growing up, although they aren't a year old yet.'

'That's marvellous. You'll have your whole family down here just as I do, except for Tom and he won't be leaving the farm in Bethlehem. I wonder how he and Amanda are getting on. I thought he said they were looking at getting married next spring, but we've heard nothing about it.'

'You know your brother. He's just as likely to change his mind. Maybe they need longer.'

'It's a pity you weren't at the ceremony, Jessie. I felt bad leaving you behind.'

'You know we couldn't take the twins on such a long trip. It would have been chaotic and too cold in that cottage. I'm sure Meg and Joe understood.'

'Well, thanks for holding the fort while we were away.'

'I've got a big day at the clinic tomorrow. There are two dogs that need neutering, and that Scotsman, McKlintoch on the deer farm has a young buck that is lame. He thinks it may have injured itself trying to get through a fence. He's bringing it down to the bus in his horse truck when I'm in Kinloch this afternoon.'

Mack flicked his wrist to see the time. 'I'll ask my mother to help your mum with the boys. She'd planned on visiting us tomorrow—sorry, I forgot to tell you. She's so keen to see them.'

'That's a great idea—I'll phone my mother and let her know to expect her. We've got so much support now, we're so blessed.'

'I also forgot to tell you—Meg and Joe are coming with us to church this Sunday and so are Mum and Dad. They're putting on a morning tea to celebrate their reconciliation.'

'Great news! Come on, Mack. The fire's almost out. Let's go to bed. I don't get to spend much time with you these days.'

He turned out the lights and led her down the hallway. It was Jessie's turn to receive a portion of her husband's love that seemed to overflow from his heart, the kind that served as a catalyst for change in the lives of so many.

Tonight Mack would sleep peacefully knowing that everything in his world seemed right. Not only had his grandfather made peace with himself and his family, but Meg had also finally redeemed herself.

***

The first day of spring arrived. Hope Rigby stood at the gate with baby Sophie and her brother, Bertie waving as Jessie arrived. Bertie ran to the car and banged on the window as she turned off her engine.

He pointed at his sister. 'Look, Sophie can walk—see!' He grabbed Jessie's hand almost pulling her over as she stepped out of the car.

Hope took his hand and moved him aside. 'Hold on, Bertie. Wait until Aunty Jessie gets the boys out of the back seat.'

Jessie unclipped each child from their car seats and let them toddle onto the grass while she reached out and hugged her friend.

'It's so long since we've caught up. I'm dying to hear all your news.' Hope lifted Sophie and coaxed Bertie up the steps with Jessie in tow with her boys.

'It's such a beautiful spring day—I love this season. Let's have tea on the veranda in the sun while the children play on the grass. It's dry now, and the garden is fenced off so we can watch them from here.'

Hope hurried back with a tray of tea and cake. She showed Jessie small pieces of fruit, and homemade bread covered in peanut butter, cut into squares.

'Okay if your boys share this with Sophie and Bertie?'

'Absolutely—go ahead.'

Hope walked down the steps with a blanket to spread on the grass, followed by Jessie who placed the plate of fruit and bread down. The two sat drinking English Breakfast tea while sampling Hope's freshly baked banana cake.

Hope's face appeared animated. 'We haven't done this since we were both pregnant. How time goes by so fast— now tell me all the juicy stuff.'

'Well, you know about Grandad's earlier estrangement with his entire family. There has been a miraculous healing, and they are reunited. As well as all that, Meg and Joe are back together again for good.'

'My goodness—how did all that come about?'

'First of all, it was Mack who brought the family completely back together and healed their relationship. He has been amazing—so compassionate and insightful for a high country farmer. That makes me love him even more. He prayerfully intervened and through his persistence and wise words, he never gave up. He convinced Meg her marriage was worth saving and just how selfish she'd been. Grandad also had an enormous impact on Meg by confessing to her what a rotter he'd been to Grandma. He had neglected her after she gave birth to Len and her health deteriorated as a result of his selfishness.'

'That's unbelievable. What a turnaround!'

'To add to that, Grandad has let go of his self-hatred of not taking care of Grandma. They are such different people now. Please thank your family for all their prayers. I'll have to tell our church prayer chain, too.'

'That's no problem. You would have done the same for us.'

'Oh-oh! Sophie's trying to pull her nappy off. I don't like to think what's inside it. She does that if it needs changing—if you know what I mean.' She walked off with Sophie while Jessie wiped peanut butter off the twins' faces. In a short time, Hope returned with her daughter tucked under one arm.

Jessie pointed to Bertie. 'I can't believe how much he has grown. How is kindergarten going—has the class increased in size much?'

'He loves it, but the class is too big. They need another classroom, and they still only have one teacher.'

'Is it still part of the little school?'

'Yes, and it's too small for all the children coming into the area. A developer has built a large subdivision on the Closeburn side of Glenorchy—mostly families live there.'

'Yes, I see that. I think that's the property developer who wanted to buy land from Meg. It's a tragedy.'

'I agree—they're an eyesore—houses made of ticky-tacky.'

'Jessie—I was wondering if Meg is ready for me to come and help with the horses. I did promise—remember? I no longer have classes at Dart River Ranch, and I kind of miss it.'

'I'm sure she'll appreciate your offer, but pony camp doesn't start until November when summer begins. You could help her train the new ponies, as they need some groundwork. Perhaps you had better call her.'

'I sure will. Thanks, Jessie—that'll be right up my alley. Mum has offered to babysit so I can get out a few days a week now.'

'You're like me—you have built-in babysitters. I'm so lucky that I'll have two lots with Mack's parents having moved down from Nelson to Willow Park and absolutely loving it. Meg's caretaker has retired so they now live in the chalet that Meg built for my parents.'

'Jeepers! Major changes going on with your family but all good, though.'

'How about you—how is the breeding program going? Are you still involved now you have two children?'

'It's doing well—only it has quietened down now as the mating season is over and most of our mares are pregnant. Cole has taken on an assistant, as Dad is pulling back and giving him more responsibility. I work a few days a week with Cole and sometimes I get requests to break in a local horse.'

'You're like me—employed both inside and outside the home. We're tough women.'

'Cole has to call on the services of the on-call vet to carry out the pre-pregnancy checks on the mares, but next season he would like you do conduct them.'

'Jeepers! I'm going to be busy, aren't I?'

'We can't let you off lightly.'

'Sorry, Hope. I must take the boys home for their afternoon nap. They'll be getting grumpy soon. Don't forget to give Meg a call about helping out with her ponies.'

'I will do. Come on, boys, I'd better get you home.'

She gathered the twins one by one and bustled them into their car seats.

'Thanks for the tea and that lovely banana cake—you haven't lost your knack.' She gave Hope a warm hug, climbed in her vehicle, and drove off tooting all the way up the driveway.

***

Jessie startled awake next morning to her alarm screaming at her on the bedside table. Mack's side of the bed was empty. He appeared in the doorway holding grizzling baby Oliver.

'Don't worry, he's had his breakfast.' Mack handed him to his mother for a cuddle.

Jessie slid into her slippers. 'I was going to get up and let you have a sleep in—that's why I set the alarm. I get more time to take breaks than you do. Why don't you go back to bed? I'll watch the boys.'

She knew that the start of the lambing season was tough for Mack. He'd been hard at it since daybreak each day checking all the ewes that they had brought down to the valley during the last muster. He found a few of them cast—weighed down by their weight because of the lush green grass after the spring rain. The sheep were heavy to lift onto their feet once they were on the ground.

Mack crawled back under the blankets. 'Thanks, love. I'll just lie here for a while and relax.'

What he usually meant by that was pray. But this time, unwanted thoughts crowded God out. He knew that before long it would be Jessie's turn to be out on the station using her veterinary expertise to assist him with difficult births. The Angus cows are another story and Jessie will have her work cut out when calving begins. The thought of their overwhelming workload caused him to pull the covers over his head and blank out, even for a short time. Sometimes he thought he'd bitten off more than he could chew when he took the job over from his grandfather but now there was no turning back.

582

She was right—her mother gave her sufficient breaks from the boys, and she didn't do full days on the station, although she was also a station manager. When Mack married Jessie, she took over the book-keeping from Walter. Now it was time to employ a bookkeeper with her trying to manage three part-time jobs, Mack said to himself. That'll be the next thing on the agenda—unless Wyatt would like to do it.

Jessie wandered down the hallway with Oliver after checking that Will was still asleep in the nursery.

Mack lay back, engulfed by the resonating stillness of the dawn. The buzzing of cicadas invaded his peace—or was it his tinnitus, the one characteristic he knew he'd inherited from his grandfather that occurred when he was tired or pressured.

Before long, a child's whimper in the next room shattered his oblivion. Should he jump out of bed and hurry to him? At once the sound of Jessie's soft voice interrupted the whine and then there was silence. Mack's body forced him to stay motionless. He deserved a day off.

Mid-morning he rose and freshened up in the bathroom ready to take on the world again. Bessie had set them a simple breakfast and was out at the henhouse collecting eggs.

Jessie had Will in his highchair while Oliver sat playing on a rug on the floor. She scooped a large dollop of strawberry jam from the glass jar and spread it on her toast.

'There's still porridge in the pot if you want some. If you are going to eat toast, would you mind popping a couple more slices in the toaster?' she asked, licking her fingers.

'I'll give the porridge a miss this morning. I tend to go off it in the warm weather. That's a fresh pot of strawberry jam, isn't it? I saw Bessie making it yesterday.'

They sat chatting over coffee and toast, revelling in Bessie's jam while still in their pyjamas.

'Grandad's sleeping late. I hope he's alright. He's been getting a few bad headaches again.'

'I wouldn't worry about it—at his age, he's bound to slow down. He's coming up eighty-six.'

Jessie unclipped the safety strap in Will's highchair and placed him on the rug next to Oliver.

'He's unbelievable—still riding his quad bike and repairing fences after having two strokes. Strong stock, the Reed family. I hope you and the boys inherit his longevity.'

'I forgot to tell you I dropped by to see Meg on my way back from the Feed Depot. They have decided to let the rooms out in the guesthouse to tourists until Christmas and start pony camp after the New Year during the school holidays. Joe has purchased a new vehicle to offer tourists mini-tours of the area and they have travel agents in Queenstown doing some promotion.'

'Gosh. What brought this on?'

'It's a great way for them to make extra income during the winter. He may continue the tours when pony camp is on, but the guesthouse will be only used for the children at that time, so they'll just be day tours.'

Jessie pushed the double baby stroller into the lounge. 'That's a great idea. It looks like it's all falling into place for them—oh, I just remembered our horses still have their covers on and it's going to be a warm day today.'

'I'll take care of it as I've got to do my rounds of the pregnant animals. I'll be taking Zoro out, but I'll take Chantilly's cover off first.'

'Your folks will be arriving soon, and your Mum wants to babysit. I can do the covers later.'

'That will be a great help. So good to have them living nearby on Meg's property instead of in Nelson.'

Jessie stroked Mack's hair and kissed him.

He cupped her face in his hands. 'It's as if God had planned it all—everything that has taken place up to now can't just be a coincidence—in fact, I no longer believe in that. It has to be divine intervention. We have been truly blessed, Jessie.' He kissed her again and walked off.

Chapter Twenty-Three

Mack wandered off down the track that led to the horses' paddocks. Chantilly and Zoro shared grazing together while Walter's horse, an old gelding was kept in his stable, as he, like Walter, was the veteran on the station. The stockmen kept their horses in another paddock on the other side of the stable-barn.

'What is it, buddy?' He looked around him and took a deep breath. Is it the stench of smoke? Probably someone burning off crop stubble, he decided.

He took the cover off both horses and put the halter with lead rope on Zoro. Chantilly pig-jumped and put her ears back. Mack knew she was annoyed he was taking Zoro out and not her.

'Don't worry, girl. Your turn's coming soon. Zoro has some work to do.'

He led his horse out of the paddock checking behind him that Chantilly didn't try to bolt through the gate. Within minutes he arrived at the stable-barn where he saddled and bridled Zoro.

'Come on, buddy. Let's go see where this smoke is coming from—just in case.'

He could see plumes of thick, black smoke in the distance but needed to get high up where he could view the surrounding area as he rode up onto a steep ridge.

His heart sank as his eyeballs widened like glass marbles. He removed his Stetson and swished his fingers back through his hair replacing the hat. The billows of smoke loomed high above his neighbour, Ned's barn.

'Walk on.' Mack wanted to race down but knew that one hasty step too many, horse and rider would roll to the bottom of the craggy hillside.

Once down on the flat, he urged Zoro into a canter back down the track to their stable-barn. Once there, after quickly removing his harness, he let him go inside his pen.

Mack rushed up to the homestead yelling out to Jessie, tripping up the steps on his way into the living room.

'Quick, phone the fire brigade. Ned's barn's on fire—I'll see if I can help.'

Jessie raced to the phone. 'Please be careful, love. You have baby boys—remember!'

Mack charged out of the house before Jessie finished her sentence and jumped into his Ute driving like a madman onto the main road. The vehicle rattled his bones as he hurtled along the loose metal road for the five-minute drive to Ned's before careering into his driveway. A cat darted in front of his wheels and into a bush.

Mack torpedoed over to the barn where layers of heavy smoke surged through the roof window. He held a handkerchief to his face as he arrived at the entrance calling out to Ned. His stomach somersaulted when he heard the shrill neigh of a horse in the corner of the barn, but as he glanced above him, he was relieved to see that the fire was still in the roof and hadn't reached the floor of the barn.

'Ned!' he screamed as he looked around, but the intense crackling of the fire raged through the wooden framework of the roof and drowned his voice.

Mack approached the horse whose ears were erect, tipping forwards while his nostrils flared. He danced around the pen throwing his head up and down whinnying, his tail swishing furiously.

Mack grabbed a lead rope hanging from a hook near the horse that now reared, his eyes bulging, rolling backwards exposing the whites.

Mack pulled back, holding onto the rope. 'Whoa, it's okay—I'll get you out of here.'

The clip on the lead rope found its home as Mack fastened it to the halter. 'Come on, Clover, you'll have to trust me.'

Yanking off his sweatshirt, he tied it around the petrified horse's head to cover his eyes and led him out the door. Trying to keep up as Clover trotted briskly alongside him, he coaxed the horse into the open until they were out of danger. Spotting an empty paddock nearby, Mack removed his sweatshirt from the horse, opened the gate and released him. The animal whinnied and took off across the paddock bucking madly.

Mack could hear dogs whining nearby and knew they weren't in the barn, but he wanted to make sure they were safe too. His throat seized with the stress of it all and dense smoke penetrated his airways causing him to gag. Running towards Ned's house he felt a deep sense of impending doom, concerned that the old man had not come out to investigate. Perhaps he had passed out in the barn overcome by smoke. Mack sprinted towards the house passing metal kennels with two sheepdogs on the way. Storming through the front door of the bungalow which was unlocked, there was Ned snoring in his armchair with his feet propped up on a leather ottoman.

Mack held back tears of relief. Ned didn't even startle at the shrill sound of sirens outside the house.

'Ned, wake up—Ned!' The farmer cringed as he woke suddenly to see a tall, muscular young man towering over him.

'What—what's this? What are you going in here, Mack?'

'Your barn's on fire—hurry! Are there any other animals in there? I got your horse out safely.'

'Clover—good heavens, man. No, there aren't any animals except for him. Where is he now?'

'I let him go in the paddock to the west of the barn. He may need some water if there's no trough.'

'Yes, there's water there. Was he hurt?'

'He's just shaken up, but I'll check on him again. The firemen are coming around the side of the house to see where they can bring the fire-engines to the fire. You'd best go and assist them right now.'

Mack left the firemen in Ned's hands and went back to check on Clover. He sidled up to him and patted him on the neck. The horse's whole body quivered.

'You're alright now, Clover. That was a close shave, wasn't it?'

He left the horse to continue grazing and wandered over to the barn which was under siege. Mack prayed silently that the fire would not destroy the whole barn, and when he arrived at the inferno, the firemen were hard at work with their hoses. He was relieved to see they had saved the external framework of the barn, apart from the roof which was severely damaged and started collapsing.

Ned leaned on his John Deere tractor parked near the fire-engines, watching the disaster unfold before him as he surveyed the wreckage.

'Can I go over, now that they have finished hosing? I need to see what's left of all my equipment and machinery,' he asked a fireman.

'You can only look from a distance, sorry, mate. For safety regulations, we can't allow you to enter the building until the fire chiefs have certified it safe to do so.'

Ned stood up when he saw Mack approach him.

'How did you know the barn was on fire? If it wasn't for you, I would have lost Clover and my house. I have little stock left now as I'm retired except for a handful of sheep up the back of the farm. It's all I have left at this time of life, including my working dogs.'

'I was riding up on the hillside to see if there were any stray sheep or cattle and saw clouds of smoke. I wouldn't have seen it from down below.' Mack guessed it must have been fate that he rode up onto the ridge to view his property at that moment.

'Well, I'm indebted to you, mate and won't forget it—I'll repay you, somehow.'

'I'm not worried about that, Ned. Seeing you are so shaken up, perhaps you'd like to come and stay with me and my family for a few days.'

Ned patted him on the back. 'There's no need for all that—thanks, anyway. I need to make sure Clover's doing alright as he'll be in shock, and I have my dogs to take care of. You're a good man and I hope this community appreciates having someone like you in their midst. You're a Godsend.'

Mack could see there was nothing else for him to do there. He would rather have Ned accompany him to Reed Station, but he could see the man was stubborn and reluctant to leave. The firemen were still busy cleaning up the debris from the roof that had caved in. Tomorrow he will return to check on him.

Chapter Twenty-Four

It was supposed to be Jessie's day off, but this was one of the busiest days on the station since lambing and calving had begun. She had to deliver intravenous fluids and oxygen to calves whose mothers had suffered difficult labour.

After Jessie finished treating the needy animals, she went home for a break and left Wyatt in the barn to watch over the calves and their mothers. She would only need to be on standby if there were complications with any of the animals.

Mack came into the house for lunch, unaccustomed to his children not bowling him over the moment they saw him appear. 'Where are the boys?'

'They're next door with my folks. Mum and I decided they were old enough to hang out at her house when she was babysitting. She and dad have been busy setting the place up, so it is safe for them to rattle around there.'

'That's great, but it doesn't matter whose house they are in as long as they don't come to any harm. When they're older, my folks might have them stay with them too, at Willow Park.'

When they had finished lunch together, Jessie started folding a pile of nappies. 'What's on your schedule for this afternoon?'

'If you don't mind, I'd like to pop over to see Ned and see if he's okay after the fire. Joe also asked if I'd drop by to see his new off-road Jeep Wagoneer. He bought one of those Sports Utility Vehicles ... SUV they're called. It even has wood grain along the side.'

'That sounds posh. What does he want with that?' Jessie said, frowning.

'Remember, I told you Joe wants to start a side business taking tourists on mini-tours? The area looks spectacular during winter.'

'I think that's a clever idea and Joe needs a job. He's too young to put out to pasture. I'll stay here in case the stockmen need me with my medical bag. Let Ben know, seeing he's second in charge when we aren't around.'

'It's just that I think Joe might need a bit of support until he settled into the community. I'll take my radiophone and if you need me, call me.' Mack kissed her on his way to the door.

'I'll try to be back as soon as possible. Wyatt is pretty clued up and so are Ben and Coran. You should manage alright with them.'

***

Mack chuckled to himself, watching Meg and Joe trudging around the stable yard in gumboots and overalls mucking out.

Meg looked up and leaned on her shovel—her wispy hair dishevelled by the southerly breeze.

'Mack! Good to see you—just in time to help us shift dung.'

Mack's eyes shot daggers at her until he burst out laughing, realising she was teasing.

'I was hoping for a cup of tea if you can spare the time.'

'We sure can,' said Joe. 'I'm dying for a break.'

They arrived on the porch and yanked off their boots by the front door.

Meg passed them both in the lounge. 'I'll put the kettle on,'

Joe pointed to a seat. 'Come on in and sit down. It's been a while since we caught up.'

Meg brought tea and biscuits through, served it to them and joined Joe on the couch.

'Excuse the old throw rug. We always sit here to protect our furniture when we are in our dirty work clothes.'

For the next hour, Joe told Mack about his business plan with his new vehicle, and now and then Meg got a word in to ask about Jessie and the boys.

She passed the biscuits around again. 'You'll have to bring the twins to visit us soon. It's been ages since we saw them last.'

'To be honest, it's probably easier for you both to come to us. It's a bit of a performance visiting with the boys as they still need a midday nap, and we can only take them out in short bursts,' said Mack.

Joe sat, rubbing his hands together, eager to get back outside.

'When you've finished your tea, I'd like to show you the Wagoneer.'

Mack sat scanning the living room. 'You've updated your wallpaper. It looks much more appealing.'

Meg stood up, pointing upstairs. 'And all the other rooms, too. You must see the guest rooms, Mack. We've also put in new bathrooms at both ends of the corridor.'

'Sure, I'll do that first and then take a look at Joe's new vehicle.'

Joe fidgeted in his seat, looking at his watch. He stayed in the living room while Meg showed her brother around.

While Mack surveyed the renovations to the building, Meg pulled him aside. 'I want to tell you something while you're here,' she whispered. 'It's about Joshua.'

He grimaced. 'You mean that doctor friend of yours—I thought that was all finished with!'

'Shh! It's all finished—I saw him in town the other day holding hands with his new fiancée. He's marrying a nurse colleague from Tekapo and apparently, they've been friends for years. He was keen to marry her before he arrived here, but she wasn't ready. She obviously is now.'

'How do you know all this?'

'One of my friends from the Country Women's Institute knows her family in Tekapo.'

'So—how did you feel when you saw him holding her hand?'

'That's just the point—I felt nothing—in fact, it was a relief to see he has someone. I realised then that I was never in love with him and how grateful I am that Joe is back.'

'Why did you fraternise with the doctor in the first place, if that's the case?'

'When Joe stayed away, I came to believe he didn't love me or want me back.'

Mack put his arm around Meg. 'Goes to show how fickle the human mind is and how assumptions can mess up our lives. Let's get back to Joe—he'll be wondering where we've got to.'

When they walked down the stairs, they bumped into Joe, who was about to come looking for them.

'Goodness! That took a long time. Talk about the grand tour. Can we go outside now and look at my new venture?'

Meg cleared up their cups while she gave Joe space to be with Mack.

The men pulled their boots on and wandered out to the oversized garage at the entrance to the property.

'I keep this here locked up with Meg's car.'

'Brand new, is it?' Mack stood with his eyes popping out, staring at Joe's new find. 'Superb! 'It even has woodgrain along the sides. Where did you come across this one?'

'That new importer, Gibson and Son in Queenstown. Take a look at the upholstery—it's all leather.'

Mack climbed into the back of the car, gliding his hand along the seats.

'Stunning! Your tourists are going to get a ride and a half in one of these. I wouldn't mind being a passenger being driven around myself.'

'Maybe we can all go on a test run out to Paradise. We can see Earnslaw there covered with snow.'

'I'm up for that—although I feel guilty about Jessie missing out and I'm sure she'd love to come, but she needs to stay at the station in case her medical expertise is needed. I don't want to be away too long, though.'

'Maybe Jessie can have a ride another time when she's free,' said Joe.

'I hoped to drop by the chalet to see my folks before I head back later, too.'

'They've gone into Queenstown for the day. I'll tell them you called in.'

Mack was grateful his mother-in-law lived on their property. When his own mother was not available to take care of the twins, Pru was always a backstop.

***

Meg peered through the window at the spring flowers on the side of the road—a technicolour of lupins—pink, blue and purple.

Sitting in the backseat, Mack stared out at Mount Alfred as they passed the snow-capped mountain that towered over the extensive farmland. He recalled the time when he first fell in love with his wife—the time when Hope and

Cole had invited him and Jessie to walk up the icy bush track to the mountain summit. Though all of them were seasoned rock climbers, Jessie slipped and fell into a deep, ice-filled crevice. At the thought of her dying, Mack realised he was smitten and, after he bravely rescued her, a romance blossomed.

Unexpectedly, Joe pulled up for a moment in front of a river ford.

'The water level is higher than usual. I don't enjoy taking vehicles through water, but this one is high off the ground, so I don't mind.'

They arrived at a lookout point where tourists can view Mount Earnslaw. Joe pointed towards a grassy hillock. 'That's where I'll take them—up there on that hill. There's a clear view of Mt Earnslaw from there.'

'Where else will you take them?' Mack rolled down his window to look at the view.

'Meg has made friends with some of the station owners here and at Kinloch who've invited me to conduct tours of their farms.'

Mack raised his eyebrows. 'Pleased to hear you've made a few friends around here. They must be pretty chummy with you to extend that kind of hospitality.'

'Some of their children have attended holiday camps here to give the parents a break. Our business set up impresses them, so I guess they want to do me a favour.'

Mack reflected on how far his sister had come socially when initially she had the entire community against her. Now they go out of their way to help her.

'I'd better get back, if you don't mind, Joe. I promised Jessie I wouldn't be too long; in case she is needed in the lambing shed.'

'Sure, no problem. Just enjoy being driven around for once—let's go.'

When Mack arrived back at Reed Station, Jessie appeared in the driveway. Concerned, he wound down his window. 'Everything alright, love?'

'The boys are fine, but I'm needed in the lambing shed again. One of them which has a complicated presentation and is exhausted. Ben has been with her for two hours.'

'I'll go and collect the boys from your mother.'

'No, don't worry—she is happy to have them for a little longer. They are home now, and Mum is inside with them. You need to take me to the ewe on the quad bike. I'll go inside first and radio Ben to let him know we're on our way.'

'Bring the radiophone back with you.'

Chapter Twenty-Five

Jessie took off inside the house for her medical bag and hurried back down the steps to climb on the bike behind Mack.

'I've got the radiophone inside my bag. Ben's waiting by the shed.'

Mack revved the engine, taking off up the track to the shed where Ben stood with his radiophone, holding open the gate.

'I'm sure glad to see you!' he said, flashing a smile at Jessie. I think this will be a prolonged labour—we've got her in the shed lying on hay.'

Jessie scrambled off the quad bike with her bag and followed Ben who carried a bucket of clean water and placed it on the ground next to her. 'Do you need soap?'

'No, thanks—I always carry my own.'

After washing her hands and arms, she took a clean hand towel from her bag to dry off and pulled on long gloves.

Mack knelt next to Jessie. 'You can see to the rest of them, Ben. I'll stay and assist Jessie.'

'Right, you are. I'll get off then.'

Jessie examined the ewe while Mack stood by to help when needed. Within minutes, the lamb's face showed.

'This is no good. I'll have to slide its head back inside and see if I can get the legs into the canal so she can deliver normally. Help me get the ewe onto her side, Mack.'

She took a thick piece of cord from her bag. After changing her gloves, she covered the lamb's head with lubricant and slid the loop of cord over the head, behind its ears and through its mouth.

'I'll ease the head back and grab hold of its legs ... wait ... here it comes.'

Before long, the lamb slid into the hay. Mack removed the cord snare from its neck, then cleared its mouth with his finger and lay the tiny creature on its side. He squeezed its ribcage a few times when he saw its chest was barely moving and within minutes, it was breathing on its own. Mack turned the ewe's head towards the limp bunch of wet fluff lying in front of the depleted mother and lifted the lamb, placing it under her nose. 'She looks like a stunned mullet—not too interested yet.'

'You would be like that too! Labour is a strenuous business—that I do know—she'll come right soon.'

After the ewe had finished licking and cleaning the lamb, Jessie cut the umbilical cord and treated it with iodine to prevent infection, while Mack checked the ewe's udder before she started feeding.

After a short time, this worn-out vet was ready to go home. She rinsed and dried her hands before closing her bag. 'Are we finished here, then?'

'Yep, we sure are. I'll take you home and then come back and check on her.'

'Tell the others to monitor this lamb. If she appears cold and weak, I may have to give her an injection of dextrose.'

'I'll let Ben know. He may need some help with some of the other ewes, as it's getting late in the day. He and Coran will take turns monitoring them, but they should know by their last visit at eleven tonight whether any of them will birth in the night.'

Mack pulled her close to him and glanced at her face.

'I'm so blessed to have married you, young lady. Who would have thought I'd have my own ready-made vet on a high country station?'

He kissed her and let it linger. 'When lambing is over, I'll see if Wyatt and Ben can hold the fort one weekend. They'll have Coran here too. If our parents can babysit, we could go to Queenstown and stay the night in one of those cabins by the lake you keep telling me about.'

Jessie climbed on the back of the bike. 'I'd love that. It has been a long while since we had any time together on our own. Let's plan it soon.'

To their delight, Pru had given the boys their evening meal. She'd taken them back to her house and raked up some meals that Bessie had pre-prepared and placed in mini containers in the fridge.

'Hope you don't mind, but they are all watered and fed. I've also changed their nappies a few minutes ago. I thought you would be tied up with the ewe for ages and the boys were getting hungry.'

Jessie threw her arms around her mother.

'Oh, Mum. What would we do without you? I'm sure Mack's mother would do the same but to have you right on our doorstep is a Godsend.'

'Enough of that—Bessie dropped by and lent a hand, bless her. Do you want a hand to bathe them?'

'No, I'll be okay. Mack and I can manage that together. I must remember to thank Bessie later.'

Pru helped fasten the boys in their double stroller. Before Jessie walked back home, she hesitated.

'Oh yes, I forgot to tell you—we've received a wedding invitation from Tom with short notice that they're getting married in a month! He said he sent one to you and Dad and will phone you.'

Pru raised her eyebrows a few times and chuckled.

'Typical, of Tom though—always leaving everything until last when we all live so far away. He just doesn't think—poor Amanda will have her work cut out for her.'

'I guess so, Mum, but perhaps he has a lot on his mind. I understand that, trying to run this station with Mack. It's so much responsibility.'

'You forget that when your father and I started out on our farm, we had no help from anyone. Wyatt's father was dead, and we were as green as grass. My parents lived miles away.'

'Maybe that's why it could be a challenge for Tom as he's so used to having Dad on the farm and now he has to stand on his own two feet. Anyway—regarding the wedding—from what he has said to me, Amanda wasn't interested in a formal wedding at all. She just wants a small, local church ceremony with family and a few friends and then a casual celebration back at the house.'

'He said nothing like that to me. Oh well, let's wait and see what transpires. I'll see you tomorrow, love.'

After she arrived home, Jessie gathered up the boys for their bath and found Mack already busy filling it.

They chatted while the twins played in the water.

'We must organise our trip to the Bay of Plenty for Tom's wedding next month. Did you see our invitation on the table?'

Mack tossed a rubber duck to Oliver while Will splashed around, drenching Mack's face.

'Could you pass the towel, please?'

He wiped his face dry and then replied. 'You mean organising staff to run this place while we're gone. We can't rely on Grandad—he's not in a fit state to leave him all the responsibility, but Ben and Coran should be able to manage. Bessie and Grandad can look after each other and I might ask Joe and Meg to visit, just to monitor things.'

'We'd best go to Queenstown this weekend and book our flights. We could look for their wedding present while we are there.'

'Wonderful stuff. Let's get these fellas out—they're shivering.'

***

They all crammed into Jessie's spacious Land Rover. The trip took a good hour going to the Queenstown Airport to catch the flights to Rotorua Airport. They left their vehicle in the secure carpark until their return and had plenty of time before the flight as they'd arrived early.

Mack dreaded taking the twins on the plane. What if they cried the whole time or messed their nappies? He detested the way they packed them in on small aircraft like dried figs in a tin. He couldn't wait to arrive.

A pretty hostess offered to help during the trip to entertain the babies during the three-hour flight that seemed to take forever for Mack.

When they arrived, Jessie and Pru changed the twins in the child-friendly bathroom at the air terminal. Wyatt and Mack waited for them at the carousel. After they all found their luggage, Mack and Jessie carried one child each in a back baby carrier.

'We should have brought their twin pushchair, Jessie,' said Pru, eyeing the weight on her daughter's back.

'No, Mum—it's cumbersome and takes up too much space. It's best this way.'

Pru knew better than to contradict her daughter who was the epitome of stubbornness.

'There he is!' Jessie waved out to Tom in the arrival lounge.

602

'Oh, no.' She eyed the ginger tufts of hair protruding from her brother's chin. 'It makes him look like an old man,' Jessie tittered.

They all greeted each other with a hug.

'No Amanda, Tom?' uttered Jessie, looking around him.

'No—she'll catch up with us later. She works on a Friday.'

The road trip to Tauranga from Rotorua crammed into Tom's Ford Falcon was not so bad as it could fit an army. Mack usually found it a nightmare taking the twins on such a long trip, but the vehicle was comfortable. The toddlers slept for half of the journey fastened in rear side-facing bench seats, already fitted by the neighbour.

Mack tapped Tom on the shoulder. 'Cool number, this vehicle, Tom. All decked out for a large family. I've been looking forward to seeing it.'

He whispered to Jessie, 'I think he's planning on having a tribe of children,' and winked at her.

Wyatt jumped in before Tom could answer. 'Yep, it was a good buy. Pru and I thought it a handsome gift—a way of saying thank you for taking over the management of our farm.'

'And what a wonderful job he is doing too,' Pru added.

'This is superb, Tom. Is this the vehicle you scored from old farmer Henderson—the one you've had your eye on for years?' quizzed Jessie, trying not to throw up in the back of the car each time the vehicle veered around the deep bends in the road. She leaned her head out the window as the green rolling hills of home became clear. 'Man, I didn't realise how much I've missed this. Still—life has to go on.'

Tom turned his head sideways. 'You know you can always come and stay for a bit, but you never take me up on the offer.'

'Dear Tom—if only you knew how tight my schedule is now we have twins. I'm working three jobs—and I can't just up sticks with two babies!'

Just at that moment, the vehicle hit a deep pothole in the long driveway that led to the farmhouse.

'Sorry about that—I heard you, Jessie, and believe me—I understand. Here we are, back home.'

***

The quaint, white-washed chapel started filling with the bridal party, families and friends. It was the size of the one in Glenorchy, a small historic building.

Pru checked Jessie's hat, attempting to tuck loose strands of hair away. 'It's a perfect summer's day. Tom couldn't have asked for anything better than this. Do I look alright—is my collar lying flat?'

'Don't fuss, mother. It's fine. Where are Dad and Mack? We had better go in and sit down.'

Before they entered the chapel, Jessie stopped to smell the gardenia bush that featured by the entrance to the church.

'Jessie!' Pru whispered, 'You can't pick those.'

Jessie frowned at her mother. 'I'm not picking them—I haven't smelled them in years.'

'Let's go inside—the men have gone in already.'

Mack and Wyatt sat together on the groom's side of the church with their wives next to them. When the service was about to start, Mack turned around to see only a small gathering of people.

'Good heavens—they've hardly invited anyone,' he murmured.

'Shh—I think that's how Amanda wanted it,' Jessie whispered.

Pru leaned over and murmured, 'Thank God Tom has shaved off that awful half-beard.'

He appeared clean-shaven in grey flannel trousers and matching waistcoat, and although he was reluctant to wear a black tie, Pru had insisted, and he changed his mind.

The nostalgic chapel reminded Mack of the old, white-washed church he attended as a young boy when his mother sent him and Meg to Sunday school. Unlike the formal Church of England of his youth, this service appeared to be laid back.

An Air from Bach burst forth from an upmarket organ, while Amanda, dressed like a nymph in a simple white dress and gypsophila in her hair, walked down the aisle next to her father. Mack looked to make sure she wore shoes and was not barefoot. He elbowed Jessie who forced herself to not laugh out loud.

The ceremony was short and formal. The wedded couple bolted out the door while the organ played on. They couldn't get away quick enough—such a far cry from Jessie and Mack's ceremony which they had planned themselves.

Amanda's folks walked out the door followed by Pru and Wyatt who simultaneously greeted Tom and Amanda with a hug. Tom's new wife seemed to strike up a conversation easily and gravitated towards Jessie. They all stood chatting for a while, and after greeting the guests, the newlyweds made a dash for it.

Tom approached Jessie. 'We're having a barn dance later. Nothing like the elaborate shindig you and Mack had on Reed Station, but we could still have some fun, though. First, a good feed put on by Amanda's folks on the veranda under cover.'

Amanda's mother seemed to be in her element, organising everyone. She approached Pru and Wyatt.

'Ah, there you are—good thing we all met at your house last night otherwise this could have been awkward. Are we all ready to go onto the reception yet?'

'Yes, I think we're all sorted, aren't we, dear?' Pru looped her arm in Wyatt's as they walked to their vehicles.

It was an afternoon wedding and still warm. They set the food out on a long trestle table covered with a white cloth.

With the help of a few friends, multiple dishes of fancy food paid for by Amanda's parents appeared on the tables.

The music from the barn bellowed until midnight and the twins slept through it all while the Mack and Jessie took turns checking on them in the house all evening.

Coloured lights flashed, illuminating a dance floor covered in fine sawdust.

'I should have brought my gumboots,' said Wyatt, grinning at his wife.

'Come, dear, let's have one more dance before I head off to bed.' Pru pulled Wyatt back into the middle of the dance floor. Afterwards, they retired to bed early, leaving the young ones to party on.

Later that night, Jessie looked around for Tom and Amanda, but they had disappeared, telling no one. Pru and Wyatt had booked them into an apartment on the ocean side at Mount Maunganui with a sea view for their wedding present. While the newlyweds were away on their honeymoon, Mack and Wyatt monitored the farm, although Tom's farm manager had it under control.

Four days later, the Glenorchy bridal party began their long trip back home. It had been a whirlwind event and Mack didn't enjoy travelling so far from home, for, in the back of his mind, he had reservations about leaving his grandfather.

Chapter Twenty-Six

Jessie yanked off her court shoes and plonked herself down into an armchair, massaging the back of her neck.

'Whew! Thank the Lord the boys went off to sleep straight away—I'm glad we're home.'

Mack carried their suitcases down to the bedroom and returned in his pyjamas.

'What a long trip that was. At least Tom didn't have too far to travel to collect us from Rotorua Airport. It's so good that Mt Cook Airlines are stopping there now, and we don't have to commute from Auckland.'

'Yes, it's great—and the twins were much better than I expected. They had everyone in the aircraft fussing over them.'

Mack yawned. 'Tom didn't give people much warning, as our invitations only arrived a month before the wedding. Especially for people like us who had so far to travel.'

Jessie bent down to pick up some of the children's toys off the floor and placed them in their toy basket.

'True—don't you think Amanda is a sweetie? When I first met her, I didn't think she was cut out to be a farmer's wife, but she proved me wrong. Tom said she helped him with lambing and didn't mind getting her hands dirty. She has her own horse and has won a few prizes at shows.'

Mack sat munching on an apple. 'I'm pleased it was a simple affair. There were only a handful of people—family and close friends, which is what they wanted. I thought Amanda was dressed like a nymph—quite liberal. As long as she is a good match for Tom, that's all that matters—listen—is that one of the boys calling out?'

Jessie tiptoed along the hallway and peeped through the door.

'No, they are sound asleep,' she said, walking back and sitting next to Mack again. 'I think it's a lamb that Grandad weaned while we were away.'

'Let's get to bed—it won't hurt to have an early night for a change. I've got an early start tomorrow with the shearing contractors arriving first thing,' Mack said, rubbing his eyes.

They turned out the lights and shuffled off down to their bedroom. Jessie sat on the edge of the bed, brushing her hair. 'We have to think about what we will do for the twins' first birthday. It will be a busy Christmas this year. Oh ... I'm worn out thinking about it. Time to get some sleep.'

***

Reed station became a flurry of activity during the shearing season. The truck arrived with shearers, shedhands and cooks all bustling about looking for their accommodation—laughing and joking in high spirits.

Jessie bounced Oliver up and down on her knee in a chair by the outdoor table, watching the workers come and go while baby Will sat playing in his mobile walker.

Holding a mug of tea, Walter wandered out onto the veranda to observe the activity. Instantly, he held a hand against his forehead and started to sway.

'Are you okay, Grandad? Come and sit down.'

Walter slumped back in a wicker chair, leaning forward with his head resting on his hands.

'What's wrong—are you unwell?' Jessie stared at him, her brow crinkling.

'Don't worry about me, lassie. It's just one of those jolly headaches I get now and then,' he mumbled, barely lifting his head.

'Let me get you your painkillers. Where do you keep them?'

'In the medicine cabinet in the bathroom above the hand basin.'

Jessie secured the gate on the veranda to stop Will escaping, propped Oliver on her hip and went looking for the tablets.

She arrived back with a glass of water. Placing Oliver on the ground, she pulled the medication from her pocket and handed it to Walter.

'Here, Grandad—you'd better take these. If it doesn't subside, I'll take you in to see the doctor.'

'No need for that now. I'm supposed to be helping Mack and Ben get those sheep into the woolshed race. I said I would be there.'

'You're not going anywhere, Grandad. We don't want you having another stroke. You're supposed to rest when you get these headaches. Have you been taking your blood pressure pills?'

'Yes—and I know all that. But you can't keep a shepherd down—you should know that by now.'

***

Jessie heard the thumping of boots on the veranda steps. It was a warm summer's evening as Mack stumbled in, lifting his arms and sniffing his armpits.

'Bah, that smells high—I'm going straight to the shower.' He began stripping off his black, woollen singlet.

A short time later, he came out of the bathroom reeking of aftershave. Jessie walked over and stroked his smooth cheeks.

'Ooh—clean-shaven, too. What's the occasion?'

'Nothing—just that it's so dirty in the woolsheds and I feel as though the stench permeates everything.'

Mack always helped Jessie bath the boys. He never once thought it was her role, as she was working three jobs.

'I've already run their bath. I'll take Olly.'

Jessie glared at him. 'Please don't start calling him that. It'll stick and Oliver's such a charming name.'

'Okay, you're right. Let's get them into the bath.'

Jessie picked up Will and carried him into the bathroom.

After they bathed the children and tucked them into their cots, Jessie expressed her concerns to Mack about Walter.

'I'm worried about him. You should try to get him to see the doctor—he had a nasty headache today and needed pain relief. I thought he was going to pass out.'

'He seemed to be a bit on the slow side with mustering earlier, even though I only gave him a handful to do. Maybe I can take him in to see the doctor late this afternoon. I'll be tied up until then.'

***

The trip to the doctor was a false alarm. All Joshua told him was to rest as he explained that dehydration causes headaches, and he had to drink more water.

In the Ute on the way home, Walter started talking about all the things he'd like to teach the boys.

'I'd like to get two miniature horses, the same as Meg has, and then I can teach them how to ride.'

'It's too soon for that yet, Grandad. Perhaps in another couple of years. I'm all for it but not yet. Wait until they're a little older.'

610

'Well, I don't want to wait too long—I might not be around for too much longer. This old body is decaying.'

Mack's brows snapped together. Don't be ridiculous—we're all decaying. Isn't that what the pastor said in the sermon on Sunday? Anyway—the doctor thinks you're as fit as a flea.'

'I'm not sure about that. I know what my body is telling me.'

After dropping his father back home, Mack climbed on his quad bike and rode off to check the calves.

Jessie agreed to let the boys sit with Walter on the tractor parked near the house where she could see them. They loved him a great deal, especially when he spent so much time with them.

Chapter Twenty-Seven

Two years later - 1986

Mack had the day off. After a belly full of Christmas cake and apple cider, he rested on the couch in the living room, reading a book by one of his favourite Suspense authors.

Jessie yawned as she reached to pick up one of Will's Tonka trucks off the floor. 'We must teach our boys to put their own toys away. I'm worn out and never thought I'd be pleased to have the house to ourselves, but today I'm glad of it.'

'They were spoilt rotten by their grandparents this Christmas. Look at how many toys they gave them. I hope they get to play with them all, but I doubt it. I think they would rather be outside with the animals with me or Grandad on the farm.'

'Where are they right now? I can't see them in the yard.' Jessie hurried over to the window.

Mack yawned and put down his book. 'Grandad took them out to show them how to feed the lambs from that dead ewe. He made a temporary pen for them in the front yard. Do you mind if I take a quick nap? I need to recharge my batteries.'

'No, you have a rest. I'll just be fussing around here keeping tabs on the boys, and that includes our big boy out there.' Jessie chuckled.

She went out through the front door to look for them and heard the lambs crying for their mother. The boys stood watching their great-grandfather coax the animals to take the teat from the bottle of warm milk.

Jessie, satisfied that they were in expert hands, went back inside to tidy up.

Bessie was away with her family for the holidays, which meant Mack and Jessie had all the housework and cooking to do between them. Walter just wasn't up to much anymore. He showed signs of slowing down.

Jessie dusted and vacuumed Walter's room. She was about to wipe down his bedside table when she discovered a book of memoirs like the ones she'd seen about the Reed family in Arrowtown Historical Museum lying on his dresser. She opened the book to see a chronological history of the gold miners, Mack's ancestors. There was a photo of the original homestead before they rebuilt it and an aerial view of the station. Jessie found the black and white photos of Walter's parents and grandparents in authentic vintage clothing intriguing. A large, coloured photo on the bedside table caught her eye. It was a handsome woman with long, jet black hair pulled softly back into a simple braid, and a long, blue dress. Hazel Reed stood in the forefront of the original Reed Station homestead.

She heard a voice and promptly closed the book, dragging the vacuum cleaner into the hallway to see Will standing there.

'Mummy! Poppa showed us how to feed Barney and Lofty. He said we can do it all by ourselves now. Come and watch us.'

Before Jessie could reply, Will bounded back out the door while his mother stood at the window smiling warmly at the boys showing their skills with a milk bottle. She waved and gave a thumbs-up of approval.

Walter, convinced that he'd taught them sufficiently how to get the lambs to take the teat and the right way to hold the milk bottle, went back up on the veranda to watch them from under the outdoor umbrella. He wiped his brow with his handkerchief and closed his eyes. Jessie stood in the living room window briefly, smiling at the sight of her three-year-old twin boys feeding twin lambs while their Poppa looked on. After she finished the vacuuming, Jessie set up the iron board and before she turned the iron on, a commotion startled her. Her sons shouted out at and as she looked up, the two of them barged through the door, trying to catch their breath.

'Mummy! We want Poppa to help us, but he won't open his eyes, cried Oliver. 'Can you tell him to wake up?'

'Yes, Mummy, quick—come! Lofty wants more milk and Poppa said he would get more if it ran out,' said Will, pulling her other arm.

Jessie almost toppled the ironing board. She switched off the iron and followed them onto the veranda.

'Quiet—don't wake him if he's taking a nap. It looks like he's exhausted. It's good you came to tell me, though. You can't stay out here on your own.'

Jessie peered at Walter as she reached up to change the slant of the umbrella to screen his face from the sun. Suddenly, she braced herself and took a step back, squinting from the glare. Edging her way along the table where he sat, she froze.

Her face paled as she bent down to speak to her sons.

'Please go inside and wake Daddy ... tell him I need him right now—go!'

The twins stood gaping, then ran inside the house.

Jessie turned to Walter. 'Grandad, wake up! Please, Grandad, open your eyes!' she yelled.

Walter lay motionless, about to slide off the seat. Jessie pressed her knuckles hard into his breastbone while he remained deathly still. She leaned over, touching his mouth with her left cheek. 'Oh, no. Please, not now!' Her eyes welled up as she held his icy hand. He had already gone.

Mack rushed out onto the veranda.

'I'm so sorry, darling, but Grandad's ... he's gone. Tell the boys to stay in the living room then help me.'

After helping Jessie slide him off his chair and onto the floor, Mack raced back to her side after he rang the flying doctor.

'Shall we start CPR?'

'I'm sorry, darling, it's too late. He died peacefully in his sleep, watching his grandsons feeding their lambs.'

Mack burst into tears. Not so much because of Walter's death, as he knew the eighty-six-year-old had lived on borrowed time following two strokes, but more so because he never had the chance to say goodbye.

Jessie took Mack's hand. 'You know our boys have had a privileged relationship with Grandad and so have we. He enhanced our lives so much and I hope he knew how much we appreciated him.'

They both kissed him on the forehead and covered him with a blanket. Jessie wrapped her arms around Mack, then called the boys who came running back with exuberance. Mack guessed they expected to see their Poppa sitting up talking.

Will tugged on Jessie's sleeve. 'Why is Poppa lying on the ground—why doesn't he wake up, Mummy? He said we could give Lofty and Barney another bottle. Please wake him for us.'

Jessie gathered the children together under her arms. They snuggled into her.

'Poppa is in a deep sleep and won't wake anymore until he is with God in Heaven. He's waiting for him and the helicopter will take him there.'

'But why is he going away—we don't want him to go?' said Oliver, teary-eyed.

'Sometimes God just lends us people so we can love them, and they can love us back. Then he gives them to others for a while. It's someone else's turn to love Poppa now. One day we'll all be together again when he has finished working for God.'

'He's freezing, Mummy,' wailed Oliver. 'Can the blanket make him better?'

'When the helicopter gets here, they will take him to a place where he will never be cold again.'

'The helicopter will take him to God, won't it?' Will asked, staring at the shape under the blanket.

'Yes, my darling. He's going to heaven where all good shepherds live. There'll be lots of lambs for him to take care of there.'

Both boys walked up to the lifeless form covered by the blanket and lay across him with their heads on his chest.

'Don't worry, Poppa. We know how to give Barney and Lofty their milk, so they won't be hungry while you're away. You wait for us, promise?' The roar of the helicopter's rotors drowned out Oliver's voice as it landed in the field next to the homestead.

As the air ambulance officers took Walter on a stretcher out to the helicopter with its engine still roaring, Mack stood on the veranda, fighting back more tears. He and Jessie held the hands of their children, saying a silent goodbye.

'Daddy—Mummy said you're a good shepherd. Are you going to go off with Poppa too?' Will gazed at him with wide eyes.

'No, I'm not going anywhere until I'm old like Poppa and you'll be grown up. We'll all see Poppa in God's pastures, and he'll be teaching other children to feed the lambs and find those that have strayed and lost their way.'

They all stood huddled together on the veranda as the helicopter churned its way into the sky with Oliver and Will blowing butterfly kisses until it disappeared behind the clouds.

THE END

EPILOGUE

Walter's funeral service was held at the Glenorchy chapel. Following his request, after his cremation, the family took his ashes, as he had requested to be buried in a plot at the Church of the Good Shepherd at Lake Tekapo next to his wife, Hazel. His family travelled to see the gravestone they had got engraved.

WALTER JOHN REED
THE GOOD SHEPHERD 1900 -1986
HUSBAND OF HAZEL, FATHER OF LEN,
GRANDFATHER OF MACK AND MEG AND GREAT-
GRANDFATHER OF WILL AND OLIVER. HE PASSED
AWAY DOING WHAT HE LOVED MOST. MAY YOU REST
IN PEACE. YOU WILL BE FOREVER IN OUR HEARTS.

Author Bio

Patricia, known as Trish, grew up in a small town in New Zealand. From the age of five, she rode horses which her family owned and trained, often winning prizes in the local horse shows. During her early life, her parents lived off the land, initially share-milking and later as horticulturists.

After completing her nursing studies and qualifying as a Registered Nurse, Patricia spent six years abroad, living in Australia and Europe, doing a variety of jobs between her nursing roles and returned to Auckland to start a family. After a forty-year nursing career, Patricia retired and now writes inspirational Cosy Mysteries, Adventure and Romantic Suspense set in beautiful New Zealand.

Visit: patriciasnelling.com for more of Patricia's books